THE
SCANDALOUS
Kolovskys

Three sensational, passionate novels from
bestselling Mills & Boon® author

CAROL MARINELLI

D1639216

Scandalous Dynasties

June 2013
THE SCANDALOUS KOLOVSKYS
Carol Marinelli

August 2013
THE SCANDALOUS ORSINIS
Sandra Marton

September 2013
THE SCANDALOUS WAREHAMS
Penny Jordan

October 2013
THE SCANDALOUS SABBATINIS
Melanie Milburne

THE
SCANDALOUS
Kolovskys

CAROL MARINELLI

MILLS
.BOON

Published in Great Britain 2013
by Mills & Boon, an imprint of Harlequin (UK) Limited, Eton House, 18-24 Paradise Road, Richmond, Surrey TW9 1SR

THE SCANDALOUS KOLOVSKYS
© Harlequin Enterprises II B.V./S.à.r.l. 2013

Knight on the Children's Ward © Carol Marinelli 2010
The Last Kolovsky Playboy © Carol Marinelli 2010
The Devil Wears Kolovsky © Carol Marinelli 2011

ISBN: 978 0 263 90672 1

009-0613

Printed and bound by
CPI Group (UK) Ltd, Croydon, CR0 4YY

KNIGHT ON THE CHILDREN'S WARD

CAROL MARINELLI

Carol Marinelli recently filled in a form where she was asked for her job title and was thrilled, after all these years, to be able to put down her answer as 'writer'. Then it asked what Carol did for relaxation. After chewing her pen for a moment Carol put down the truth—'writing'. The third question asked—'What are your hobbies?'. Well, not wanting to look obsessed or, worse still, boring, she crossed the fingers on her free hand and answered 'swimming and tennis'. But, given that the chlorine in the pool does terrible things to her highlights, and the closest she's got to a tennis racket in the last couple of years is watching the Australian Open, I'm sure you can guess the real answer!

PROLOGUE

'CAN I ask what happened, Reyes?'

Ross didn't answer his mother for a moment—instead he carried on sorting out clothes, stray earrings, books, make-up, and a shoe that didn't have a partner. He loaded them into a suitcase.

He'd been putting the job off, and when he'd finally accepted his mother's offer to sort Imelda's things, he had accepted also that with her help might come questions.

Questions that he couldn't properly answer.

'I don't know.'

'Were you arguing?' Estella asked, and then tried to hold back a sigh when Ross shook his head. 'I loved Imelda,' Estella said.

'I know,' Ross said, and that just made it harder—Imelda had loved his family and they had loved her too. 'She was funny and kind and I really, really thought I could make it work. I can't honestly think of one thing that was wrong… It was just…'

'Just what, Reyes?' His mother was the only person who called him that. When he had arrived in Australia aged seven, somehow his real name had slipped away. The other children, fascinated by the little dark-haired, olive-skinned

Spanish boy who spoke no English, had translated Reyes to Ross—and that was who he had become.

Ross Wyatt.

Son of Dr George and Mrs Estella Wyatt. Older brother to Maria and Sophia Wyatt.

Only it was more complicated than that, and all too often far easier *not* to explain.

Sometimes he *had* to explain—after all, when he was growing up people had noticed the differences. George's hair, when he had had some, had been blond, like his daughters'. George was sensible, stern, perfectly nice and a wonderful father—but it wasn't his blood that ran in Ross's veins.

And he could tell from his mother's worried eyes that she was worried *that* was the problem.

Estella's brief love affair at sixteen with a forbidden Gitano, or Romany, had resulted in Reyes. The family had rallied around. His grandmother had looked after the dark baby while his mother had worked in a local bar, where, a few years later, she'd met a young Australian man, just out of medical school. George had surprised his rather staid family by falling in love and bringing home from his travels in Europe two unexpected souvenirs.

George had raised Reyes as his own, loved him as his own, and treated him no differently from his sisters.

Except Reyes, or rather Ross, *was* different.

'It wasn't…' His voice trailed off. He knew his mother was hoping for a rather more eloquent answer. He knew that she was worried just from the fact she was asking, for his mother never usually interfered. 'There wasn't that…' He couldn't find the word but he tried. He raked his mind but couldn't find it in English and so, rarely for Ross, he reverted to his native tongue. *'Buena onda.'* His mother tensed when he said it, and he knew she understood—for that was the phrase she used when she talked about his father.

His real father.

Buena onda—an attraction, a connection, a vibe from another person, from *that* person.

'Then you're looking for a fairytale, Reyes! And real-life fairytales don't have happy endings.' Estella's voice was unusually sharp. 'It's time you grew up. Look where *buena onda* left me—sixteen and pregnant.'

Only then, for the first time in his thirty-two years did Ross glimpse the anger that simmered beneath the surface of his mother.

'Passion flares and then dims. Your father—the father who held you and fed you and put you through school—stands for more than some stupid dream. Some gypsy dream that you—' She stopped abruptly, remembering perhaps that they were actually discussing him. 'Imelda was a good woman, a loyal and loving partner. She would have been a wonderful wife and you threw it away—for what?'

He didn't know.

It had been the same argument all his life as his mother and George had tried to rein in his restless energy. He struggled with conformity, though it could hardly be called rebellion.

Grade-wise he had done well at school. He had a mortgage, was a paediatrician—a consultant, in fact—he loved his family, was a good friend.

On paper all was fine.

In his soul all was not.

The mortgage wasn't for a bachelor's city dwelling—

though he had a small one of those for nights on call, or when he was particularly concerned about a patient— no, his handsome wage was poured into an acreage, with stables and horses, olive and fruit trees and rows of vines, and not another residence in sight.

Just as there had been arguments about his attitude at school, even as a consultant he found it was more of the same. Budgets, policies, more budgets—all he wanted to do was his job, and at home all he wanted to do was *be*.

There was nothing wrong that he could pin down.

And there was no one who could pin him down.

Many had tried.

'Should I take this round to her?' Ross asked.

'Put it in the cupboard for now,' Estella said. 'If she comes for her things, then at least it is all together. If she doesn't…' She gave a little shrug. 'It's just some clothes. Maybe she would prefer no contact.'

He felt like a louse as he closed the zipper. Packed up two years and placed it in the cupboard.

'Imelda wanted to decorate the bedroom.' Task over, he could be a bit more honest. 'She'd done the bathroom, the spare room…' It was almost impossible to explain, but he had felt as if he were being slowly invaded. 'She said she wanted more of a commitment.'

'She cared a lot about you, Reyes…'

'I know,' he admitted. 'And I cared a lot about her.'

'It would have hurt her deeply, you ending it.'

It had. She had cried, sobbed, and then she had hit him and he'd taken it—because he deserved it, because she had almost been the one. He had hoped she was the one and then, when he could deny no longer that she wasn't… What was wrong with him?

'She loved you, Reyes!'

'So I should have just let it carry on? Married her…?'

'Of course not,' Estella said. 'But it's not just Imelda…'

It wasn't.

Imelda was one of a long line of women who had got too close—and, despite his reputation, Ross hated the pain he caused.

'I don't like it that my son hurts women.'

'I'm not getting involved with anyone for a while,' Ross said.

'You say that now…'

'I've never said it before,' Ross said. 'I mean it; I've got to sort myself out. I think I need to go back.' It took a lot of courage to look at his mum, to watch her dark eyes widen and her lips tighten. He saw the slight flinch as he said the words she had braced herself to hear for many years. 'To Spain.'

'What about your work in Russia?' Estella asked. 'All your annual leave is taken up with that. You said that it's the most important thing to you.'

It had been. As a medical student he had taken up the offer to work in a Russian orphanage on his extended summer break, with his fellow student Iosef Kolovsky. It had changed him—and now, all these years on, much of his spare time was devoted to going back. Even though Iosef was married now, and had a new baby, Ross had been determined to return to Russia later in the year. But now things had changed.

'I want to go to Spain, see my *abuelos*…' And that was a good reason to go—his grandparents were old now—but it didn't quite appease his mother. 'I'm going back next month, just for a few weeks….'

'You want to find him, don't you?'

He saw the flash of tears in her eyes and hated the

pain he was causing, but his mother, whether she believed it or not, simply didn't understand.

'I want to find myself.'

CHAPTER ONE

'THERE is room for improvement, Annika.' Heather Jameson was finding this assessment particularly difficult. In most areas the student nurse was doing well. In exams, her pass-rates had been initially high, but in her second year of study they were now merely *acceptable*. In her placements it was always noted how hard she worked, and that she was well turned out, on time, but there were still a couple of issues that needed to be addressed.

'It's been noted that you're tired.' Heather cleared her throat. 'Now, I know a lot of students have to work to support themselves during their studies, but…'

Annika closed her eyes, it wouldn't enter Heather's head that she was amongst them—no, she was a Kolovsky, why on earth would *she* have to work?

Except she did—and that she couldn't reveal.

'We understand that with all your family's charity work and functions…well, that you have other balls to juggle. But, Annika, your grades are slipping—you have to find a better balance.'

'I am trying,' Annika said, but her assessment wasn't over yet.

'Annika, are you enjoying nursing?'

No.

The answer was right there, on the tip of her tongue, but she swallowed it down. For the first six months or so she had loved it—had, after so much searching, thought that she had found her vocation, a purpose to her rich and luxurious life. Despite the arguments from her mother, despite her brother Iosef's stern warning that she had no idea what she was taking on, Annika had dug in her heels and, for six months at least, she had proved everyone wrong.

The coursework had been interesting, her placements on the geriatric and palliative care wards, though scary at first, had been enjoyable, and Annika had thought she had found her passion. But then gradually, just as Iosef had predicted it would, the joy had waned. Her surgical rotation had been a nightmare. A twenty-one-year-old had died on her shift and, sitting with the parents, Annika had felt as if she were merely playing dress-up.

It had been downhill since then.

'Have you made any friends?'

'A few,' Annika said. She tried to be friendly, tried to join in with her fellow students' chatter, tried to fit in, but the simple truth was that from the day she had started, from the day her peers had found out who she was, the family she came from, there had been an expectation, a pressure, to dazzle on the social scene. When Annika hadn't fulfilled it, they had treated her differently, and Annika had neither the confidence nor the skills to blend in.

'I know it's difficult for you, Annika...' Heather really didn't know what else to say. There was an aloofness to Annika that was hard to explain. With her thick blonde hair and striking blue eyes, and with her family's connections, one would expect her to be in constant demand, to be outgoing and social, yet there was a coldness in her that had to be addressed—because it was apparent not just to staff but to the patients. "A large part of nursing is about putting patients at ease—'

'I am always nice to the patients,' Annika interrupted, because she was. 'I am always polite; I introduce myself; I...' Annika's voice faded. She knew exactly what Heather was trying to say, she knew she was wooden, and she didn't know how to change it. 'I am scared of saying the wrong thing,' Annika admitted. 'I'm not good at making small talk, and I also feel very uncomfortable when people recognize my name—when they ask questions about my family.'

'Most of the time people *are* just making small talk, not necessarily because of who you are,' Heather said, and then, when Annika's eyes drifted to the newspaper on the table, she gave a sympathetic smile, because, in Annika's case people would pry!

The Kolovsky name was famous in Melbourne. Russian fashion designers, they created scandal and mystery and were regularly in the tabloids. Since the founder, Ivan, had died his son Aleksi had taken over the running of the business, and was causing social mayhem. There was a picture of him that very morning on page one, coming out of a casino, clearly the worse for wear, with the requisite blonde on his arm.

'Maybe nursing is not such a good idea.' Annika could feel the sting of tears behind her eyes but she would not cry. 'At the start I loved it, but lately...'

'You're a good nurse, Annika, and you could be a *very* good nurse. I'm more concerned that you're not happy. I know you're only twenty-five, but that does mean you're older than most of your group, and it's a bit harder as a mature student to fit in. Look…' She changed tack. This wasn't going the way Heather had wanted it—she was trying to bolster Annika, not have her consider quitting. 'You're starting on the children's ward today. Most of them won't have a clue about the Kolovsky name, and children are wonderful at…'

'Embarrassing you?' Annika volunteered, and managed a rare smile. 'I am dreading it.'

'I thought you might be. But children are a great leveller. I think this might be just the ward for you. Try and enjoy it, treat it as a fresh start—walk in and smile, say hello to your colleagues, open up a little, perhaps.'

'I will try.'

'And,' Heather added in a more serious tone, because she had given Annika several warnings, 'think about managing your social engagements more carefully around your roster. Request the weekends off that you need, plan more in advance.'

'I will.' Annika stood up and, unlike most other students, she shook Heather's hand.

It was little things like that, Heather thought as Annika left the room, which made her stand apart. The formal handshake, her slight Russian accent, even though she had been born in Australia. Heather skimmed through Annika's personal file, reading again that she had been home tutored, which explained a lot but not all.

There was guardedness to her, a warning that came from those blue eyes that told you to keep out.

And then occasionally, like she had just now, Annika would smile and her whole face lifted.

She was right about one thing, though, Heather thought, picking up the paper and reading about the latest antics of Annika's brother Aleksi. People did want to know more. People were fascinated by the Kolovsky family—even Heather. Feeling just a touch guilty, she read the article and wondered, not for the first time, what someone as rich and indulged as Annika was trying to prove by nursing.

There was just something about the Kolovskys.

There was still half an hour till Annika's late shift started and, rather than walk into an unfamiliar staffroom and kill time, unusually for Annika she decided to go to the canteen. She had made a sandwich at home, but bought a cup of coffee. She glanced at the tables on offer, and for perhaps the thousandth time rued her decision to work at Melbourne Bayside.

Her brother Iosef was an emergency doctor at Melbourne Central. His wife, Annie, was a nurse there too, but Iosef had been so discouraging, scathing almost, about Annika's ability that she had applied to study and work here instead. How nice it would be now to have Annie wave and ask to join her. Perhaps too it would have been easier to work in a hospital where there were already two Kolovskys—to feel normal.

'Annika!'

She felt a wash of relief as one of her fellow students waved at her. Cassie was down for the children's ward rotation too and, remembering to smile, Annika made her way over.

'Are you on a late shift?' asked Cassie.

'I am,' Annika said. 'It's my first, though. You've

already done a couple of shifts there—how have you found it?'

'Awful,' Cassie admitted. 'I feel like an absolute beginner. Everything's completely different—the drug doses, the way they do obs, and then there are the parents watching your every move.'

It sounded awful, and they sat in glum silence for a moment till Cassie spoke again. 'How was your assessment?'

'Fine,' Annika responded, and then remembered she was going to make more of an effort to be open and friendly 'Well, to tell the truth it wasn't great.'

'Oh?' Cassie blinked at the rare insight.

'My grades and things are okay; it is more to do with the way I am with my peers...' She could feel her cheeks burning at the admission. 'And with the patients too. I can be a bit stand-offish!'

'Oh!' Cassie blinked again. 'Well, if it makes you feel any better, I had my assessment on Monday. I'm to stop talking and listen more, apparently. Oh, and I'm to stop burning the candle at both ends!'

And it did make her feel better—not that Cassie hadn't fared well, more that she wasn't the only one who was struggling. Annika smiled again, but it faded when she looked up, because there, handing over some money to the cashier, *he* was.

Dr Ross Wyatt.

He was impossible not to notice.

Tall, with thick black slightly wavy hair, worn just a touch too long, he didn't look like a paediatric consultant—well, whatever paediatric consultants were supposed to look like.

Some days he would be wearing jeans and a T-shirt,

finished off with dark leather cowboy boots, as if he'd
just got off a horse. Other days—normally Mondays,
Annika had noticed—it was a smart suit, but still with
a hint of rebellion: his tie more than a little loosened,
and with that silver earring he wore so well. There was
just something that seemed to say his muscled, toned
body wanted out of the tailored confines of his suit.
And then again, but only rarely, given he wasn't a
surgeon, if he'd been on call he might be wearing scrubs.
Well, it almost made her dizzy: the thin cotton that ac-
centuated the outline of his body, the extra glimpse of
olive skin and the clip of Cuban-heeled boots as she'd
walked behind him in the corridor one morning….

Ross Wyatt was her favourite diversion, and he was certainly diverting her now. Annika blushed as he pocketed
his change, picked up his tray and caught her looking. She
looked away, tried to listen to Cassie, but the slow, lazy
smile he had treated her with danced before her eyes.

Always he looked good—well, not in the conven-
tional way: her mother, Nina, would faint at his choices.
Fashion was one of the rules in her family, and Ross
Wyatt broke them all.

And today, on her first day on the paediatric ward,
as if to welcome her, he was dressed in Annika's personal favourite and he looked divine!

Black jeans, with a thick leather belt, a black crew-
neck jumper that showed off to perfection his lean
figure, black boots, and that silver earring. The colour
was in his lips: wide, blood-red lips that curved into an
easy smile. Annika hadn't got close enough yet to see
his eyes, but he looked like a Spanish gypsy—just the
sort of man her mother would absolutely forbid. He
looked wild and untamed and thrilling—as if at any

minute he would kick his heels and throw up his arms, stamp a flamenco on his way over to her. She could almost smell the smoke from the bonfire—he did that to her with a single smile…

And it was madness, Annika told herself, utter madness to be sitting in the canteen having such flights of fancy. Madness to be having such thoughts, full stop.

But just the sight of him did this.

And that smile *had been* aimed at her.

Again.

Maybe he smiled at everyone, Annika reasoned—only it didn't feel like it. Sometimes they would pass in the corridor, or she'd see him walking out of ICU, or in the canteen like this, and for a second he would stop…stop and smile.

It was as if he was waiting to know her.

And that was the other reason she was dreading her paediatric rotation. She had once let a lift go simply because he was in it. She wanted this whole eight weeks to be over with, to be finished.

She didn't need any more distractions in an already complicated life—and Ross Wyatt would be just that: a huge distraction.

They had never spoken, never even exchanged pleasantries. He had looked as if he was going to try a couple of times, but she had scuttled back into her burrow like a frightened rabbit. Oh, she knew a little about him—he was a friend of her brother's, had been a medical student at the same time as Iosef. He still went to the orphanages in Russia, doing voluntary work during his annual leave—that was why he had been unable to attend Iosef and Annie's wedding. She had paid little attention when his name had been mentioned at the time, but since last year, when she had put his face to his name, she had yearned for snippets from her brother.

Annika swallowed as she felt the weight of his eyes still on her. She had the craziest notion that he was going to walk over and finally speak to her, so she concentrated on stirring her coffee.

'There are compensations, of course!' Cassie dragged her back to the conversation, only to voice what was already on Annika's mind. 'He's stunning, isn't he?'

'Who?' Annika flushed, stirring her coffee, but Cassie just laughed.

'Dr Drop-Dead Gorgeous Wyatt.'

'I don't know him.' Annika shrugged.

'Well, he's looking right over at you!' Cassie sighed. 'He's amazing, and the kids just love him—he really is great with them.'

'How?'

'I don't know…' Cassie admitted. 'He just…' She gave a frustrated shrug. 'He *gets* them, I guess. He just seems to understand kids, puts them at ease.'

Annika did not, would not, look over to where he sat, but sometimes she was sure he looked over to her— because every now and then she felt her skin warm. Every now and then it seemed too complicated to move the sandwich from her hand up to her mouth.

Ross Wyatt certainly didn't put Annika at ease.

He made her awkward.

He made her aware.

Even walking over to empty out her tray and head to work she felt as if her movements were being noted, but, though it was acutely awkward, somehow she liked the feeling he evoked. Liked the thrill in the pit of her stomach, the rush that came whenever their paths briefly crossed.

As she sat in handover, listening to the list of patients and their ages and diagnoses, he popped his head around the door to check something with Caroline, the charge nurse, and Annika felt a dull blush on her neck as she heard his voice properly for the first time.

Oh, she'd heard him laugh on occasion, and heard his low tones briefly as they'd passed in the corridor when he was talking with a colleague, but she'd never fully heard him speak.

And as he spoke now, about an order for pethidine, Annika found out that toes did curl—quite literally!

His voice was rich and low and without arrogance. He'd made Caroline laugh with something he said— only Annika couldn't properly process it, because instead she was feeling her toes bunch up inside her sensible navy shoes.

'Back to Luke Winters…'

As the door closed so too did her mind on Ross, and she began concentrating carefully on the handover, because this rotation she *had* to do well.

'He's fifteen years old, Type 1 Diabetes, non-compliant…'

Luke Winters, Annika learnt, was causing not just his family but the staff of the children's ward a lot of problems.

It was his third admission in twelve months. He was refusing to take his insulin at times, ignoring his diet, and he had again gone into DKA—a dangerous, toxic state that could kill. He had an ulcer on his leg that had been discovered on admission, though had probably been there for some time. It would take a long time to heal and might require a skin graft. His mother was frantic—

Luke had come to the ward from ICU two days ago and was causing chaos. His room was a mess, and he had told the domestic this morning, none too politely, to get out.

He was now demanding that his catheter be removed, and basically both the other patients and the staff wanted him taken to an adult ward, though Ross Wyatt was resisting.

'"Teenagers, even teenagers who think they are adults, are still children."' Caroline rolled her eyes. 'His words, not mine. Anyway, Luke's mum is at work and not due in till this evening. Hopefully we can have some order by then. Okay…' She stared at the patient sheet and allocated the staff, pausing when she came to Annika. 'I might put you in cots with Amanda…' She hesitated. 'But you haven't been in cots yet, have you, Cassie?'

When Cassie shook her head and Caroline changed her allocation Annika felt a flood of relief—she had never so much as held a baby, and the thought of looking after a sick one petrified her.

'Annika, perhaps you could have beds eight to sixteen instead—though given it's your first day don't worry about room fifteen.'

'Luke?' Annika checked, and Caroline nodded.

'I don't want to scare you off on your first day.'

'He won't scare me,' Annika said. Moody teenagers she could deal with; it was babies and toddlers that scared her.

'His room needs to be sorted.'

'It will be.'

'Okay!' Caroline smiled. 'If you're sure? Good luck.'

Lisa, who was in charge of Annika's patients, showed her around the ward. It was, as Cassie had said, completely different. Brightly painted, with a detailed mural running the length of the corridor, and divided pretty much into three.

There were cots for the littlest patients—two large rooms, each containing four cots. Then there were eight side rooms that would house a cot or a bed, depending on the patient's age. Finally there were three large four-bedded rooms, filled with children of various ages.

'Though we do try to keep ages similar,' Lisa said, 'sometimes it's just not possible.' She pointed out the crash trolley, the drug room, and two treatment rooms. 'We try to bring the children down here for dressings and IV's and things like that.'

'So they don't upset the other children?' Annika checked.

'That, and also, even if they are in a side room, it's better they have anything unpleasant done away from their bed. Obviously if they're infectious we can't bring them down, but generally we try to do things away from the bedside.'

Annika was offered a tabard to replace her navy one. She had a choice of aprons, all brightly coloured and emblazoned with cartoon characters, and though her first instinct was to politely decline, she remembered she was making an effort, so chose a red one, with fish and mermaids on it. She felt, as she slipped it over her head, utterly stupid.

Annika started with the obs. Lunches were being cleared away, and the ward was being readied for afternoon rest-time.

The children eyed her suspiciously—she was new and they knew it.

'What's that for?' A mother demanded angrily as her first patient burst into tears when Annika went to wrap a blood pressure cuff around her arm.

Lisa moved quickly to stop her.

'We don't routinely do blood pressure,' Lisa said, showing her the obs form. 'Unless it's stated on the chart.'

'Okay.'

'Just pulse, temp and respirations.'

'Thank you.'

The little girl wouldn't stop crying. In fact she shrieked every time Annika tried to venture near, so Lisa quickly took her temperature as Annika did the rest of the obs. In the room, eight sets of eyes watched her every awkward move: four from the patients, four from their mothers.

'Can I have a drink?' a little boy asked.

'Of course,' Annika said, because that was easy. She checked his chart and saw that he was to be encouraged to take fluids. 'Would you like juice or milk…?'

'He's lactose intolerant!' his mother jumped in. 'It says so above his bed.'

'Always look at the whiteboard above the bed,' Lisa said. 'And it will say in his admission slip too, which is clipped to his folder.'

'Of course.' Annika fled to the kitchen, where Cassie was warming a bottle.

'Told you!' Cassie grinned when Annika told her all that had happened. 'It's like landing on Mars!'

But she wasn't remotely nervous about a sullen Luke. She knew he had no relatives with him, and was glad to escape the suspicious eyes of parents. It was only when she went into the side ward and realised that Ross was in there, talking, that she felt flustered.

'I can come back.'

'No.' He smiled. 'We're just having a chat, and Luke needs his obs done.'

'I don't want them done,' Luke snarled as she approached the bed.

That didn't ruffle her either—her extra shifts at the nursing home had taught her well, because belligerence was an everyday occurrence there!

'I will come back in five minutes, then,' Annika said, just as she would say to Cecil, or Elsie, or any of the oldies who refused to have their morning shower.

'I won't want them done then either.'

'Then I will come back five minutes later, and five minutes after that again. My name is Annika; it would seem that you'll be seeing a lot of me this afternoon.' She gave him a smile. 'Every five minutes, in fact.'

'Just take them now, then.'

So she did.

Annika made no attempt at small talk. Luke clearly didn't want it, and anyway Ross was talking to him, telling him that there was no question of him going home, that he was still extremely ill and would be here for a few weeks—at least until the ulcer on his leg was healed and he was compliant with his medication. Yes, he would take the catheter out, so long as Luke agreed to wee into a bottle so that they could monitor his output.

Luke begrudgingly agreed to that.

And then Ross told him that the way he had spoken to the cleaner that morning was completely unacceptable.

'You can be as angry as you like, Luke, but it's not okay to be mean.'

'So send me home, then.'

'That's not going to happen.'

Annika wrote down his obs, which were all fine, and

then, as Ross leant against the wall and Luke lay on the bed with his eyes closed, she spoke.

'When the doctor has finished talking to you I will come back and sort out your room.'

'And I'll tell *you* the same thing I said to the cleaner.'

She saw Ross open his mouth to intervene as Luke snarled at her, but in this Annika didn't need his help.

'Would you rather I waited till children's nap-time is over?' Annika asked. 'When you feel a little less grumpy.'

'Ha-ha…' he sneered, and then he opened his eyes and gave a nasty sarcastic grin. 'Nice apron!'

'I hate it,' she said. 'Wearing it is a bit demoralising and…' She thought for a moment as Luke just stared. 'Well, I find it a bit patronising really. If I were in cots it would maybe be appropriate. Still…' Annika shrugged. 'Sometimes we have to do things we don't want to.' She replaced his chart. 'I'll be back to clean your room shortly.'

Ross was at the nurses' station writing notes when she came over after completing the rest of the obs. He grinned when he saw her.

'Nice apron.'

'It's growing on me!' Annika said. 'Tomorrow I want to wear the one with robots!'

'I can't wait!' he replied, and, oh, for a witty retort— but there wasn't one forthcoming, so instead she asked Lisa where the cleaning cupboard was and found a bin liner. She escaped to the rather more soothing, at least for Annika, confines of Luke's room.

It was disgusting.

In the short time he had been in the room he had accumulated cups and plates and spilt drinks. There were used tissues on the floor. His bed was a disgrace because he refused to let anyone tidy it, and there were loads of cards from friends, along with all the gadgets fifteen-year-olds seemed to amass.

Luke didn't tell her to leave—probably because he sensed she wouldn't care if he did.

Annika was used to moods.

She had grown up surrounded by them and had chosen to completely ignore them.

Her father's temper had been appalling, though it had never been aimed towards her—she had been the apple of his eye. Her brothers were dark and brooding, and her mother could sulk for Russia.

A fifteen-year-old was nothing, *nothing*, compared to that lot.

Luke ignored her.

Which was fine by Annika.

'Everything okay?' Lisa checked as she finally headed to the kitchen with a trolley full of used plates and cups.

'All's fine.' The ward was quiet, the lights all dimmed, and Ross was still at the desk. 'Do you need me to do anything else, or is it okay if I carry on with Luke's room?'

'Please do,' Lisa said.

Luke wasn't ignoring her now—instead he watched as she sorted out his stuff into neat piles and put some of it into a bag.

'Your mum can take these home to wash.'

Other stuff she put into drawers.

Then she tacked some cards to the wall. All that was messy now, Annika decided as she wiped down the sur-faces in his room, was the patient and his bed.

'Now your catheter is out it will be easier to have a shower. I can run it for you.'

He said neither yes nor no, so Annika headed down the ward and found the linen trolley, selected some towels and then found the showers. She worked out the taps and headed back to her patient, who was a bit wobbly but refused a wheelchair.

'Take my arm, then.'

'I can manage,' Luke said, and he said it again when she tried to help him undress.

'You have a drip…'

'I'm not stupid; I've had a drip before.'

Okay!

So she left him to it, and she didn't hover outside, asking if he was okay every two minutes, because that would have driven Luke insane. Instead she moved to the other end of the bathroom, so she could hear him if he called, and checked her reflection, noting the huge smudges under her eyes, which her mother would point out to her when she went there for dinner at the weekend.

She was exhausted. Annika rested her head against the mirror for a moment and just wanted to close her eyes and sleep. She was beyond exhausted, in fact, and from this morning's assessment it seemed it had been noticed.

Heather would never believe that she was working shifts in a nursing home, and the hardest slots too—five a.m. till eight a.m. if she was on a late shift at the hospital, and seven p.m. till ten p.m. if she was on an early. Oh, and a couple of nights shifts on her days off.

She was so tired. Not just bone-tired, but tired of arguing, tired of being told to pack in nursing, to come home, to be sensible, tired of being told that she didn't need to nurse—she was a Kolovsky.

'Iosef is a doctor,' Annika had pointed out.

'Iosef is a fool,' her mother had said, 'and as for that slut of a wife of his…'

'Finished.'

She was too glum thinking about her mother to smile and cheer as Luke came out, in fresh track pants and with his hair dripping wet.

'You smell much better,' Annika settled for instead, and the shower must have drained Luke because he let Annika thread his T-shirt through his IV.

'What are you looking so miserable about?' Luke asked.

'Stuff,' Annika said.

'Yeah,' Luke said, and she was rewarded with a smile from him.

'Oh, that's *much* better!' Lisa said, popping her head into the bathroom. 'You're looking very handsome.' Annika caught Luke's eyes and had to stop herself from rolling her own. She sort of understood him—she didn't know how, she just did. 'Your mum's here, by the way!' Lisa added.

'Great,' Luke muttered as Annika walked him back. 'That's all I need. You haven't met her yet…'

'You haven't met mine!' Annika said, and they both smiled this time—a real smile.

Annika surprised herself, because rarely, if ever, did she speak about her family, and especially not to a patient. But they had a little giggle as they walked, and she was too busy concentrating on Luke and pushing his IV to notice Ross look up from the desk and watch the unlikely new friends go by.

* * *

'Are you still here?' Caroline frowned, quite a long time later, because, as pedantic as Ross was, consultants didn't usually hang around all day.

'I just thought I'd catch up on some paperwork.'

'Haven't you got an office to go to?' she teased.

He did, but for once he didn't have that much paperwork to do.

'Annika!' Caroline called her over from where Annika was stacking the linen trolley after returning from her supper break. 'Come and get started on your notes. I'll show you how we do them. It's different to the main wards.'

He didn't look up, but he smelt her as she came around the desk.

A heavy, musky fragrance perfumed the air, and though he wrote it maybe twenty times a day, he had misspelled *diarrhoea*, and Ross frowned at his spiky black handwriting, because the familiar word looked completely wrong.

'Are you wearing perfume, Annika?' He didn't look up at Caroline's stern tone.

'A little,' Annika said, because she'd freshened up after her break.

'You can't wear perfume on the children's ward!' Caroline's voice had a familiar ring to it—one Ross had heard all his life.

'What do you mean—you just didn't want to go to school? You can't wear an earring. You just have to, that's all. You just don't. You just can't.'

'Go and wash it off,' Caroline said, and now Ross did look up. He saw her standing there, wary, tight-lipped, in that ridiculous apron. 'There are children with allergies, asthma. You just *can't* wear perfume, Annika—didn't you think?'

Caroline was right, Ross conceded, there were children with allergies and, as much as he liked it, Kolovsky musk post-op might be a little bit too much, but he wanted to step in, wanted to grin at Annika and tell her she smelt divine, tell her *not* to wash it off, for her to tell Caroline that she wouldn't.

And he knew that she was thinking it too!

It was a second, a mere split second, but he saw her waver—and Ross had a bizarre feeling that she was going to dive into her bag for the bottle and run around the ward, ripping off her apron and spraying perfume. The thought made him smile—at the wrong moment, though, because Annika saw him and, although Ross snapped his face to bland, she must have thought he was enjoying her discomfort.

Oh, but he wanted to correct her.

He wanted to follow her and tell her that wasn't what he'd meant as she duly turned around and headed for the washroom.

He wanted to apologise when she came back unscented and sat at her stool while Caroline nit-picked her way through the nursing notes.

Instead he returned to his own notes.

DIAOR… He scrawled a line through it again.

Still her fragrance lingered.

He got up without a word and, unusually for Ross, closed his office door. Then he picked up his pen and forced himself to concentrate.

DIARREA.

He hurled his pen down. Who cared anyway? They knew what he meant!

He was not going to fancy her, nor, if he could help it, even talk much to her.

He was off women.

He had sworn off women.

And a student nurse on his ward—well, it couldn't be without complications.

She was his friend's little sister too.

No way!

Absolutely not.

He picked up his pen and resumed his notes.

'The baby has,' he wrote instead, *'severe gastro-enteritis.'*

CHAPTER TWO

HE DID a very good job of ignoring her.

He did an excellent job at pulling rank and completely speaking over her head, or looking at a child or a chart or the wall when he had no choice but to address her. And at his student lecture on Monday he paid her no more attention than any of the others. He delivered a talk on gastroenteritis, and, though he hesitated as he went to spell *diarrhoea*, he wrote it up correctly on the whiteboard.

She, Ross noted, was ignoring him too. She asked no questions at the end of the lecture, but an annoying student called Cassie made up for that.

Once their eyes met, but she quickly flicked hers away, and he, though he tried to discount it, saw the flush of red on her neck and wished that he hadn't.

Yes, he did a very good job at ignoring her and not talking to her till, chatting to the pathologist in the bowels of the hospital a few days later, he glanced up at the big mirror that gave a view around the corridor and there was Annika. She was yawning, holding some blood samples, completely unaware she was being watched.

'I've been waiting for these...' Ross said when she

turned the corner, and she jumped slightly at the sight of him. He took the bloodwork and stared at the forms rather than at her.

'The chute isn't working,' Annika explained. 'I said I'd drop them in on my way home.'

'I forgot to sign the form.'

'Oh.'

He would rather have taken ages to sign the form, but the pathologist decided they had been talking for too long and hurried him along. Annika had stopped for a moment to put on her jacket, and as his legs were much longer than hers somehow, despite trying not to, he had almost caught her up as they approached the flapping black plastic doors. It would have been really rude had she not held it open—and just plain wrong for him not to thank her and fall into step beside her.

'You look tired,' Ross commented.

'It's been a long shift.'

This had got them halfway along the corridor, and now they should just walk along in silence, Ross reasoned. He was a consultant, and he could be as rude and as aloof as he liked—except he could hear his boots, her shoes, and an endless, awful silence. It was Ross who filled it.

'I've actually been meaning to talk to you...' He had—long before he had liked her.

'Oh?' She felt the adrenaline kick in, the effect of him close up far more devastating than his smile, and yet she liked it. She liked it so much that she slowed down her pace and looked over to him. 'About what?'

She could almost smell the bonfire—all those smiles, all that guessing, all that waiting was to be put to rest now they were finally talking.

'I know your brother Iosef,' Ross said. 'He asked me to keep an eye out for you when you started.'

'Did he?' Her cheeks were burning, the back of her nose was stinging, and she wanted to run, to kick up her heels and run from him—because all the time she'd thought it was her, not her family, that he saw.

'I've always meant to introduce myself. Iosef is a good friend.' It was her jacket's fault, Ross decided. Her jacket smelt of the forbidden perfume. It smelt so much of her that he forgot, for a second, his newly laid-down rules. 'We should catch up some time…'

'Why?' She turned very blue eyes to him. 'So that you can report back to Iosef?'

'Of course not.'

'Tell him I'm doing fine,' Annika snapped, and, no, she didn't kick up her heels, and she didn't run, but she did walk swiftly away from him.

A year.

For more than a year she'd carried a torch, had secretly hoped that his smile, those looks they had shared, had meant something. All that time she had thought it had been about her, and yet again it wasn't.

Again, all she was was a Kolovsky.

It rankled. On the drive home it gnawed and burnt, but when she got there her mother had left a long message on the answer machine which rankled rather more.

They needed to go over details, she reminded her daughter.

It was the charity ball in just three weeks—as if Annika could ever forget.

When Annika had been a child it had been discovered that her father had an illegitimate son—one who was being raised in an orphanage in Russia.

Levander had been brought over to Australia. Her father had done everything to make up for the wretched years his son had suffered, and Levander's appalling early life had been kept a closely guarded family secret.

Now, though, the truth was starting to seep out. And Nina, anticipating a public backlash, had moved into pre-emptive damage control.

Huge donations had been sent to several orphanages, and to a couple of street-kid programmes too.

And then there was *The Ball*.

It was to be a dazzling, glitzy affair they would all attend. Levander was to be excused because he was in England, but the rest of the family would be there. Iosef and his wife, her brother Aleksi, and of course Annika. They would all look glossy and beautiful and be photographed to the max, so that when the truth inevitably came out the spin doctors would be ready.

Already were ready.

Annika had read the draft of the waiting press release.

The revelation of his son Levander's suffering sent Ivan Kolovsky to an early grave. He was thrilled when his second-born, Iosef, on qualifying as a doctor, chose to work amongst the poor in Russia, and Ivan would be proud to know that his daughter, Annika, is now studying nursing. On Ivan's deathbed he begged his wife to set up the Kolovsky Foundation, which has gone on to raise huge amounts (insert current figure).

Lies.

Lies based on twisted truths. And only since her father's death had Annika started to question them.

And now she had, everything had fallen apart.

Her mother had never hit her before—oh, maybe a slap on the leg when she was little and had refused to converse in Russian, and once as a teenager, when her mother had found out she was eating burgers on her morning jog, Annika had nursed a red cheek and a swollen eye…but hardly anything major…

Until she had asked about Levander.

They had been sorting out her father's things, a painful task at the best of times, and Annika had come across some letters. She hadn't read them—she hadn't had a chance to. Nina had snatched them out of her hands, but Annika had asked her mother a question that had been nagging. It was a question her brothers had refused to answer when she had approached them with it. She asked whether Ivan and Nina had known that Levander was in an orphanage all those years.

Her mother had slapped her with a viciousness that had left Annika reeling—not at the pain but with shock.

She had then discovered that when she started to think, to suggest, to question, to find her own path in life, the love and support Annika had thought was unconditional had been pulled up like a drawbridge.

And the money had been taken away too.

Annika deleted her mother's message and prepared a light supper. She showered, and then, because she hadn't had time to this morning, ironed her white agency nurse's uniform and dressed. Tying her hair back, she clipped on her name badge.

Annika Kolovsky.

No matter how she resisted, it was who she was— and *all* she was to others.

She should surely be used to it by now.

Except she'd thought Ross had seen something else—thought for a foolish moment that Ross Wyatt had seen her for herself. Yet again it came back to one thing.

She was a Kolovsky.

CHAPTER THREE

'SLEEP well, Elsie.' Elsie didn't answer as Annika tucked the blankets round the bony shoulders of the elderly lady.

Elsie had spat out her tablets and thrown her dinner on the floor. She had resisted at every step of Annika undressing her and getting her into bed. But now that she was in bed she relaxed, especially when Annika positioned the photo of her late husband, Bertie, where the old lady could see him.

'I'll see you in the morning. I have another shift then.'

Still Elsie didn't answer, and Annika wished she would. She loved the stories Elsie told, during the times when she was lucid. But Elsie's confusion had worsened because of an infection, and she had been distressed tonight, resenting any intrusion. Nursing patients with dementia was often a thankless task, and Annika's shifts exhausted her, but at least, unlike on the children's ward, where she had been for a week now, here Annika knew what she was doing.

Oh, it was back-breaking, and mainly just sheer hard work, but she had been here for over a year now, and knew the residents. The staff of the private nursing home had been wary at first, but they were used to Annika now. She had proved herself a hard worker and, frankly, with a skeleton staff, so long as the patients were clean and dry, and bedded at night or dressed in the morning, nobody really cared who she was or why someone as rich as Annika always put her hand up for extra shifts.

It was ridiculous, though.

Annika knew that.

In fact she was ashamed that she stood in the fore-court of a garage next to a filthy old ute and had to pre-pay twenty dollars, because that was all she had until her pay from the nursing home went in tomorrow, to fill up the tank of a six-figure powder-blue sports car.

It had been her twenty-first birthday present.

Her mother had been about to upgrade it when Annika had declared she wanted to study nursing, and when she had refused to give in the financial plug had been pulled.

Her car now needed a service, which she couldn't afford. The sensible thing, of course, would be to sell it—except, despite its being a present, technically, it didn't belong to her: it was a company car.

So deep in thought was Annika, so bone-weary from a day on the children's ward and a twilight shift at the nursing home, that she didn't notice the man crossing the forecourt towards her.

'Annika?' He was putting money in his wallet. He had obviously just paid, and she glanced around rather than look at him. She was one burning blush, and not just because it was Ross, but rather because someone from work had seen her. She had done a full shift on the children's ward, and was due back there at midday tomorrow, so there was no way on earth she should be cramming in an extra shift, but she clearly was—two, actually, not that he could know! The white agency nurse dress seemed to glow under the fluorescent lights.

He could have nodded and left it there.

He damn well *should* nod and leave it there—and maybe even have a quiet word with Caroline tomorrow, or Iosef, perhaps.

Or say nothing at all—just simply forget.

He chose none of the above.

'How about a coffee?'

'It's late.'

'I know it's late,' Ross said, 'but I'm sure you could use a coffee. There's an all-night cafe a kilometre up the road—I'll see you there.'

She nearly didn't go.

She was *extremely* tempted not to go. But she had no choice.

Normally she was careful about being seen in her agency uniform, but she didn't have her jacket in the car, and she'd been so low on petrol… Anyway, Annika told herself, it was hardly a crime—all her friends did agency shifts. How the hell would a student survive otherwise?

His grim face told her her argument would be wasted.

'I know students have to work…' he had bought her a coffee and she added two sugars '…and I know it's probably none of my business…'

'It *is* none of your business,' Annika said.

'But I've heard Caroline commenting, and I've seen you yawning…' Ross said. 'You look like you've got two black eyes.'

'So tell Caroline—or report back to my brother.' Annika shrugged. 'Then your duty is done.'

'Annika!' Ross was direct. 'Do you go out of your way to be rude?'

'Rude?'

'I'm trying *not* to talk to Caroline; I'm trying to talk to *you*.'

'Check up on me, you mean, so that Iosef—'

He whistled in indignation. 'This has nothing to do with your brother. It's my ward, Annika. You were on an early today; you're on again tomorrow…'

'How do you know?'

'Sorry?'

'My shift tomorrow. How do you know?'

And that he couldn't answer—but the beat of silence did.

He'd checked.

Not deliberately—he hadn't swiped keys and found the nursing roster—but as he'd left the ward he had glanced up at the whiteboard and seen that she was on tomorrow.

He had noted to himself that she was on tomorrow.

'I saw the whiteboard.'

And she could have sworn that he blushed. Oh, his cheeks didn't flare like a match to a gas ring, as Annika's did—he was far too laid-back for that, and his skin was so much darker—but there was something that told her he was embarrassed. He blinked, and then his lips twitched in a very short smile, and then he blinked again. There was no colour as such to his eyes—in fact they were blacker than black, so much so that she couldn't even make out his pupils. He was staring, and so was she. They were sitting in an all-night coffee shop. She was in her uniform and he was telling her off for working, and yet she was sure there was more.

Almost sure.

'So, Iosef told you to keep an eye out for me?' she said, though more for her own benefit—that smile wouldn't fool her again.

'He said that he was worried about you, that you'd pretty much cut yourself off from your family.'

'I haven't,' Annika said, and normally that would have been it. Everything that was said stayed in the family, but Ross was Iosef's friend and she was quite sure he knew more. 'I see my mother each week; I am attending a family charity ball soon. Iosef and I argued, but only because he thinks I'm just playing at nursing.'

This wasn't news to Ross. Iosef had told him many things—how Annika was spoilt, how she stuck at nothing, how nursing was her latest flight of fancy. Of course Ross could not say this, so he just sat as she continued.

'I have not cut myself off from my family. Aleksi and I are close...' She saw his jaw tighten, as everyone's did these days when her brother's name was mentioned. Aleksi was trouble. Aleksi, now head of the Kolovsky fortune, was a loose cannon about to explode at any moment. Annika was the only one he was close to; even his twin Iosef was being pushed aside as Aleksi careered out of control. She looked down at her coffee then, but it blurred, so she pressed her fingers into her eyes.

'You *can* talk to me,' Ross said.

'Why would I?'

'Because that's what people do,' Ross said. 'Some people you know you can talk to, and some people...' He stopped then. He could see she didn't understand, and neither really did Ross. He swallowed down the words he had been about to utter and changed tack. 'I am going to Spain in three, nearly four weeks.' He smiled at her frown. 'Caroline doesn't know; Admin doesn't know. In truth, they are going to be furious when they find out. I am putting off telling them till I have spoken with a friend who I am hoping can cover for me…'

'Why are you telling me this?'

'Because I'm asking you to tell *me* things you'd rather no one else knew.'

She took her fingers out of her eyes and looked up to find *that* smile.

'It would be rude not to share,' he said.

He *was* dangerous.

She could almost hear her mother's rule that you discussed family with no one breaking.

'My mother does not want me to nurse,' Annika tentatively explained. And the skies didn't open with a roar, missiles didn't engage. There was just the smell of coffee and the warmth of his eyes. 'She has cut me off financially until I come back home. I still see her, I still go over and I still attend functions. I haven't cut myself off. It is my mother who has cut me off—financially, anyway. That's why I'm working these shifts.'

He didn't understand—actually, he didn't fully believe it.

He could guess at what her car was worth, and he knew from his friend that Annika was doted upon. Then there was Aleksi and his billions, and Iosef, even if they argued, would surely help her out.

'Does Iosef know you're doing extra shifts?'

'We don't talk much,' Annika admitted. 'We don't get on; we just never have. I was always a daddy's girl, the little princess… Levander, my older brother, thinks the same…' She gave a helpless shrug. 'I was always pleading with them to toe the line, to stop making waves in the family. Iosef is just waiting for me to quit.'

'Iosef cares about you.'

'He offers me money,' Annika scoffed. 'But really he is just waiting for this phase to be over. If I want money I will ask Aleksi, but, really, how can I be independent if all I do is cash cheques?'

'And how can you study and do placements and be a Kolovsky if you're cramming in extra shifts everywhere?'

She didn't know how, because she was failing at every turn.

'I get by,' she settled for. 'I have learnt that I can blowdry my own hair, that foils every month are not essential, that a massage each week and a pedicure and manicure...' Her voice sounded strangled for a moment. 'I am spoilt, as my brothers have always pointed out, and I am trying to learn not to be, but I keep messing up.'

'Tell me?'

She was surprised when she opened her screwed up eyes, to see that he was smiling.

'Tell me how you mess up?'

'I used to eat a lot of takeaway,' she admitted, and he was still smiling, so she was more honest, and Ross found out that Annika's idea of takeaway wasn't the same as his! 'I had the restaurants deliver.'

'Can't you cook?'

'I'm a fantastic cook,' Annika answered.

'That's right.' Ross grinned. 'I remember Iosef saying you were training as a pastry chef...in Paris?' he checked.

'I was only there six months.' Annika wrinkled her nose. 'I had given up on modelling and I so badly wanted to go. It took me two days to realise I had made a mistake, and then six months to pluck up the courage

to admit defeat. I had made such a fuss, begged to go...
Like I did for nursing.'

He didn't understand.

He thought of his own parents—if he'd said that he
wanted to study life on Mars they'd have supported
him. But then he'd always known what he wanted to do.
Maybe if one year it had been Mars, the next Venus and
then Pluto, they'd have decided otherwise. Maybe this
was tough love that her mother thought she needed to
prove that nursing was what she truly wanted to do.

'So you can cook?' It was easier to change the subject.

'Gourmet meals, the most amazing desserts, but a
simple dinner for one beats me every time...' She gave
a tight shrug. 'But I'm slowly learning.'

'How else have you messed up?'

She couldn't tell him, but he was still smiling, so
maybe she could.

'I had a credit card,' she said. 'I have always had one,
but I just sent the bill to our accountants each month...'

'Not now?'

'No.'

Her voice was low and throaty, and Ross found himself leaning forward to catch it.

'It took me three months to work out that they
weren't settling it, and I am still paying off that mistake.'

'But you love nursing?' Ross said, and then frowned
when she shook her head.

'I don't know,' Annika admitted. 'Sometimes I don't
even know why I am doing this. It's the same as when
I wanted to be a pastry chef, and then I did jewellery
design—that was a mistake too.'

'Do you think you've made a mistake with nursing?'
Ross asked.

Annika gave a tight shrug and then shook her head—
he was hardly the person to voice her fears to.

'You can talk to me, Annika. You can trust that it
won't—'

'Trust?' She gave him a wide-eyed look. 'Why would
I trust you?'

It was the strangest answer, and one he wasn't expecting. Yet why should she trust him? Ross pondered.
All he knew was that she could.

'You need to get home and get some rest,' Ross
settled for—except he couldn't quite leave it there.
'How about dinner…?'

And this was where every woman jumped, this was
where Ross always kicked himself and told himself to
slow down, because normally they never made it to
dinner. Normally, about an hour from now, they were
pinning the breakfast menu on the nearest hotel door or
hot-footing it back to his city abode—only this was
Annika, who instead drained her coffee and stood up.

'No, thank you. It would make things difficult at work.'

'It would,' Ross agreed, glad that one of them at least
was being sensible.

'Can I ask that you don't tell Caroline or anyone
about this?'

'Can I ask that you save these shifts for your days off,
or during your holidays?'

'No.'

They walked out to the car park, to his dusty ute and
her powder-blue car. Ross was relaxed and at ease,
Annika a ball of tension, so much so that she jumped at
the bleep of her keys as she unlocked the car.

'I'm not going to say anything to Caroline.'

'Thank you.'

'Just be careful, okay?'

'I will.'

'You can't mess up on any ward, but especially not on children's.'

'I won't,' Annika said. 'I don't. I am always so, so careful…' And she was. Her brain hurt because she was so careful, pedantic, and always, *always* checked. Sometimes it would be easier not to care so.

'Go home and go to bed,' Ross said. 'Will you be okay to drive?'

'Of course.'

He didn't want her to drive; he wanted to bundle her into his ute and take her back to the farm, or head back into the coffee shop and talk till three a.m., or, maybe just kiss her?

Except he was being sensible now.

'Night, then,' he said.

'Goodnight.'

Except neither of them moved.

'Why are you going to Spain?' Unusually, it was Annika who broke the silence.

'To sort out a few things.'

'I'm staying here for a few weeks,' Annika said, with just a hint of a smile. 'To sort out a few things.'

'It will be nice,' Ross said, 'when things are a bit more sorted.'

'Very nice,' Annika agreed, and wished him goodnight again.

'If you change your mind…' He snapped his mouth closed; he really mustn't go there.

Annika was struggling. She didn't want to get into her car. She wanted to climb into the ute with him, to forget about sorting things out for a little while. She wanted him to drive her somewhere secluded. She wanted the passion those black eyes promised, wanted out of being staid, and wanted to dive into recklessness.

'Drive carefully.'

'You too.'

They were talking normally—extremely politely, actually—yet their minds were wandering off to dangerous places: lovely, lovely places that there could be no coming back from.

'Go,' Ross said, and she felt as if he were kissing her. His eyes certainly were, and her body felt as if he were.

She was shaking as she got in the car, and the key was too slim for the slot. She had to make herself think, had to slow her mind down and turn on the lights and then the ignition.

He was beside her at the traffic lights. Ross was indicating right for the turn to the country; Annika aimed straight for the city.

It took all her strength to go straight on.

CHAPTER FOUR

ELSIE frowned from her pillow when Annika awoke her a week later at six a.m. with a smile.

'What are you so cheerful about?' Elsie asked dubiously. She often lived in the past, but sometimes in the morning she clicked to the present, and those were the mornings Annika loved best.

She recognised Annika—oh, not all of the time, sometimes she spat and swore at the intrusion, but some mornings she was Elsie, with beady eyes and a generous glimpse of a once sharp mind.

'I just am.'

'How's the children's ward?' Elsie asked. Clearly even in that fog-like existence she mainly inhabited somehow she heard the words Annika said, even if she didn't appear to at the time.

Annika was especially nice to Elsie. Well, she was nice to all the oldies, but Elsie melted her heart. The old lady had shrunk to four feet tall and there was more fat on a chip. She swore, she spat, she growled, and every now and then she smiled. Annika couldn't help but spoil her, and sometimes it annoyed the other staff, because many showers had to be done before the day shift appeared, and there really wasn't time to make drinks, but Elsie loved to have a cup of milky tea before she even thought about moving and Annika always made her one. The old lady sipped on it noisily as Annika sorted out her clothes for the day.

'It's different on the children's ward,' Annika said. 'I'm not sure if I like it.'

'Well, if it isn't work that's making you cheerful then I want to know what is. It has to be a man.'

'I'm just in a good mood.'

'It's a man,' Elsie said. 'What's his name?'

'I'm not saying.'

'Why not? I tell you about Bertie.'

This was certainly true!

'Ross.' Annika helped her onto the shower chair. 'And that's all I'm saying.'

'Are you courting?'

Annika grinned at the old-fashioned word.

'No,' Annika said.

'Has he asked you out?'

'Sort of,' Annika said as she wheeled her down to the showers. 'Just for dinner, but I said no.'

'So you're just flirting, then!' Elsie beamed. 'Oh, you lucky, lucky girl. I loved flirting.'

'We're not flirting, Elsie,' Annika said. 'In fact we're now ignoring each other.'

'Why would you do that?'

'Just leave it, Elsie.'

'Flirt!' Elsie insisted as Annika pulled her nightgown over her head. 'Ask him out.'

'Enough, Elsie,' Annika attempted, but it was like pulling down a book and having the whole shelf toppling down on you. Elsie was on a roll, telling her exactly what she'd have done, how the worst thing she should do was play it cool.

On and on she went as Annika showered her, though thankfully, once Annika had popped in her teeth, Elsie's train of thought drifted back to her beloved Bertie, to the sixty wonderful years they had shared, to shy kisses at the dance halls he had taken her to and the agony of him going to war. She talked about how you must never let the sun go down on a row, and she chatted away about Bertie, their wedding night and babies as Annika dressed her, combed her hair, and then wheeled her back to her room.

'You must miss him,' Annika said, arranging Elsie's table, just as she did every morning she worked there, putting her glasses within reach, her little alarm clock, and then Elsie and Bertie's wedding photo in pride of place.

'Sometimes,' Elsie said, and then her eyes were crystal-clear, 'but only when I'm sane.'

'Sorry?'

'I get to relive our moments, over and over...' Elsie smiled, and then she was gone, back to her own world, the moment of clarity over. She did not talk as Annika wrapped a shawl around her shoulders and put on her slippers.

'Enjoy it,' Annika said to her favourite resident.

He had his ticket booked, and four weeks' unpaid leave reluctantly granted. They had wanted him to take paid leave but, as Ross had pointed out, that was all saved up for his trips to Russia. This hadn't gone down too well, and Ross had sat through a thinly veiled warning from the Head of Paediatrics—there was no such thing as a part-time consultant and, while his work overseas was admirable, there were plenty of charities here in Australia he could support.

As he walked through the canteen that evening, the conversation played over in his mind. He could feel the tentacles of bureaucracy tightening around him. He wanted this day over, to be back at his farm, where there were no rules other than to make sure the animals were fed.

His intention had been to get some chocolate from the vending machine, but he saw Annika, and thought it would be far more sensible to keep on walking. Instead, he bought a questionable cup of coffee from another machine and, uninvited, went over.

'Hi!'

He didn't ask if he could join her; he simply sat down.

She was eating a Greek salad and had pushed all the olives to one side.

'Hello.'

'Nice apron.' She was emblazoned with fairies and wands, and he could only laugh that she hated it so.

'It was the only one left,' Annika said. 'Ross, if I do write my notice—if I do give up nursing—in my letter there will be a long paragraph devoted to being made to wear aprons.'

'So you're thinking of it?'

'I don't know,' she admitted. 'I asked for a weekend off. There is a family function—there is no question that I don't go. I requested it ages ago, when I found out that I would be on the children's ward. I sent a memo, but it got lost, apparently.'

'What are you going to do?'

'Caroline has changed my late shift on Saturday to

an early, and she has changed the early shift on Sunday to a late. She wasn't pleased, though, and neither am I.' She looked over to him. 'I have to get ready….' And then her voice trailed off, because it sounded ridiculous, and how could he possibly know just what getting ready for a family function entailed?

And he didn't understand her, but he wanted to.

And, yes, he was sworn off women, and she had said no to dinner, and, yes, it could get very messy, but right now he didn't care.

He should get up and go.

Yet he couldn't.

Quiet simply, he couldn't.

'I told them I'm going to Spain.'

She looked at his grim face and guessed it hadn't gone well. 'It will be worth it when you're there, I'm sure.'

'Do you ever want to go to Russia?' Ross asked. 'To see where you are from.'

'I was born here.'

'But your roots…'

'I might not like what I dig up.'

He glanced down at her plate, at the lovely ripe olives she had pushed aside. 'May I?'

'That's bad manners.'

'Not between friends.'

He would not have taken one unless she'd done what she did next and pushed the plate towards him. She watched as he took the ripe fruit and popped it in his mouth, and Annika had no idea how, but he even looked sexy as he retrieved the stone.

'They're too good to leave.'

'I don't like them,' she said. 'I tried them once…' She pulled a face.

'You were either too young to appreciate them or you got a poor effort.'

'A poor effort?'

'Olives,' Ross said, 'need to be prepared carefully. They take ages—rush them and they're bitter. I grow them at my farm, and my grandmother knows how to make the best... She's Spanish.'

'I didn't think you were Spanish, more like a pirate or a gypsy.'

It was the first real time she had opened the conversation, the first hint at an open door. It was a glimpse that she did think about him. 'I am Spanish...' Ross said '...and I prefer Romany. I am Romany—well, my father was. My real father.'

His eyes were black—not navy, and not jade; they were as black as the leather on his belt.

'He had a brief affair with my mother when they were passing through. She was sixteen...'

'It must have caused a stir.'

'Apparently not,' Ross said. 'She was a wild thing back then—she's a bit eccentric even now. But wise...' Ross said reluctantly. 'Extremely wise.'

She wanted to know more. She didn't drain her cup or stand. She was five minutes over her coffee break, and never, ever late, yet she sat there, and then he smiled, his slow lazy smile, and she blushed. She burnt because it was bizarre, wild and crazy. She was blue-eyed and blonde and rigid, and he was so very dark and laid-back and dangerous, and they were both thinking about black-haired, blue-eyed babies, or black-eyed blonde babies, of so many fabulous combinations and the wonderful time they'd have making them.

'I have to get back.'

Annika had never flirted in her life. She had had just one boring, family-sanctioned relationship, which had ended with her rebellion in moving towards nursing, but she knew she was flirting now. She knew she was doing something dangerous and bold when she picked up a thick black olive, popped it in her mouth and then removed the pip.

'Nice?' Ross asked

'Way better than I remember.' And they weren't talking about olives, of that she was certain. She might have to check with Elsie, but she was sure she was flirting. She blushed—not from embarrassment, but because of what he said next.

'Oh, it will be.'

And as she sped back to the ward late, she was burning. She could hardly breathe as she accepted Caroline's scolding and then went to warm up a bottle for a scream-ing baby. Only when he was fed, changed and settled did she pull up the cot-side and let herself think.

Oh, she didn't need to run it by Elsie.

Ross had certainly been flirting.

And Annika had loved it.

CHAPTER FIVE

'I DON'T want a needle.'

Hannah was ten and scared.

She had flushed cheeks from crying, and from the virus that her body was struggling to fight, and Annika's heart went out to her, because the little girl had had enough.

Oh, she wasn't desperately ill, but she was sick and tired and wanted to be left alone. However, her IV site was due for a change, and even though cream had been applied an hour ago, so that she wouldn't feel it, she was scared and yet, Annika realised, just wanted it to be over and done with.

So too did Annika.

Ross was putting the IV in.

'I'll be in in a moment,' he had said, popping his head around the treatment room door—and Annika had nodded and carried on chatting with Hannah, but she was exhausted from the hyper-vigilant state he put her in. She knew he was in a difficult position; he was a consultant, she a student nurse—albeit a mature one. She also knew a relationship was absolutely the last thing she needed. Chaos abounded in her life; there was just so much to sort out.

Yet she wanted him.

Elsie, when Annika had discussed it with her, had huffed and puffed that it should be Ross who asked *her* out, Ross who should take her out dancing. But things were different now, Annika had pointed out, and she'd already said no to him once.

'Ask him,' Cecil had said when she had taken him in his evening drink. He had a nip of brandy each night, and always asked for another one. 'You lot say you want equal rights, but only when it suits you. Why should he risk his job?'

'Risk his job?'

'For harassing you?' Cecil said stoutly. 'He's already asked you and you said no—if you've changed your mind, then bloody well ask him. Stop playing games.'

'How do you know all this?' Annika had demanded, and then gone straight to Elsie's room. 'That was a secret.'

'I've got dementia.' Elsie huffed. 'You can't expect me to keep a secret.'

'You cunning witch!' Annika said, and Elsie laughed.

She hadn't just told Cecil either!

Half of the residents were asking for updates, and then sulking when Annika reported that there were none.

So, when Ross had asked her to bring Hannah up to the treatment room to have her IV bung replaced, even though Cassie had offered to do it for her, Annika had bitten the bullet. Now she was trying to talk to her patient.

'The cream we have put on your arm means that you won't feel it.'

'I just don't like it.'

'I know,' Annika said, 'but once it is done you can go back to bed and have a nice rest and you won't be worrying about it any more. Dr Ross is very gentle.'

'I am.'

She hadn't heard him come in, and she gave him a small smile as she turned around to greet him.

'Hannah's nervous.'

'I bet you are,' Ross said to his patient. 'You had a tough time of it in Emergency, didn't you? Hannah was too sick to wait for the anaesthetic cream to work,' he explained to Annika, but really for the little girl's benefit, 'and she was also so ill that her veins were hard to find, so the doctor had to have a few goes.'

'It hurt,' Hannah gulped.

'I know it did.' Ross was checking the trolley and making sure everything was set up before he commenced. Hannah was lying down, but she looked as if at any moment she might jump off the treatment bed. 'But the doctor in Emergency wasn't a children's doctor…' Ross winked to Hannah, 'I'm used to little veins, and you're not as sick now, so they're going to be a lot easier to find and because of the cream you won't be able to feel it…'

'No!'

She was starting to really cry now, pulling her arm away as Ross slipped on a tourniquet. The panic that had been building was coming to the fore. He did his best to calm her, but she wasn't having it. She needed this IV; she had already missed her six a.m. medication, and she was vomiting and not able to hold down any fluids.

'Hannah, you need this,' Ross said, and as she had

done for several patients now, Annika leant over her, keeping her little body as still as she could as Ross tried to reassure her.

'Don't look,' Annika said, holding the little girl's frightened gaze. 'You won't feel anything.'

'Just because I can't see it, I still know that you're hurting me!' came the pained little voice, and something inside Annika twisted. She felt so hopeless; she truly didn't know what to say, or how to comfort the girl.

'Watch, then,' Ross said. 'Let her go.'

He smiled to Annika and she did so, sure that the little girl would jump down from the treatment bed and run, but instead she lay there, staring suspiciously up at Ross.

'I know you've been hurt,' he said, 'and I know that in Emergency it would have been painful because the doctor had to have a few goes to get the needle in, but I'm not going to hurt you.'

'What if you can't get the needle in, like last time?'

'I'm quite sure I can,' Ross said, pressing on a rather nice vein with his olive-skinned finger. 'But if, for whatever reason, I can't, then we'll put some cream elsewhere—you're not as sick now, and we can wait…'

His voice was completely serious; he wasn't doing the smiling, reassuring thing that Annika rather poorly attempted.

'I am going to do everything I can not to hurt you. If for some reason there's ever a procedure that will hurt, I will tell you, and we'll work it out, but this one,' Ross said, 'isn't going to hurt.'

He tightened the tourniquet and Hannah watched. He swabbed the vein a couple of times and then got out the needle, and she didn't cry or move away, she just watched.

'Even I'm nervous now.' Ross grinned, and so too did

Annika, that tiny pause lifting the mood in the room. Even Hannah managed a little smile. She stared as the needle went in, and flinched, but only because she was expecting pain. When it didn't come, when the needle was in and Ross was taping it securely in place, her grin grew much wider when Ross told her she had been very brave.

'Very brave!' Annika said, like a parrot, because she could never be as at ease with children as he was. She was attaching the IV and Ross was looking through his drug book, working out the new medication regime that he wanted Hannah on.

Brighter now it was all over, Hannah looked up at Annika.

'You're pretty.'

'Thank you.' She hated this. It was okay when Elsie said it, or one of the oldies, but children were so probing. Annika was still trying to attach the bung, but the little hard bit of plastic proved fiddly, and the last thing she wanted was to mess up the IV access. She almost did when Hannah spoke next.

'Have you got a boyfriend?'

'No.' Her cheeks were on fire, and she could feel Ross looking at her, though she was *so* not going to look at him.

'I thought you did, Annika.' He spoke then to Hannah. 'He's a very nice guy, apparently.'

'It's very early days.' The drip was attached, and now she had to strap it in place.

'I like a boy in my class,' Hannah said, with a confidence Annika would never possess. 'He sent me a card, and he wrote that he's coming to visit me once I'm allowed visitors that aren't my mum.'

'That's nice.'

'So, where does your boyfriend take you?' Hannah probed.

'I'm more a stay-at-home person…' Annika blew at her fringe and pressed in the numbers. Ross was beside her, checking that the dosage was correct and signing off on the sheet. She could feel that he was laughing, knew he was enjoying her discomfort—and there and then she decided to be brave.

Exceptionally brave—and if it didn't work she'd blame Cecil and Elsie.

'I was thinking of asking him over for dinner on Saturday.' Annika swallowed. She knew her face was on fire, she was cringing and burning, and yet she was also excited.

'That sounds nice. I'm sure he'd love it,' was all Ross said.

She got Hannah back to bed, and then, as she went back into the treatment room to prepare Luke's dressing, Ross came in.

'I don't want to talk at work.'

'Fine.'

'So can we just keep things separate?'

'No problem, Annika.'

'I mean it, Ross.'

'Of course,' he said patiently. 'Annika, do you know where the ten gauge needles are kept? They've run out on the IV trolley…'

And he was so matter-of-fact, so absolutely normal in his behaviour towards her, that Annika wondered if she actually had asked him out at all. At six a.m. on a Saturday, when he hadn't asked for a time, or even an address, she wasn't sure that she had.

CHAPTER SIX

'How's the children's ward?' Elsie was wide awake before Annika had even flicked the lights on.

'It's okay,' Annika said, and then she admitted the truth. 'I'll be glad when it's over.'

'What have you got next?'

'Maternity,' Annika said, as Elsie slurped her tea.

She seemed to have caught her second wind these past few days: more and more she was lucid, and the lucid times were lasting longer too. She was getting over that nasty UTI, Dianne, the Div 1 nurse had explained. They often caused confusion in the elderly, or, as in Elsie's case, exacerbated dementia. It was good to have her back.

'I'm not looking forward to it.'

'What *are* you looking forward to?'

'I don't know,' Annika admitted.

'How's your boyfriend?' Elsie asked when they were in the shower, Annika in her gumboots, Elsie in her little shower chair. 'How's Ross?'

'I don't know that either,' Annika said, cringing a little when Elsie said his name. 'It's complicated.'

'Love isn't complicated,' Elsie said. 'You are.'

And they had a laugh, a real laugh, as she dried and dressed Elsie and put her in her chair. Then Annika did something she had never done before.

'I've got something for you.' Nervous, she went to the fridge and brought out her creation.

It was a white chocolate box, filled with chocolate mousse and stuffed with raspberries.

'Where's my toast?' Elsie asked, and that made Annika laugh. Then the old lady peered at the creation and dipped her bony finger into the mousse, licked it, and had a raspberry. 'You bought this for me?'

'I made it,' Annika said. 'This was my practice one…' She immediately apologised. 'Sorry, that sounds rude…'

'It doesn't sound rude at all.'

'You have to spread the white chocolate on parchment paper and then slice it; you only fill the boxes at the end. I did a course a few years ago,' Annika admitted. 'Well, I didn't finish it…'

'You didn't need to,' Elsie said. 'You could serve this up every night and he'd be happy. This is all you need…it's delicious…' Elsie was cramming raspberries in her mouth. 'This is for your man?'

'I'm worried he'll think I've gone to too much effort.'

'Is he worth the effort?' Elsie asked.

'Yes.'

'Then don't worry.'

'I think I've asked him to dinner tonight.'

'You think?' Elsie frowned. 'What did he say?'

'That it sounded very nice.' Annika gulped. 'Only we haven't confirmed times. I'm not even sure he knows where I live…'

'He can find out,' Elsie said.

'How?'

'If he wants to, he will.'

'So I shouldn't ring him and check…?'

'Oh, no!' Elsie said. 'Absolutely not.'

'What if he doesn't come?'

'You have to trust that he will.'

'But what if he doesn't?'

'Then you bring in the food for us lot tomorrow,' Elsie said. 'Of course he's coming.' She put her hands on Annika's cheeks. 'Of *course* he'll come.'

CHAPTER SEVEN

IT KILLED her not to ring or page him, but Elsie had been adamant.

She had to trust that he would come, and if he didn't... Well, he had never been going to.

So, when she finished at the nursing home at nine a.m., she went home and had a little sleep, and then went to the Victoria Market. She bought some veal, some cream, the most gorgeous mushrooms, some fresh fettuccini and, of course, some more raspberries.

It was nice to be in the kitchen and stretching herself again.

Melting chocolate, whisking in eggs—she really had loved cooking and learning, but cooking at a high level had to be a passion. It was an absolute passion that Annika had realised she didn't have.

But still, she could love it.

She didn't know what to wear. She'd gone to so much trouble with the dessert that she didn't want to make too massive an effort with her clothes, in case she terrified him.

She opened her wardrobe and stared at a couple of Kolovsky creations. She had a little giggle to herself, wondering about his reaction if she opened the door to him in red velvet, but settled for a white skirt and a lilac top. She put on some lilac sandals, but she never wore shoes at home—well, not at this home—and ten minutes in she had kicked them off. She was dusting the chocolate boxes and trying not to care that it was ten past eight. She checked her hair, which was for once out of its ponytail, and put on some lip-gloss. Then she went to the kitchen, opened the fridge. The chocolate boxes hadn't collapsed, and the veal was all sliced and floured and waiting—and then she heard the knock at her door.

'Hi.' His voice made her stomach shrink.

'Hi.'

He was holding flowers, and she was so glad that she had taken Elsie's advice and not rung.

He kissed her on the cheek and handed her the flowers—glorious flowers, all different, wild and fragrant, and tied together with a bow. 'Hand-picked,' he said, 'which is why I'm so late.'

And she smiled, because of course they weren't. He'd been to some trendy place, no doubt, but she was grateful for them, because they got her through those first awkward moments as he followed her into the kitchen and she located a vase and filled it with water.

Ross was more than a little perplexed.

He hadn't known quite what to expect from tonight, but he hadn't expected this.

Okay, he'd known from her address that she wasn't in the smartest suburb. He hadn't given it that much thought till he'd entered her street. A trendy converted townhouse, perhaps, he'd thought as he'd pulled up— a Kolovsky attempt at pretending to be poor.

Except her car stuck out like a sore thumb in the

street, and as he climbed the steps he saw there was nothing trendy or converted about her flat.

There was an ugly floral carpet, cheap blinds dressed the windows, and not a single thing matched.

The kitchen was a mixture of beige and brown and a little bit of taupe too!

There was a party going on upstairs, and an argument to the left and right. Here in the centre was Annika.

She didn't belong—so much so he wanted to grab her by the hand and take her back to the farm right now, right this minute.

'I'll start dinner.'

She poured some oil in a large wok, turned the gas up on some simmering water, and then glanced over and gave him a nervous smile, which he returned. Then she slipped on an apron.

And it transformed her.

He stood and watched as somehow the tiny kitchen changed.

She pulled open the fridge and put a little meat in the wok. It was rather slow to sizzle, so she pulled out of the fridge some prepared plates, and he watched as she tipped coils of fresh pasta into the water and then threw the rest of the meat into the wok. Her hair was in the way, so she tied it back in a knot. He just carried on watching as this awkward, difficult woman relaxed and transformed garlic, pepper, cream and wine. He had never thought watching someone cook could be so sexy, yet before the water had even returned to the boil Ross was standing on the other side of the bench!

'Okay?' Annika checked.

'Great,' Ross said.

In seven minutes they were at the table—all those

dishes, in a matter of moments, blended into a veal sca-
loppini that was to die for.

'When you said dinner…'

'I love to cook…'

And she loved to eat too.

With food between them, and with wine, somehow,
gradually, it got easier.

He told her about his farm—that his sisters didn't get
it, but it must be the gypsy blood in him because there
he felt he belonged.

'I've never been to a farm.'

'Never?'

'No.'

'You're a city girl?'

'I guess,' Annika said.

She intrigued him.

'You used to model?'

'For a couple of years,' Annika said. 'Only in-house.'

'Sorry?'

'Just for Kolovsky,' she explained. 'I always thought
that was what I wanted to do—well, it was expected of
me, really—but when I got there it was just hours and
hours in make-up, hours and hours hanging around,
and…' she rolled her eyes '…no dinners like this.' She
registered his frown. 'Thin wasn't thin enough, and I
like my food too much.'

'So you went to Paris…?'

'I did.'

'What made you decide to do nursing?'

'I'm not sure,' Annika admitted. 'When my father
was ill I watched the nurses caring for him…' It was
hard to explain, so she didn't. 'What about you? Are you
the same as Iosef? Is medicine your vocation?'

'Being a doctor was the only thing I ever wanted to be.'

'Lucky you.'

'Though when I go to Russia with your brother, sometimes I wonder if there is more than being a doctor in a well-equipped city hospital.'

'You're not happy at work?'

'I'm very happy at work,' Ross corrected. 'Sometimes, though, I feel hemmed in—often I feel hemmed in. I just broke up with someone because of it.' He gave her a wry smile. 'I'm supposed to be sworn off women.'

'I'm not good at hemming.'

Ross laughed. 'I can't picture you with a needle.' And then he was serious. 'Romanys have this image of being cads—that is certainly my mother's take. I understand that, but really they are loyal to commitment, and virginity is important to them, which is why they often marry young...' He gave an embarrassed half-laugh. 'There is more to them than I understand...'

'And you need to find out?'

'I think so,' Ross answered. 'Maybe that is why I get on with the orphans in Russia. I am much luckier, of course, but I can relate to them—to that not knowing, never fully knowing where you came from. I don't know my father's history.'

'You could have a touch of Russian in you!' Annika smiled.

'Who knows?' Ross smiled. 'Do you go back to Russia?'

She shook her head. 'Levander does, Iosef as you know does work there...'

'Aleksi?' Ross asked.

'He goes, but not for work...' She gave a shrug. 'I don't really know why. I've just never felt the need to.'

'You speak Russian, though?'

'No.' She shook her head. 'Only a little—a very little compared to my family.'

'You have an accent.'

'Because I refused to speak Russian…' She smiled at his bemusement. 'I was a very wilful child. I spoke Russian and a little English till I was five, and then I realised that we lived in Australia. I started to say I didn't understand Russian—that I only understood English, wanted to speak English.' He smiled at the image of her as a stubborn five-year-old. 'It infuriated my mother, and my teacher… I learnt English from Russians, which is why I have an accent. Do you speak Spanish?'

'Not as much as I'd like to.'

'You're going in a couple of weeks?'

'Yeah.' And he told her—well, bits… 'Mum's upset about it. I think she's worried I'm going to find my real father and set up camp with him. Run away and leave it all behind…'

'Are you?'

'No.' Ross shook his head. 'I'd like to meet him, get to know him if I can find him. I only have his first name.'

'Which is?'

'Reyes,' Ross said, and then he gave her a little part of him that he didn't usually share. 'That's actually my real name.'

'I lived with my father. Every day I saw him,' Annika said, giving back a little part of herself, 'but I don't think I knew him at all.'

'I know about Levander.' He watched her swallow. 'I know that Levander was raised in the Detsky Dom.'

'Iosef shouldn't talk.'

'Iosef and I have spent weeks—no, months, working

in Russian orphanages. It's tough going there—sometimes you need to talk. He hates that Levander was raised there.'

'My parents were devastated when they found out…' She was glad she'd read that press release now. 'On his deathbed my father begged that we set up the foundation…' Her voice cracked. She was caught between the truth and a lie, and she didn't know what was real any more. 'We are holding a big fundraiser soon. If nursing doesn't work out then I am thinking of working full-time on the board…'

'Organising fundraisers?'

'Perhaps.' She shrugged. 'I'll get dessert…'

'You made these?' He couldn't believe it. He took a bite and couldn't believe it again—and then he said the completely wrong thing. 'You're wasted as a nurse.'

And he saw her eyes shutter.

'I'm sorry, Annika; I didn't mean it like that.'

'Don't worry.' She smiled. 'You're probably right.'

'Not wasted…'

'Just leave it.'

'I can't leave it,' Ross said, and her eyes jerked up to his. 'But I ought to.'

'At least till I have finished on the ward,' Annika said, and her throat was so tight she didn't know how to swallow, and her chocolate box sat unopened.

'I'll be in Spain,' Ross said.

'Slow is good.' Annika nodded. 'I don't want to rush.'

'So we just put it on hold?' Ross checked, and she nodded. 'Just have dinner?' He winced. 'When I say *just*…'

'Maybe one kiss goodnight,' Annika relented, because Elsie would be so disappointed otherwise.

'Sounds good,' Ross said. 'Now or later?'

'You choose.'

Four hours of preparation: tempering the chocolate, slicing the boxes, choosing the best raspberries. And the mousse recipe was a complicated one. All that work, all those hours, slipped deliciously away as he pulled her across the table and her breast sank into her own creation.

His tongue tasted better than anything she could conjure. They both had to stretch, but it was worth it. He tasted of chocolate, and then of him. His hair was in her fingers and she was pressing her face into him, the scratch of his jaw, the press of his lips. She wanted more, so badly she almost climbed onto the table just to be closer, but it was easier to stand. Lips locked, they kissed over the table, and then did a sort of crab walk till they could properly touch—and touch they did.

The most touching it was possible to do with clothes on and standing. She felt his lovely bum, and his jeans, and she pressed him into her. It was still just a kiss, one kiss, but it went on for ever.

'Oh, Annika,' he said, when she pulled back for a gulp of air, and then he saw the mess on her top and set to work.

'That's not kissing…' He was kissing her breast through the fabric, sucking off the mousse and the cream, and her fingers were back in his hair.

'It is,' he said.

And the raspberries had made the most terrible stain, so he concentrated on getting it out, and then she had to stop him. She stepped back and did something she never did.

She started to laugh.

And then she did something really stupid—something she'd cringe at when she told Elsie—well, the edited version—but knew Elsie would clap her approval.

She told him to dance—ordered him, in fact!

She lay on the sofa and watched, and there was rather more noise than usual from Annika's flat—not that the neighbours noticed.

She lay there and watched as his great big black boots stamped across the floor, and it was mad, really, but fantastic. She could smell the gypsy bonfire, and she knew he could too—it was their own fantasy, crazy and sort of private, but she would tell Elsie just a little.

And she did only kiss him—maybe once or twice, or three times more.

But who knew the places you could go to with a kiss?

Who knew you could be standing pressed against the door fully dressed, but naked in your mind?

'Bad girl,' Ross said as, still standing, she landed back on earth.

'Oh, I will be!' Annika said.

'Come back to the farm…'

'We said slowly.'

So they had—and there was Spain, and according to form he knew he'd hurt her, but he was suddenly sure that he wouldn't. She could take a sledgehammer to his bedroom wall if she chose, and he'd just lie on the bed and let her.

'Come to the farm.' God, what was he doing?

'I've got stuff too, Ross.'

'I know, I know.'

'Don't rush me.'

'I know.' He was coming back to earth as well. He'd never been accused of rushing things before. It was always Ross pulling back, always Ross reluctant to share—it felt strange to be on the other side.

'And I've never been bad.'

He started to laugh, and then he realised she wasn't joking.

'The rules are different if you're a Kolovsky girl, and till recently I've never been game enough to break them.'

Oh!

Looking into her troubled eyes, knowing what he knew about her family, suddenly he was scared of his own reputation and knew it was time to back off.

Annika Kolovsky he couldn't risk hurting.

CHAPTER EIGHT

AT HER request, things slowed down.

Stopped, really.

The occasional text, a lot of smiles, and a couple of coffees in the canteen.

It was just as well, really. There was no time for a relationship as her world rapidly unravelled.

Aleksi had hit a journalist and was on the front pages again.

Her mother was in full charity ball mode, and nothing Annika could say or do at work was right.

'He's *that* sick from chicken pox?' Annika couldn't help but speak up during handover. Normally she kept her head down and just wrote, but it was so appalling she couldn't help it. An eight-year-old had been admitted from Emergency with encephalitis and was semi-conscious—all from a simple virus. 'You can get *that* ill from chicken pox?'

'It's unusual,' Caroline said, 'but, yes. If he doesn't improve then he'll be transferred to the children's hospital. For now he's on antiviral medication and hourly obs. His mother is, of course, beside herself. She's got two others at home who have the virus too. Ross is just checking with Infectious Diseases and then he'll be contacting their GP to prescribe antivirals for them too.' Caroline was so matter-of-fact, and Annika knew she had to be too, but she found it so hard!

Gowning up, wearing a mask, dealing with the mum.

She checked the IV solutions with a nurse and punched in the numbers on the IVAC that would deliver the correct dosage of the vital medication. She tried to wash the child as gently as she could when the Div 1 nurse left. The room was impossibly hot, especially when she was all gowned up, but any further infection for him would be disastrous.

'Thank you so much.' The poor, petrified mum took time to thank Annika as she gently rolled the boy and changed the sheets. 'How do you think he's doing?'

Annika felt like a fraud.

She stood caught in the headlamps of the mother's anxious gaze. How could she tell her that she had no idea, that till an hour ago she hadn't realised chicken pox could make anyone so ill and that she was petrified for the child too?

'His observations are stable,' Annika said carefully.

'But how do *you* think he's doing?' the mother pushed, and Annika didn't know what to say. 'Is there something that you're not telling me?'

The mother was getting more and more upset, and so Annika said what she had been told to in situations such as this.

'I'll ask the nurse in charge to speak with you.'

It was her first proper telling-off on the children's Ward.

Well, it wasn't a telling-off but a pep talk—and rather a long one—because it wasn't an isolated incident, apparently.

Heather Jameson came down, and she sat as Caroline tried to explain the error of Annika's ways.

'Ross is in there now.' Caroline let out a breath. 'The mother thought from Annika's reaction that there was bad news on the way.'

'She asked me how I thought he was doing,' Annika said. 'I hadn't seen him before. I had nothing to compare it with. So I said I would get the nurse in charge to speak with her.'

She hadn't done anything wrong—but it was just another example of how she couldn't get it right.

It was the small talk, the chats, the comfort she was so bad at.

'Mum's fine.' Ross knocked and walked in. 'She's exhausted. Her son's ill. She's just searching for clues, Annika.' He looked over to her. 'You didn't do anything wrong. In fact he is improving—but you couldn't have known that.'

So it was good news—only for Annika it didn't feel like it.

'It's not a big deal,' Ross said later, catching her in the milk room, where she was trying to sort out bottles for the late shift.

'It is to me,' Annika said, hating her own awkwardness. She should be pleased that her shift was over, and tonight she didn't have to work at the nursing home, but tonight she was going to her mother's for dinner.

'Why don't we—?'

'You're not helping, Ross,' Annika said. 'Can you just be a doctor at work, please?'

'Sure.'

And she wanted to call him back—to say sorry for

biting his head off—but it was dinner at her mother's, and no one could ever understand what a nightmare that was.

'How's the children's ward?'

Iosef and Annie were there too, which would normally have made things easier—but not tonight. They had avoided the subject of Aleksi's latest scandal. They had spoken a little about the ball, and then they'd begun to eat in silence.

'It's okay,' Annika said, pushing her food around her plate.

'But not great?' Iosef checked.

'No.'

They'd been having the same conversation for months now.

She'd started off in nursing so enthusiastically, raving about her placements, about the different patients, but gradually, just as Iosef had predicted, the gloss had worn off.

As it had in modelling.

And cooking

And in jewellery design.

'How's Ross?' Iosef asked, and luckily he missed her blush because Nina made a snorting sound.

'Filthy gypsy.'

'You've always been *so* welcoming to my friends!' Iosef retorted. 'He does a lot of good work for your chosen charity.' There was a muscle pounding in Iosef's cheek and they still hadn't got through the main course.

'Romany!' Annika said, gesturing to one of the staff to fill up her wine. 'He prefers the word Romany to gypsy.'

'And I prefer not to speak of it while I eat my dinner,' Nina said, then fixed Annika with a stare. 'No more wine.'

'It's my second glass.'

'And you have the ball soon—you'll be lucky to get into your dress as it is.'

There was that feeling again. For months now out of nowhere it would bubble up, and she would suddenly feel like crying—but she never, ever did.

What she did do instead, and her hand was shaking as she did it, was take another sip of wine, and for the first time in memory in front of her mother she finished everything on her plate.

'How are you finding the work?' Iosef attempted again as Nina glared at her daughter.

'It's a lot harder than I thought it would be.'

'I was the same in my training,' Annie said happily, sitting back a touch as seconds were ladled onto her plate.

Annika wanted seconds too, but she knew better than to push it. The air was so toxic she felt as if she were choking on it, and then she stared at her brother, and for the first time ever she thought she saw a glimmer of sympathy there.

Annie chatted on. 'I thought about leaving—nursing wasn't at all what I'd imagined—then I did my Emergency placement and I realised I'd found my niche.'

'I just don't know if it's for me,' Annika said.

'Of course it isn't for you,' Nina said. 'You're a Kolovsky.'

'Is there anything you want help with?' Iosef offered, ignoring his mother's unhelpful comment. 'Annie or I can go over things with you. We can go through your assignments…'

He was trying, Annika knew that, and because he was

her brother she loved him—it was just that they had never got on.

They were chalk and cheese. Iosef, like his twin Aleksi, was as dark as she was blonde. They were both driven, both relentless in their different pursuits, whereas all her life Annika had drifted.

They had teased her, of course, as brothers always did. She'd been the apple of her parents' eyes, had just had to shed a tear or pout and whatever she wanted was hers. She had adored her parents, and simply hadn't been able to understand the arguments after Levander, her stepbrother, had arrived.

Till then her life had seemed perfect.

Levander had come from Russia, an angry, displaced teenager. His past was shocking, but her father had done his best to make amends for the son he hadn't known about all those years. Ivan had brought him into the family and given him everything.

Annika truly hadn't understood the rows, the hate, the anger that had simmered beneath the surface of her family. She had ached for peace, for the world to go back to how it was before.

But, worse than that, she had started to wonder why the charmed life she led made her so miserable.

She had been sucked so deep into the centre of the perfect world that had been created for her it had been almost impossible to climb out and search for answers. She couldn't even fathom the questions.

Yet she *was* trying.

'You could do much better for the poor orphans if you worked on the foundation's board,' Nina said. 'Have you thought about it?'

'A bit,' Annika admitted.

'You could be an ambassador for the Kolovskys. It is good for the company to show we take our charity work seriously.'

'And very good for you if it ever gets out that Ivan's firstborn was a Detsky Dom boy.' Iosef had had enough; he stood from his seat.

'Iosef!' Nina reprimanded him—but Iosef was still, after all these years, furious at what had happened to his brother. He had worked in the orphanages himself and was struggling to forgive the fact that Levander had been raised there.

'I'm going home.'

'You haven't had dessert.'

'Annie is on an early shift in the morning.'

Annie gathered up the baby, and Annika kissed her little niece and tried to make small talk with Annie as Iosef said goodbye to her mother, who remained seated.

'Can I hold her?' Annika asked, and she did. It felt so different from holding one of the babies at work. She stared into grey trusting eyes that were like the baby's father's, and smiled at the knot of dark curls that came from her mother. She smelt as sweet as a baby should. Annika buried her face in her niece's and blew a kiss on her cheek till she giggled.

'Annika?' Iosef gestured her out to the hall. 'Would some money help?'

'I don't want your money.'

'You're having to support yourself,' Iosef pointed out. 'Hell, I know what she can be like—I had to put myself through medical school.'

'But you did it.'

'And it was hard,' Iosef said. 'And…' He let out a breath. 'I was never their favourite.' He didn't mean it as an insult; he was speaking the truth. Iosef had always been strong, had always done his own thing. Annika was only now finding out that she could. 'How *are* you supporting yourself?'

'I'm doing some shifts in a nursing home.'

'Oh, Annika!' It was Annie who stepped in. 'You must be exhausted.'

'It's not bad. I actually like it.'

'Look…' Iosef wrote out a cheque, but Annika shook her head. 'Just concentrate on the nursing. Then—*then*,' he reiterated, 'you can find out if you actually like it.'

She could…

'Give your studies a proper chance,' Iosef said.

She stared at the cheque, which covered a year's wage in the nursing home. Maybe this way she *could* concentrate just on nursing. But it hurt to swallow her pride.

'We've got to go.'

And they did. They opened the front door and Annika stood there. She stroked Rebecca's cheek and it dawned on her that not once had Nina held or even looked at the baby.

Her own grandchild, her own blood, was leaving, and because she loathed the mother Nina hadn't even bothered to stand. She could so easily turn her back.

So what would she be like to a child that wasn't her own?

'Iosef…' She followed him out to the car. Annie was putting Rebecca in the baby seat and even though it was warm Annika was shivering. 'Did they know?'

'What are you talking about, Annika?'

'Levander?' Annika gulped. 'Did they know he was in the orphanage?'

'Just leave it.'

'I can't leave it!' Annika begged. 'You're so full of hate, Levander too…but in everything else you're reasonable. Levander would have forgiven them for not knowing. You would too.'

He didn't answer.

She wanted to hit him for not answering, for not denying it, for not slapping her and telling her she was wrong.

'You should have told me.'

'Why?' Iosef asked. 'So you can have the pleasure of hating them too?'

'Come home with us,' Annie said, putting her arm around Annika. 'Come back with us and we can talk…'

'I don't want to.'

'Come on, Annika,' Iosef said. 'I'll tell Mum you're not feeling well.'

'I can't,' Annika said. 'I can't just leave…'

'Yes, Annika,' Iosef said, 'you can—you can walk away this minute if you want to!'

'You still come here!' Annika pointed out. 'Mum ignores every word Annie ever says but you still come for dinner, still sit there…'

'For you,' Iosef said, and that halted her. 'The way she is with Annie, with my daughter, about my friends… Do you really think I want to be here? Annie and I are here for you.'

Annika didn't fully believe it, and she couldn't walk away either. She didn't want to hate her mother, didn't want the memory of her father to change, so instead she ate a diet jelly and fruit dessert with Nina, who started crying when it was time for Annika to go home.

'Always Iosef blames me. I hardly see Aleksi unless I go into the office, and now you have left home.'

'I'm twenty-five.'

'And you would rather have no money and do a job you hate than work in the family business, where you belong,' Nina said, and Annika closed her eyes in exhaustion. 'I understand that maybe you want your own home, but at least if you worked for the family... Annika, think about it—think of the good you could do! You are not even *liking* nursing. The charity ball next week will raise hundreds of thousands of dollars—surely you are better overseeing that, and making it bigger each year, than working in a job you don't like?'

'You knew about Levander, didn't you?' Had Annika thought about it, she'd never have had the courage to ask, but she didn't think, she just said it—and then she added something else. 'If you hit me again you'll never see me again, so I suggest that you talk to me instead.'

'I was pregnant with twins,' Nina hissed. 'It was hard enough to flee Russia just us two—we would never have got out with him.'

'So you left him?'

'To save my sons!' Nina said. 'Yes.'

'How could Pa?' Still she couldn't cry, but it was there at the back of her throat. 'How could he leave him behind?'

'He didn't know...' Annika had seen her mother cry, had heard her wail, but she had never seen her crumple. 'For years I did not tell him. He thought his son was safe with his mother. Only I knew...'

'Knew what?'

'We were ready to leave, and that *blyat* comes to the door with her bastard son...' Annika winced at her mother's foul tongue, and yet unlike her brothers she listened, heard that Levander's mother had turned up one night with a small toddler and pleaded that Nina take him, that she was dying, that her family were too poor to keep the little boy…

'I was pregnant, Annika…' Nina sobbed. 'I was big, the doctor said there were two, I wanted my babies to have a chance. We would never have got out with Levander.'

'You could have tried.'

'And if we'd failed?' Nina pleaded. 'Then what?' she demanded. 'So I sent Levander and his mother away, and for years your father never found out.'

'And when he did Levander came here?'

'No.' Nina was finally honest. 'We tried for a few more years to pretend all was perfect.' She looked over to her daughter. 'So now you can hate me too.'

CHAPTER NINE

BUT Annika didn't want to hate her mother.

She just didn't know how to love her right now.

She wanted Ross.

She wanted to hide in his arms and fall asleep.

She wanted to go over and over it with him.

The truth was so much worse than the lies, and yet she could sort of understand her mother's side.

The family secret had darkened many shades, and her mother had begged her not to tell anyone.

Oh, Annie knew, and no doubt so did Millie, Levander's wife, but they were real partners. Ross and Annika…they were brand spanking new!

How could she land it on him?

And anyway, he would soon be heading off for Spain!

For the first time in her life she had a tangible reason to sever ties with her mother. Instead she found herself there more and more, listening to Nina's stories, understanding a little more what had driven her parents, what had fuelled their need for the castle they had built for their children.

* * *

'I haven't seen you so much,' Elsie commented.

'I've cut down my shifts,' Annika said, with none of her old sparkle. 'I need to concentrate on my studies.'

Cashing the cheque had hurt, but then so too did everything right now. When push had come to shove, she'd realised that she actually *liked* her shifts at the nursing home, so instead of cutting ties completely, she'd drastically reduced her hours.

Ross was around, and though they smiled and said hello she kept him at a distance.

She had spent the past week in cots, which didn't help matters.

The babies were so tiny and precious, and sometimes so ill it terrified Annika.

She was constantly checking that she had put the cot-sides up, and double- and triple-checking medicine doses.

She longed to be like the other nurses, who bounced a babe on their knee and fed with one hand while juggling the phone with the other.

She just couldn't.

'How's that man of yours?' Elsie asked, because Annika was unusually quiet.

'He goes to Spain soon—when he gets back we will maybe see each other some more.'

'Why wait?'

'You know he's a doctor—a senior doctor on my ward?'

'Oh.' Elsie pondered. 'I'm sure others have managed—you can be discreet.'

'There's stuff going on.' Annika combed through her hair. 'With my family. I think it's a bit soon to land it all on him.'

'If he's the right one for you, he'll be able to take it,' Elsie said.

'Ah, but if he's not...' Annika could almost see the news headlines. 'How do you know if you can trust someone?'

'You don't know,' Elsie said. 'You never know. You just hope.'

CHAPTER TEN

Ross always liked to get to work early.

He liked a quick chat with the night staff, if possible, to hear from them how things were going on the ward, rather than hear the second-hand version a few hours later from the day nurses.

It was a routine that worked for him well.

A niggle from a night nurse could become a full-blown incident by ten a.m. For Ross it was easier to buy a coffee and the paper, have a quick check with the night staff and then have ten minutes to himself before the day began in earnest. This morning there was no such luxury. He'd been at work all night, and at six-thirty had just made his way from ICU when he stopped by the nurses' station.

'Luke's refused to have his blood sugar taken,' Amy, the night nurse, explained. 'I was just talking him round to it and his mum arrived.'

'Great!' Ross rolled his eyes. 'Don't tell me she took it herself?'

'Yep.'

It had been said so many times, but sometimes working on a children's ward would be so much easier without the parents!

'Okay—I'll have another word. What else?'

There wasn't much—it was busy but under control—and so Ross escaped to his office, took a sip of the best coffee in Australia and opened the paper. He stared and he read and he stared, and if *his* morning wasn't going too well, then someone else's wasn't, either.

His pager went off, and he saw that it was a call from Iosef Kolovsky. He took it.

'Hi.'

'Sorry to call you for private business.' Iosef was, as always, straight to the point. 'Have you seen the paper?'

'Just.'

'Okay—now, I think Annika is on your ward at the moment…' Iosef had never asked for a favour in his life. 'Could you just keep an eye out for her—and if the staff are talking tell them that what has been written is nonsense? You have my permission to say you know me well and that this is all rubbish.'

'Will do,' Ross said, and, because he knew he would get no more from Iosef, 'How's Annie?'

'Swearing at the newspaper.'

'I bet. I'll do what I can.'

He rang off and read it again. It was a scathing piece—mainly about Iosef's twin Aleksi.

On his father's death two years ago he had taken over as chief of the House of Kolovsky, and now, the reporter surmised, Ivan Kolovsky the founder must be turning in his grave.

There had been numerous staff cuts, but Aleksi, it was said, was frittering away the family fortune in casinos, on long exotic trips, and on indiscretions with women. A bitter ex, who was allegedly nine weeks pregnant by him, was savage in her observations. Not only had staff been cut, but his own sister, a talented jewellery designer, had been cut off from the family trust and was now living in a small one-bedroom flat, studying nursing. Along with a few pictures of Aleksi looking rather the worse for wear were two of Annika—one of her in a glamorous ballgown, looking sleek and groomed, and the other... Well, it must have been a bad day, because she was in her uniform and looking completely exhausted, teary even, as she stepped out into the ambulance bay.

There was even a quote from an anonymous source that stated how miserable she was in her job, how she hated every moment, and how she thought she was better than that.

How, Ross had fathomed, was she supposed to walk into work after that?

She did, though.

He was sitting in the staffroom when she entered, just as the morning TV news show chatted about the piece. An orthopaedic surgeon was reading the paper, and a couple of colleagues were discussing it as she walked in. Ross felt his heart squeeze in mortification for her.

But she didn't look particularly tense, and she didn't look flushed or teary—for a moment he was worried that she didn't even know what was being said.

Until she sat down, eating her raisin toast from the canteen, and a colleague jumped up to turn the television over.

'It's fine,' she said. 'I've already seen it.'

The only person, Ross surmised as the gathering staff sat there, who didn't seem uncomfortable was Annika.

Ross called her back as the day staff left for handover. 'How are you doing?'

'Fine.'

'If you want to talk…?'

'Then I'll speak with my family.'

Ross's lips tightened. She didn't make things easy, but he didn't have the luxury of thinking up a smart retort as his pager had summoned him to a meeting.

'I'm here if you need me, okay?'

The thing with children, Annika was fast realising, was that they weren't dissimilar from the residents in the nursing home. There, the residents' tact buttons had long since been switched off—on the children's ward they hadn't yet been switched on.

'My mum said you were in the paper this morning!' A bright little five-year-old sang out as Annika did her obs.

'What's "allegedly" mean?' asked another.

'Why don't you change your name?' asked Luke as she took down his dressing just before she was due to finish. Ross wanted to check his leg ulcer before it was re-dressed, and Annika was pleased to see the improvement. 'Then no one would know who you are.'

'I've thought about it,' Annika admitted. 'But the papers would make a story out of that too. Anyway, whether I like the attention or not, it is who I am.'

His dressing down, she covered his leg with a sterile sheet and then checked off on his paperwork before the end of her shift.

'What's your blood sugar?'

'Dunno.'

It had been a long day for Annika, and maybe her own tact button was on mute for now, but she was tired of reasoning with him, tired of the hourly battles when it was really simple. 'You know what, Luke? You can argue and you can kick and scream and make it as hard as you like, but why not just surprise everyone and do it for yourself? You say you want your mum to leave you alone, to stop babying you—maybe it's time to stop acting like one.'

It was perhaps unfortunate that Ross came in at that moment.

'His dressing's all down,' Annika gulped.

'Thanks. I'll just have a look, and then you can re-dress.'

'Actually, my shift just ended. I'll pass it on to one of the late staff.'

She turned to go, but Ross was too quick for her.

'If you could wait in my office when you've finished, Annika,' Ross said over his shoulder. 'I'd like a quick word.'

Oh, she was really in trouble now.

She hadn't been being mean—or had she?

Maybe she should have been more tactful with Luke…

She couldn't read Ross's expression when he came in.

He was dressed in a suit, even though he hadn't been in one this morning, and he looked stern and formidable. Unusually for Ross, he also looked tired, and he gave a grim smile when she jumped up from the chair at his desk.

'Is Luke okay?'

'He's fine. I asked Cassie to do his dressing.'

'Was he upset?'

'Upset?'

'Because I told him he should be taking his own blood sugars?'

'He just took it.'

'Oh.'

Ross frowned, and then he shook his head in bewilderment. 'Do you think you're here to be told off?'

'I told him he was acting like a baby.'

'I've told him the same,' Ross said. 'Many times. You were fine in there—would you please stop doubting yourself all the time?'

'I'll try.'

'How come you're finishing early?'

'I worked through lunch; I'm going home at three.' She let out a breath. 'It's been a long day.'

'That offer's still there.' He saw her slight frown. 'To talk.'

'Thank you.'

And when she didn't walk off, neither did Ross.

'Do you want to come riding?' There was an argument raging in his head—he was going away soon, they had promised to keep things on ice till he returned, and yet he couldn't just leave her like this.

'Riding?'

'At the farm.'

'I've never ridden.'

'It's the best thing in the world after a tough day,' Ross said. 'You'll love it.'

'How do you know?' Annika said.

'I just know.' He watched her cheeks darken further. 'Annika, I will not lay a finger on you. It's just a chance to get away…'

'I don't like talking like this when I'm on duty.'

'Then give me half an hour to call in a favour and I'll meet you in the canteen.'

She *wasn't* going back to the farm with him. Her hand was shaking as she opened her locker, and then she picked up her phone and turned it on. She saw missed calls from her mother, her family's agent, her brother Iosef, a couple from Annie and four from Aleksi. She turned it off. Right now she was finding it very hard to breathe.

She didn't want to go home.

Didn't want to give a comment.

Didn't want a spin doctor or a night out at some posh restaurant with her family just to prove they were united.

Which was why she turned left for the canteen.

He drove; she followed in her own car. He had a small flat near the hospital, Ross had explained, for nights on call, but home was further away, and by the time they got there it was coming up for five. As they slid into his long driveway, she saw the tumbled old house and sprawling grounds. For the first time since she had been awoken by a journalist at five a.m., asking her to offer a comment, Annika didn't have to remember to breathe.

It just happened.

And when she stepped out of the car she saw all the flowers waving in the breeze—the same kind of flowers he had brought for her.

Ross *had* picked them.

The inside was scruffy, but nice: boots in the hallway, massive couches, and a very tidy kitchen, thanks to the cleaner who was just leaving.

'Hungry?' Ross asked, and she gave a small shrug.

'A bit.'

'I'll pack a picnic.'

'Am I to learn to ride in my uniform?'

He laughed and found her some jodhpurs that he said belonged to one of his sisters, some boots that belonged to someone else, though he wasn't sure who, and an old T-shirt of his.

Annika didn't know what she was doing here.

But it was like a retreat and she was grateful for it.

She was grateful too for familiarity in the strangest of places. There were pictures of Iosef there with Ross, from twenty years old to the present day. They grew up before her eyes as she walked along the hallway—and, though she had never really discussed the Detsky Dom with her brother, somehow with Ross she could.

'I expected them to be more miserable,' Annika said, staring at a photo of some grinning, pimply-faced teenagers, with Ross and Iosef beaming in the middle. It was a Iosef she had never seen.

'Our soccer team had just won!' Ross grinned at the memory. 'It's not all doom and gloom.'

'I know,' Annika said, glad that now she did, because there were so many questions she felt she couldn't ask her brothers.

'There's an awful lot of love there,' Ross said, 'there's just not enough to go around. The staff are wonderful…'

And she was glad to hear that.

She was glad too when she walked back into the kitchen. They had had very little conversation—she was too tired and confused and brain-weary to talk—but he got one essential thing out of the way.

He held her.

It was as if he had been waiting for her, and she stepped so easily into his arms. She never cried, and she certainly wouldn't now, but it had been a horrible day, a rotten day, and although Iosef, Annie, Aleksi, her friends, would all do their best to offer comfort—she was sure of that—Ross was far nicer. He didn't ask, or make her explain, he just held her, and the attraction that had always been there needed no explanation or discussion. It just was. It just *is*, Annika thought.

His chest smelt as she remembered. He was, she decided as she rested in his arms, an absolute contradiction, because he both relaxed and excited her. She could feel herself unwind. She felt the hammer of his heart in her ear and looked up.

'One kiss,' she said.

'Look where that got us last time.'

'Just one,' Annika said, 'to chase away the day.'

So he kissed her. His lovely mouth kissed hers and her wretched day disappeared. He tasted as unique as he had the first time he'd kissed her, as if blended just for her. His mouth made hers an expert. They moved as if they were reuniting, tongues blending and chasing. His body was taut, and made hers do bold things like press a little into him. Her fingers wanted to hook into the loop of his belt and pull him in harder, and so she did. Their breathing was ragged and close and vital, and when he pulled back he gave her that delicious smile.

'Come on.'

He gave her his oldest, slowest, most trustworthy horse to ride, and helped her climb on, but even as the horse moved a couple of steps she felt as if the ground was giving way and let out a nervous call.

'Sit back in the saddle.' Ross grinned. 'Just relax back into it.'

She felt as if she would fall backwards, or slide off, every muscle in her body tense as they clopped at a snail's pace out of the stables.

'Keep your heels down,' Ross said, as if it were that

easy. Every few steps she lost a stirrup, but the horse, along with Ross, was so endlessly patient that soon they were walking. Annika concentrated on not leaning forward and keeping her heels down, and there was freedom, the freedom of thinking about nothing other than somehow staying on. After a little while Ross goaded her into kicking into a trot.

'Count out loud if it helps.' He was beside her, holding his own reins in one hand as she bumped along. It was *exciting* for maybe thirty seconds, as she found her rhythm and then lost it. She pulled on the reins to stop, and then the only thing Annika could do was laugh. She laughed with a strange freedom, exhilaration ripping through her, and Ross was laughing too.

'Better?'

'Much.' She was breathless—from laughing, from riding, from dragging in the delicious scent of dusk, and then, when she slid off the horse and he spread out a picnic, she was breathless from just looking at him.

'It helped,' Annika said. 'You were right.'

'After a bad day at work,' Ross said, 'or a difficult night, this is what I do and it works every time.' He gave her a smile. 'It worked for me today.'

'Was today a bad day?' Annika asked, and he looked at her.

'Today was an exceptionally bad day.'

'Really?' She cast her mind back. Was there something she had missed on the ward? An emergency in ICU, perhaps?

But Ross smiled. 'I had a meeting with the CEO!'

'I wondered what was with the suit.'

'On my return they want me to commit to a three-year contract. So far I have managed to avoid it...'

'Does a three-year contract worry you?'

'More the conditions.' He gave a tight smile. 'I'm a good doctor, Annika, but apparently wearing a suit every day will make me a better one.'

'At least it's not an apron,' she joked, but then she was serious. 'You *are* a good doctor—but why would you commit if you are not sure it is what you want?'

And never, not once, had he had that response.

Always, for ever and always, it had been, 'It's just a suit. What about the mortgage? What if…?'

'I love my job,' Ross said.

'Do you love the kids or the job?' Annika checked, and Ross smiled again. 'There will always be work for you, Ross.'

'I've also been worrying about you.'

'You don't have to worry about me.'

'Oh, but I do.'

They ate cold roast beef and hot mustard sandwiches and drank water. The evening was so still and delicious, so very relaxing compared to the drama waiting for her at home.

'I should get back…' She was lying on her back, staring up at an orange sky, inhaling the scent of grass, listening to the sounds of the horses behind them. Ross was so at ease beside her—and she'd never felt more at home with another person.

She looked over to him, to the face that had taken her breath away for so long now, and he was there, staring back and smiling.

A person, Annika reminded herself, who barely knew her—and if he did…

If she closed her eyes, even for a moment, she knew she would remember his kiss, knew where another kiss might lead, right here, where the air was so clear she could breathe, the sky so orange and the grass so cool.

'I should get back,' she said again. She didn't want to, but staying would be far too dangerous.

'You don't have to go,' Ross said.

'I think I do,' was her reluctant reply. 'Ross, it's too soon.'

'Annika, you are welcome to stay. I'm not suggesting a weekend of torrid sex.' Low in her stomach, something curled in on itself. 'Though of course...' he grinned '...that can be an optional extra...' And then he laughed, and so too did she. 'There's a spare room, and you're more than welcome to use it. If you want a break, a bit of an escape, here's the perfect place for it. I can go and stay at the flat if you prefer...'

'You'd offer me your home?'

'Actually, yes!' Ross said, surprised at himself, watching as she turned on her phone again and winced at the latest flood of incoming messages. 'Hell, I can't imagine what you have to go home to.'

'A lot,' Annika admitted. 'I have kept my phone off all day.'

'You can keep it off all weekend if you like.'

Oh, she could breathe—not quite easily, but far more easily than she had all day.

'I don't want to stay here alone.'

'Then be my guest,' he said.

'I have a shift at the nursing home tomorrow night.'

'I'm not kidnapping you—you're free to come and go,' Ross replied, and after a moment she nodded.

'I'd love to stay, but I should let Aleksi know.'

She rang her brother, and Ross listened as she checked if he was okay and reassured him that she was fine.

'I'm going to have my phone off,' Annika said. 'Tell Mum not to worry.'

He busied himself packing up the picnic, but he saw her run a worried hand through her hair.

'No, don't—because I'm not there,' she said. 'I'm staying with a friend.' She caught his eye. 'No, I'd rather not say. Just don't worry.'

She clicked off her phone and stood. Ross called the horses, and they walked them slowly back.

'It's nice,' Annika said. 'This…' She looked over to him. 'Do your grandparents have horses?'

'They do.'

And he'd so longed for Spain, longed for his native land, yearned to discover all that had seemed so important, so vital, but right now he had it all here, and the thought of Spain just made him homesick.

Homesick for here.

It was relaxing, settling the horses for the night, then heading back to his house.

'Have a bath,' Ross suggested.

'I have nothing to change into. Maybe I should drive back and pack. I haven't got anything.'

'You don't need anything,' Ross said. 'My sisters always leave loads of stuff—they come and stay with the kids some weekends when I'm on call.' He went upstairs and returned a few moments later with some items of clothing and a large white towelling robe. 'Here.' He handed her a toothbrush. 'Still in its wrapper—you're lucky I did a shop last week.'

'Very lucky.'

'So now you have no excuse but to relax and enjoy.'

He poured her a large glass of wine and told her to

take it up to the bath, and then he showed her the spare room, which had a lovely iron bed with white linen.

'You have good taste.'

'Spanish linen,' Ross said, 'from my grandmother… She's the one who has good taste.' On the way to the bathroom he kicked open another door. 'I, on the other hand, have no taste at all.'

His bedroom was far more untidy than his office, with not a trace of crisp linen in sight. It was brown on black, with boots and jeans and belts, a testosterone-laden den, with an unmade bed and a massive music system.

'This reminds me of Luke's room.'

'You can come in with your bin liner any time,' Ross said. 'My door is always open…' Then he laughed. 'Unless family's staying.'

The bathroom was lovely. It had a large freestanding bath that took for ever to fill, a big mirror, and bottles of oils, scents and candles.

His home confused her—parts looked like a rustic country home, other parts, like his bedroom, were modern and full of gadgets. It was like Ross, she thought. He was doctor, farmer, gypsy—an eclectic assortment that added up to one incredibly beautiful man.

Settling into the warm oily water, she could, as she lay, think of no one, not one single other person, whose company could have soothed her tonight.

His home was like none she had ever been in.

His presence was like no other.

She washed out her panties and bra, but stressed for a moment about hanging them over the taps to dry. They were divine: Kolovsky silk in stunning turquoise. In fact all her underwear was divine—it was one of the genuine perks of being a Kolovsky. It was seductive, suggestive, and, Annika realised, she could *not* leave it in the bathroom!

 So she hung it on the door handle in her bedroom and then headed downstairs, where he sat, boots on the table, strumming at a guitar, a dog looking up at him. She thought about using her fingers as castanets and dancing her way right over to his lap, but they'd both promised to be good.

'Why would you do this for me?' She stood at the living room door, wrapped in his sister's dressing gown, and wondered why she wasn't nervous.

'Because my life's not quite complicated enough,' Ross said, with more than a dash of sarcasm. 'Just relax, Annika, I'm not going to pounce.'

So she did—or she tried to.

They watched a movie, but she was so acutely aware of the man on the sofa beside her that frankly her mother would have been more relaxing company. When she gave in at eleven and went to bed, it was almost frustrating when he turned and gave her a very lovely kiss, full on the lips, that was way more than friendly but absolutely going nowhere. It was, Annika realised as she climbed the steps, a kiss goodnight.

She could taste him on her lips.

So much so that she didn't want to remove the toothbrush from its wrapper. But she did, and she brushed her teeth, and then when she heard him coming up the stairs she raced to her bedroom. She slipped off her dressing gown and slid naked into bed, then cursed that she hadn't been to the loo.

He was filling the bath.

She could hear it, so she decided to make a quick dash for it, but she came out to find him walking down the landing wearing only a black towel round his loins. His body was delicious, way better than her many imaginings, and his hair looked long, and his early-morning shadow was a late-night one now. She just gave a nod.

'Feel free…' He grinned at her awkwardness.

'Sorry?'

'To wash your hands…'

'Oh.'

So she had to go into the bathroom, where his bath was running, as he politely waited outside. She washed her hands and tried not to look at the water and imagine him naked in it.

'Night, Annika.'

'Night.'

How was she to sleep? He was in the bath for ever, and then she heard the pull of the plug and the lights ping off. She lay in the dark silence and knew he was just metres away. And then, just as she thought she might win, as a glimpse of sleep beckoned, she heard music.

There was no question of sleeping here in a strange house, with Ross so close. She couldn't sleep, so instead she did a stupid thing—she checked her phone.

Even as she turned it on it rang, and foolishly she answered. She listened as her mother demanded that she end this stupidity and come home immediately—not to the flat, but home, where she belonged. She was wreaking shame on her family, and her father would be turning in his grave. Annika clicked off the phone, her heart pounding in her chest, and headed out for a glass of water.

The low throb of music from his room somehow beckoned, and his door was, as promised, open. She glanced inside as she walked past.

'Sorry.'

'For what?'

'I'm just restless.'

'Get a drink if you want…' He was lying in the bed reading, hardly even looking up.

'I'll just go back to bed.'

'Night, then.'

She just stood there.

And Ross concentrated on his book.

His air ticket was his bookmark. He'd done that very deliberately—ten days and he was out of here; ten days and he would be in Spain. And then, when he returned—well, then maybe things could be different.

'Night, Annika.'

She ignored him and came and sat on the bed. They kept talking. And it was hard to talk at two a.m. without lying down, so she did, and even with her dressing gown on it was cold. So she went under the covers, and they talked till her eyes were really heavy and she was almost asleep, and then he turned out the light.

'The music…'

'It will turn itself off soon.'

She turned away from him; there were no curtains on the window, just the moon drifting past, and he spooned right into her. She could feel his stomach in her back, and the wrap of his arms, and it was sublime—so much so that she bit on her lip. Then he kissed the back of her head, pulled her in a little bit more, and she could feel every breath he took. She could feel the lovely tumid length of him, and just as she braced herself for delicious attack, just as she wondered how long it would be polite to resist, she felt him relax, his breathing even, as she struggled to inhale.

'Ross, how can you just lie there…?' He wasn't even pretending; he really was going to sleep!

'Relax,' he said to her shoulder. 'I told you, nothing's going to happen—I had a *very* long bath.'

And she laughed, on a day she had never thought she would, on a day she had done so many different things. She lay in bed and counted her firsts: she had been cuddled, and she had hung up the phone on her mum.

The most amazing part of it all, though, was that for the first time in ages she slept properly.

CHAPTER ELEVEN

IT WAS midday when she woke up.

Annika never overslept, and midday was unthinkable, but his bed was so comfortable, and it held the male scent of him even though he had long since gone. Instead of jumping guiltily out of bed she lay there, half dozing, a touch too warm in her dressing gown, smiling at the thought that there was really no point getting up as she had nothing to wear—and there was no way she was getting on a horse today!

She hurt in a place she surely shouldn't!

'Afternoon!' He pushed the bedroom door open, and the door to her heart opened a little wider too. He hadn't shaved, and looked more gypsy-like, dark and forbidden, than she had ever seen him, but he was holding a tray and wearing a smile that she was becoming sure was reserved solely for her. She smiled back at him.

'What did I do to deserve breakfast in bed?'

'You didn't snore, which is very encouraging,' he said, waiting till she sat up before placing a tray on her lap, 'and it's actually *lunch* in bed.'

It was *the* nicest lunch in the world: omelette made from eggs he had collected that morning, with wild mushrooms and cheese. The coffee was so strong and sweet that if she had given orders to the chef at her mother's home he could not have come up with better.

'You're yesterday's news, by the way,' Ross said. 'In case you were wondering.'

She had been.

'Lucky for you some bank overseas has gone into liquidation and the papers have devoted four pages to it—you don't even get a mention.'

'Thank you.'

She had finished her lunch, and he took the tray from her, but instead of heading off he put it on the floor and lay on top of the bed beside her.

'I like having you here.'

'I like being here.'

She could feel his thigh through the sheet. She felt so safe and warm and relaxed, in a way she never would have at the movies with him, or across the table in some fancy restaurant—so much so that she could even get up and go to the loo, brush her teeth and then come to the warm waiting bed.

'I am being lazy,' Annika said as she crossed the room.

'Why not?' Ross said. 'You have to work tonight.'

And he might never know how nice that sentence was—for surely he could never understand the battle of wills, the drama it entailed, merely for her to work.

Ross accepted it.

It was warm. The sun was streaming through the window, falling on the crumpled bed. After hot coffee and the omelette, wearing a thick dressing gown under the covers was suddenly making her feel way too hot. She stared at him, wanting to peel her dressing gown off, to stand naked before him and climb in bed beside him.

He stared back for the longest time. The air was thick with lust and want, but with patience too.

'Sleep.' He answered the heavy unvoiced question by standing up. He stood in front of her, and she thought he would go, but she didn't want him to.

There was a mire of confusion in her mind, because it was too soon and sometimes she wondered if she was misreading him. What if he was just a very nice guy who perhaps fancied her a little?

And then he answered her fleeting doubt.

His hands untied the knot of her dressing gown, and she stood as he slid it over her shoulders. She saw his calm features tighten a fraction, felt the caress of his gaze over her body and the arousal in the air.

She was naked in front of him, and he was dressed, and yet it felt appropriate. She could not fathom how, but if felt right that he should see her, that they glimpsed the future even if it was too soon to reach for it. She felt safe as he pulled the bedcovers over her.

Only then did he kiss her. He kissed the hollows of her throat, sitting on the bed, leaning over where she lay. He kissed her till she wanted him to lie down beside her again, but he didn't. He kissed her until her hands were in his thick black hair, her body stretched to drag him down, but he didn't lie down. He just kissed her some more, till her breath was as hard and as ragged as his. It was just a kiss, but it brought with it indecent thoughts, because they both explored what they knew was to come. Their faces and lips met, but their minds were meshed too. It was a dangerous kiss, that went on and on as her body flared for him, and then he lifted his head and smiled down.

'Go back to sleep.'

'You are cruel.'

'Very.' He smiled again, and then he left her, a twitching mass of desire, but relaxed too. She had never slept more, never felt more cherished or looked after. The horrors were receding with every hour she spent in his presence.

She slept till seven, and then showered and pulled on her uniform. She made his bed before heading downstairs. He offered her some dinner but she wasn't hungry.

'I need to go home and get my agency uniform, and perhaps...'she blushed a little at her own presumption '...perhaps I should pack a change of clothes for tomorrow.'

'Here.' He handed her a key. 'I lie in on Sunday. Let yourself in.' And he handed her something else—a brown paper bag. 'For your break.'

He had made her lunch—well, a lunch that would be eaten at one a.m., after she had helped to get twenty-eight residents into bed and answered numerous call bells.

She deliberately didn't look inside until then. She sat down in the staffroom and took the bag out of the fridge and opened it as excited as a kid on Christmas morning.

He had made her lunch!

A bottle of grapefruit juice, a chicken, cheese and salad sandwich on sourdough bread, a small bar of chocolate and, best of all, a note.

Hope you are having a good shift.
R x
PS I am no doubt thinking about you. R xx

* * *

He *was* thinking of her.

Even though she had slept for most of the day, it had been nice knowing Annika was there, and without her now the house seemed empty and quiet.

He had never felt like this about anyone, of that he was sure.

Gypsy blood did flow in his veins, and it wasn't just his looks that carried the gene. There was a restlessness to him that so many had tried and failed to channel into conventional behaviour.

He didn't feel like that with Annika.

Yet.

Her vulnerability unnerved him, his own actions sideswiped him—it had taken Imelda months to get a key; he had handed it to Annika without thought.

He was going away in little more than a week, digging deep into his past, thinking of throwing in his job… He could really hurt her, and that was the last thing he wanted to do.

Ross headed upstairs and stepped into his room. He smiled at the bed she had made. The tangled sheets were tucked into hospital corners, his pillows neatly arranged. If it been Imelda it would have incensed him, but it was Annika, and it warmed him instead.

And that worried him rather a lot.

CHAPTER TWELVE

SHE flew through the rest of her shift.

There would be no words of wisdom from Elsie, though.

As Annika flooded the room with light at six the following morning, Elsie stared fixedly ahead, lost in her own little world. And though, as Elsie had revealed, she enjoyed being there, this morning Annika missed her. She would have loved some wise words from her favourite resident.

Instead she propped Elsie up in bed and chatted away to her as she sorted out clothes from Elsie's wardrobe, her stockings, slippers, soap and teeth. Then Annika frowned.

'Drink your tea, Elsie.'

No matter Elsie's mood, no matter how lucid she was, every morning that Annika had worked there the old lady had gulped at her milky tea as Annika prepared her for her shower.

'Do you want me to help you?'

She held the cup to her lips, but Elsie didn't drink. The tea was running down her chin.

'Come on, Elsie.'

Worried, Annika went and found Dianne, the Registered Nurse.

'Perhaps just leave her shower this morning,' Dianne said when she came at Annika's request and had a look at Elsie. Instead they changed her bed, combed her hair, and Annika chatted about Bertie and all the things that made Elsie smile—only they didn't this morning.

Annika checked her observations, which were okay. The routine here was different from a hospital: there was no doctor on hand. There was nothing to report, no emergency as such.

Elsie just didn't want her cup of tea.

It was such a small thing, but Annika knew that it was vital.

It felt strange, driving home to *someone*.

Strange, but nice.

Since her mother had refused to talk to her about her work since she had supposedly turned her back on her family to pursue a 'senseless' career, Annika had felt like a ball-bearing, rattling around with no resting place, careering off corners and edges with no one to guide her, no one to ask where she was.

It felt different, driving to someone who knew where you had been.

Different letting herself in and knowing that, though he was asleep, if the key didn't go in the lock she would be missed.

She felt responsible, almost, but in the nicest way.

She dropped the bag she had packed on the bathroom floor, and then slipped out of her uniform and showered, using her own shampoo that she had brought from home. It felt nice to see it standing by his shampoo, to wrap herself in his towel and brush her hair and teeth, then put her toothbrush beside his.

The house was still and silent, and she had never felt peace like it.

Nothing like it.

She had never felt so sure that the choice she made now would be right, no matter what it was. The decision was hers.

She could step out of the bathroom and turn right for the spare room and that would be okay.

She could go downstairs and make breakfast and that would be fine too.

Or she could slip into bed beside him and ask for nothing more than his warmth, and that would be the right choice too.

It was her choice, and she was so grateful he was letting her make it.

His door *was* always open, and she stepped inside and stood a moment.

He needed to shave—his jaw was black and he looked like a bandit. His eyes were two slits and she knew he was deeply asleep. He was beautiful, dark and, no doubt—according to her mother—completely forbidden, but he was hers for the taking—and she wanted to take.

Annika slipped in bed beside him, her body cool and damp from the shower, and he stirred for a moment and pulled her in, spooned in beside her, awoke just enough to ask how her shift had been.

'Good.'

And then she felt him fall back to sleep.

His body was warm and relaxed, and hers was cold, tired and weary, drawing warmth from him. She felt him unfurl, felt him harden against her, and then he turned onto his back. She lay there for a moment, till his breathing evened out again, and then she rested her wet hair on his chest and wrapped her cold foot between his warm calves. She slid her hand down to his hardening place, heard his breath held beneath her ear, and turned her head and kissed his flat nipple. Her hand stroked him boldly—because this was no sleepy mistake.

'Annika…'

'I know.' She did—she knew they were supposed to be taking it slow, knew he was going away, knew it was absolutely bad timing—but… 'I want it to be you.'

'What if…?'

'Then I still want it to be you.'

Her virginity, in that moment, was more important to Ross than it was to her. To him it denoted a commitment that he thought he wasn't capable of making, yet he had never felt more sure in his life.

She traced his lovely length to the moist tip, and then he lifted her head, gently pulled at her hair so that he could kiss her. His hand was on her breast, warming it, holding its weight. Then he was stroking her inside, her warm centre was moist, and she was glad his mouth had left hers because she wanted to bite on her lip.

He kissed her low in the neck, a deep, slow kiss, and he was restraining himself in case he bruised her, but she wanted his bruise, so she pushed at his head, rocking a little against him as his lips softly branded her.

'Put something on,' she begged, because she wanted to part her legs so badly.

'Are you sure?' It was the right thing to say, but it seemed stupid, and Annika clearly thought the same.

'Yes!' she begged. 'Just put something on.'

He was nuzzling at her breasts now, as his fingers still slid inside her, and his erection was there too, heavy on her inner thigh, teasing her as his other hand frantically patted at the bedside drawer.

She was desperate.

Little flicks of electricity showered her body. She was wanton as he suckled at her breast and searched unseeing in the drawer. Then she held him again, because she wanted to. She took his tip and slid it over her, and he moaned in hungry regret because he wanted to dive in. Side by side they explored each other's bodies as still he searched for a condom.

'Here…' He waved it as if he had found the golden ticket, his hand shaking as he wrestled with the foil.

Still she held him, slid him over and over the place he wanted to be till it was almost cruel. He was so hard, so close, and she didn't want him sheathed. She wanted to see and feel—but he had a shred of logic and he used it. He sheathed himself more quickly than he ever had, but he didn't dive in, because he didn't want to hurt her. He claimed her breast again with his mouth, and she cupped him and stroked him again. She teased him, but she could only tease for so long—and then she got her reaction: he was gently in. She was breaking every ingrained rule and it felt divine.

'Did I hurt you?' he checked.

'Not yet.'

And he swore to himself that he wouldn't.

Yes, he'd made that promise more than a few times before, but this time he hoped he meant it.

She wanted more, and he pushed so hard into her that she had to lie back. She wanted to accommodate him, to orientate herself to the new position. Those little flicks of electricity had merged into a surge—she couldn't breathe. He was bucking inside her and she was frantic. She thought she might swear, or cry out his name, but she held back from that. She could feel his rip of release and she wanted to scream, but she wouldn't allow herself. She bit on his shoulder instead, sucked his lovely salty flesh and joined him—*almost*.

Not with total abandon, because she didn't yet know what that was, but she joined him with a rare freedom she had never envisaged.

Then, after, he waited.

As she fell asleep, still he waited.

For the thump of regret, the sting of shame, for him to convince himself that he was just a bastard—but it never came.

CHAPTER THIRTEEN

HE WAS a very patient teacher—and not just in the bedroom. Round and round the field she bobbed, trot, trot, and she even, to her glee, got to gallop. Then Ross showed her the sitting trot, in which her bottom wasn't to lift out of the seat. He did it with no hands, made it look so easy, but it was actually hard work.

Around Ross she was always starving.

'It's all the exercise!'

She laughed at her own little joke and he kissed her. Then, when she wanted so much more than a kiss, very slowly he took off her boots and she lay back. She could feel the sun on her cheeks and the breeze in the trees, and life was, in that moment, perfect. He sorted out her zip and she let him. In everything she was inhibited—at work, with friends, with family— but not with Ross.

In this, with him, there was no fear or shame, just desire.

'There,' she told him, because where he was kissing her now was perfect.

'Again,' she said, when she wanted it there again.

'More,' she said, when she wanted some more.

She pulled his T-shirt over his head, berating him the second his mouth stopped working so it resumed duty again.

She wanted more—and not just for herself, so she pulled at her own T-shirt till all she wore was a bra. Then she didn't care what she was wearing. She could feel his ragged breathing on her tender skin and sensed her pleasure was his.

He was unshaved, and she was tender, so she had to push him back, just once, and yet she so much wanted him to go on.

And he dived in again, but she was still too tender.

So she pulled at his jodhpurs and freed him instead.

He was divine, his black curls neat and manicured, the erection glorious and dark, so that she had to touch. Her fingers stroked, guided, and he was there at her entrance, moistening it a little. It was so fierce to look at, yet on contact more gentle than his lips.

'Please…' She was so close to coming she lifted her hips.

'They're in there…' He was gesturing to the backpack, a lifetime away, or more like ten metres, but it was a distance that was too far to fathom. He might just as well have left the condoms in the bathroom.

It was the most delicious tease of sex to come. He was stroking against her and she was purring, her hips rising, begging that he fill her and for it not to stop.

'Just a little way…' Her voice was throaty, and he stared down at her, so pink and swollen. How could he not? He entered her just a little.

He was kneeling up, holding her buttocks, and his eyes roamed her body. He thought he would come. She was all blonde and tumbled, and in underwear that would make working beside her now close to impossible, because if he even pictured her in that… He pushed it in just a little bit more as Annika—shy, guarded Annika—gave him a bold, wanton smile that had his heart hammering. He pulled down the straps on her bra and freed her breasts, and she boldly took his head and led him there. She kissed his temple as he suckled her. He moved within her till he wanted more than just a little way, and so too did she.

He leant back and guided her, up and down his length. She had never felt more pliant, moving as his hands guided her. She could see his dark skin against her paleness, and she felt as if she were climbing out of her mind and watching them, released from inhibition. She cried out, could see her thighs trembling, her back arching. Then she climbed back into her body and felt the deep throb of an orgasm that didn't abate. It swelled and rolled like an ocean, took away her breath and dragged her under, and she said his name, thought she swore. Still he was pounding within her, so fast and hard that even as her orgasm faded she thought it would happen again.

And it did—because he was mindful. Just as he satisfied her he gave in, pulled out of her warmth and shivered outside her. She watched. It was startling and beautiful and intimate.

Their intimacy shocked her.

It shocked her that this was okay, that *they* were okay, that they could do all that and afterwards he could just pull her to him.

They lay for a long time in delicious silence, and all Ross knew was that they had completely crossed a line—it wasn't about condoms, or trips to Spain, or families, or all things confusing.

It was, in that moment, incredibly simple.

They were both home.

CHAPTER FOURTEEN

'YOU might want to get dressed…' They were both half dozing when Ross heard the crunch of tyres. 'I think we've got visitors.'

And, though they were miles from being seen, Annika was horrified. As she dressed quickly Ross took his time and laughed. She tripped over herself pulling on her jodhpurs.

'No one can see,' he assured her.

'Who is it?'

'My family, probably…' Ross said, and then there were four blasts of a horn, which must have confirmed his assumption because he nodded. 'There's no rush; they'll wait.'

'I'll go home.' Annika was dressed now. The horses were close by, and she would put up with *any* pain just to make it to the safety of her car. 'I'll just say a quick hello and then go.'

'Don't rush off.' For the first time ever he looked uncomfortable.

'What will they think, though?' Annika asked, because if *her* mother had turned up suddenly on a

Sunday evening to find a man at her home she would think plenty—and no doubt say it too.

'That I've got a friend over for the afternoon,' Ross said, but she knew he was uncomfortable.

As they rode back her heart was hammering in her chest—especially when another car pulled up and several more Wyatt family members piled out. His father was very formal, his sisters both much paler in colouring than Ross, and his mother, Estella, was raven-haired and glamorous. Grandchildren were unloaded from the car. His sisters said hi and bye, and relieved them of their horses before heading out for a ride in what was left of the sun.

'Hi, Imelda!'

The sun must have gone behind a cloud, because it was decidedly chilly.

'This is Annika,' Ross said evenly. 'She's a friend from the hospital. Iosef's sister…'

'Oh, my mistake.' His mother gave a grim smile. 'It's just with the blonde hair, and given that she's wearing Imelda's things, you'll forgive me for being confused.'

Ross's brain lurched, because never before had his mother shown her claws.

She had never been anything other than a friend to him, but now she was stomping inside. A row that had never before happened between them was about to start—and it was terrible timing, because he had to deal with Annika as well.

'Imelda?'

'My ex,' Ross said.

'How ex?'

'A few weeks.'

And she wasn't happy with that, so she demanded dates and he told her.

'Was there time to change the sheets?'

'Annika, I never said I didn't have a past.'

'And I'm standing here dressed in her things!'

'It's not as bad as it sounds...'

'It's worse,' Annika said. 'Can you get my keys?'

'Don't go.'

'What—do you expect me to go in and make small talk with your family? Can you please go and get my things?'

It was like two patients collapsing simultaneously at work. Two blistering things he had to deal with.

Annika refused to bend—she wanted her keys and no more.

Ross stomped into the house.

'What the hell?' His voice was a roar. 'How *dare* you do that to her?'

'She'll thank me!' Estella shouted. 'And don't, Reyes—don't even try to justify it to me. "I've got to sort myself out." "I want to find myself." "I'm not getting involved with anyone..."' She hurled back everything he had said, and then she called him a *cabrón* too! He vaguely remembered it meant a bastard. 'I had Imelda on the phone last night, and again this morning. You shred these girls' hearts and we're supposed to say *nothing*?'

'Annika's different!'

'Oh, it's *different* this time, is it?' Estella shouted, and the windows were open, so Ross knew Annika could hear. 'Because apparently you said that to Imelda too!'

And then she really let him have it.

Really!

She called him every name she could think of. Later, Ross would realise that she had probably been talking to Reyes senior. Every bit of hurt his biological father had caused his mother, all the shame, anger and fury that had never come out, had chosen that afternoon to do so.

And his time was up. Annika was storming through the house, finding her keys for herself as his mother continued unabated.

Ross raced out behind her to the car.

'It's not that bad…'

'Really?' Annika gave him a wide-eyed look as she turned the key in the ignition. 'From the sounds inside your home, you're the only who thinks that way.'

'You're just going to drive off…?' He couldn't believe it. He didn't like rows, but he didn't walk away from them either. 'All that's happened between us and you'll just let it go…?'

'Watch me!' Annika said, and she did just that. She gunned the car down his drive, still dressed in Imelda's things. His mother's words about her own son still ringing in her ears.

It was only when she went into her flat, kicked off her boots and ripped off those clothes that she calmed down.

Well, she didn't calm down, exactly, but she realised it wasn't that she had been wearing Imelda's things, or what his mother had said, or anything straightforward that had made her so angry. It was that, just like her family, he had fed her a half-truth.

And, as she had with her family, she had been foolish enough to trust him.

CHAPTER FIFTEEN

ELSIE was right—you should never let the sun go down on a row, because as the days moved on life got more complicated. It was cold and lonely up there on her high horse, and next Tuesday Ross flew out to Spain. More importantly, her midway report on her time with the children's ward was less than impressive, and she was considering the very real good she could do working on the family foundation board.

She wanted his wisdom.

She attempted a smile, even tried to strike up a conversation. She finally resorted to wearing the awful wizard apron that always garnered comment. But Ross didn't bat an eye.

Because Ross was sulking too.

Yes, he'd messed up, but the fact that she hadn't let him explain incensed him. His mother, two minutes after Annika had left, had burst into tears, and George had had to give her a brandy.

Then George, who had always been a touch lacking in the emotion department, had started to cry and revealed he was dreading losing his son!

Ross had problems too!

So he ignored her—wished he could stop thinking about her, but ignored her.

Even on Saturday.

Even as she left the ward, still he didn't look up.

'Enjoy the ball!' Caroline called. 'You can tell us all about it tomorrow.'

'I will,' Annika said. 'See you then.'

He could feel her eyes on the top of his head as he carried on writing his notes.

'See you, Ross.'

Consultants didn't need to look up; he just gave her a very clipped response as he continued to write.

'Yep.'

Annika consoled herself that this was progress.

'You're not working this afternoon, are you?' Dianne frowned as Annika came into the office.

'No,' Annika said. 'I just popped in to check my roster.'

It was a lie and everyone knew it. She wasn't due for a shift for another week, and anyway she could have rung to check. She had, to her mother's disgust, worked on the children's ward this morning, but they had let her go home early. Instead of taking advantage of those extra two hours, and racing to her mother's to have her hair put up and her make-up applied for the ball, she'd *popped in to check her roster*.

'How's Elsie?' Annika asked. 'I rang yesterday and the GP was coming in…'

'She's not doing so well, Annika,' Dianne said. 'She's got another UTI, and he thinks she might have had an infarct.'

'Is she in hospital?'

'She's here,' Dianne said, 'and we're making her as comfortable as we can. Why don't you go in and see her?'

Annika did. Elsie wasn't particularly confused, but she didn't recognize Annika out of uniform.

'Is any family coming?' Annika asked Dianne.

'Her daughter's in Western Australia, and she's seventy,' Dianne said. 'She's asked that we keep her informed.'

Annika sat with Elsie for a little while longer, but her phone kept going off, which disturbed the old lady, so in the end Annika kissed Elsie goodbye and asked Dianne if she could ring later.

'Of course,' Dianne said. 'She's your friend.'

CHAPTER SIXTEEN

STARING out of her old bedroom window, Annika felt the knot in her stomach tighten at the sight of the luxury cars waiting lined up in the driveway.

She could hear chatter and laughter downstairs and was loath to go down—but then someone knocked at the door.

'Only me!' Annie, her sister-in-law, popped her head round and then came in. 'You look stunning, Annika.'

'I don't feel it.' She stared in the mirror at the curled blonde ringlets, at the rouge, lipstick, nails and the thousands of dollars worth of velvet that hugged her body and felt like ripping it off.

'But you look gorgeous,' Annie protested.

How did Annie balance it? Annika wondered. She had probably spent half an hour getting ready. Her dark curls were damp at the ends, and she was pulling on a pair of stockings as she chatted. Her breasts, huge from feeding little Rebecca, were spilling out her simple black dress. And her cheeks had a glow that no amount of blusher could produce—no doubt there was a very good reason why she and Iosef were so late arriving for pre-dinner drinks!

'It's going to be fun!' Annie insisted. 'Iosef was

dreading it too, but I've had a fiddle and we're on the poor table.'

'Pardon?'

'Away from the bigwigs!' Annie said gleefully. 'Well, we're not sitting with the major sponsors of the night.'

And then Annie was serious.

'Iosef meant it when he said if you needed a hand.'

'I cashed the cheque.'

'We meant with your studies.' Annie blew her fringe out of her eyes. Iosef's family were all impossible—this little sister too. There was a wall that Annie had tried to chip away at, but she'd never even made a dint. 'I know it must be hell for you now—finding out what your mother did…'

'Had she not…' Annika's blue eyes glittered dangerously '…your beloved Iosef wouldn't be here. Do you ever think of *that* when you're so busy hating her?'

'Annika, please, let us help you.'

'No!' Annika was sick of Annie—sick of the lot of them telling her how she felt. 'I don't need your help. I'm handing in my notice, and you'll get your money back. All my mother did was try and look after her family—well, now it's my turn to look after her!'

She stepped out of the car and smiled for the cameras. She stood with her mother and smiled ever brighter, and then she walked through the hotel foyer and they were guided to the glittering pre-dinner drinks reception.

Diamonds and rare gems glittered from throats and ears, and people sipped on the finest champagne. Annika dazzled, because that was what was expected of her, but it made no sense.

Hundreds of thousands would have been spent on tonight.

Aside from the luxury hotel and the fine catering, money would have been poured into dresses, suits, jewels, hairdressers, beauticians, prizes and promotion. All to support a cluster of orphanages the Kolovskys had recently started raising funds for.

All this money spent, all this gluttony, to support the impoverished.

Sometimes, to Annika, it seemed obscene.

'You have to spend it to make it,' her mother had said.

'Annika…' Her mother was at her most socially vigilant. Everything about tonight had to be perfect. The Kolovskys had to be seen at their very best—and that included the daughter. 'This is Zakahr Belenki, our guest speaker…'

'*Zdravstvujte*,' he greeted her formally, in Russian, and Annika responded likewise, but she was relieved when he reverted to English.

He was a Detsky Dom boy made good—a self-made billionaire and the jewel in the crown that was tonight. He poured numerous funds into this charity, but he was, Zakahr said, keen to raise awareness, which was why he had flown to the other side of the world for this ball.

This, Nina explained, was what tonight could achieve, proof of the good they could do. But though Zakahr nodded and answered politely to her, his grey eyes were cold, his responses slightly scathing.

'I've heard marvellous things about your outreach programme!' Annika attempted.

'What things?' Zakahr asked with a slight smirk, but Annika had done her homework and spoke with him about the soup kitchen and the drop-in centre, and the regular health checks available for the street children. She had heard that Zakahr was also implementing a casual education programme, with access to computers...

'We would love to support that,' Nina gushed, and then dashed off.

'Tell me, Annika?' Zakahr said when they were alone. 'How much do you think it costs to clear a conscience?'

She looked into the cool grey eyes that seemed to see right into her soul and felt as if a hand was squeezing her throat, but Zakahr just smiled.

'I think our support for the education programme is assured,' she said.

He knew, and he knew, and it made her feel sick.

Soon everyone would know, and she could hardly stand it. She wanted to hide, to step off the world till it all blew over, but somehow she had to live through it and be there for her mother too.

'Excuse me...' She turned to go, to escape to the loo, to get away from the throng—except there was no escape tonight, because she collided into a chest and, though she didn't see his face for a second, the scent of him told her that a difficult night had just become impossible.

'Ross.' Annika swallowed hard, looked up, and almost wished she hadn't.

Always she had considered him beautiful; tonight he was devastatingly handsome.

He was in a dinner suit, his long black hair slicked back, his tie knotted perfectly, his shirt gleaming against his dark skin, his earring glittering. His face was, for the first time, completely cleanshaven. She looked for the trademark mockery, except there was none.

'How come...?' She shook her head. She had never for a second factored him into tonight, had never considered that their worlds might collide here.

'I work in the orphanages with your brother.' Ross shrugged. 'It's a very good cause.'

'Of course.' Annika swallowed. 'But…' She didn't continue. How could she? This was her world, and she had never envisaged him entering it.

'I'm also here for the chance to talk to you.'

'There's really not much to say.'

'You'd let it all go for a stupid misunderstanding? Let everything go over one single row?'

'Yes,' Annika said—because her family's shame was more than she could reveal, because it was easier to go back to the fold alone than to even try to blend him in.

'Hello!' Nina was all smiles. Seeing her daughter speaking to a stranger, she wormed her way in for a rapid introduction, lest it be someone famous she hadn't met, or a contact she hadn't pursued.

'This is my mother, Nina.' Annika's lips were so rigid she could hardly get the words out. 'Mother, this is Ross Wyatt—Dr Ross Wyatt.'

'I work at the hospital with Annika; I'm also a friend of Iosef's.' Ross smiled.

Only in her family was friendship frowned upon; only for the Kolovskys was a doctor, a *working* doctor, considered common.

Oh, Nina didn't say as much, and Ross probably only noticed her smile and heard her twenty seconds of idle chatter, but Annika could see the veins in her mother's neck, see the unbreakable glass that was her mother's eyes frost as she came face to face with the 'filthy gypsy' Iosef had spoken so often about.

She glanced over to Annika.

'You need to work the room, darling.'

So she did—as she had done many times. She

made polite conversation, laughing at the right moment and serious when required. But she could feel Ross's eyes on her, could sometimes see him chatting with Iosef, and a job that had always been hard was even harder tonight.

She was the centre of attention, the jewel in the Kolovsky crown, and she had to sparkle on demand.

Just as she had been paraded for the grown-ups on her birthdays as a child, or later at dinner parties, so she was paraded tonight.

Iosef, Aleksi, and later Levander had all teased her, mocked her, because in her parents' eyes Annika had been able to do no wrong. Annika had been the favourite, Annika the one who behaved, who toed the line. Yes, she had, but they just didn't understand how hard that had been.

And how much harder it would be to suddenly stop.

She stood at the edge of the crowd, heard the laughter and the tinkle of glass, felt the buoyant mood, and how she wanted to head over to Ross, to Iosef and Annie, to relax. She almost did.

'Aleksi isn't here…' Her mother's face was livid behind her bright smile, her words spat behind rigid teeth. 'You need to speak to the Minister, and then you need to—'

'I'm just going to have a drink with my friends, with Iosef…'

'Have you *any* idea what people are paying to be here tonight?' Nina said. 'Any idea of the good we can do? And you want to stop and *have a drink*?'

'Annie and Iosef are.'

'You know what I think of *them*. You are better than that, Annika. Your father wanted more for you. Iosef thinks his four weeks away a year helping the orphans excludes him from other duties. Tonight *you* can make a real difference.'

So she did.

She spoke to the Minister. She laughed as his revolting son flirted with her. She spoke fluent French with some other guests, forgetting that she was a student nurse and that she wiped bums in a nursing home. She shone and made up for the absent Aleksi and she impressed everyone—except the ones that mattered to her the most.

'It's going well!' Annika said, slipping into her seat at their table, putting her hand over her glass when the waiter came with wine. 'Just water, thanks.'

'Ross was just saying,' Iosef started, 'that you're…' His voice trailed off as his mother appeared and spoke in Annika's ear.

'I have to go and sit with them…' Annika said.

'No, Annika, you don't,' Iosef said.

'I want to.' She gave Ross a smile, but he didn't return it.

'It's hard for her,' Annie said, once Annika had gone, but Iosef didn't buy it. He had done everything he could to keep Annika in nursing, and his mother had told him earlier today that Annika was quitting.

'No, she loves this,' he said. 'She always has.' He looked over to his wife. 'Has she told you that she's handing in her notice at the end of her rotation?'

'Sort of.'

'I told you she wouldn't stick at it.' He glanced at Ross. 'Model, pastry chef, jewellery designer, student nurse…' He looked to where his sister was laughing at something the Minister's son had said. 'I think she's found her vocation.'

Aleksi did arrive. Dinner had already been cleared

away, and the speeches were well underway, but because it was Aleksi, everyone pretended not to notice his condition.

A stunning raven-haired beauty hung on his arm and he was clearly a little the worse for wear—and so was she. Their chatter carried through the room, once at the most inappropriate of times, when Zakahr Belenki was speaking of his time in the Detsky Dom.

Abandoned at birth, he had been raised there, but at twelve years of age he had chosen the comparative luxury of the streets. The details were shocking, and unfortunately, as he paused for effect, Aleksi's date, clearly not listening to the speaker, called to the waiter for more wine.

And Ross watched.

Watched as the speaker stared in distaste at Aleksi.

Watched as a rather bored Annika played with her napkin and fiddled with the flower display, or occasionally spoke with her brother's revolting date.

He saw Aleksi Kolovsky yawn as Zakahr spoke of the outreach programme that had saved him.

Clothed him.

Fed him.

Supported him.

Spoke of how he had climbed from the gutters of the streets to become one of Europe's most successful businessmen.

He asked that tonight people supported this worthy cause.

And then Ross watched as for the rest of the night Annika ignored him.

He'd clearly misread her. Here she was, being how he had always wanted her to be—smiling, talking, dancing, laughing—she just chose not to do it with him.

'Why don't I give you a lift home?'

'There's an after-party event.'

'How about we stay for an hour and then…?'

'It's exclusive,' Annika said.

And he got the point.

Tonight he had seen her enjoying herself in a way that she never had with him.

For once instinct had failed him.

He had been sure there was more, and was struggling to accept that there wasn't.

'It was a good speech from Zakahr…' Ross said, carefully watching her reaction.

'It was a little over the top,' Annika said, 'but it did the job.'

'Is that what this is to you?'

'Ross.' Annika's cheeks were burning. 'You and Iosef are so scathing, but you don't mind spending the funds.'

'Okay.' She had a point, but there was so much more in the middle.

Iosef and Annie were leaving, and they came over and said their goodnights.

'You've got work tomorrow,' Iosef pointed out, when Annika declined a lift from them and said where she was heading.

And then it was just the two of them again, and, though he had no real right to voice an opinion, though she had promised him nothing, he felt as if he had been robbed.

'Are you giving up nursing?'

'Probably,' Annika answered, but she couldn't look at him. Why wouldn't he just leave her? Why, every time she saw him, did she want to fall into his arms and weep? 'Ross, I need to be here for my mother, and there's a good work opportunity for me. Let's face it—

I'm hardly nurse of the year. But I haven't properly made up my mind yet. I'm going to finish my paediatric rotation—'

'Come back with me,' Ross interrupted.

How badly she wanted to—to go back to the farm, where she could breathe, where she could think. Except Ross would be gone on Tuesday, and all this would still be here.

Her mother was summoning her over and Annika took her cue. 'I have to go.'

'I'll see you at work on Monday,' Ross said, and suddenly he was angry. 'If you can tear yourself away from the Minister's son!'

CHAPTER SEVENTEEN

Ross's words rang in her ears as she raced home and pulled on her uniform. After this afternoon, she knew it would confuse Elsie to see Annika in anything else.

Yes, she was supposed to be at the after-party event, and, yes, her mother was furious, but even though she wouldn't get paid for tonight, even though she wasn't on duty, she *had* to be here.

'How is she?' Annika asked, as Shelby, one of the night nurses, let her in.

'Close to the end,' Shelby said. 'But she's lucid at times.'

'Hi, Elsie.'

They were giving her some morphine when Annika walked in, and the smile on the old lady's face was worth all the effort of coming. Now she was in her uniform Elsie recognised her. Yes, Annika would be tired tomorrow, and, no, she didn't have to be here, but she had known and cared for the old lady for over a year now, and it was a very small price to pay for the friendship and wisdom Elsie had imparted.

'My favourite nurse,' Elsie mumbled. 'I thought you weren't on for a while…'

'I'm doing an extra shift,' Annika said, so as not to confuse her.

'That's good.' Elsie said. 'Can you stay with me?'

She couldn't.

She really couldn't.

She'd only popped in to check on her, to say goodnight or goodbye. She had to be at work at twelve tomorrow. The charity do would be all over the papers— it was unthinkable that she call in sick.

But that was exactly what she did.

She spoke to a rather sour voice on the other end of the phone and said she was getting a migraine and that she was terribly sorry but she wouldn't be in.

There was going to be trouble. Annika knew that.

But she'd deal with it tomorrow. Tonight she had other things to do.

Elsie's big reclining seat was by her bed, and Annika put a sheet over it and sat down beside her. She took the old bony hand in hers and held it, felt the skinny fingers hold hers back, and it was nice and not daunting at all.

She remembered when her father had been so ill. Annie had been his nurse on his final night. How jealous Annika had been that Annie had seemed to know what to do, how to look after him, how to take care of him on his final journey.

Two years on, Annika knew what to do now.

Knew this was right.

It was right to doze off in the chair, to hold Elsie's hand and wake a couple of hours later, when the morphine wore off a little and Elsie started to stir. She walked out to find Shelby.

'I think her medication's wearing off.'

And Shelby checked her chart, and then Elsie's, and agreed with Annika's findings.

Gently they both turned Elsie, and Annika combed her hair and swabbed her mouth so it tasted fresh, put some balm on her lips. Elsie was lucid before the medicine started to kick in again.

'How's Ross?' Elsie asked.

'Wonderful,' Annika said, because she knew it would make Elsie happy.

'He's good to you?' the old lady checked.

'Always.'

'You can be yourself?'

And she should just say yes again, to keep Elsie happy, but she faltered.

'Be yourself,' Elsie said, and Annika nodded. 'That's the only way he can really love you.'

The hours before dawn were the most precious.

Elsie slept, and sometimes Annika did too, but it was nice just to be there with her.

'I'm very grateful to you,' Elsie said, her tired eyes meeting Annika's as the nursing home started to wake up. The hall light flicked on and the drug trolley clattered. 'You're a wonderful nurse.'

Annika was about to correct her, to say she wasn't here as a nurse but as a friend, and then it dawned on her that she could be both. Here, she knew what she was doing, and again Elsie was right.

She *was*, at least to the oldies, a wonderful nurse.

'I'm very grateful to you too,' Annika said.

'For what?'

'You've worked it out for me, Elsie.' And she took Bertie's photo and gave it to Elsie, who held it instead of Annika's hand.

The next dose of morphine was her last.

Annika stepped out into the morning without crying. Death didn't daunt her, it was living that did, but thanks to Elsie she knew at least something of what she was doing.

Her old friend had helped her to map out the beginnings of her future.

CHAPTER EIGHTEEN

'ANNIKA.' Caroline had called her into the office immediately after handover. 'I appreciate that you have commitments outside of nursing, and I know that your off-duty request got lost, but I went out of my way to accommodate you. I changed your shift to a late and you accepted it!'

'I thought I would be able to come in.'

'Your photo is in the paper—dining with celebrities, drinking champagne...' Caroline was having great trouble keeping her voice even. 'And then you call at four a.m. to say you're unable to come in. Even this morning you're...' Her eyes flicked over Annika's puffy face and the bags under her eyes. 'Do you even want to be here, Annika?'

Just over twenty-four hours ago her answer would have been very different. Had it not been for Elsie, Annika might well have had her notice typed up in her bag.

But a lot had changed.

'Very much so.' Annika saw the dart of surprise in her senior's eyes. 'I have been struggling with things for a while, but I really do want to be here.' Annika was trying to be honest. It wasn't a Kolovsky trait, in fact her life was a mire of lies, but Annika took a deep breath. All she could do was hope for the best. 'I wasn't sick yesterday.'

'Annika, I should warn you—'

'I am tired on duty at times but that is because I have been doing shifts at a private nursing home. Recently I have tried to arrange it so that it doesn't impinge on my nursing time, but on Saturday I found out that my favourite resident was dying. She has no visitors, and I went in to see her on my way home from the party. I ended up staying. Not working,' she added, when Caroline was silent. 'Elsie had become a good friend, and it didn't seem right to leave her. I'm sorry for letting everyone down.'

'Keep us informed in the future,' Caroline said. 'You've got a lecture this morning in the staffroom—why don't you get a coffee?'

She had expected a reprimand, even a written warning. She was surprised when neither came, and surprised, too, when Ross caught up with her in the kitchen.

'Caroline said you were at the nursing home on Saturday night?'

'I'm surprised she discusses student nurses with you.'

'I heard her on the phone to Heather Jameson.'

'Oh.'

'Is that the truth?' He didn't know. 'Or did it take you twenty-four hours to come up with a good excuse?'

'It's the truth.' She filled her mug with hot water.

'So why couldn't you tell me that?' Ross demanded. 'Why did you make up some story about an after-party event?'

'I thought I was just going to drop in on Elsie; I didn't realise that I'd stay the night.'

'You could have told me.'

'And have you tell Caroline?' Annika said. 'Or Iosef? He's given me some money so that I don't have to work there any more.' She swallowed hard. 'I wasn't actually working. I don't expect you to understand, but Elsie has been more than a patient to me, and it didn't seem right to leave her—'

'Hey.' He interrupted her explanations with a smile. 'Careful—you're starting to sound like a nurse.'

'I thought I would be in trouble,' Annika admitted. 'I didn't expect Caroline to understand.'

'You could have told me,' Ross said. 'You could have trusted me…'

'I don't, though,' Annika said.

Her tongue could be as sharp as a razor at times, but this time it didn't slice. He stared at her for a long moment.

'Why do you push everything good away?'

He didn't expect an answer. He was, in fact, surprised when she gave one.

'I don't know.'

Each Monday, patients permitting, one of the senior staff did an informal lecture for the nursing staff, and particularly the students. As they sat in the staffroom and waited for a few stragglers to arrive, Ross struggled to make small talk with the team. His mind was too full of her.

He watched as she came in and took a seat beside Cassie. She smiled to her fellow student, said hello, and then put down her coffee, opened her notebook, clicked on her pen and sat silent amidst the noisy room.

Her eyes were a bit puffy, and he guessed she must have spent the night crying. How he wished he had known—how he wished she had been able to tell him.

Ross waited as the last to arrive took their seats. It was all very informal, even though it was a difficult subject: 'Recognising Child Abuse in a Ward Environment.'

Ross was a good teacher; he didn't need to work from notes. He turned off the television, told everyone to get a drink quickly if they hadn't already. As he talked, he let his eyes roam around the room and not linger on her. She was probably uncomfortable because it was Ross giving the lecture—not that she ever showed it. She nodded and gave a brief smile at something Cassie said, and she glanced occasionally at him as he spoke, but mainly—rudely, perhaps—she looked at the blank television screen or took the occasional note on the pad in her lap.

'Often,' Ross said, 'by the time a child arrives on the ward there is a diagnosis—perhaps from a GP, or Emergency, or perhaps you have a chronically ill child that has been in many times before. It is your responsibility to look beyond the diagnosis, to always remember to keep an open mind.' He glanced around and saw her writing. 'Babies can't tell you what is wrong, and older children often won't. Perhaps they are loyal to their parents, or perhaps they don't even know that something is wrong…'

'How can they not know?' Cassie asked.

'Because they know no different,' Ross said patiently. 'This is particularly the case with emotional abuse, which is hard to define. Neglect is a hard one too. They are used to being neglected. They have grown up thinking this is normal.'

It was a complicated talk, with lots of questions. None from Annika, of course. She just took her notes and sometimes gazed out of the window or down at her hands. Once she yawned, as if bored by the subject, but this time Ross didn't for a moment consider it rude.

He remembered the way she had sat at the charity ball, ignoring the speaker, oblivious to his words. Now, standing in front of everyone, he started to understand.

'A frozen look?' Cassie asked, when he explained what he looked for in an abused child, and Ross nodded.

'You come to recognise it...' he said, then corrected himself. 'Or you sometimes do.'

There were more questions from the floor, and all of a sudden he didn't feel qualified to answer, although he had to.

'These children sometimes present as precocious. Other times,' Ross said, 'they are withdrawn, or lacking in curiosity. You may go to put in an IV and instead of resistance or fear there is compliance, but often there is no one obvious clue...'

He wanted his lecture over; he wanted a moment to pause and think—and then what?

He felt sick. He thought about wrapping things up, but Cassie was like a dog with a bone, asking about emotional abuse—what did he mean? What were the signs?

'"*Just because I can't see it, I still know you are hurting me.*"' He quoted a little girl who was now hopefully happy, but had summed it up for so many.

And you either understood it or you didn't, but he watched Annika's mouth tighten and he knew that she did.

'How can you get them to trust you?' another student asked.

'How do you approach them?' Cassie asked.

But Ross was looking at Annika.

'Carefully,' he said. 'Sometimes, in an emergency,

you have to wade in a bit, but the best you can do is hope they can trust you and bit by bit tell their story.'

'What if they don't know their story?' Annika asked, her blue eyes looking back at him, and only Ross could see the flash of tears there. 'What if they are only just finding out that the people they love have caused them hurt, have perhaps been less than gentle?'

'Then you work through it with them,' Ross said, and he saw her look away. 'Or you support them as they work through it themselves. It's hard for a child to find out that the people they love, that those who love them—'

'They *can't* love them…' Cassie started. 'How can you say they love them?'

'Yes,' Ross said, 'they can—and that is why it's so bloody complicated.'

He had spoken for an hour and barely touched the sides. He didn't want her to be alone now, he wanted to be with her, but it was never that easy.

'Sorry to break up the party.' Lisa's voice came over the intercom. 'They need you in Emergency, Ross. Two-year-old boy, severe asthma. ETA ten minutes…'

And the run to Emergency would take four.

As everyone dispersed Annika sat there, till it was only the two of them left.

'You have to go.'

'I know.'

Her head was splitting.

Don't tell. Don't tell. Don't tell.

Family.

No one else's business.

How much easier it would be to walk away, to shut him out, to never tell rather than to open her heart?

'You know that my brother, Levander, was raised in the orphanages…'

He did, but Ross said nothing.

'We did not know—my parents said they did not know—but now it would seem that they did.' It was still so hard to believe, let alone say. 'I thought my parents were perfect—it would seem I was wrong. I was told my childhood was perfect, that I was lucky and had a charmed life. That was incorrect too.'

'Annika…'

'You want me to be open, to talk, and to give you answers—I don't know them. When I met my brothers' wives, when I saw what "normal" was, I realised how different my world was…' She shook her head at the hopelessness of explaining something she didn't herself understand. 'I was sheltered, my mind was closed, and now it is not as simple as just walking away. Every day it is an effort to break away. I don't like my mother, and I hate what she did, but I love her.'

'You're allowed to.'

'I realise now my parents are far from perfect. I see how I have been controlled…' She made herself say it. 'How conditional their love actually was. I am starting to see it, but I still want to be able to sustain a relationship with my mother and remember my father with love.'

'I'm sorry.' He had never been sorrier in his life. 'For rushing you, for…'

'It can't be rushed,' Annika said. 'And I am not deliberately not telling you things. Some of it I just don't know, and I don't know how to trust you.'

'You will,' Ross said.

She almost did.

His pager was shrilling, and he had to run to the

152   KNIGHT ON THE CHILDREN'S WARD

patient instead of to her. He had to keep his mind on the little boy and, though he was soon sorted, though the two-year-old was soon stable, it was, Ross decided, the hardest patient he had dealt with in his career.

So badly he wanted to speak with her.

CHAPTER NINETEEN

'HI, ANNIKA?'

'Yes.'

'I'm ringing for a favour.' Now that he understood her a little bit, he could smile at her brusqueness. 'A work favour.'

'What is it?'

'I've got this two-year-old with asthma. Emergency is steaming. There's some poor guy in the next bed after an MVA, and the kid's getting upset.'

'Bring him up, then.'

'The bed's not ready. Caroline says you need an hour,' Ross explained. 'Look, can you ring Housekeeping and ask them...?'

'Just bring him up,' Annika said. 'I'll get the bed ready. Caroline is on her break. It can be my mistake.'

'You'll get told off.'

'I'm sure I will survive.'

'It will be *my* mistake,' Ross said. 'Just make sure the bed's made—that would be great.' He paused for a moment. 'I need another favour.'

'Yes?'

'This one isn't about work.'

'What is it?'

'I'd like…' He was about to say he'd like to talk, but Ross stopped himself. 'I'd like to spend some time with you.'

The silence was long.

'Tonight,' Ross said.

And still there was silence.

'You don't have to talk,' he elaborated. 'We can listen to music…wave to each other…' He thought he heard a small laugh. 'I just want to spend some time with you.'

'I'm busy on the ward at the moment. I don't have time to make a decision.'

She was like no one he had ever met, and she intrigued him.

She would not be railroaded, would not give one bit of herself that she didn't want to, and he admired her for that. It also brought him strange comfort, because when she had been with him she had therefore wanted to be there—the passionate woman that he had held had been Annika.

He had wanted more than she was prepared to give.

And now he was ready to wait. However long it took for her to trust him.

'He can go up…' Ross said to one of the emergency nurses. 'I've cleared it with the ward.'

The emergency nurse looked dubious, as well she might. The children's ward had made it perfectly clear that it would be an hour at least, but the resuscitation area was busy, with doctors running in to deal with the patient from the car accident, neurologists, anaesthetists… The two-year-old was getting more and more distressed.

He could hear the noise from behind the curtains and gave the babe's mum a reassuring smile, blocking the gap in the curtains just a touch with his body as the toddler and his mother where wheeled out.

'Thanks so much for this.'

'No problem.' He gave her a small grimace. 'They might be a bit put out on the ward when you arrive, but don't take it personally—he's better up there than down here.'

He'd left his stethoscope on the trolley and went over to retrieve it. He considered walking up to the paediatric ward to take the flak, just in case Annika was about to get told off on his account, but then he smiled.

Annika could take it, *would* take it—she had her own priorities, and a blast from Caroline… The smile froze on his face, everything stilled as he heard a colleague's voice from behind the curtain.

'Kolovsky, Aleksi…'

Ross could hear a swooshing sound in his ears as he pictured again the mangled, bloodied body that had been rapidly wheeled past twenty minutes or so ago. His legs felt like cotton wool as he walked back across the resus unit and parted the curtains.

The patient's face had been cleaned up a bit, though Ross wasn't sure he would have recognised him had he not heard his name, but, yes, it was him.

His good friend Iosef's identical twin.

Annika's brother.

'Aleksi…' His voice was a croak and he had to clear it before he continued. 'Aleksi Kolovsky.'

'His sister works here, doesn't she?' A nurse glanced up. 'Annika? One of the students…?'

He stood and watched for a few moments, more stunned than inquisitive. He watched as the powerful, arrogant man he had met just the once extended his arms, indicative of a serious head injury, and grunted with each breath. The anaesthetist had decided to intubate, but just before he did, Ross went over.

'I'm going to get Annika for you,' he said, 'and you're going to be okay, Aleksi.'

CHAPTER TWENTY

THE hospital grapevine worked quickly, and Ross was aware not just that he had to let Annika know, but his good friend Iosef too.

The Kolovskys were famous. It would be breaking news soon—not just on the television and the internet, but the paramedics and emergency personnel would be talking, and both Iosef and his wife Annie worked in another emergency department across the city.

As he walked he scrolled through his phone. He didn't have Annie's number, only Iosef's, but, deciding it would be better for his friend to hear it from his wife, he called their emergency department. He found out that Iosef was just being informed and would be there to see Aleksi for himself shortly.

Ross moved faster, walked along the long corridor at a brisk pace, bracing himself for Annika's reaction and wondering what it would be.

He spoke briefly with Caroline, informed her of the news he would be imparting, and then headed down to room eleven.

'He's settled.' She was checking the asthma baby's

oxygen saturation; he was sleeping now, his mother by his side.

'That's good,' Ross said. 'Annika, could I have a word, please?'

'Of course.' She nodded to the mother and stepped outside. 'There was no trouble with Caroline—the cot was prepared…'

'Thanks for that. Would you mind coming into my office?'

Her eyes were suddenly wary.

'It's a private matter.'

'Then it can wait till after work,' Annika said.

'No, it's not about that…' He blew out a breath, wondered if perhaps he should have taken up Caroline's suggestion and let her be the one to tell Annika, but, no, he wanted it to come from him—however little he knew her, still he knew her best. 'Just come into my office, please, Annika.'

She did as told and stood, ignoring the seat he offered, so he stood too.

'There was a patient brought into Emergency,' Ross said. 'After a motor vehicle accident. It's Aleksi, Annika.'

'Is he alive?'

'Yes.' Ross cleared his throat. 'He's unconscious; he has multiple injuries and is still being assessed.' She was pale, but then she was always pale. She was calm, but then she was mostly calm. She betrayed so little emotion, and for Ross it was the hardest part of telling her. She just took it—she didn't reach out, didn't express alarm. It was almost as if she expected pain.

'I'll tell Caroline that I need to…'

'She knows,' Ross said. 'I'll take you down there now.'

Annika only wavered for a second. 'Iosef…'

'He's been informed and is on his way.'

They walked to Emergency. There was no small talk. He briefed her on the little he knew and they walked in relative silence. A nurse took them to a small interview room and they were told to wait there.

'Could I see my brother?' Annika asked.

'Not at this stage,' the nurse said. 'The trauma team are trying to stabilise him. As soon as we know more, a doctor will be in to speak with you.'

'Thank you.'

And then came Iosef and Annie, and Nina, their mother, who was hysterical. Iosef and Annika just sat there, backs straight, and waited as more and more Kolovskys arrived.

And still there was no news.

A doctor briefly popped in to ask the same questions as a nurse had ten minutes previously—was there any previous medical history that was relevant? Had Aleksi been involved in any other accidents or had any illnesses?

'Nothing!' Nina shouted. 'He is fit; he is strong. This is his first time sick—please, I need to see my son.'

And then they went back to waiting.

'Do *we* keep relatives waiting as long as this?' Iosef's patience was finally running out. 'Do they *know* I'm an emergency consultant?'

'I'll ask again,' Annie said.

'I'll come with you.' Ross went with her.

'God!' Annie said, once they were outside, blowing her dark curls to the sky as she let out a long breath. 'I can't stand it in there—I can't stand seeing Iosef…' She started to cry, and all Ross could do was pull a paper towel out of the dispenser and watch as she blew her nose. 'It was the same when his dad died. You know he's bleeding inside, but he just won't say…'

'He will,' Ross said. 'Maybe later—to you.'

'I know.' Annie nodded and forced a smile. 'I should warn you. They're bloody hard work, that family.'

'But worth it, I bet?' Ross said. Then he crossed a line—and he would only do it once. He looked at Annie, and stared till she looked back at him. 'Annika isn't a lightweight.'

'I know she's not.' Annie blushed.

'That family *is* bloody hard work, and Annika's right in the thick of it…'

He watched her cheeks redden further.

'Imagine if you woke up and found out that the grass was red and not green.'

'I don't get you.'

'Imagine if you'd been told all your life how lucky you were, how spoiled and indulged and precious you were, how grateful you should be.'

Annie just frowned.

'Grateful for what?' Ross demanded, and he wasn't sure if he and Annika would make it, because at any moment she was likely to turn tail and run, so he took the opportunity to tell Annie. 'Go and tell your doctor husband, my good friend, to look up emotional abuse. I can't stand the board at the hospital, but maybe on this they're right—there are charities closer to home. Tell him to wake up and see what's been going on with his own sister.'

He watched her face pale.

'They controlled what she ate, how she spoke, what she thought—have you ever stopped to think how hard it must be to break away from that?'

'We try to help!'

'Not good enough,' Ross said. 'Try harder.'

CHAPTER TWENTY-ONE

THEY could get no information at the nurses' station, so, before Iosef did, Ross pulled rank. He sent Annie back to the relatives' room and walked into resus, past the huddle around the bed, and up to Seb, the emergency consultant, who was also a friend. He was carefully examining X-ray films.

'How's it looking?'

'Not great,' Seb said, 'but there's no brain haemorrhage It's very swollen, though, and it's going to be a while till we know if there's brain damage.'

He was bringing up film after film.

'Fractured sternum, couple of ribs...' Seb was scanning the X-rays and he looked over to Ross, who was scanning them too, looking at the fractures, some old, some new. 'His left leg's a mess, but his pelvis and right leg look clear...' Seb said. The X-rays were just a little harder to read than most. There was an old fracture on Aleksi's right femur, and when he pulled up the chest film Ross looked again and there were a few old fractures there too.

'Any skull fracture?'

'One,' Seb said. 'But, again, it's old.'

'How old?'

'Not sure—there's lots of calcification… The mum says he's never been in hospital. Poor bastard.' Seb cleared his throat. 'Twenty years ago I'd have been calling you.'

'And Social Services,' Ross said, his lips white. 'What happens when it's all these years on?'

'Look, he could have been in an accident they don't know about…' But these fractures were old, and in a child they would have caused huge alarm. 'Let's get him through this first,' Seb said. 'I'll come and talk to the family.'

Nina sobbed through it; the aunts were despairing too. Iosef and Annika just sat there.

Seb was tactful, careful and thorough. He mentioned almost in passing that there were a couple of old injuries, and Nina said he had been in a lot of fights recently, but Seb said no, some looked older. And Iosef remembered a time his brother was ill, the time he came off his bike…

Nina remembered then what had happened.

'Oh, yes…' she said, but her English was suddenly poor, and an aunt had to translate for her.

'Just before the long summer holidays one year he had a nasty tumble. His leg…' she gestured '…his head. But it was nothing too serious.'

Iosef excused himself for some air, and Annika looked at her hands, sometimes at the door, and once or twice at Ross. When he went and sat beside her he gave her hand a little squeeze, and when he started to remove it she held it back. She kept holding it till they moved Aleksi up to ICU.

'Levander's flying over from England,' Iosef said, as he clicked off his phone in yet another waiting room.

'He moved there when he got married,' Annika explained. 'That is when Aleksi took over the company.'

Her face was as white as chalk, Ross noted. When she came out from seeing her brother, he saw her fingers go to her temples.

'Can you take me home?'

'Of course.'

'Will you tell my mother for me?'

'Of course,' Ross said, though he wasn't particularly looking forward to it. He turned to Nina. 'Annika's not feeling great; I'm going to take her home…'

Nina shot up from her seat. 'You need to be here—for your brother.'

'I am here for my brother,' Annika said. 'But the doctor said it is going to be at least forty-eight hours.'

'If he gets worse…'

'I have said everything I need to to him,' Annika said, and suddenly her eyes held a challenge. 'Have you?'

'You should stay.'

'I can't.'

She was so white he thought she might faint, and he put his arm around her.

'Can you give them the phone number?' she said.

He frowned.

'Your phone number at the farm—my phone battery's flat.'

'I've got Ross's number,' Iosef said, and he gave his sister a small hug. 'Look after her,' he said to Ross.

'I will.'

Ah, but Nina hadn't finished, because Nina hadn't yet got her way. 'If you had any respect for my daughter you would not flaunt this in front of her own mother.'

'I have *so* much respect for your daughter.' It was all

he could say, the only way he could respond and remain civil, and it was also true. He had so much respect for Annika—and never more so than now.

A few hours in her mother's company was enough for him.

Annika had had a lifetime.

He took her to his car, held her hair when she threw up in the bin, and then stopped at the all-night chemist for headache tablet and a cold drink too. He promised himself as they drove home in silence that he would never question her, never ask for more than he needed to know, and that if she didn't trust him, then that was okay.

He trusted himself. For the first time he trusted himself with a woman. Trusted that he would do the right thing by her, always, and that one day, he was sure, she would see it.

CHAPTER TWENTY-TWO

'WHAT time's your flight?'

A massive backpack was half filled in the living room, and only then did she remember that he was going to Spain tomorrow. She looked up at the clock and amended that to today.

'It just got cancelled,' Ross said. 'Family crisis.'

'You don't have to do that.' She meant it—she would be okay. She was making decisions for herself, seeing things for herself. She didn't need Ross to get her through this.

'I want to,' Ross said, and though she didn't need him, she *wanted* him.

'You need to find your family.'

'I think I just did.' Ross grinned. 'Heaven help me.'

'She *is* difficult.' Annika had had two headache tablets and a bath, had refused a cup of coffee and asked for a glass of wine. 'I don't know if I love her, Ross. I am trying to work it out.'

'You will.'

'Can I ask something?' He nodded. 'What do you think will happen with Aleksi?'

'As a doctor, or as a friend?'

'Can you be both?'

'I can try,' Ross said, and he did try. He stood for a full minute, trying to separate the medical from the personal, then trying to put it back together. 'I don't know,' he admitted. 'As Seb said, we won't know for a couple of days yet…' He hesitated, then made himself continue. 'If he can hang in there for a couple of days, that is. He's been unresponsive since they found him. I spoke to him,' Ross said, 'before I came and got you, and I don't know, I can't prove it, it's more gut than brain, but I think he heard…'

He almost hated the hope that flared in her eyes, but what he had said was true. 'I think he was a little bit aware.'

'I want to go to bed.'

'Okay—you have my room. I'll sleep on the couch.'

'Pardon?'

'I've got some explaining to do,' Ross reminded her. 'I was supposed to be apologising about Imelda, the clothes…'

'I accept.' She gave a tight smile. 'If it's okay with you, I would like you to make love to me.'

'Okay…' he said slowly.

'I don't want to think about today,' Annika explained. 'And I know I can't sleep.' Her very blue eyes met his. 'And I'm not really in the mood to talk.' She gave him a very brief smile. 'And you're very good at it.'

'You're a strange girl.'

'I am.'

'Impossible to work out.'

'Very.'

'But I do love you.'

'Then get me through this.'

His love was more than she could fathom right now, its magnitude too much to ponder, yet it was something she accepted—a beautiful revelation that she would bring out and explore later. Right now, she gratefully accepted the gift.

And Ross took loving her very seriously too.

He had never felt more responsible in his life.

He wanted his kiss to right a thousand wrongs, but no kiss was that good, no kiss could. He wanted to show her how much she meant to him.

She couldn't believe she had asked for sex.

Was it wrong?

Should she be sitting with her mother, being seen to do the right thing?

Did she love her brother less because she was not in a room next door?

She was dreading the days that would follow—the pain, the vigil, the hope, the fear—and she knew she had to prepare, to rest, and to get strong for whatever lay ahead.

His kiss made her tremble. It shocked her that even in misery she could be held, kissed, made to feel a bit better, that she could be herself—whoever that was.

He kissed her so deep, slow and even, and when she stopped kissing him back he kissed her some more. He kissed her face, her neck, and then her breasts, and then he kissed her mouth again.

His bed was a tumble.

There was music, books by the bedside, and a dog scraping on the door down the hall.

But there were coffee beans in the fridge and there would be warm eggs in the morning.

There was a soft welcome any time she wanted it.

And she wanted it now.

He took her away, but he let her come back, and then he took her away again.

She had a fleeting image of being old, of a nurse wheeling her into the shower as she ranted about Ross.

Let me rant.

She coiled her legs around him.

Let me rant about the night when I couldn't survive and I came to his home.

She lost herself in a way she had never envisaged.

She lost herself, and this time she didn't hold back—she dived into oblivion. She swore she could smell the bonfire as she felt the magic and the gypsy in him.

He brought her back to a world that was scary, but there was music still playing, and Ross was beside her, and she knew she'd get through. Then she did something she hadn't been able to do at the hospital, that she so rarely did—she cried, and he held her, and it didn't make things better or worse, it just released her.

'I'm sorry about my family.'

She poured it all out, and it probably didn't make much sense, but she said sorry for the past, and the stuff that was surely to come, because Zakahr Belenki knew the truth and so must others. Between gulps she told him that it was only a matter of time, warned him what he was taking on if he was mad enough to get involved with her.

'You don't have the monopoly on crazy families.' Ross grinned. 'Do you remember meeting mine?'

This made her laugh. Then she stared out of the window and thought about Aleksi. She couldn't be more scared for him if she tried.

'What are you thinking?'

'That you need curtains.'

'He'll be okay.'

'You don't know that.'

But he did.

And so he told her—stuff he had never told anyone.

He told her about intuition, and that some of the stories about gypsies were real, and that, like it or not, she was saddled with someone who was a little bit different too.

CHAPTER TWENTY-THREE

HE WOKE her at six, saw her eyes open with a smile to his, and then the pain cloud them as she remembered.

'No change,' Ross said quickly. 'I just called Iosef.'

'We should go.'

All she had was her uniform, or a suitcase of clothes that belonged to Imelda.

So she settled for his rolled-up black jeans, and a lovely black jumper, and a belt that needed Ross to poke another hole in it—but she did, to her shame, borrow Imelda's boots.

They drove to the hospital. Annika was talking about Annie, how good she had been with her father. It was this that had first made Annika think about nursing. It was a little dot, but it went next to another dot, and then she told him about Elsie. One day he would join up the complicated dots that were Annika.

Or not.

It didn't change how he felt.

'It's going to be difficult these next weeks,' Annika said as they neared the city. 'Mum will want me to move home. I can just see it…'

'You do what you have to.'

'She's so determined that I give up nursing.'

'What do *you* want, Annika?'

'To finish my training.'

'Then you will.'

They were at the hospital car park now.

'She'll want me there, back in the family business, away from nursing.' They were walking up to ICU. 'I'm so much stronger, but I'm worried that once I'm back there…'

'You've got me now,' Ross said. 'Whatever you need, whatever might help, just say.'

And that helped.

It helped an awful lot.

It helped when they got to the hospital and Nina was so tired that she was the one who had to go home, with a few of the aunties too. Annie was ringing around for a hotel nearby.

'Use my flat,' Ross said, and handed them the keys.

It helped when she kissed him goodbye and went and took her position next to Aleksi and held his hand. She told him he'd better get better. It helped to know that Ross was in the building—that he wasn't at all far away.

Every minute of every day was made better knowing that Ross Wyatt loved her.

CHAPTER TWENTY-FOUR

BEING a doctor brought strange privileges.

It brought insight and knowledge gleaned when a person was at their most vulnerable, and it weighed heavily on Ross. He loved Annika, which meant he cared about Aleksi.

And, he didn't want to keep secrets from Annika, but, like it or not, he knew something that she didn't.

He had spoken with his colleague, Seb, who had revealed that Aleksi had refused any attempt to discuss his past. Ross considered, long into the lonely nights while Annika was at her mother's, if perhaps he should take the easy option and just leave it.

Then one day, checking in on a patient in the private wing of the hospital, Ross saw the Kolovsky clan leaving. The door to Aleksi's room was slightly open. A nurse was checking his obs, but apart from that Aleksi was alone.

Ross walked away, and then turned around and walked back again just as the nurse was going out.

'How are you doing?' He wasn't offended by Aleksi's frown as he attempted to place him—after all, they'd met only once, and Aleksi was recovering from a head injury. 'I was in Emergency when you came in.'

'You'll forgive me if I don't remember, then,' Aleksi said

'I'm also a friend of Annika's; I was at the charity function. Ross Wyatt…'

He shook his hand.

'Annika's spoken about you,' Aleksi said, then closed his eyes and lay back on the pillows. Just as Ross thought he was being dismissed, as he realised the impossibility of broaching the subject of Aleksi's old injuries, Aleksi spoke, though his eyes stayed closed. 'How is Annika doing?'

'Okay.'

'She's moved back home?' Aleksi asked.

'Your mum was upset, with the accident and everything. She wanted Annika close.'

'She should be back at her own flat.' Grey eyes opened. 'Try and persuade her…'

'Annika will be fine,' Ross said, because that much he knew. 'You don't need to worry.'

'For her, I do.'

'Let me do the worrying on that score,' Ross said, and Aleksi gave a small grimace of pain as he tried to shift in the bed. Ross saw his opening. 'That's got to hurt. I saw the X-rays…'

'I'm going to bleep for ever going through security at airports,' Aleksi said. 'I'm full of wires and pins.'

'It was a bit of a mess.'

'So, are you an emergency doctor?'

'No.' Ross shook his head. 'I'm a paediatrician. I was just in Emergency when you came in—and I broke the news to Annika. She asked me to find out more.' He held his breath in his lungs for just a second. 'I was trying to get more information for her. I was speaking to Seb when he was looking over your X-rays.'

'The emergency consultant?' Aleksi checked, and Ross nodded. 'He was up a couple of days ago to see how I was doing.'

And then Aleksi looked at Ross, and Ross looked back, and the conversation carried on for a full two minutes but not a single word was uttered. Finally Aleksi cleared his throat.

'What happens to patient confidentiality if I'm not your patient?'

'You still have it.'

'Even if you're screwing my sister?' Aleksi was savage for a moment, but Ross was expecting it—even if Annika's brother was a generation older than Ross's usual patients, his reaction was not dissimilar.

'I'm a doctor,' Ross said. 'It's my title at home, at work, in bed; it's not a badge I can ever take off. Some conversations with your sister might be more difficult for me—I will have to think hard before I speak, and I will have to remember that I know only what she chooses to tell me—but I'm up to it.'

'Thanks, but no thanks.'

Aleksi closed his eyes and Ross knew he had been dismissed. Inwardly cursing, he turned to go, wondering if he'd made things worse, if he could have handled it better, if he should have just left well alone. And then Aleksi's voice halted him.

'It was only me.'

Ross turned around.

'You don't have to worry that Annika was beaten.' He gave a low mirthless laugh. 'She had it tougher in many ways. My father was the sun, my mother the moon, and they revolved around her. She had the full beam of their twisted love, but they never laid a finger on her. It was just me.'

'I'm sorry,' Ross said, because he was.

'It was my own stupid fault for knowing too much…' He looked up at Ross. 'Every family has their secrets, Ross,' Aleksi said, 'and Levander thinks he knows, and Iosef is sure he knows, but they don't….' He gave a thin smile at Ross's frown.

'Annika told me…' He faltered for a moment. 'Some…'

'About Levander being raised in an orphanage—and my parents conveniently not knowing he was there?'

Ross nodded.

'That isn't the half of it. And I'll save you from future awkward conversations with my sister by not telling you. Suffice to say I know more than any of them. That's why my father beat me to within an inch of my life, and that's why my mother, instead of taking me to hospital, kept me at home.'

'Any time,' Ross said. 'Any time you can talk to me. And I promise I'll keep it confidential.'

He'd had enough. Ross saw the anger and the energy leave him, knew Aleksi had revealed all that he was going to—for now.

It was almost a relief when Annika walked in, for a quick visit at the end of her shift. She smiled and frowned when she saw Ross with her brother.

'I thought I'd see for myself how he was doing,' Ross said by way of explanation. 'I was just saying to Aleksi that he looks a hell of a lot better than he did last time I saw him.'

'I was wondering why they'd sent a paediatrician to see me.' Aleksi gave a rare smile to his sister. 'I didn't realise at first it was your boyfriend.'

'Boyfriend?' Annika wrinkled her nose. 'He's thirty-two.'

And Ross laughed and left them to it.

He nodded to a colleague in the corridor, chatted to Caroline when he got back to the ward, and then he went into his office and closed the door and sat there.

The cleaner got the fright of her life when she came in to empty the bin and he was still there, in the dark.

'Sorry, Doctor. I didn't realise you were here. Do you want me to turn on the light?'

'No, thanks.'

And he was alone again, in the dark.

With Annika he might always be in the dark.

Might never know the full truth—what she knew, what Aleksi knew... It was like a never-ending dot-to-dot picture he might never be able to join up.

Buena onda. He felt what it meant this time—that vibe, that feeling, that connection. Finally he had it with Annika, and it belonged with Annika.

An ambulance light flashed past and Ross looked around his office. The blue and red lights from the ambulance danced on the walls. He realised he wasn't completely in the dark—there were shades and colour, the glow of the computer, a chink of light under the door, the streetlight outside, the reflective lights of the hospital foyer.

There was light in the dark.

And he didn't have to see it all to know what was there.

He didn't need neat answers, because for Ross there were no longer questions.

There was nothing that could happen, nothing that could be said, nothing that could be revealed that would change how he felt.

More light—his phone glowed as his inbox filled.

And he smiled as he read her meticulous text—no slang for Annika.

My mother just left the building.
I have been told for the last hour how bad you
are for me.
When can we be bad? x

He smiled because everything he wanted and needed he already had—everything she was was enough.

Okay, so she had never said she loved him, and she probably didn't yet fully trust him—but slowly she would.

Ross swore there and then that one day she would, and replied to her text.

ASAP x

CHAPTER TWENTY-FIVE

'Is IT possible to request first lunch break?' Annika asked during handover. 'Only, my elder brother is coming from the UK this morning.'

'That shouldn't be a problem,' Caroline said. 'How is Aleksi doing?'

'Better.' Annika nodded. 'A little slower than he would like, but he is improving.'

It had been a tough few weeks.

But full of good times too.

Levander had flown in at the time of the accident and stayed till Aleksi had shown improvement, but had had to return to the UK. Now, though, he was coming with his wife, Millie, and little Sashar for a six-month stay. Levander would take over the running of the Kolovsky empire while Aleksi recuperated. But though it had been wonderful to see Aleksi make such rapid progress, it had been draining too.

Nina had wept and wailed, had made Annika feel so wretched for leaving her alone that she had moved back home. The daily battle just to go to work had begun again.

The control her mother exerted, the secrets of the

past, had all sucked her back to a place where she didn't want to be.

The papers had been merciless. It had been proved that neither drugs nor alcohol had been a factor in the accident, but still they had dredged up every photo of Aleksi's wild ways.

And she'd hardly seen Ross.

She'd seen him at work, of course, and they'd managed to go out a couple of evenings, but Nina always managed to produce a drama that summoned her home. Ross had been so patient…

'Oohh, look at you!' Caroline gave a low wolf-whistle as Ross walked past, and Annika gave a rare laugh at his slight awkwardness as nurses, domestics and physios all turned and had a good look!

He *was* particularly spectacular this morning.

Black jeans, black belt, a sheer white cotton shirt and Cuban-heeled boots. His hair was still damp and he had a silver loop in his ear. He looked drop-dead sexy.

'Will your brother be here yet?' Ross asked a while later.

'I would think so.' Annika glanced at her watch. 'Iosef is going to the airport to collect them.'

'So what's your mum got planned for you tonight?'

'Probably a big family reunion dinner, somewhere glitzy where the press can see us all smiling and laughing.'

'I'll give it a miss.' Ross gave her a wink. 'But thanks for the invite.'

'There was no invite.' Annika shot him a short smile back. 'You're a bad influence, remember?'

* * *

It was a busy morning, made busier because it was her last day on the ward and time for her end-of-rotation assessment.

'Well done.' Heather Jameson ticked all the boxes this time. In the last few weeks, though it had been hard at home, Annika had made work her solace, had put her head down, or sometimes up, had smiled when she didn't really feel like it and had been rewarded in a way she had never expected. 'I know you've had a difficult time personally, and that it took you a bit of time to settle, but you have. The staff are all delighted with you.'

'I've liked working on the children's ward,' Annika said. 'I never thought I would, but I truly have.'

'What do you like about it?'

'It's honest,' Annika said. 'The children cry and they laugh and they don't pretend to be happy.' She gave a small smile. 'They forgive you if you are not happy too,' Annika said, 'and so long as you are kind, they don't mind if you are quiet.'

'You've got Maternity next,' Heather said, and blinked when Annika rolled her eyes.

'You might like it—remember you weren't looking forward to Paeds?'

'I think I am too stoic to be sympathetic,' Annika said, 'but of course I will be. Now I know where I'm going.'

It was things like that that set her apart.

There was still an aloofness, a hard edge that bewildered Heather, but, yes, Annika was intriguing.

'Do you think Paediatrics is where you might specialise?' Heather said.

'No,' Annika said. 'I've decided what I want to do.'

'And?'

'Geriatrics or palliative care.' Annika smiled at

Heather's slight frown. 'It has everything the children's ward has and a lot of wisdom too. I guess as you near the end of your life the mask slips away and you can be honest again.'

'You did very well in your geriatric rotation.'

'I thought it was because nursing was new,' Annika admitted. 'I thought the gloss had worn off over the last eighteen months or so. But now I realise nothing was ever as good as my time there, because geriatrics is the area of nursing where I belong.'

She thought of Elsie.

Of a white chocolate box filled with mousse and raspberries—and that nothing could taste so perfect, so why bother searching?

Idle chatter had come easily with Elsie and the oldies, and silence had been easy too.

'I want to qualify,' Annika explained. 'I want to get through the next year. I am not looking forward to Maternity, nor to working in Theatre, but I will do my best, and when I get my qualification I have decided that I would like to specialize in aged care.'

Oh, it wasn't as exciting as Emergency, or as impressive sounding as Paediatrics or ICU—but it was, Annika realised, an area of nursing she loved. She had been searching for something and had found it—so quickly, that she hadn't recognised it at first.

It was the care Annie had shown her father that had first drawn her into nursing—the shifts at the nursing home that had sustained her.

She liked old people.

For the most part they accepted her.

It was very hard to explain, but she tried.

'Those extra shifts that I did in the nursing home,'

Annika admitted, 'they were busy, and it was hard work, but…' Still she could not explain. 'I like the miserable ones, the angry ones, the funny ones, even those I don't like, I like… They teach me, and I can help them just by stopping to listen, by making sure they have a chance to talk, or making sure they are clean and comfortable. It's a different sort of nursing.'

And Heather looked at a very neat, very well turned out, sometimes matter-of-fact, often awkward but always kind nurse, and realised that Geriatrics would be very lucky to have her. To be old, to have someone practical tend to the practical and then to have the glimpse of her warmth—well, they would be lucky to have her and also she would be lucky to have them.

She needed a few golden oldies bolstering her up, mothering her, gently teasing her, showing her how things could be done, how life could be funny even when it didn't feel it. It might just bring a more regular smile to those guarded lips.

'You'll be wonderful.'

It was the first compliment Annika had truly accepted.

'Thank you.'

'But you have to get through the next year.'

'I will,' Annika said. 'Now I know where I'm heading.'

'Right, you'd better get off for lunch.'

Was it already lunchtime?

Annika dashed into the changing room, opened her locker and ran a brush through her hair and then tied it back into its ponytail. She added some lip-gloss and went to squirt on some perfume—but remembered it was forbidden on the children's ward.

She couldn't wait to see Levander. Last time it had been so stressful, but with Aleksi improving there was much to celebrate, and she was looking forward to seeing Millie too, and little Sashar.

She dashed down the corridor and saw Ross, standing talking to some relatives, and he caught her eye, gave her that smile, and it was as if he was waiting for her, had always been waiting patiently for her.

'Levander.' She hugged her brother when she reached Aleksi's room. It was so good to see him looking well and happy, and Sashar came to her easily. Millie was talking to Annie, who was holding Rebecca.

All the family were together, yet still her mother was not happy, still she could not just relax and enjoy it. She was talking in Russian, even though neither Millie nor Annie understood, telling her children her restaurant of choice for the Kolovsky dinner tonight.

'The hairdresser is at five, Annika.' Nina still spoke in Russian. 'Make sure that you come straight home.'

'I'll come too.'

Annika frowned as Annie, for the first time in living memory, volunteered for a non-essential hour at the Kolovsky family home.

'If Iosef takes Rebecca home, I can hang around here and you can give me a lift.'

Annika looked to Iosef, who nodded.

'Hey!' Annika turned to Aleksi and kissed him. His face was pale and it worried her. 'Any better?'

'I'm fine,' Aleksi said, because he said the same each day. He was so tough, so removed from everyone, and so loathing this prolonged invasion of his privacy.

'You'll be home soon.'

'Nope!' A thin smile dusted his pale features. 'I'm sick of bloody family…' He turned to his PA who was there, a large, kind woman, always calm and unruffled, and whispered in her ear. 'Tell them, Kate.'

'Your brother's off to recover at a small island in the West Indies.'

'Very nice.' Annika smiled.

'I'm going into hiding,' Aleksi explained, with just a hint of a wink. That dangerous smile, Annika saw with relief, was starting to return. 'I refuse to be photographed like this—it will ruin my reputation.'

'It's irreparable!' Annika joked, and yet she was worried for him—more worried than he would want her to be, more worried than she could show. She would talk to Kate later—check out as best she could the details of his rehabilitation.

'Come and visit?' Aleksi said, but Annika shook her head.

'I can't. I'm going to Spain for my honeymoon,' Annika said, enjoying her brother's look of confusion.

The door opened, and Nina frowned as a forbidden doctor walked in.

'Family.' Nina said it like a curse. 'Family only.'

'Ross is family,' Annika said. 'Or rather he's about to be.'

She swallowed as the celebrant walked in behind Ross.

'Mrs Kolovsky.' Ross's voice was neither nervous nor wavering as the relatives he had been talking to in the corridor came in—*his* relatives, all happily in on the plan. 'Annika and I want no fuss, but we do want everyone we love present.'

She felt Aleksi's hand squeeze hers, saw Levander smile, and Iosef too. She was scared to see her mother's reaction, so she looked at Ross instead.

It was the teeniest, tiniest of weddings. But she was

getting stronger and, with or without Ross, she would make it.

But as he took her hand and slipped on a heavy silver ring she knew that with Ross beside her she would get there sooner.

'By the power vested in me, I pronounce you man and wife.'

He kissed her, a slow, tender kiss that was patient and loving, and then he pulled her back and smiled.

The same smile that had kept her guessing all this time and would keep her guessing for years to come.

'I love you.' It was the first time she had ever said it, Annika realised. He had married her without the confirmation of those three little words.

'I always knew that one day you would,' Ross said. 'What's not to love?'

He made her stomach curl; he made her want to smile. There was excitement from just looking at him, and she wanted to look at him for ever, but for now there was duty.

'We would love to be there tonight,' Annika said to her mother's rigid face. 'Just for a little while.'

For her mother she would face the cameras and allow it to be revealed in the newspapers tomorrow that the Kolovsky heiress was married. She would smile, and she would have her hair done and wear a fabulous dress, but it would be one of her choosing.

'And I would like it if Ross's family could join in the celebration.'

'Of course…' Nina choked.

'Look after her,' Iosef said to Ross.

'I intend to.'

And Iosef could see his wife's tears, and understood all that she had been trying to say to him these past weeks.

His spoiled, lightweight, brat of a little sister was actually a woman of whom he should be proud—and he told her so.

'I am so proud of you.'

She had needed to hear it, and she smiled back at her brother and her sister-in-law, and then to Levander and Millie—and it dawned on her then.

They were all survivors.

Survivors who were busy pulling their own oars, rather than being dragged down—but how much easier it would be now if they pulled together.

There was only one who was still going it alone.

'Aleksi.' She smiled to her brother. 'I was going to speak to the nurse in charge, see if maybe we could come back here after dinner...' And then, much to her mother's annoyance, she changed the plans again. 'Or we could ring the restaurant and eat here.'

Aleksi wouldn't hear of it. 'Go out,' he said, and then gestured to his infusion. 'I'll be knocked out by seven anyway.'

He was, Annika realised, still rowing all by himself.

'Congratulations,' Aleksi said, and kissed his sister.

'The last single Kolovsky,' Annika teased. 'And still the Kolovsky wedding gown has not been worn.'

'It never will be, then.' He shook his new brother-in-law's hand. 'Take care of her.'

'He already has,' Annika said.

Yes, the tiniest of weddings—and still duty called.

But sometimes duty was a pleasure too.

They walked back down the corridor, laughing and chatting. A nurse and a doctor returning from their lunch break.

The ward was nice and quiet, darkened for the afternoon's quiet time, but Caroline wasn't best pleased. She was talking to Heather Jameson and was stern in her greeting to her student. Good report or not, it was inexcusable to be thirty minutes late back from lunch without good reason.

'Annika, it's forty-five minutes for lunch. I know your brother just arrived, but...'

'I am sorry,' Annika said. 'I was at Security; I had to pick up my new ID.'

Lifting up her lanyard, she offered it to Caroline.

'Well, next time...' Her voice trailed off. 'Annika Wyatt?'

Her neck almost snapped as she turned to Ross, then back to Annika.

'We just got married,' Annika explained, as if that was what people always did in their lunch break.

It seemed the strangest way to spend your wedding day, and no one but the two of them would understand, but there was freedom, real freedom, as she excused herself from the little gathering, smiled to her husband and colleagues, and did what she had fought so hard and for so long to do.

She started to live life her way.

THE LAST
KOLOVSKY PLAYBOY

CAROL MARINELLI

PROLOGUE

SHE couldn't go back in there.

Or rather she couldn't go back in there like this.

Kate's heart was hammering, her face burning in a blush, and her hands were shaking as she frothed the coffee for her boss, Levander Kolovsky, and his younger half brother, Aleksi.

Never, *never*, had she reacted so violently to someone.

And, at thirty-six weeks pregnant, she certainly hadn't been expecting to today!

Aleksi Kolovsky was over from London for a working visit to the Australian head office and she had thought she'd known what to expect. After all, he had an identical twin brother, whom Kate had met, so she basically knew what he looked like and she'd heard all about his reputation with women.

It wasn't his good-looks she had reacted to, though—the House of Kolovsky head office was swarming with beauties. Kate had been petrified when the temp agency had sent her there, and she was quite sure Levander had only kept her on because she was brilliant at her job and because she *was* temporary. A permanent PA to a Kolovsky needed to be more than brilliant at her job; she needed to be stunning, and Kate was nowhere near that.

No, it was something other than Aleksi's looks that had caused this reaction.

Something else that had made her heart trip as she'd walked into Levander's office—something else that had caused her body to flood with heat as the rogue bad brother had looked up from the papers he'd been skimming through and given her a wide-eyed look.

'Should you really be here?' His voice was deep and low, with just a hint of accent, and those grey eyes with their black depths skimmed over her pregnant stomach and then back to her face.

He had a point! She was massive with child, rather than possessing a nice little bump like some of the Kolovsky maternity models, whose only indication of pregnancy was a lovely round abdomen and an extra size to their AA bra cup. No, pregnancy for Kate Taylor meant that her whole body was swollen from her breasts to her ankles. She was so obviously, uncomfortably, heavily pregnant that Aleksi was right—she really shouldn't be here.

'I'm sorry?' Kate had surprised herself with her own response. Normally she would have given him a brief, polite smile. After four months of working for the Kolovsky fashion house she was more than used to making polite small talk with the rich and famous, more than used to melting into the background, but for some reason the real Kate had answered. For some reason she hadn't been able to help but sustain a tiny tease.

'You look as if you're due any moment,' Aleksi persisted.

'Due for what?' Kate frowned, and she watched those

impassive features flutter in brief panic, watched that haughty, confident expression suddenly falter as for one appalling moment Aleksi Kolovsky thought he had made the worst social gaffe—that she wasn't in fact pregnant at all!

'Due for a raise.' Levander gave a rare laugh as he watched his brother squirm. 'You've certainly earned it. Not many people can make my brother blush.'

'She *is* pregnant though?' Kate had heard Aleksi ask as she'd slipped out to make the coffee.

'What do you think?' Levander's smile lingered after Kate had left, enjoying his brother's rare moment of discomfort. 'Sadly, yes.'

'Sadly?'

'I'm trying to ignore the fact that she could give birth at any moment. This place was in chaos till Kate started, and now she's sorted everything out. I actually know where I'm supposed to be for the next few weeks, and she's great with even the most difficult client.'

'She'll be back...'

'Nope.' Levander shook his head. 'She's just a temp. She only wanted a few weeks' work. She broke up with her boyfriend and moved to Melbourne. She's just trying to get ahead, and has no intention of coming back once the baby arrives.'

That was all Levander said before their attention turned back to work, and Kate needn't have worried about Aleksi noticing her blush or shaking hands. The two men were immersed in some project when she returned with the coffee a few moments later. Aleksi's head was down, black fringe flopping forward as he skimmed through a document. He didn't even murmur thanks.

Still, for the next two weeks he came every day, and

generally stopped by her desk and said hello—asked
how she was getting on as they waited for Levander to
return from his morning run. Sometimes he told her a
little about London, where he lived, heading up the UK
branch of Kolovsky, and sometimes, rarely for Aleksi, he
asked a little about herself. Maybe it was because she'd
never see him again, maybe because she was so bone-
weary and so lonely, but Kate was honest in her replies.

She was honest, all right, Aleksi discovered.

About how petrified she was at the prospect of being
a single mum, how her family were miles away, how she
dreaded the hospital…

Then, on his last morning before he headed back for
the UK, when there was an important meeting with
Levander, his father, Ivan, and his mother, Nina, and the
prospect of three hours in his parents' company was
causing black rivers of bile to churn in his stomach, he
found the one thing he was actually looking forward to
as he stepped out of the lift was Kate's kind smile and
the endless stream of coffee she'd bring to the meeting.

Instead, five feet ten inches of whippet-like flesh, a
mask of make-up and a head that looked too big for its
body smiled from behind the desk.

'Good morning, Mr Kolovsky, everyone's waiting for
you. Can I bring you in a coffee?'

'Where's Kate?' Aleksi asked as the lollipop head
blinked.

'Oh?' She frowned. 'You mean the temp… She had
her baby last night.'

'What did she have?'

The lollipop shrugged, and Aleksi wondered if her
clavicles might snap.

'I'm not sure. Actually, thanks for reminding me.

I'll ring the hospital and find out. Levander said to arrange a gift.'

It was the longest meeting. Coffee, and then morning coffee, and then lunch at the desk—it wasn't often the three Kolovsky sons and their parents were together. Aleksi's identical twin, Iosef, had taken a day off from the hospital where he was a doctor, and they had all sat in silence as Ivan told them about his illness, his sketchy prognosis, and the necessity that no one must know.

'People get sick,' Iosef had stated. 'It's nothing to be ashamed of.'

'Kolovskys cannot be seen as weak.'

And they spoke about figures and projections, and a new line that was due for release, and the fact that Aleksi would appear at all the European fashion shows while Ivan underwent his treatment. Levander would cover Australasia.

Iosef, by then, had long since left.

Despite the gloomy subject matter, it was a meeting devoid of emotion and the coffee tasted absolutely awful.

'Shto skazeenar v ehtoy komnarteh asstoyotsar v ehtoy komnarteh.' His mother's eyes met his as Aleksi stood to leave for London. No *Have a nice trip* from her, just a cold warning that what was said in this room was to stay in the room. The trickles of bile turned into one deep dark lake and Aleksi felt sick—felt as if he were a child again, back in his bedroom with his parents standing over him, warning him not to speak of his pain, not to reveal anything, not to weep.

Kolovskys were not weak.

Levander said goodbye to him as if he were going out to the shops rather than heading to the other side of the world.

As Aleksi headed out through the plush foyer he saw a vast basket, filled with flowers, champagne and a thick, blush-pink silk Kolovsky blanket, waiting for the courier to collect it.

Kate must have had a girl.

Rarely did Aleksi question his motives, rarely did he stop for insight, and he didn't now, as he went through the gold revolving doors to the waiting car that would speed him to the airport. He went around again, stepped back into the foyer, and with a few short words at the bemused receptionist, picked up the basket. When he was seated in the back of the luxury car, he read out the address to his driver.

'I can take it in for you, sir,' his driver said as they arrived at the large, sprawling concrete jungle of a hospital.

But somehow he wanted something he could not define.

His father was dying and he was so numb he couldn't feel.

He didn't understand why he was standing at a desk asking for directions to Kate's room, didn't really stop to pause as he took the lift, was only aware that the place smelt nothing like the private wings he occasionally graced. And, yes, he was just a touch nervous as to her reaction, what her visitors might say, if he'd be intruding, but he wanted to say goodbye to her.

For Kate, the last twenty-four hours had been hell.

Twelve hours of fruitless labour, followed by an emergency Caesarean. Her daughter lay pink and pretty in her crib beside her, but Kate was the loneliest she had ever been in her life.

Her parents would be in to visit tonight, but after her phone conversation with Craig she held out little hope that he would appear.

No, the pain of labour and surgery was nothing compared to the shame and loneliness she felt at visiting time.

She could see the curious, sympathetic stares from the other three mothers and their visitors at her unadorned bed, devoid of balloons, flowers and cards.

She was just alone and embarrassed to be seen alone. Unwanted.

She'd asked the nurse to pull the curtains, but she'd misunderstood and had pulled them right back—exposing the bed, exposing her shame.

And then there he was.

He read her in an instant.

Read the other mothers too, saw the dart of incredulity in their eyes as he smiled over to her, as they realised that he was there to see her. Could he be…? Surely not! But then again…

'I am so sorry, darling!'

His voice had a confident ring as he strode across the drab four-bed ward, and he looked completely out of place, still in a suit, his tie pulled loose. He came over to the bed, deposited the glorious Kolovsky basket on her bedside table and looked down to where she lay.

Her face was swollen, her eyes bloodshot from the effort of pushing. Aleksi had thought women lost weight when they gave birth, but Kate seemed to have doubled in size. Her dark wavy hair was black with grease and sweat, but she gave him a half-smile and Aleksi was glad that he had come.

'Can you ever forgive me for not being there?' He said it loud enough for the others to hear.

'Stop it.' She almost giggled, but it hurt too much to laugh. 'They think you're the father.'

'Well, given that's never going to be true…' he lowered his voice and, so as not to hurt her, very gently lowered himself on the bed '…it might be fun to pretend.' He looked at her poor bloodshot eyes. 'Was it awful?'

'Hell.'

'Why all the drips?'

'I had to have surgery.' She watched him wince.

'When do you go home?'

'In a couple of days.' Kate shivered at the prospect. She couldn't even lift her baby; the thought of being completely responsible for her was overwhelming.

'That's way too soon!' Aleksi was appalled. 'I think my cousin had a Caesarean and she was in for at least a week…' He thought back to the plush private ward, the baby he had glimpsed from behind the glass wall of the nursery. He glanced into the crib, about to make a cursory polite comment, and then he actually smiled, because struggling to focus back at him was surely the cutest baby in the world. Completely bald, she had big, dark blue eyes and her mother's full pink lips.

'She's gorgeous.' He wasn't being polite; he was being honest.

'Because she's a Caesarean, apparently,' Kate said. 'I think her eyes will be brown by the time I get her home.' And then she asked him, 'Aleksi, what on earth are you doing here?'

'I'm on my way to the airport.' When she didn't look convinced he gave a shrug. 'Five hours in my parents' company and maybe I needed something different.' He stared back to the baby. 'She's awake.'

'Do you want to hold her?'

'God, no!' Aleksi said, and then he changed his mind, because maybe he *did* need something different. 'Won't I disturb her?'

'She's awake,' Kate pointed out.

'I thought they were supposed to cry.' He knew nothing about babies, had no intention of finding out about babies, and yet he was curious to hold her—and so he did.

Big hands went into the clear bassinette and lifted the soft bundle. Kate's immediate instinct was to remind him to support her head, yet she bit on her lip and silenced the warning, because he already had, and for a stupid blind moment she wished the impossible.

Wished, from the tender way he held her baby, that somehow her baby was his too.

'My dad's sick,' he told her. It was top secret information, and he knew she could sell those words for tens of thousands, yet at that moment he was past caring. He held new life in his hands and he smelt an unfamiliar sweet fragrance. He ran a finger over a cheek he could only liken to a new kitten's paw—before it was let outside to a world that would roughen and harden it.

'I'm sorry.'

'No one's allowed to know,' Aleksi said, still looking down at the baby. 'What's she called?'

'Georgina,' Kate said.

'Georgie.' Aleksi smiled at his new friend.

'Georgina!' Kate corrected.

'I wonder if I was this cute.' Aleksi frowned. 'Imagine two of them.'

Kate rolled her eyes. Two identical Kolovskys in a crib—they'd have had the maternity ward at a standstill!

'I can't imagine you cute,' she said instead.

'Oh, I was!' Aleksi grinned. 'Iosef was the serious

one.' He put Georgina down and his grin turned to a very nice, slightly pensive smile. 'You're going to be wonderful as a mother.'

'How?' And whether it was hormones, exhaustion or just plain old fear, tears shot from her eyes as her bravery crumbled. 'I want it to be wonderful for her, but how will I manage it?'

'It will be,' Aleksi said assuredly. 'My parents had everything and they managed to completely mess us all up. You, on the other hand…' he stared into her soft brown eyes and didn't see the bloodshot whites, just tears and concern and a certain stoicism there, laced with kindness too '…are going to get it so right.' And then it was over. 'I've got to go.'

'Thank you.'

She braced herself for him to stand, tightened up her non-existent abdominal muscles as he went to stand, anticipating pain but getting something else. His arms came around her, that gorgeous face moved in and she smelt him—smelt Kolovsky cologne and something else, something male and unique that made her blush just as it had on that first day, just as she knew it always would.

'Let's leave your audience with no room for doubt.'

And then he kissed her.

Terribly, terribly tenderly—she was, after all, just twelve hours post-op—but there was this taste and this passion and this heaven that she found on his lips…this gorgeous, delicious escape that was delivered with his mouth and then the cool danger of his tongue. And to the nay-sayers on the ward he proved this wasn't a duty call.

'I have to get this flight.'

He should have been on the stage, Kate thought, because there was regret in his eyes and voice as he walked out of the ward. She lay back on the pillow, eyes closed, but basking in the glow of the curious looks from the other mothers and their oh, so plain partners.

Only she didn't get to enjoy them for very long.

Lost in a dream, still basking in the memory, she was very rudely interrupted as a porter kicked off the brakes on her bed.

'You're being moved.'

'Where?'

Oh, God—she so didn't want this. Didn't want to start again with three other mothers—or, worse, maybe she was being moved to an eight-bed ward.

'You're being upgraded.'

Five years ago, on a business flight to Singapore, her stingy boss had been overruled by ground staff and she had been invited to turn left, not right, as she stepped onto the plane.

It happened again that afternoon.

Her bed slid easily out of the public section, over the buffed tiles, and then stuck a little as it hit the soft carpets of the private wing, as if warning the porter— warning everyone—that she didn't really belong there.

But who cared?

Not the staff.

Aleksi Kolovsky had covered her for a full week.

It was bliss to move into the large double bed.

Heaven to stare at the five-star menu as Georgina was whisked to the nursery to be brought back later for feeding.

It was, Kate reflected later that night, as a *lovely* midwife took Georgina for the night and clicked off the light, the second nicest thing that had ever happened to her.

The first nicest thing had been his kiss.

CHAPTER ONE

IT DIDN'T hurt as much as everyone said that it should.

His leg, fractured and mangled in a road accident, would, he had been told, mean six months of extensive rehabilitation—and then perhaps he might walk with an aid.

Four months to the day since the accident that had almost taken his life, Aleksi Kolovsky waded through the glittering Caribbean ocean unaided. The doctor had suggested two fifteen-minute sessions a day.

It was his third hourly session, and it was not yet midday.

Whatever he was advised to do, he did more of it.

Whatever the treatment, he headed straight for the cure.

After all, he had done this once before—under circumstances far worse than this.

He had been a child without doctors, without physios, without this stunning backdrop and the cool ocean that now soothed his aching muscles. He had rehabilitated his fractured body himself—first in the confines of his room till the bruises had faded, and then, without grimacing, without wincing, he had walked and returned to schooling. Not even his twin, Iosef, had been aware of his struggles; Aleksi had privately continued his healing behind the closed walls of his mind.

Iosef—his identical twin.

He smiled a wry smile. He had watched a show last night on the television. Well, he hadn't exactly watched it, it had been on in the background, and he had not paid it full attention. His attention had instead been on the skilled lips working on his tumescent length to raise it to its splendid glory. It had been a different attention, though. Normally he switched off, sex the balm—not any more. The television had been too loud as it spoke of telepathic bonds between twins, and the woman's sighs had been grating. Since the accident, chatter annoyed him, conversation irritated him, and last night her lips had not soothed him. He had hardened, but it had been just mechanical, an automated response that, despite her delight, had not pleased Aleksi. Though he'd yearned for relief, he had realised he wouldn't get it from her. However, there was a reputation to be upheld, so he'd shifted their position.

He'd heard her cries as he did the right thing, pleasuring her with his mouth, and then had feigned reluctance at the disturbance from his phone.

His phone buzzed regularly.

There had been no need to answer it—except last night he had chosen to. Chosen to make excuses as to why she must leave, rather than give that piece of himself to her.

Was even the escape of sex to be denied him?

The sun beat on his shoulders—his skin was brown, his body lean and toned, and he appeared a picture of health above the water. But the scars stung beneath as he stretched his limits and made himself run in the water.

Now it hurt.

It hurt like hell, but he pushed through it.

Could his brother in Australia feel this? Aleksi thought as he sliced the water and forced himself on. Was Iosef, working in an Emergency ward in Australia, suddenly sweating and gripped by pain as he went about his day?

Aleksi doubted it.

Oh, he had no animosity towards Iosef—he admired that he had broken away from the company and gone on to study medicine. Still they chatted, and met regularly. Aleksi liked him, in fact. But there was no telepathic bond, no sharing of minds, no sixth sense…

Where had the twin bond been when his father had beaten him to a pulp when he was only seven years old?

Where had the sixth sense been when a week later his brother had been allowed in to see him?

'Some fall…' Iosef had said, in Russian of course—because even in Australia the Kolovskys had spoken in Russian.

'Dad is getting you a new bike.' Iosef had come to sit on the bed, laughing and chatting, but as the mattress had indented a white bolt of pain had shot through Aleksi and he had gone to cry out. Then he had seen the warning in his mother's eyes.

'Good,' he had said instead.

There *was* no special bond Aleksi realised.

You did not ache, you did not bleed just because your brother did.

He ran faster.

Riminic, Riminic, Riminic.

Even the gulls taunted him with the name.

A brother whose existence he had denied.

A brother he had chosen to forget.

There was no end to his shame, and his leg wouldn't let him outrun it.

Sprint over, he was spent, and glad to be exhausted. Maybe now he could get some rest.

The nurse had his pills waiting when he returned to the lavish chalet, but he refused them. He drank instead a cocktail of vitamins and fresh juice and headed for his bedroom.

'I'm going to rest.'

'Would you like me to come in?' She smiled. 'To check on you?'

He growled out a refusal of her *kind* offer—could he not just recover? Could he not have some peace?

He lay on the silk sheets, the fan cooling his warm skin, yet his blood felt frozen.

The pain did not scare him—it was the damage to his mind. He had passed every test, had convinced the doctors that he was fine—could at times almost convince himself that he was—but there was a blur of memories, conversations that he could not recall, images that he could not summon, knowledge that lay buried.

The phone buzzed.

He went to turn it off.

Tired, he needed to rest.

And then he saw her name.

Kate.

Aleksi hesitated before answering. Kate was one of the reasons he was in the West Indies recovering—he had grown accustomed to her by his bedside, looked forward rather too much to her visits in the hospital and started to rely on her just a little too heavily. And Aleksi had long since chosen to rely on no-one.

'What?' His voice was curt.

'You said to tell you if…'

Her voice came to him over the phone from halfway around the world. He could hear that she was nervous and he didn't blame her. Nina would go berserk if she found out that Kate was calling. Aleksi was not to be disturbed with mundane work matters—except Aleksi had told Kate that he wanted to be disturbed.

'Tell me what, Kate?' Aleksi said. He could picture her round, kind face, and was quite sure that she was blushing. Kate blushed a lot—she was a large girl, surrounded by whip-thin models. The House of Kolovsky was a bitchy place to work at the best of times, and at the worst of times it was a snake pit—right now it was the worst of times. 'Remember, no matter what my mother says, your loyalty is to me—you are *my* PA.'

She had been his PA for over a year now. He had cajoled her into taking the position when yet another PA of his had been so stupid as to confuse sex with love. Safe in the knowledge that he would never cross the line with an overweight single mum, he had contacted her. Georgie was now nearly five years old and at school, and Kate was even bigger than before—no, there was absolutely no question of his fancying her.

'Your brother Levander…' Kate stammered. 'You know he and Millie were looking to adopt an orphan…?'

'And?'

'They went to Russia last week; they met him— their new son…'

Aleksi closed his eyes; he had feared this day would come sooner than was convenient. Levander had run the House of Kolovsky head branch in Australia. He had been sensible, and on their father's death a couple of years ago he had got out. Now he worked in London, taking over

Aleksi's old role, while Aleksi had taken over the running of Kolovsky—effectively a swap. Levander had only returned to Australia while Aleksi recuperated.

'I've heard Nina talking; *she* is going to run it…'

'Run what?'

'House of Kolovsky.' Kate gulped. 'She has these ideas…'

'Levander would never—' Aleksi started, but then again Levander now would. Since he had met Millie, since they had had Sashar, his priorities had shifted. Money had never been Levander's god. Raised in Detsky Dom, an orphanage in Russia, he had no real allegiance to the Kolovskys—Nina wasn't his mother, and with Ivan dead Aleksi knew that Levander's priorities were with his own family now—his new family, one that wanted to save a child from the hell Levander had endured.

'She has told Levander not to tell you,' Kate explained. 'That no one is to disturb you with this—that you need this time to heal.'

'The board will not pass it.'

'Nina has new plans, ideas that will generate a lot of money…'

She had stopped stammering now. Despite her shyness at times, Kate was an articulate, intelligent woman, which was why he had bent over backwards to get her on staff. She was different from all the others. Her only interest at work was *work*—which she did very capably, so she could earn the money to single-handedly raise her daughter.

'She will convince the board, and she has ideas that they like.'

'Ideas?' Aleksi snorted.

'She makes them sound attractive,' Kate said. 'I sat in on a meeting last week. She put forward a proposal from Zakahr Belenki…'

Despite the warmth of the room Aleksi felt his blood chill. 'What sort of proposal?'

'One that will benefit both Kolovsky and Belenki's charity,' Kate said. 'They are talking of a new range— bridal dresses in the Krasavitsa outlets with a percentage of profit…'

Aleksi didn't hear much more. He was aware of his racing heart, as if he were pounding his battered body through the ocean this very minute, except he was lying perfectly still on the bed. The Krasavitsa offshoot of the Kolovsky business was *his* baby—his idea, his domain. But it wasn't just that Nina was considering tampering with his baby that had Aleksi's heart hammering like this.

What was the problem with Belenki?

His mind, though Aleksi had denied it both to his family and to the doctors, *was* damaged.

Thoughts, images, and memories were a mere stretch from his grasp. He could remember the charity ball just before his accident—Belenki had flown in from Europe and had been the guest speaker, that much he remembered. And he remembered the fear he had felt at the time too. Iosef had had harsh words with him—for his poor behaviour at the ball, for talking through the speeches, which, yes, he had. Zakahr Belenki had been talking about his life in Detsky Dom, how he had chosen to live instead on the streets, about what he had done to survive there.

It had been easier to have another drink that night than to hear Zakahr's message. Levander had never really spoken of his years there, and part of Aleksi didn't want to hear it. He didn't want to hear how his half-brother had suffered so.

'Has Belenki been back to Australia?'

'No,' Kate said. 'But he has been talking daily with Nina. They are coming up with new ideas all the time.'

Why, Aleksi begged himself, did that name strike fear inside him?

He tried to pull up the man's image—yet, like so much else in his mind, it was a blur…as if it had been pixilated…like the many other shadowy areas in his mind that he must allow no one else to know about.

'Nina will run the House of Kolovsky into the ground—she cannot run it,' he declared.

'Who else is there?'

'Me,' Aleksi ground out. 'I will be back at my desk on Monday.'

'Aleksi!' Kate's voice was exasperated. 'I didn't ring for that; I just rang because you made me promise to keep you informed. It's way too soon for you to return. Look…'

She lowered her voice and he could just picture her leaning forward, picture her finger toying with a curl of her hair as she tried to come up with a solution, and despite the direness of the situation the image made him smile. The sound of her voice soothed him, and it moved him too, in the way it sometimes did—never more so than now.

'I can ring you every day…'

He stared down at the sudden, unexpected passionate reaction of his body and did not answer.

'Can you hear me, Aleksi?'

'Go on.'

'I can ring you all the time…tell you things…and then you can tell me what to do.'

He wanted to close his eyes. He wanted her to tell him things. Hell, how he wanted at this moment to tell her exactly what to do. He didn't want to think about the House of Kolovsky and his family, didn't want to face what he was trying to forget. How much nicer would it be to just lie here and let her tell him things that he wanted to hear?

'Kate…' His voice was ragged. He wanted her on a plane this minute—he wanted her here, wanted her now—but instead he forced himself to sit upright, to ignore the fire in his groin and concentrate on what was necessary. 'I'll be back on Monday. Don't tell anyone, don't act any different. Just go along with whatever Nina says.'

It wasn't her place to argue, and she didn't.

'Fine,' she said. 'Do you want me to organize—?'

'I'll sort everything out from this end,' Aleksi interrupted. 'Kate…?'

'Yes?'

'Nothing.' He clicked off the phone and tried to keep his mind on necessary business. Turned on his laptop and raced through figures. He knew only too well that the House of Kolovsky was on a collision course and that he was the only one who could stop it.

He just couldn't quite remember why.

And for the first time in ages he didn't try to. The figures he was analysing blurred in front of his eyes, so instead he clicked on company photographs—a who's who of the House of Kolovsky.

Ivan, his deceased father; Nina, his mother; Levander, his half-brother, whom his parents had conveniently forgotten about and left in an orphanage in Russia when they fled to Australia; Iosef, his twin, and his sister Annika. Then Aleksi clicked on his own image, saw his scowling, haughty face before hurriedly moving on. Finally, for the first time in weeks he allowed himself the respite of *her* face.

Kate Taylor.

Smiling, her face round and shiny, dark hair curling under the heat of the photographer's lights, nervous at having her photo taken—though it was just a head-and-shoulders corporate shot.

He must be losing his mind.

Imagine *that* bulk on his healing thigh, he told himself, trying to calm his excited body. He tried in vain to reel in his imagination—except he just grew harder at the thought of Kate on top of him...

He had the most beautiful women on tap—warm, eager flesh on the other side of his bedroom door—yet all he could think of was that in a week he would again see Kate.

'Aleksi?' The nurse knocked, her voice low, the door opening just a fraction. 'Is there anything at all you need?'

'Not to be disturbed,' he growled, and as the door reluctantly closed he turned off the computer and lay in the darkness, willing sleep to invade. Then he gave in.

Once, he decided.

Just this once he would allow himself to go there—to think about Kate and imagine himself with her. Or rather, Aleksi corrected as his hand slid around his heated length, just one last time.

Just one time more.

CHAPTER TWO

'YOU look pretty!' Georgie said as Kate sliced off the top of her boiled egg.

'Thank you,' Kate replied with a half-smile. After all, Georgie was her number one fan, and it was a compliment that was regularly given.

'Really pretty.' Georgie frowned. 'You're wearing lots of lipstick.'

'Am I?' Kate said vaguely.

'Is that new?' Her knowing little eyes roamed over Kate's new suit.

'I've had it for ages.' Kate shrugged, adding two sweeteners to her cup of tea and wishing, wishing, *wishing* she'd kept to her diet. She'd consoled herself that it would be another two months at least before he came back, and now, thanks to the lousy Nina, Aleksi would be back in the office *today!*

'Is Aleksi coming back today?' Her daughter's shrewd eyes narrowed.

'I'm not sure…' Kate was at a loss as to what to say, stunned at the mini-witch she had created. She half expected her to wrinkle up her nose and cast a spell— but then Georgie liked Aleksi.

No, Georgie *adored* Aleksi.

Kate had thought that day at the hospital would be the last time she would see him—had almost managed to put him to the far recesses of her mind, where he would have stayed had the occasional card not arrived from him.

The occasional hotel postcard, from far-flung places around the globe, in less than legible writing.

The odd, completely child-unfriendly toys for Georgie—like a set of Russian dolls when she was eighteen months old, and a jewellery box with a little ballerina. Oh, they'd been few and far between over the years, but, given Aleksi's communication was only slightly more erratic than Georgie's father's, they had lit up the little girl's day when occasionally they came.

Kate had struggled through part-time jobs, watching the unfolding saga of the Kolovskys in all the magazines, and when Ivan had died and Levander had renounced the Kolovsky throne the news that Aleksi was moving back to Australia had had Kate on tenterhooks—until finally, *finally,* long after his return, he had called and offered her a job she couldn't refuse.

And such was the nature of the job she had been unable to refuse, despite thorough prior negotiation that she could only work school hours, sometimes Georgie could be found in the early hours of a Sunday morning sitting by Kate's desk at work, with a takeaway breakfast in her lap, as Kate gritted her teeth and worked on the latest crisis that had erupted.

'I like Aleksi!'

'Well, you would,' Kate said drily. 'He's always nice to *you*.' Even when he was at his meanest, even when Kate had somehow managed to erase six months of figures and had tearfully been trying to retrieve them as he hovered like a black cloud over her shoulder one very early morning, still he'd managed a smile and an eye-roll for Georgie.

'Mummy will find them, Georgie,' he had assured the little girl.

'Mummy damn well can't,' Kate had growled.

'Yes, Kate,' Aleksi had said, 'you can. And,' he had added, winking to his latest fan, 'don't swear in front of your daughter.'

'Does Aleksi have a girlfriend?' Georgie probed, and Kate hesitated.

Aleksi cast new meaning on the term 'playing the field', and Georgie was way too young for that. Still, she didn't want her daughter getting too many ideas on her mother's behalf.

'Aleksi's very popular with the ladies,' Kate settled for, and then tried to hurry things along. 'Come on, eat up—you've got school.'

'I don't want to go.'

'You'll enjoy it when you're there,' Kate said assuredly. But, seeing Georgie's eyes fill up with tears, she had trouble wearing that brave smile.

'They don't like me, Mum.'

'Do you want me to have another word with Miss Nugent?'

Kate had had many words with the teacher. Georgie was gifted—incredibly clever. She could read, she could write, but she was also funny and naughty and almost five years old. And Miss Nugent had more pressing problems than a child who *could* read and write.

'Then they'll be more mean to me.' Her voice wobbled and tore straight through Kate's heart. 'Why don't they like me?'

There was no simple answer. Georgie had had a miserable year at kindergarten and now school was proving no better. Though her daughter ached to join in with the other children at playtime, the other little girls didn't include her, because in the classroom she didn't fit in. She could read and write already; she could tell the time. Bored, she annoyed the other students, and the teachers too with her incessant questions, and there had been a few *incidents* recently where Georgie—Kate's sweet, happy little Georgie—had been labeled as 'difficult'.

Shamefully, it was almost a relief to Kate that Georgie didn't want her to speak to Miss Nugent!

Bruce the dog got most of Georgie's egg and toast, and as they drove to school it took all Kate's effort to keep wearing that smile as she walked a reluctant Georgie across the playground and into her classroom.

'Come on now, Georgie!' Miss Nugent said firmly as Georgie lingered by the pegs—though at least today she didn't cry. 'Say goodbye—Mum has to go to work.'

'Bye, Mum,' Georgie duly said, and it almost broke Kate's heart.

All the little girls were in groups, chatting and laughing, whereas Georgie sat alone, looking through her reader, her pencil case in front of her. How Kate wished Georgie could just join in and play. How Kate wished her daughter could, for once, fit in.

As she drove to work, not for the first time she reconsidered Aleksi's offer—if she worked full-time for him, he had told her, then he would pay for Georgie's education. Kate had already found the most wonderful school—a school with a gifted children's programme—one that understood the problems along with the rewards of having a child that was exceptionally bright.

But, more importantly, Kate had known the moment she had stepped into the class during the tour that Georgie would instantly fit in.

There, Georgie would be just a regular child.

Hitting a solid wall of traffic on the freeway, she shook her head and turned on the radio. Georgie needed a mum more than Aleksi needed a full-time, permanently on call PA, and Aleksi's moods changed like the wind—Kate couldn't let Georgie glimpse a future that might so easily be taken away if Aleksi Kolovsky suddenly changed his mind about paying for her education.

Kate wouldn't be so beholden to him.

'It's good to see you, sir.'

Normally Aleksi would have at least nodded a greeting to the doorman, but not this morning. As his driver had opened the car door he had remembered the steps that led up to the golden revolving doors of the impressive city building that was the hub of the House of Kolovsky.

He had not yet mastered steps—but he would this morning.

It had taken an hour to knot his tie—that once effortless, simple task had been an exercise in frustration this Monday morning—but no one would have guessed from looking at him. Immaculate, he walked from the car to the entrance, negotiating the steps as if it had not been four months of hell since he'd last done it. But the ease of his movements belied the supreme effort and concentration Aleksi was inwardly exerting.

'Aleksi?' Kate heard the whisper race through the building. 'What do you mean he's here?'

She could sense the panic, the urgency, but she pretended not to notice. Instead she sat at her desk, coolly typing away, glad—so glad—for the extra layer of foundation she had put on this morning, and wondering if it would stand up to Nina's scrutiny.

Aleksi's area was always a flurry of activity. He had his own vast office, but around that was an open-plan area which he often frequented—Kate worked there, as did Lavinia, the assistant PA. Kate could feel several sets of eyes on her as Aleksi's mother approached.

'Did you know about this?' Nina demanded as she stopped beside Kate's desk.

'Know what?' Kate frowned.

'Aleksi is on his way up!' Nina hissed, her eyes narrowing. 'If I find out you had anything to do with this, you can kiss your perky little job goodbye.'

'I don't know what you're talking about.' Kate swallowed and tried to feign genuine shock at the news. 'Aleksi isn't supposed to back for months yet.'

Just his presence in the building set off a panic.

There was a stampede for the restrooms as everyone dashed to fix their face. Accountants, who had been resting on their laurels, seemingly safe in the knowledge that the astute Aleksi's return was ages away, suddenly flooded Kate's e-mail inbox and phone voicemail with demands for reports, figures, meetings.

Though outwardly unruffled, inside Kate was a bundle of nerves, her heart hammering beneath her new jacket and blouse, her lips dry beneath the glossy new lipstick, her hands shaking slightly as she tapped out a response to one of the senior buyers. Even as her head told her to stay calm, her body struggled with the knowledge that, after the longest time, in just a few seconds, finally she would see him again.

She sensed him, smelt him, tasted him almost, before she faced him.

His formidable, unmistakable presence filled the entire room and her eyes jerked up as he approached— and she remembered.

Remembered the shock value of his presence—how the energy shifted whenever he was close.

It wasn't precisely that she had forgotten. She'd merely refused to let herself remember.

'What are you doing here, Aleksi?' Kate didn't have to feign the surprise in her voice; the sight of him ensured that it came naturally. A couple of months ago there had been a single photo of him captured by a *paparazzo* that had been sold for nearly half a million dollars. It had showed a chiselled and pale Aleksi recuperating in the West Indies, his wasted leg supported on pillows, and that was the Aleksi Kate had been expecting—a paler version of his old self.

Instead he stood, toned, taut and tanned and radiating health, his rare beauty amplified.

'It's good to have you back, Aleksi,' Lavinia purred. 'You've been missed.'

He just nodded and headed to his office, calling over his shoulder for a coffee. Then, as Lavinia jumped up, he specified his order. 'Kate.'

'Poor you!' Lavinia's cooing baby voice faded as Kate made his brew. 'If Nina finds out you had anything to do with him coming back she'll make your life hell.'

'I didn't,' Kate said. 'Anyway, Aleksi's head of Kolovsky, not Nina.'

'This week.' Lavinia smirked. 'Don't you realise times are changing? Aleksi's days are numbered.'

Which was the reason Kate had summoned him back.

When the youngest male Kolovsky, the head of the empire, had spectacularly crashed his car and come close to losing his life, the population of Australia had held its breath as Aleksi had lain unconscious—although rumors of brain damage and amputation had been quickly squashed. Still, the spin doctors had had other things to deal with at the same time. The news that Levander Kolovsky had been raised in an orphanage in Russia while his father had lived in luxury with his wife had slipped out.

The House of Kolovsky had faced its most telling time, and yet somehow it had risen above it—Nina, a tragic figure leaving the hospital after seeing Aleksi, had somehow procured sympathy. Her almost obscene fortune and the rash of scandals had been countered by her recent philanthropic work in Russia. Her daughter's wedding, followed by the news that Levander was about to adopt a Russian orphan, and now her involvement with the European magnate Zakahr Belenki, who ran outreach programmes on the streets of Russia, all boded well for Nina. Suddenly the tide of bad opinion had turned, and Kolovsky could do no wrong.

'Tell the press that the House of Kolovsky is riding high.' Nina had said at a recent decisive board meeting. 'At the moment we can do no wrong.'

'And Aleksi?' the press officer had asked. 'We should give an indication as to his health—assure the shareholders his return is imminent.'

But instead of moving to communicate Aleksi's chances of full recuperation, Nina had chosen the 'no comment' route. Sitting in on the meeting, Kate had been stunned to hear his own mother's words.

'Without Aleksi at the helm,' Nina had clarified, 'Kolovsky can do no wrong.'

Two hours later, Kate had made the call to her boss.

'It's Nina you want to keep sweet! Not Aleksi!' Lavinia broke into Kate's thoughts, and suddenly she'd had enough.

'Actually, it's you I feel sorry for, Lavinia,' Kate shot back. 'We all know what *you* have to do to keep in with the boss—I can't imagine the taste of Nina after Aleksi!'

'You're shaking,' Aleksi noted as the coffee cup rattled to a halt on his desk.

'Don't give yourself the credit!' Kate blew her fringe skywards. More than anything she hated confrontation, yet it was all around, and she simply couldn't avoid it any longer. 'I just had words with Lavinia.'

'Not long ones, I hope,' Aleksi said. 'They'd be wasted on her.'

'Oh, they were pretty basic.'

For once, there was no witty retort from Aleksi. The walk had depleted him. His leg was throbbing, the muscles in spasm, but he did not let on. Instead he took a sip of his brew and finally—after weeks of hospital slop and maids in the West Indies attempting to get it right—finally it was. He liked his coffee strong and sweet, and was tired of explaining that that didn't mean adding just a little milk. Aleksi liked a lot of everything. He took another sip and leant back in his chair, returning her smile when she spoke next.

'The place is in panic!' Kate gave a little giggle. 'I had a frantic call from Reception to alert me you were on your way up, and then the place just exploded! I even saw Nina running for the first time.'

'Running to delete all the files she is so busy corrupting,' he said cynically.

'She wants Kolovsky to do well.' Kate frowned.

'Money is her only god.' Aleksi shrugged. 'Three more months and there would have been no more House of Kolovsky ,' he sneered. 'Or not one to be proud of.'

'Things aren't that bad,' Kate answered dutifully, but she struggled to voice the necessary enthusiasm. On paper everything was fine—fantastic, in fact—but since Levander had returned to the UK and Nina had taken over things were fast unravelling. 'I should never have called you.'

'I'm glad that you did. I've been on the phone with Marketing—"Every woman deserves a little piece of Kolovsky!"' Aleksi scorned. 'That is my mother's latest suggestion. Apart from tampering with the bridal gowns and *Krasavitsa*, she is considering a line of bedlinen for a supermarket chain.'

'An *exclusive* chain,' Kate attempted, but Aleksi just cursed in Russian.

'Chush' sobach'ya!' He glanced down at the coffee and found she was setting out an array of pills beside it. 'I don't need them.'

'I've looked at your regime,' Kate said. 'You are to take them four-hourly.'

'That was my regime when lying on a beach—here, I need to think.'

'You can't just stop taking them,' Kate insisted. She had known this was coming. Even in hospital he had resisted every pill, had stretched the time out between them to the max, refusing sedation at night. Always he was rigid, alert—even when sleeping.

So many hours she had spent by his bed during his recovery—taking notes, keeping him abreast of what was going on, assuring him she would keep him informed but that surely he should rest. She had watched as sleep continually evaded him. Sometimes, regretfully almost, he had dozed, only to be woken by a light flicking on down the hall, or a siren in the distance.

She had hoped his time away in the Caribbean would mellow him—soften him a little, perhaps. Had hoped that the rest would do him good. Instead he was leaner and if anything meaner, more hungry for action, and, no matter how he denied it, he was savage with pain.

'Get my mother in here.'

'I'm here.' Nina came in. She was well into her fifties, but she looked not a day over forty—as if, as Aleksi had once said to Kate, she had stepped straight out of a wind tunnel. She had lost a lot of weight since Ivan's death, and was now officially tiny—though her size belied her sudden rise in stature at House of Kolovsky. Dressed in an azure silk suit, her skinny legs encased in sheer black stockings and her feet dressed up in heels, with diamonds dripping from her ears and fingers, her new-found power suited her. She swept into the room, ignoring Kate as she always did. Lavinia came in behind her.

'It is good to see you back, Aleksi,' Nina said without sentiment, and Kate could only wonder.

This was her son—her son who had been so very ill, who had clawed his way back from the most terrible accident—and this was how she greeted him.

'Really?' Aleksi raised an eyebrow. 'You don't sound very convincing.'

'I'm concerned,' Nina responded. 'As any mother would be. I think that it's way too soon.'

'It's almost too late,' Aleksi snapped back. 'I've seen your proposals.'

'I specifically said you were *not* to be worried with details!' She glared over to Kate, who stood there blushing. 'Leave us!' she ordered. 'I will deal with you later. I assume this is your doing.'

'It was *your* doing,' Aleksi corrected. '*Your* grab for cash that terminated my recuperation. You may leave,' he told Kate, and she did.

It was a relief to get out of there, to be honest.

And oh, so humiliating too. Before the door closed she heard Nina's bitchy tones. 'Tell your PA she is supposed to remove the coat hanger *before* she puts on her skirt.' Kate heard Lavinia's mirthless laugh in response to Nina's cruel comment and fled to the loos, but there was no solace there.

Mirrors lined the walls and she saw herself from every angle.

Even her well-cut grey suit couldn't hide the curves—curves that wouldn't matter a jot anywhere else, but at the House of Kolovsky broke every rule. She turned heads wherever she went, and not in a good way. And by the end of the day, no matter how she tamed it, or smothered it in serum or glossed it and straightened it, her hair was a spiral mass of frizzy curls. Her make-up, no matter how she followed advice, no matter how carefully she applied it, had slid off her face by lunchtime, and her figure—well, it simply didn't work in the fashion industry.

Kate pretended to be washing her hands as an effortless beauty came in and didn't even pretend she was here for the loo. She just touched up her make-up, hoiked her non-existent breasts a little higher in her bra and played with her hair for a moment before leaving.

She didn't acknowledge Kate—didn't glance in her direction.

Kate was nothing—no challenge, no competition. Nothing.

If only she knew, Kate thought, watching in the mirror as the trim little bottom wiggled out on legs that should surely snap.

If only *they* knew her secret.

That sometimes… Kate stared in the mirror at the glitter in her eyes, a small smile on her lips as she recalled the memories she and Aleksi occasionally made. Sometimes, when Georgie was at her grandparents', Aleksi would come to her, would leave the glitz and the glamour and arrive on her doorstep in the still of the night.

They never discussed it. He was always gone by the morning. And it wasn't as if they slept together. In fact in their entire history they'd shared just two kisses—one when Georgie was born; one the night before the accident.

And, yes, a kiss from a Kolovsky meant very little. It was currency to them, easily earned, carelessly spent, but for Kate it was her most treasured memory.

Oh, if only they knew that sometimes, late in the night, Aleksi Kolovsky came to *her* door, wanting *her* company.

'You're to go in.' Lavinia sat scowling when Kate returned, clearly annoyed at having been asked to leave the meeting.

Stepping into the room, had she not known, Kate would never have guessed the two people in there were mother and son. The air sizzled with hatred, and the tension was palpable. Aleksi was on the telephone, speaking in Arabic—just one of his impressive skills—but when he replaced the receiver he wasted no time getting straight to the point.

'Nina has agreed to delay a formal proposal to the board for a fortnight, but she will then propose her takeover of the company, with the board to vote in two months.'

Kate couldn't look at him as he spoke, so her eyes flicked to Nina instead—not a muscle flickered in her Botoxed face.

'My mother says the board is concerned by my behaviour, and that she is worried about my health and the pressure.' He dragged out each syllable, his lips curling in distaste, but still Nina sat impassive. 'I want Kolovsky and Krasavitsa to be treated as two separate entities in the vote. In return, Nina wants the full trajectory reports for Krasavitsa, along with past figures…'

Krasavitsa meant *beautiful woman*, and was a clothing and accessories range aimed at the younger market. The garments and jewels were still extravagant and expensive, still eagerly sought, but not, as was Kolovsky, exclusive.

The idea and its inception had been Aleksi's. In fact it had been his first major project when he had taken over the helm. The launch had gone well. Krasavitsa was the toast of Paris—and every young, beautiful, rich girl, according to their figures, surely by now had at least one piece in their wardrobe, or in their underwear drawer.

And when that beautiful young woman matured into full womanhood, as Aleksi had said at numerous board meetings, she would crave Kolovsky.

It had been Aleksi's pet, and he had nurtured it from the very start—but, it would seem, not satisfied just with Kolovsky, Nina wanted Krasavitsa too.

'Nina has all the figures,' Kate said, and then swallowed as Nina snorted.

'The *real* figures,' Nina said. 'Not the doctored version. I want the real figures.'

'It might take a while.' Aleksi's voice was tart. 'There are other things I need to sort out before I go through figures. The call I just took was from Sheikh Amallah's private secretary...'

Kate watched as only then did Nina show a hint of nervousness, her tongue bobbing out to moisten her lower lip.

'It would take thousands of the cheap, rubbish wedding dresses you have in mind to match the price of his daughter's Kolovsky gown.' Even though he wasn't shouting, it was clear Aleksi was livid. 'Yet you couldn't even be bothered to meet her at the airport!'

'I had Lavinia go!' Nina said defensively.

'Lavinia!' Aleksi gave a black laugh, then whistled through his teeth. 'You just don't get it, do you? You really don't understand.' He looked over to Kate. 'Arrange dinner, and then tell them Nina is looking forward to it.'

'I'm not going to dinner tonight!' Nina spoke as if he'd gone completely mad. 'You go,' she said. 'You speak their language.'

'I hardly think the Sheikh will want his virgin daughter going out for dinner with me!' Now *he* shouted. Now he *really* shouted! 'For now, *I'm* in charge, and don't forget it. For now, at least, we do things *my* way.'

'Well, I want those figures by next Monday.' Nina glowered at Aleksi. 'Only then will I make my decision.'

'You can fight me on Kolovsky,' Aleksi said. 'But I will never concede Krasavitsa. That was *my* idea.'

'Krasavitsa would be *nothing* without *my* husband's name...'

And that, Kate realised as she watched a muscle leap in Aleksi's cheek, was what appeared to hurt the most.

A blistering row with his mother didn't dent him, but the insinuation that without Kolovsky he was nothing was the thing that truly galled him.

'You have *no* idea what you are doing.' Aleksi stared at his mother. 'Follow your plans and the Kolovsky name will be worth nothing in a few years.'

'These are tough times Aleksi,' Nina stood to leave. 'We have to do what it takes to survive.'

He just sat there when she had left.

'*Is* Kolovsky in trouble?' Kate couldn't help but ask.

'It will be.' Aleksi shook his head in wonder. 'We are doing well—but she strikes fear where there is none.' He rested his elbows on his desk and pressed his fingers to his temples. 'Belenki has suggested these off-the-peg bridal gowns and the bedding range. It is supposed to be a one-off—just for a year—with ten percent of the profits going to both our charities: his outreach work in Russia and the orphanages my mother sponsors.' He looked up to her. 'What do you think, Kate?'

He'd never asked her opinion on work before, but before she could reply he did so for her.

'It sounds like a good idea,' he said, and reluctantly she nodded. 'But I know it will be the beginning of the end for Kolovsky. Belenki surely also knows that; exclusivity is why Kolovsky has survived this long. I don't like him...' He halted, then frowned when Kate agreed.

'You said you didn't trust him.'

Aleksi's eyes shot to hers. 'When?'

'The night before the accident...' Her face was on fire. 'When you came to my home.' But clearly he was uncomfortable with the memory, because he snapped back into business mode.

'Get the figures ready for me,' Aleksi said. 'The real figures. But don't give them to Nina until I've gone through them.'

'She'll know if you change them.'

'She couldn't read STUPID if it was written in ten-foot letters on the wall,' Aleksi said. 'Just get them ready for me.' As she turned to go, he called her back. 'You're in or you're out.'

'I'm sorry?' Kate turned around.

'You're on my side, or you pack your bags and go now.'

She frowned at him. 'You know I'm on your side.'

'Good.' Aleksi said, but he didn't let it drop there. 'If you choose to stay, and I get even a hint that you're looking for work elsewhere, not only will I fire you on the spot, don't even *think* to put me down as a reference—you won't like what I say.'

'Don't threaten me, Aleksi. I do have rights!' Her blush wasn't just an angry one, it was embarrassment too, because, given the conversation they'd just had, she'd already decided her night would be spent online, firing off her résumé. But he had no idea what she was going through right now—no idea just how dire her finances were at this moment.

'Exercise your rights.' Aleksi shrugged. 'Just know I don't play nice.'

'I don't get your skewed logic, Aleksi.' Kate was more than angry now. 'All you had to do was *ask* that I stay, but instead you go straight for the jugular each time!'

'I find it more effective.' He looked over to where she stood. 'So you weren't considering leaving?'

'Not really.' Kate swallowed. 'But if Nina does win…' She closed her eyes. 'Not that she will—but if she does…' Hell, maybe she wouldn't get an award for dogged devotion to her boss, but it came down to one simple fact. 'I've got a daughter to support.'

'Then back a winner.' Aleksi said. 'Are you in or out?'

God, he gave her no room, no space to think. But that was Aleksi—he hurled his orders and demanded rapid response.

'I'm in.'

'Good,' Aleksi responded. 'But if I find out—'

'Aleksi,' Kate broke in, 'I've said that I'm in, that I'm not going to look for anything else. You're just going to have to trust me.'

His black smile didn't even turn the edges of his mouth. 'Why would I?'

She just loathed him at times.

Back at her desk, she loathed him so much she was tempted to have a little surf and find a job—just to prove him right!

Just to prove her word wasn't enough.

Just to convince him that his eternally suspicious mind was again merited.

And then he walked past, his leg dragging just slightly, and she watched as Lavinia gave him an intimate smile and tried to engage him in conversation that would be fed back to Nina.

His own mother was trying to destroy him.

Why would he trust anyone?

Why would he even contemplate trusting her?

All Kate knew was that he could.

CHAPTER THREE

Riminic Ivan Kolovsky.

Aleksi put the name into an internet search engine and got nothing.

He didn't really know where to start, and then he glanced over to his mother, who was going through the messages on her phone, and toyed with flicking the name on an e-mail to her, just to watch her reaction—except Lavinia was buzzing like an annoying fly around him, asking for a password so she could get some figures that were needed for tonight.

'Kate will sort it out,' Aleksi uttered, without looking over from the computer, saying the same words he spoke perhaps a hundred times a day.

It was Friday afternoon, but there was no end-of-week buoyancy filling the building. Aleksi had been back for a week now, and had made it exceptionally clear that, whatever Nina or the board might think, for now he was certainly in charge.

There had been several sackings—anyone who had dared question him had been none too politely shown the door—and everyone was walking on eggshells around him.

Everyone, that was, but Kate. She had long since learnt that Aleksi smelt fear like a shark smelt blood, and she refused to bend to his will.

Refused to be beholden to him.

It was the only way she knew how to survive.

'I really need to get things prepared for your conference call with Belenki,' Lavinia insisted. 'The meeting won't be till six p.m. our time, and Kate leaves at five…'

There was more than a slight edge to her voice, and Kate looked up, saw the dart of worry in Lavinia's eyes, and knew for certain then that Lavinia was gathering information for Nina.

'She *has* to pick up Georgie.'

'Actually, I don't tonight,' Kate said sweetly. 'So there's no problem, Lavinia. I'll sort out the meeting.'

Aleksi chose not to notice the toxic current, but carried on with his work. He didn't look over, and neither did Kate look up as Lavinia huffed out.

'You look tired,' he commented.

Which dashed the forty minutes that she'd spent that morning in front of the mirror!

'I haven't been getting much sleep.'

'Look…' Aleksi was a smudge uncomfortable. 'What I said on Monday—'

'Has nothing to do with it,' Kate interrupted. 'I've been up at night with Georgie.'

'How is she?' Aleksi asked.

'She's just having a few problems settling in at school.' Kate tried to sound matter-of-fact. 'But she's doing well.'

'Still too well?' Aleksi asked, and Kate managed a smile at the fact that he had remembered her plight from before the accident. 'You were going to speak with the school?'

'I did,' Kate said. 'They've tried to be accommodating. They're going to see how she goes and then assess her. They might put her up a year…'

'She's not even five yet.'

'But she's so bright.'

'She should still be mixing with five-year-olds—laughing and playing with them—not sitting with the six and seven-year-olds who think she's a baby and whose work she can already do!'

Aleksi got it.

He was the one person who truly got it.

'Did you look at the school I suggested?'

'Yes,' Kate said. 'But I wish I hadn't.'

'The offer is still there. You can work full-time—I have told you that I will fund Georgie's education if you are able to make more of a commitment.' He must have read her worried frown. 'With or without the House of Kolovsky, Kate, I'll more than survive. I'll always need a full-time PA.'

'The size of the commitment you require, Aleksi, is one I can only give my daughter.' She hated him sometimes—hated the carrot he dangled in front of her because she so badly wanted it. She *wanted* that education for Georgie, but what she didn't want was a nanny for when Kate inevitably had to traipse around the world following Aleksi, when she worked till midnight, or had to leave mid-race at the school athletics carnival because some VIP had arrived and couldn't negotiate the walk from Arrivals to the awaiting limo without her…

Aleksi Kolovsky's full-time PA could not be the mother she wanted to be to her little girl.

'She'll be fine where she is,' Kate said, without any hope of believing herself.

'Please!' Aleksi snorted. 'She'll be cleverer than her teachers soon!' He said it with a conviction that came from experience. 'Bored and restless and getting into trouble.'

'I'm saving for a good secondary school.'

She would be. Aleksi knew that. He admired her for it, and for her decision not to work full-time for him too—but it also annoyed him. He wanted her full time, wanted her quiet efficiency. It galled him that the one PA he could work with refused to commit to him.

Aleksi always, *always* got what he wanted. 'She needs her peers. She needs children her own age to play with.'

'*You* didn't have that,' Kate said, because Aleksi had been home-schooled. 'And you seem to have done all right. Iosef too!'

'I hated every moment.' He looked over to her. 'By the time I was fourteen there was nothing my tutor could teach me. By the time I was sixteen... Well, at that point there was a little more. While Iosef studied to be a doctor, I worked with my teacher one-to-one on...we'll call it lessons in human biology...'

Her cheeks were flaming. Sometimes she didn't know if he said things to get a reaction from her—to shock her, to embarrass her.

'She was a very good teacher!' Aleksi said, and then smirked. 'But, again, by seventeen already I knew more than her. At seventeen and a half I was showing her how things could better be done...'

Cheeks still flaming, Kate stood up. Aleksi laughed. 'Have I embarrassed you, Kate?'

'Not at all,' Kate said coolly, 'I'd love to stay and reminisce about your depraved childhood, but I've got the Princess arriving and I need to escort her to her fitting and make sure everything is in order.'

'Given she's already met her, surely Lavinia can do it?'

'But I'll do it better,' Kate said firmly.

'Really?'

And then their eyes locked and her blush wouldn't fade and her lungs were hot with breath that tasted of fire and she felt as if they'd just crossed a line.

It hadn't been anything other than a point she often made—Lavinia *was* rubbish with the dignitaries. She didn't get the nuances, especially with Arabian visitors. It would be far, far easier for Kate to greet their esteemed guests—see the father to the elevator and then walk with the mother of the bride and the Princess herself to the hallowed fitting rooms, which only the most pampered bride ever glimpsed.

A Kolovsky bridal gown was worth a fortune, and not a small one either.

The PAs of the newly rich and famous often had to put up with tantrums and tears when their spoiled brides-to-be finally understood that the price of a per-sonally designed and fitted Kolovsky gown worked out to cost more than their luxurious wedding and honey-moon combined.

Both Ivan and Levander had refused to include a bridal range in Kolovsky's ready-to-wear lines. Even Aleksi, with the opening of Krasavitsa, would not put bridalwear in it.

If the bride wore Kolovsky she was someone—but not if Nina had her way.

Only they weren't talking about bridal gowns now.

'I'm quite sure,' Aleksi said, his dark eyes searing into hers, 'that you'd be wonderful.'

It was Kate who looked away first.

Never had they flirted.

Not once at work had there been an exchange.

She blushed often—but only at his debauchery.

Not once had there been…

She couldn't even really work out what had happened as she walked away from him to greet the bride-to-be. And she might just as well have sent Lavinia, because with her mind still on Aleksi it was almost impossible to concentrate on the Princess as Security opened up and they walked into the bridal area.

It was a jewel of a place that few witnessed.

Every House of Kolovsky boutique was a work of art in itself—but this was not a boutique; this was Kolovsky Bridal and it was hallowed ground indeed.

There were no walls or ceiling as such. As they walked towards the centre there were simply endless stretches of the most divine silks—the palest of blush-pinks, and every shade of cream—handmade silk that the skin ached to feel. It was like being pulled into a silken womb with each step. The huge antique mirrors were not just for aesthetics. Already the team were watching the soon-to-be bride—her posture, her figure, her gait—their brilliant minds already working on the ultimate creation for this woman, whose beauty, hidden or otherwise, was as of this moment the only thing on their minds.

There was no second store, no chain, no Kolovsky designers jetting overseas to take measurements.

Kolovsky did not chase anyone—to wear their art, you had to be present.

Of course their client would stay in Melbourne for a few days—being pampered, going through designs, being measured, seeing portrayed images of the creation on the screen—and finally there would be a follow-up visit to the bride. Then, only then, did Kolovsky come to them.

A team was dispatched a week prior to the date with the creation to wherever the wedding was to be—not just style consultants for the dress, but hair and make-up artists, an entire team to ensure that the bride who wore Kolovsky was the most beautiful.

'This…' The Princess spoke only broken English as they passed lavish display cabinets which held tiaras and shoes and jewels. Those weren't what she noticed, however. The Princess did what every woman who entered this chamber did. She walked or rather was hypnotically drawn to the divine dress in the centre. 'This one. I choose this one.'

'This is not to be reproduced,' Kate explained. 'This is the Kolovsky dress, designed for a Kolovsky or a soon-to-be Kolovsky bride.'

'I want,' the princess said, and her mother nodded—because there was nothing on God's earth that this family could not afford…except what was not for sale.

'Your dress will be designed with only you in mind,' Kate explained. 'This dress was designed for someone else.'

The design team took over then, coming out to greet the bride and her mother, pulling her into the very centre, and as the Princess went Kate watched as she gave one last lingering look at the gown on display.

There could never be anything more beautiful.

Georgie never wrapped herself in sheets or put a towel on her head as a make-believe veil—but Kate had done. She had adored dressing up as a child and, watching a royal wedding on the television, had wanted, wished, *hoped* that one day she would be as beautiful as the bride who walked blushing up the aisle towards her prince. Her mother had said that she had a good imagination—which she had—but even if her imagination could somehow transform her from tubby and serious to petite and pleasing, her secret, wildest dreams could never have conjured up this dress…

Kolovsky silk, so rumour had it, was like an opal—it changed with the mood of the woman whose skin it clung to. Each time Kate saw the dress it seemed slightly different—golden, silver, white, even transparent. Sewn into the bodice were tiny jewels, and there were more hidden in the hem, just as Ivan and Nina had hidden their treasures when they fled Russia for the haven of Australia.

This dress should have been passed, like a revered christening gown, down through the brothers' brides and then to Annika, Ivan and Nina's daughter.

But instead in turn each had shunned it.

Millie, Levander's wife, had come the closest to being married in it, but on her wedding day she had taken off the gown, left it like a puddle on the floor, and fled—only to marry Levander hours later in a jeans-clad ceremony.

Second son Iosef's wedding had taken place in the weeks after Ivan's death, and he and his wife, Annie, had felt it improper to have a lavish celebration while everyone was grieving, so the bride had worn off-the-peg lilac.

His sister Annika's wedding had taken place at Aleksi's bedside, after the accident.

Only Aleksi remained—so presumably the dress would stay where it was: locked behind glass.

'Daydreaming?' Aleksi made her jump as he walked up behind her.

'No,' Kate lied. 'What are you doing down here?'

'Just making sure everything's in place for our esteemed guest.'

'It's all going smoothly—she's in with the design team. They're looking forward to dining with Nina again tonight. Oh, and I rang your sister. Annika's agreed to go along too this time—I thought it better that we make an extra effort, given that we might have offended.'

'You've got more of an idea than Nina. Imagine her at the helm! We'll have name badges and cash registers…'

'And charge extra for a carrier bag!' Kate joined in the joke and then stared back to the dress, a question on the tip of her tongue. But she swallowed it.

'What,' Aleksi demanded, 'is your question?'

'Is there any point asking?'

'Probably not,' he said, and then relented. 'Try.'

'Why did Millie run away from her wedding?'

'You know I'm not going to answer that.' He saw her eyes narrow. 'The House of Kolovsky is a house of secrets.'

'And of course *your* secrets are far better than anyone else's.' She was annoyed.

The past weeks had been hell—toying with whether or not to ring Aleksi, risking her job by doing so, because if Aleksi had been unable to return and her indiscretion had been outed Nina would have dismissed her in a heartbeat. And yet Aleksi strolled in, asked her about her daughter, about her problems, her life, and gave her nothing of his.

'You're a snob, Aleksi, even with your family shame.'

'But our secrets *are* so much better than yours,' Aleksi teased, as he often did. Except this time, instead of enjoying the banter as she always had in the past, Kate promptly burst into tears. He was a mite taken aback. He had never seen her cry, not once—not even the day he had visited her in the hospital, where she'd lain alone after a long, arduous birth…

'What is it?' he demanded.

'What do you think?' She was suddenly angry. 'What the hell do you *think* is wrong?'

'Oh!' Aleksi suddenly looked uncomfortable. 'I'm sorry. I forget these things…'

'I don't believe you!' She didn't. 'You think I've got PMT?' Her mouth was agape, because that was *so* Aleksi! 'How about I'm suffering from YND!'

'YND?' Aleksi frowned.

'You Nearly Died!' It tumbled out of her—and he just didn't get it. Didn't get how hellish this past week had been, these past *months*, Kate clarified to herself, and realised she had never fathomed all that she was holding in. There was Georgie, up at night with bad dreams, Nina being poisonous at work, money problems, Aleksi hurt and on top of all that—or rather buried beneath all that—the hell of his accident, the sheer fright that had come, which had still not been processed, when she had been informed by Iosef that Aleksi had had an accident and might not make it through the night.

There was a fabulous coffee area on the second floor but she couldn't face that, so they headed out of the golden doors and across the street, and she sat in a coffee shop as he fed her napkins and she snivelled into them.

'I thought you were going to die!' Kate wailed. 'We were told you *could* well die.'

'But I didn't,' came his logical reply.

'And now here you are—back, as if nothing has happened…'

'Kate.' Aleksi shook his head, moved to correct her, then halted himself. He certainly wasn't going to reveal to her, or to anyone, just how much *had* changed. How he struggled with so many things that sometimes he wondered if he *should* be back at work. Because he was running a massive empire, yet without thinking really hard he couldn't even remember how many sugars he had in his own coffee. 'I'm fine…'

'I know you are!' She was being unreasonable, illogical. She wished she had fled to the loos to weep, instead of sitting in this public place with him. 'It was just…'

'Just what?'

'Seeing you like that,' she settled for. 'You were still so badly hurt when you went to rehab, and now…' She struggled to describe just how confusing it all was. 'Now you're back. As if nothing happened. All this stuff with your mother, Krasavitsa, the arguments, Belenki…' She screwed her eyes closed, took a deep breath, and tried to articulate what she was thinking. 'Everyone's straight back to business, but I'm just taking a little while longer than everyone else to forget just how bad things were. You nearly *died*!'

There had been no downtime, Aleksi acknowledged. No reflection, really.

Yes, he had lain in that hospital bed, but his brain had been too messed with trauma for contemplation, and in the Caribbean his mind had been too blurred with painkillers to allow anything other than for him to aim at one fixed goal: to get well, to return, to be as good as—no, better than—before.

But now, sitting in a café, perhaps for the first time he saw what he had almost lost—saw too the emotion that had been so lacking in his recovery, in his life.

'Thank you.' So rarely he said it, it felt strange to his lips. 'For all your kind thoughts and help. I hadn't realised how hard all this was on you. But I'm back now and I'm well.'

She nodded—felt a bit stupid, in fact.

'Now…' Aleksi stood. 'I have to show the world just how well I am.'

'Meaning?'

'The old Aleksi is back.'

'Shouldn't you…?'

He was about to stand to go, but when she frowned, Aleksi remained seated.

'Shouldn't I what?'

'Calm things down, perhaps?' It was far from her place to tell him how to live his life, but given the circumstances Kate took the plunge. 'Just till the board make their decision.'

'I think it might take a bit more than a few early nights to convince them I've changed. No.' Now he stood up. 'I'm not going to change just to appease them.'

'Will you think about it?'

'I just did,' Aleksi said, and gave her *that* smile that always made her stomach curl.

Although she returned it, her heart sank as they headed back and up to his office, because the moment they stepped back into the building all tenderness was gone and he was back to his usual cold, businesslike self—though he did remember to check if she was okay to stay when the clock nudged past five.

'It's no problem,' Kate said. 'My sister's picking her up from after-school care.'

'She lives in the country?'

Kate nodded, her throat just a touch dry, a dull blush spreading on her cheeks, but she hid it well, busying herself on the computer and trying, desperately trying, to keep her voice light. 'Yes, Georgie's staying there this weekend.'

He made no comment. She wasn't even sure if he'd heard her—didn't even know if he'd factored it in.

Kate had.

Going over and over and over the nights he'd come to her place, the only common denominator was that Georgie hadn't been home.

Had she been, Kate might not have let him in.

So she had the figures ready for the meeting with Belenki, and afterwards, when he came out with a face like thunder, she informed him she had arranged the best table at the casino for him and his date to dine that night. Then finally, after a very long day, she picked up her bag as Aleksi left for his very public night out.

He was dressed in a dinner suit.

Freshly washed, his hair was slicked back, gorgeous yet slightly unkempt, and Kate frowned.

'Did you keep your appointment?'

'Sorry?'

She glanced down at his hands, at nails that were spotless but just not as polished as usual. Every other Friday without fail Aleksi headed over to the trendiest of trendy salons, sat and drank green tea as his thick black hair was washed and trimmed, his nails buffed, his designer stubble made just a little bit more so. She had rung them during the week to say the appointments would now resume, and had told Aleksi the same.

Except his five o'clock shadow was a natural one and his hair was still just a touch too long.

'The salon—' Kate started, but Aleksi just screwed up his nose.

'Tell them they are to come to me now—I'm tired of going there.'

'Sure.' She made a quick note in her diary and said

goodnight—it wasn't an unusual request. Aleksi often changed his mind, and it was her job to sort it out when he did. 'Have a good night, then,' she said to him.

'You too,' Aleksi said. 'Any plans?'

'A bath and then bed,' Kate admitted, and then she smiled. 'Or I might just hit the clubs!'

'Oh, that's right,' Aleksi said. 'You don't have Georgie tonight.'

'No.' She was standing by the lifts, and had to turn her face to concentrate on the lift buttons rather than let him see her blush. 'I'll see you on Monday.'

'Sure.'

She would, Aleksi told himself.

She would see him on Monday, and not a moment before.

He watched her leave, watched her yawn as she pressed the lift button and could, for a dangerous moment, imagine her slipping out of those shoes, peeling off that suit, sinking into a bath, relishing the end of the week, the end of the day.

For Aleksi the night had just started.

He was tired, but he blocked that thought.

He was in pain, but he refused to take another pill. It had been twenty-four hours without them and it was getting harder by the minute, but he would not take another—they messed with his head.

He headed for the lift and stared for a full three seconds. He didn't want Ground he wanted Reception. He had made the same mistake so many times this week.

Not that anyone could have guessed.

Not even Kate.

He raked back his hair with his hands, and as he stepped into the lift he closed his eyes and tried and tried again in vain to picture the location of the hair salon. His eyes snapped open as the lift doors did the same.

'Goodnight, Mr Kolovsky.'

He nodded to the receptionist. Actually responded to the doorman tonight. Made the steps with apparent ease and then slid into the back of his waiting car.

Tonight he would prove to the world he was back.

Put paid to all the rumours.

He kissed his date thoroughly. They'd been out a few times before the accident and she was delighted, she said, pressing herself into him as they sped to the casino, that he was back.

'It's good to be back,' Aleksi said, and then he kissed her again—but only because it was easier than talking. It was far easier to kiss her than to tell her that he couldn't remember her name.

CHAPTER FOUR

THERE was no thrill.

Aleksi put a million on black and just stared as the wheel went round.

Win, lose.

There was just no thrill any more.

He didn't need the money, and he didn't need Kolovsky.

Wasn't sure if he wanted either.

He won.

He could hear the cheers, turned to what was surely the most beautiful woman on this planet and accepted the kiss on his lips, but he still couldn't remember her name. He kissed her back, could taste her champagne on his sober tongue, and for a moment he pulled her in, wanted her smell, her breasts, her body to do something to cure the numbness.

Yet he couldn't even accept the toast that was raised to him, let alone raise one himself.

He was back!

His suite awaited.

Paradise awaited.

Oblivion, even.

He was fifty million richer and he couldn't even

become aroused by the beautiful woman he held in his arms.

Ah, but he knew his body. Like his Midas touch, it had never once failed him—and it didn't now.

There it was—that primal response, the Kolovsky legend that never dimmed—and there was her triumphant smile as she finally felt his surge of arousal…

What *was* her name?

'Excuse me one moment.'

He had been born in Australia but schooled at home, surrounded by his family, his history, and despite his perfectionism still there was just a hint of Russian to his voice.

He walked to the restroom.

The door was held open.

He relieved himself, zipped himself back into his exquisite suit pants and then washed his hands. Then, because it was numb and it felt like plastic, he washed his face as well. He pressed it into a fluffy towel and caught his reflection in the mirror.

Black hair, thick and glossy—check.

Slate-grey eyes, not a hint of blood in their whites—check.

Smooth, unblemished skin—check.

Designer stubble—check.

The chief of Kolovsky.

He loosened his tie, because he could feel his pulse leaping against his collar.

He knew.

What it was, he couldn't remember—but he knew something important!

More than his brother Levander, who had lived it.

More than his twin, Iosef, who had *dealt* with it.

More than his sister Annika, who had worked through it.

He was cleverer than the lot of them—and being clever was a curse.

He *knew*. He knew so much more than any of them, and though he denied it—though his father had beaten him into silence because the truth would change everything—it was harder and harder to hide from it now.

There was a memory—an image, just a breath, just a realization away—yet no matter how he reached out to it, over and over it slipped from his grasp.

Why couldn't he remember?

He pressed his face into the cool mirror, willed clarity to come, and stared into the murky depths of his mind, hoping to God that coming off the pain medication would help clear it somehow. Because Aleksi knew that something had to be done.

He just didn't know what.

His phone was bleeping in his pocket, summoning him back to his immaculate world. He took a breath and headed out there, and then it bleeped again and he looked at the screen.

Brandy.

Yes, that was her name. The word was suddenly there in front of him as she called him, no doubt wondering where he was, and now he remembered her name and also a ridiculous rhyme.

Whisky makes you frisky; brandy makes you randy.

Well, not tonight.

He turned left instead of right, ended up in the kitchen instead of the high rollers' bar, ignored the exasperated attempts to turn him around, and then, when his phone beeped again, instead of answering it he rang his personal driver and told him to ensure that Brandy was taken home or put up in the hotel—whatever it was she required.

'Any message?' his driver asked.

'None,' Aleksi said, and then clicked off his phone, tossed it into a deep fat fryer and pushed open a door.

He walked down the fire escape stairs, past the skips and dumpsters, out to a side street and into a cab.

'Where to?' the driver wanted to know.

Aleksi didn't answer at first

'Where to?' the cab driver asked again.

'The airport,' Aleksi said, and as they made their way along the freeway it was all so familiar. He had been here before—he remembered then, the night of the accident, driving as if the devil was chasing him towards the airport, only he couldn't remember why. Maybe it was because it would have given him time to think, Aleksi decided. Maybe that was what he had craved that night— what he craved right now. Except the freeway was clear, the streetlights shortening, and they were there in less than thirty minutes. 'Take me back to the city.'

The cab driver started to argue, but stopped as a wad of notes silenced his protest.

'Just drive.'

So they did.

One a.m. Two a.m. They drove around.

'Left,' Aleksi said as once again the city lights receded. 'Take the exit here,' he commanded as they swerved into suburbia. 'Right at the roundabout. And right again.'

Then he saw Kate's house, nondescript in the darkness. The little streak of grass needed a cut, her car needed a wash, and a 'For Sale' sign was posted outside.

'Stop here.'

Money talked, so the taxi driver didn't—just stopped there, for five, ten, fifteen minutes, as Aleksi waited for normal services to resume, for this madness to abate, to tap the driver on the shoulder and tell him to take him back.

He had said never again.

He had sworn to himself he'd never come here again.

Hated himself for leading her on—because nothing could ever come of it.

Three times he had ended up here—and loathed himself for it.

Tomorrow, when the sun rose, he would surely regret it again.

Don't make the same mistake again, he begged himself. But…

'Go.' He stepped out of the cab.

'I can wait,' the driver offered. 'Make sure someone's home…'

'Go,' Aleksi repeated.

He stood there, in the middle of suburbia at three a.m., with no phone, watching the cab drive off and wondering to himself what the hell he was doing here.

Again.

He quashed that thought, tried to dismiss memories of his other late night visits to this house, but they rose to the surface again, demanding an answer he struggled to give.

He'd known her the longest.

It was the first time he'd considered it, thought about it, pondered it.

Apart from family, Kate had been in his life the longest of any woman—their fractured five-year history was the furthest back he'd ever gone. Aleksi travelled light; when a relationship was over it was over, and as for female friends—well, he'd never quite worked out how to keep it at that…

But he'd had to with Kate.

He walked up the path. Stared at the door. Told himself he could handle it.

And then took a breath and knocked.

Hearing the knocking on the door, Bruce barking just a couple of moments too late to earn the title of guard dog, Kate turned on the light. Half awake and half asleep, even as she headed down the hall she told herself not to hope.

Kate sometimes wondered if she imagined these visits.

There was never any mention of them—and certainly no acknowledgment of them—afterwards.

She didn't really understand why he came, yet three times before now he had arrived on her doorstep.

Once, a couple of weeks after she had started back at Kolovsky, he had said that the press had been chasing him and he had shaken them off and ended up here. She had loaned him her sofa. His silver car had looked ridiculous in her drive and he had been gone by the time she had awoken the next morning.

Then, a few weeks later, there had been a row and she had resigned when he'd demanded she stay at work late. He had arrived in a taxi, a little the worse for wear, and had asked her to reconsider handing in her notice—had offered to more rigorously uphold the part-time conditions he had previously agreed to and then, when she had agreed to return, promptly fallen asleep on her sofa.

He had returned a third time after the charity ball, incoherent, clearly the worse for wear and at odds with everyone—furious with Belenki, with his family, and with the world. They had shared their second kiss—a sweet, confusing kiss, because even as it had ended she'd seen the conflict in his eyes. What had taken place would not be open to discussion, and again he had been gone by morning. Then the accident had happened.

But now he was back—not just at work, but in her home, too.

Cruel, restless, angry—and never more so than now—again he was at her door.

'My leg…'

She could see the sweat beading on his forehead as he limped over the threshold—which told her of the pain he was in, because this week he had hidden his limp so well. 'Have you had a pill?' She had never seen him like this. Not since the early days at the hospital, when they had been trying to get his pain medication under control. 'Maybe you need an injection?'

'I've stopped taking anything!' he gasped.

He was so pale beneath his tan she thought he might pass out.

'You're supposed to be on a reducing dose.'

'I have reduced—I've stopped completely.'

'When?'

'Today.'

'Aleksi!' She was truly horrified. 'They said you had to reduce slowly—that it would be months before you could manage without them. You can't just stop like that.'

'Well, I just did.' Aleksi said. 'I need to think straight.'

'You can't think straight if you're in pain!' Kate insisted.

'Listen!' His hand closed around her wrist, his voice urgent. 'Listen to me. Since the accident I have not been able to think straight…'

'That's to be expected.'

'Exactly.' His eyes were grey, the whites bloodshot, and she had never seen him look more ill. 'They do not want me to think straight. Since that new doctor, always there are more pills…'

'He's the best,' Kate insisted. 'Your mother researched…' Her voice trailed off—surely Nina wouldn't stoop that low? But from the way she was acting now, maybe she could.

'I am going back under the care of the hospital. I have an appointment on Monday. Once I can think, once I am off this medication, I will get them to manage things— not a doctor of my mother's choosing.' He looked over to her, and she could see pain there that was so much more than physical. 'You must think I'm being completely paranoid…'

She was silent for the longest time before she spoke. 'Regretfully, no.' She thought a moment longer. 'I think maybe we're *both* being paranoid but, yes, I can see you don't trust her.'

'If I can get through tonight then I can think straight…'

That much she understood.

There was still so much she didn't.

It should have been uncomfortable—awkward, perhaps, but when he was here in her home. It wasn't.

Oh he was scathing and loathsome and everything Aleksi, yet he travelled lighter here—even if he was in pain, it was as if all his baggage had been checked and left at the door.

'How,' he said, standing at the bathroom door, 'can you lose a plug?'

She'd suggested a bath and, given he'd probably

never run one in his life, for tonight she'd made allowances and offered to run it for him. Except she couldn't find the plug!

'Maybe Georgie...' Kate started. But, no, she'd had a bath herself tonight.

'Retrace your footsteps!' was his most unhelpful suggestion.

'What about a shower?'

'You've just talked me into a bath, Kate,' Aleksi said. 'You spent the last ten minutes telling me how it would relax me, how—'

'Here!' The plug was in one of its regular hiding places—between the pages of a book she'd been reading—and of course he didn't let her get away with it that easily. As she put in the plug and turned on the taps, having checked for towels and the like, she tried to beat a hasty retreat. But Aleksi blocked the door, holding out his hand and taking the novel from her reluctant hands.

'I might like to read in the bath too,' he told her.

He must, because he was gone for an age.

She didn't really know what he was doing here—what it was that made him come. She just knew that he did.

Knew, somehow, that to question him would close the tiny door that occasionally opened between them.

The suave, sophisticated thing to do would be not to answer the door.

To pretend perhaps that she was out.

But she was in.

Definitely in to Aleksi.

She had a life.

A career.

A family.

But he was her thrill.

A guilty, delicious secret. An endless question that delivered no answers. But how nice he was to ponder. Unattainable to her, but for a while, at least, here with her in her home.

Oh, she knew what Aleksi was going through tonight—going cold turkey from his medication—and tomorrow, when she awoke to him gone, it would once again be Kate battling withdrawal symptoms from the loss of Aleksi.

'Does she go back to him?' He stood, leaning in her doorway, dripping wet, a towel around his hips, and Kate jumped where she lay on the bed and tried to scramble her thoughts into order. 'Jessica?'

He really had been reading it! 'For a little while,' Kate said as he walked over. Really, there was no question of the sofa for either of them; somehow she knew that tonight they were both staying here in her bedroom. 'Then…'

'Then what?' Aleksi asked, sitting on the bed. 'Then she realised she was better off without him?' He lay down beside her, stretched out, just a towel covering his loins, and she couldn't look—how she wanted to look, but she couldn't.

'I haven't got that far yet.' He closed his eyes and now she *could* look at him. Sitting up against the pillows, she stared at the most beautiful specimen of a man, lying beside her, one of her small towels a sash around his groin, his cheekbones—oh, God, his perfect cheekbones—two dark slashes on his cheeks, and the spike of wet eyelashes closed. But it was his nearly naked body that was new to her tonight—many nights of imaginings hadn't sufficed. Up close and personal, he was nothing but stunning.

'You're selling your home?' Somehow he managed to talk normally, and Kate tried for the same.

'My landlord is selling.'

Eyes still closed, he frowned, because of course he didn't really understand what it meant to her.

'That's why I asked my sister to have Georgie—I need to find somewhere this weekend.' She watched the edge of his eyes scrunch to deepen his frown.

'Surely he must give you notice?'

'I got given a month's notice,' Kate said. 'Last weekend you informed me you were flying home. This weekend I start looking. Next weekend I hope I find somewhere…' She stopped herself before her voice cracked. Kate never took the woe-is-me route, and suddenly she didn't need to to stop herself from getting upset, because then she got a little bit angry and it crept into her voice. 'That's if my employer will give me a reference.'

He opened his eyes to her.

'I came on too strong, perhaps?'

'There's no perhaps about it,' she retorted indignantly.

'I can't afford for you to leave just now.'

'That's all you had to say.'

When she looked back on this night—and it was certain that over and over she would—Kate wondered if she'd remember how she came to be touching him. But now, living it, feeling it, when it actually came to it, it was so seamless, so natural, that after a while of talking, after another while of silence and then talking again, when his leg was racked with painful cramping, it was more a response than a thought that led her hand to his thigh. Once it was there, once that jump had been made, she didn't want to return to a world without the feel of him beneath her fingers, even if she knew that tomorrow she would.

His skin was warm, firm and taut beneath her fingers, the contact firing her nerves into a frenzied alert. She wrestled to calm them, had to concentrate on slowing her breathing down as she slid her hand over the tight muscle, and then slowly the sirens in her body hushed a little, grew deliciously accustomed to the feel of him, and Kate could breathe more normally as she worked his spasmed flesh. She could see the scars where the pins and bolts had been. She took some baby oil—it was all she could think of—and squirted it on, rubbing the tense mound of flesh, tentatively at first and then more firmly. It took ages, and she wasn't even sure it was helping, but the muscle finally gave beneath her fingers. Then just after it relaxed it tensed again. She heard his curse, saw him grit his teeth, and she actually knew something about how he felt.

'When I had Georgie…'

'Don't!' He both laughed and warned her at the same time. 'Don't say you know how it feels…'

'But I do.' Still her hand worked on. 'I was on my own, and the nurses kept telling me that I was doing fine, that it was all completely normal, but I was begging for something. I couldn't believe how much it hurt. I knew childbirth was supposed to hurt, but it was agony. The pain just kept coming…'

'For how long?'

'All night,' Kate said. 'And I thought I'd never get through it, but I did.'

'I don't want drugs,' Aleksi said, and Kate smiled.

'I said the same.' She pressed her fingers harder into the tight knot of his thigh muscle, heard his hiss of breath, saw his hand go to remove hers. But the muscle finally relented, the tight spasm loosened, and she worked on.

'Did you give in?' Aleksi asked.

'Absolutely.' Kate smiled. 'I screamed the place down for everything.'

And Aleksi smiled, too. 'I won't give in.'

He wouldn't—that much she knew.

'Is it agony?'

'No.' His answer surprised her. 'It's not so much the pain…more the thoughts.'

'Thoughts?' Still her hands worked on.

'It would be easier to knock myself out,' Aleksi explained. 'But I just need to get through this.'

He'd put on muscle in his leg. The last time she had seen it, it had been withered and wasted, studded with pins and bolts. Now it was tanned and lean, with fresh scars and dark hair. When his thigh muscle was pliant she worked down, as the physio had done, and unknotted the calf muscle that bore so much of the strain of his healing thigh.

'You'll get there.' She was absolutely sure of it. 'Just relax.'

'Easier said than done,' he said wryly.

'Just try,' she pleaded.

So he did.

He lay there and thought only of her hands.

Listened to the tick, tick, tick of her little alarm clock.

He had loathed this in hospital—the invasion of his body, being told to relax, not to fight—but right now he got what they had been trying to tell him, because when he did relax, when he did let go, it was as if his muscles were melting.

He had never been better looked after.

Aleksi lay back on her bed and stared at the ceiling.

He had never been more relaxed, more comfortable with another soul.

Always he performed.

At dinner, in business, in bed, in hospital—always it was Aleksi driving the conversation, the deal, the orgasm, the recovery. Whatever the goal, he was relentless in pursuing it, but tonight—this morning—he lay there and for a little while just let her…

Let his mind, let his body, let himself just be—till the spasm hit again, his leg contracting, his mind tightening with the pain of recall, memories awakening. The screech of tyres and the smell of burning rubber, his car spinning out of control because his mind had been so full of other things. And as he lay there it was so vivid he had to clench his fists to prevent his arms flying up to shield his face.

Her hands were at the back of his thigh now, working the tight hamstring, and he wanted to shout out because it was sheer hell to remember.

'Don't think of anything,' she said gently.

So he looked at her instead of looking inside his mind. Her eyes were down in concentration. His moved lower too, to her cleavage, and he focused on that for a soothing moment, willing the gown to part, to reveal just a little bit more, but desire alone couldn't do that. Then he watched her hands work, saw his flesh move with each stroke to his thigh, felt his breathing slow down, and it was almost hypnotic the effect she had on him.

He was covered now by just the small towel which had loosened. His thigh was soft, but her tender ministrations had been recognised by his body elsewhere.

'Don't worry.' Embarrassed, she turned her face away, went to stand, tried to be matter-of-fact. 'I'm sure it happens…' Well, it must—all the physiotherapists, nurses who had touched him…

'Not once.'

And so here was her guilt.

Her never again.

Because each time he came to her door the bar shifted.

First a kiss.

Then a conversation.

Each a guilty memory that she took out and examined now and then like a precious hidden treasure.

And now this.

Her hand was still on his thigh, not moving. She could have walked away at that point, except she didn't.

This was the bit she would never understand.

Because here, alone with him in her house, away from it all and only for a short while, she felt beautiful.

For the first time in her life, when those grey eyes looked into hers, she felt as if she were another person entirely.

A bold, sensual woman.

Only she wasn't.

Sex had been mired in shame for Kate. Her first attempt with Craig had resulted in Georgie, followed closely by Craig insisting that her intention had been to trap him into marriage, then cruelly berating her for putting on weight and finally, on Kate's insistence, leaving.

Craig's relief to be leaving her had been palpable; she had actually seen his tension evaporate as she'd exonerated him of any duty to their unborn child. His parents had some contact with Georgie, and on occasion he saw his daughter there. He did send birthday presents and Christmas cards, but that was the sum total of his involvement.

As she had closed the door on him, Kate had sworn *never again*.

She was a mother, and she'd be the best mother she could be, and she'd do it without a man rather than subject Georgie to her mistakes.

But now Aleksi lay in her bed, and she was more than a mother tonight. For the first time in the longest time she was a woman again.

His eyes were on her face, and she just stared back at him, her hand still on his thigh. She moved it again, stroked him again, but it was more than a healing touch and they both knew it. She could feel his thigh contract beneath her fingers, feel the waves of pain rising within him again. But she would soothe him with a different touch now.

'Kate…' His hand moved over hers as it crept up his thigh. 'You don't have to…'

'I know.' Except she was mired in want. Yes, this would change things—but they had changed already.

Yes, she knew she could never keep him—but she wanted to have had him, at least for a little while.

She had never held a man in her hand, but she did so now. She held him as if it was her right—her fingers warm from the oil as she slid them around his thick length.

'Kate…' He said it again, almost urging her to stop, because there was a strange nervousness for Aleksi. His pain, his guilt and his shame would still be there tomorrow, but for now it all melted away with the bliss of her touch. A touch that wasn't greedy or demanding, but was instead a slow, rhythmic touch that had him staying silent and instead closing his eyes.

It was an inexperienced touch that he almost wanted to correct—to place his hand over hers in order to show her how, a better how. Except, Aleksi realised as he gave in to her ministrations, it couldn't be better than this.

There was a deep pleasure in the unexpected.

A lack of expertise brought a surprise with every delicious stroke.

It was too light.

She was scared to hurt him.

Too rough.

She couldn't help herself.

Not there.

She cupped him in her hand.

Be careful. His mind said what his mouth held back from.

Only Kate didn't hold back.

She cupped him and stroked him and was just so bowled over by his beauty, so lost in this intimate place. He was more beautiful than anyone had a right to be— *this* was more wonderful than she had ever dreamt—and this was real and he was here and she grew bolder.

She stroked him more easily now, finding her rhythm, and she felt a deep pool of excitement swell within her. Now her hands were busy, her mouth craved contact with him.

Guided by want rather than logic, she lowered her lips, kissed his flat nipple, anticipating what she didn't know—for him to tell her enough? To warn her off? But she heard his ragged breath, and she kissed it as delicately and then as hungrily as she wished he would kiss her.

She felt his hand creep into her dressing gown but she brushed it off. Hungry now for herself, she kissed down his chest and down his flat stomach. She relished each caress, each lick, savoured them because she knew she would live on this for weeks.

Till the master called for her again this would be her escape, this the moment she would relive.

Her mouth was neither skilled nor practised, but it didn't confuse.

There was a pleasure in its simplicity. He lay there, staring at the ceiling, and for a moment he wanted to climb from the bed, to tell her…what?

Yet he lay there.

She kissed him—not to impress or to please, but to appease her own building need. She tasted and she licked and she felt his fingers knot in her hair as she grew bolder, taking him deeper and relishing him.

For Aleksi it was a revelation.

To just lie there, to do no more than that.

To lie and think of nothing but her lips on him. This from a man who merely tolerated massages—though he was booked in each week.

Always he lay there, willing the hour over. Gave a huge tip, said he felt marvelous. Slipped back into his suit feeling the same, just oiled.

Till now, he had felt the same with this.

Yet for the first time all he did was lie there—no rush, no feigned moans, no urgency.

He lay there.

And then his hips rose.

Except he didn't want it over so soon.

So he lay there for a moment longer and climbed into a void where all there was was this sensation, just this moment in time.

'Kate,' he gasped, and his hips rose again. He felt moisture in his eyes, which he screwed closed.

He could feel her tender ministrations and he didn't want them to stop—but finally his body was beating its blessed relief. He had never been in a place like it—a still, silent place, where there was just her tongue and her lips and her breath and an endless night that was now only a little way from dawn.

He didn't know this place that was devoid of demand, of reciprocal rights—this unfamiliar place where he opened his eyes and looked at his generous bedfellow without resentment, of one with whom he actually still wanted to share a bed.

He pulled her up beside him, liked the curves and the flesh that he tangled into, liked the scent of her hair and the weight of her breast on his chest.

The right word had often evaded him these past months, and he did the usual search, trawled through his mind's thesaurus in a brain that had gone over its download limit. The search too slow; the answer when it came was surely wrong.

Calm.

He'd never known it or felt it, but even as he disputed it, even as he tried to come up with another word, it remained in his mind as sleep finally invaded and claimed him.

CHAPTER FIVE

SHE awoke to a bed that was, apart from her, empty. She waited for the tsunami of shame to sweep in, waited for regret, for remorse to arrive. But instead Kate just lay for a quiet moment, blinking as she realised those feelings were absent.

There wasn't a minute of last night that she regretted.

Oh, she did momentarily consider a full-face tattoo to hide her blushes when she faced him on Monday, but even as she climbed out of bed still regret was absent, still she considered that last night was very possibly the most wonderful of her life.

Kate pulled on her dressing gown, splashed her face with water, and on autopilot brushed her teeth.

She had three rental properties to look at this morning, plenty to get on with today, and she would do everything in her power not to think about Aleksi till later tonight, when she could quietly sit and go over the night they had shared.

Refusing to check her phone to see if he'd texted her, she padded out to the mail box and collected the newspaper, then headed into the kitchen.

'I've been thinking…'

'Ah!' she gasped, and almost dropped the newspaper.

It hadn't even occurred to Kate that he might still be here! Always he was gone by dawn, and the dark hours prior were conveniently forgotten by Monday. Yet here he was, in the morning sun, in her kitchen, pouring scalding water into two mugs!

'Where are the coffee beans?' he asked.

'In Kenya,' Kate said, opening a jar of instant and trying not to let him see how rattled his presence made her feel. The sight of him in her dingy kitchen brought her no comfort; she didn't actually want her two worlds colliding. Last night had been fantasy, escape—it suited her that they didn't speak about it, didn't acknowledge it, that their private moments weren't analysed in the cold light of day.

But here he was.

He had on only the bottom half of his suit. Despite arduous work-outs to regain his strength he had lost weight, and the pants sat a touch lower on his hips. Usually that would have been sorted. He had an army of designers at his disposal, after all, and Aleksi Kolovsky would have utilised them.

It was the tiniest detail, yet she noticed it.

Liked it, even.

Liked the extra glimpse of toned flat stomach and the glimpse of dark hair that led to where she had kissed him last night.

No, she did *not* like her dreams invading reality like this!

Didn't like facing him in her tatty dressing gown with her morning hair, and was painfully aware of her shabby kitchen, and that he was no doubt regretting coming to her door.

Again.

'I thought you'd be gone,' she commented.

Aleksi had thought he would be gone by now too.

Always he rose early, but since the accident it had been ridiculous. His eyes snapped open long before dawn and he listened to the world wake up as he lay there, racked with exhaustion but unable to rest. Except this morning. For the first time since the accident, for the first time since way before then, even, the sun had beaten him in rising.

Refreshed, even relaxed, he had left Kate sleeping, his intention to call a cab. Yet he had been reluctant to leave, reluctant to face what needed to be faced, and, attempting to locate coffee, had seen the neat stack of bills by the microwave, recalled the 'For Sale' sign outside the house and his solution had been found.

Aleksi didn't slowly form ideas, but neither did he mull. His mind was too rapid for rumination; he scanned details most legal eyes would take hours to ponder. He cut straight to the chase. 'Move in with me.'

Kate rolled her eyes.

'You have to find somewhere to live. I have a huge home you could stay in for a couple of months…' His idea stalled as the scruffiest dog he had ever seen strolled past and Kate let him out to the back yard. 'You're not saying anything.'

'Because it doesn't warrant a response,' Kate said dryly, and got on with making a much needed cup of coffee.

'You, Georgie…' he hesitated, but only for a second '…the dog…'

'Bruce.'

'I'm going to London in a few days, to meet with Belenki,' Aleksi said. 'We need to do some straight

talking. So I'll be away and you and Georgie will have the place to yourself for a while—I'd hardly be there...'
Still she didn't respond. 'It could help us both out.'

'Ah, now we're getting somewhere.' Kate handed him a mug. 'How, precisely, would a single mother and her entourage living in your home help you, Aleksi?'

'It would show responsibility. It would prove to the board...' He hesitated. 'I thought about what you said— maybe I do need a change of attitude to win the board over. Let them see that I am settling down, that I am serious about the business of Kolovsky.'

'Settling down?' she repeated flatly.

'We could say you were my fiancée. Just for a couple of months—just till I get the board's vote.'

'No.'

It was a definite answer, but one Aleksi refused to accept. 'The board thinks—'

'You've never cared what the board thinks before.'

'I've never needed to. They know I do a brilliant job, they know I can run the place blindfolded, but always there is greed.'

'No.' She said it again, even shot out an incredulous laugh at his ridiculous thought process.

'You would be remunerated.'

'Two months' worth of free rent in exchange for messing up my life? I don't think so!'

'Of course not.'

And then a dream came true.

Or rather the fantasy that soothed her late in the night sometimes—the times when she lay racked with worry, scared for Georgie's future. The dream where all that was waved away by some strange miracle—only this wasn't a winning lottery ticket, nor some unknown ancient relative's legacy.

No, six feet two inches of arrogant male Kolovsky looked her straight in the eye and offered her such an outlandish sum that the third no, though on the tip of her tongue, wasn't quite so speedily delivered. The synapses in her brain were firing in rapid calculation of the future she could achieve if only she had the nerve to say yes to him.

'No,' Kate said again, except it was preceded by a swallow.

'Think about it.' He drained his mug and then walked over to her, shrinking the kitchen and making her feel impossibly claustrophobic as he stood before her. He leant forward a touch, to place his mug on the bench behind her. She could smell him, smell the danger of him, and in that moment Kate knew he was deadly serious—she had worked with him long enough to know that Aleksi didn't make idle offers.

To know that Aleksi *always* got his way.

'I've given you my answer.' She would not be intimidated. She refused to look at him, and took a sip of her drink instead.

'If I don't sort out this chaos my mother is creating, if I don't halt Belenki in the next few days, then I'm walking away from the company completely,' he said.

She felt as if she were standing on a trampoline, unsteady and unsure, watching as the springs snapped away one by one. 'You'd never leave Kolovsky!'

'Oh, I'd leave it in a heartbeat,' Aleksi responded.

'It's your life.'

'It's just business,' Aleksi answered.

Another spring snapped and any minute she'd be

falling. Without Aleksi there, she'd certainly be fired. Where else could she earn so much for so few hours?

'You'd get another job, of course.' Aleksi smiled.

'You're blackmailing me,' she whispered.

'Not at all.' He shook his head. 'Before I leave I'd give you a glowing reference, saying what a brilliant PA you are—you know a Kolovsky reference will open any door. How could I possibly be blackmailing you?'

Because she didn't want to be a full-time PA—didn't want to work from seven till seven and then spend half the night on the computer and the phone.

'I am offering you a future—whatever happens at Kolovsky your future can be secured.' Aleksi's voice was like silk—raw silk, though. 'Georgie's future…'

'What about Georgie?' She was angry now—angry at him offering this without true thought, angry at herself for even letting her mind dance down the delicious path he was offering. She tried to push past him, but he caught her arms. 'What would I tell her, Aleksi? *Oh, Mummy's engaged, we're moving in…*'

'If she sees you happy and relaxed…'

'And when it ends?' Still the springs snapped and, glimpsing the ending, she felt as if she were finally falling. 'What do I tell her then?'

'Relationships don't work out sometimes.' Aleksi shrugged, and then his voice was serious. He held her elbows, spoke very slowly, very clearly, because there was one thing it was imperative she understood. 'So long as you're okay, Georgie will be okay. But it *will* end, Kate. You're right about that. I don't do love. I don't do for ever.'

'You're not going to break my heart, Aleksi.' Kate's voice was firm. She almost managed condescending—only inside she didn't feel so brave, because seeing him for a few hours did enough damage to her mind. To live with him, to sleep with him, to be with him all the time with the guarantee of losing him…

She was hurting already, and he must have picked up on that.

'I'm a good lover, Kate.'

'Oh, so sex is part of the deal?'

'Of course it's not mandatory…' Aleksi said, but then he pulled apart her dressing gown.

The belt was still tight, so only her breasts were exposed, and he pulled her just a small fraction closer, not enough to be touching, but almost, *almost*, and her breasts yearned for more, instantly hardening till his skin grazed her.

'What, Kate?' His whisper was cool on her flaming cheek. 'Do you want me to say that we share a bed and don't touch? That we deny ourselves such an obvious pleasure?' He was stroking her nipple now, caressing it as he had last night, only his movements were more skilful than intuitive, driven by a goal other than lust.

She flicked his hand off. 'It's not going to happen.'

'As I was saying…' He ignored her words and lifted her onto the bench as if she was as featherlight as Lavinia, and suddenly she was at eye level with him. 'We get on, Kate, and I am a good lover. I know what to say…' he was playing with the tie of her dressing gown '…and I know how to make you happy—but you have to know that it can't last.'

'Haven't you heard a word I've said?' she demanded.

He just smiled that slightly mocking smile, and then it widened as a thought struck him.

'You're on the pill.'

'If you think—'

'I'm as clean as a whistle, Kate—had it confirmed at the hospital. I knew anyway. I always wear protection.'

'There's been no one since the hospital?'

'Actually, no!' He sounded as surprised with that fact as Kate was. Then that devilish smile was one of the cat with the cream. 'We can play at monogamy…'

'It's all just a game to you!' She went to climb down but he held her waist.

'What's wrong with that?' Aleksi challenged. 'I play nicely…'

And then he wasn't nice at all. A skilled negotiator, Aleksi knew *exactly* when to change his tune. He dropped his hands, released the pressure and showed her a different way. 'Carry on with your life, Kate. Go and spend your weekend looking for a rental that takes pets. Oh, and in a couple of weeks you can look for work— because after all this trouble with Nina I won't be there much longer.' She could have stepped down but instead she sat. 'And don't forget to keep looking for schools for Georgie…' He mocked her with a wicked smile then. 'Only you've already found the one you want, haven't you? The offer's there, Kate. You can have everything you want for Georgie.'

'You're rushing me!'

'How?' Aleksi challenged. 'I'm not demanding a response—think about it over the weekend, let me know next week. I'm not rushing you into anything…'

He did this.

Kate had watched him work and she knew he did this.

He was both good cop and bad cop rolled into one— his words were like a relentless slap on alternate cheeks and then the confusion of a soothing palm. Only she had never been the recipient of his tactics before.

'Carry on juggling and living in dreary homes, paying someone a mortgage or rent.'

Slap.

'I'm offering a solution.'

Soothe.

'Promise yourself that you'll find Georgie a tutor in a couple of years to make up for the education she's missing…'

Slap.

'I can help you do better for Georgie.'

Soothe.

'And sex isn't part of the deal. I don't need to pay you for that.'

Slap.

'We can make love because we *want* to…'

He soothed her not with words but with his mouth, kissing her hard till she was too dizzy to think, muddling her, blurring all the edges. And then those hands were back, only lower, visiting a place they had never been, and had she had time to think she might have guessed that tenderness would be his next weapon, that his hands would gently beguile, but this was Aleksi and she'd just been soothed.

His fingers were precise, insistent, the pad of his thumb bringing her rapidly close to a place she had never shared with another, his mouth on her neck sucking her, almost bruising her, his other hand at his zipper and…

What did this man do to her?

Whatever it was—he just did.

She was putty in his warm, skilful hands.

She was strong and independent and a survivor—

yet in this, only in this, she was weak and needy and it was delicious.

'Take it off.' He wanted to see her, but his hands were too busy. He felt her momentarily freeze, but he wanted this. He had only had glimpses before, and he wanted the full view now. His mouth was nuzzling her breasts, his forehead butting and pushing the fabric of her dressing gown apart, and he did not care if she was embarrassed—did not give a thought to her hang-ups about her figure. All he could think of was her, and the lush spill of flesh as she shrugged off her robe, and he was lost.

Sex for Aleksi was an escape, but this was different. He could hear the little whimpers from her throat and feel the swell of her breasts in his mouth, feel this shy, guarded woman ripple into sensual life. And he wasn't escaping— he was gone. Lost in a world that was absent from pain and the bleak abyss of confusion. He remembered her soft lips last night and he wanted her to have the same.

'Aleksi, no…'

It wasn't a no that meant yes, and it wasn't a no that meant no. It was a no that said she could never enjoy it, a no that said this was not how he could pleasure her— because, naked on her kitchen bench, she felt the world coming back into focus. She felt as big and as bulky and as shiny and red as a Russian nesting doll—until he cracked that image with his mouth, dispelled it with a flick of his tongue, and eked from her the prettier woman inside. And then he did it again, till she was back in her head and alive in her body.

It was perhaps the abstinence from medication, Aleksi concluded, that had ended his abstinence from a more basic, once frequent pleasure.

It could not be *her*, could it? For Aleksi relied on no one. And yet...

There was no one else he would consider entering unprotected, yet he relished that thought now.

'Aleksi, please...' She wanted him as she had never wanted another. She wanted—no, needed to finally know the bliss of him inside her. Yet he wouldn't give her that satisfaction just yet.

He would give her another kind first.

Aleksi knew how to pleasure women. He had been taught, and he had listened well. God, but he'd loved those lessons. He listened to the moans and the trip of the rhythm in his lovers' breathing and there was always an unseen smile of triumph on his busy lips as he took her to the edge—except there were no mechanics in play today. Aleksi was as lost as she.

He could feel her orgasm, he could hear it and taste it, feel the beats of her climax on his lips, and there was no smile of triumph, just unadulterated satisfaction in his mind. Her pleasures were his—till a lush, greedy selfishness invaded.

And she shared in that selfishness.

The pure pleasure of an individual want that *could* be shared. Her nails dug into his shoulders, pushing him away, pulling him in, and she was writhing as he broke her open further, to reveal the prettiest of them all, to expose a Kate that she hadn't known was there.

A Kate who sobbed and begged and whimpered and relished. And still, even as she gathered herself up, even as she tried to put all the little Kates back inside themselves, he did not relent.

Oh, he dragged his mouth up her stomach to her neck, he held her as she came back to the world, but he did not abate. She was weak, and she wanted to regroup. Her head was on his shoulder now, but he pushed it back.

He smiled at her, and then he slipped down the zipper of his pants, unfurled his magnificent self—not discreetly, instead very deliberately—and she felt the startle of a starter's gun. Staring down at his glorious erection, she felt as if she were being propelled, unready, out of the gate—she wanted to slow down, to savour, to come back to the world after the decadent escape his lips had allowed her. Yet there he was.

Her boss, her dream, and now her lover.

She wanted to discuss, to think, to question—only not as much as she wanted him.

Wanted more than the shudder of an orgasm and the freedom of exploration.

He *was* beautiful.

Kisses in the dark didn't do him justice.

He was at her entrance, and she ran a finger around the tip of him, felt a helpless excitement at his rare beauty, and her own, too.

Why didn't she feel shy under such intense scrutiny?

Why was only a teeny, irrelevant part of her thinking of the slim, childless beauties he must be so much more used to?

Because his delight in her was so obvious.

He stroked his tip along her pretty, wet place and she shuddered involuntarily.

So he stroked her again and again, and let her glimpse just how good this was going to be, made her squirm with fresh want till he was sure she was more than ready.

'Please.' She was begging now. 'Aleksi, please.'

But since when did Aleksi play nice?

'All this can be yours.'

She'd never know the massive effort it took for him
to step back from her, to somehow contain himself, to
get himself back into his pants and pull up his zipper—
but he had been ruthless at getting his own way for a very
long time, and Aleksi *really* wanted things his way now.

'You—!' She didn't say it—she didn't have to. All
he did was shrug.

'Let me know on Monday.' She could see the scratches
from her nails on his back as he turned and pulled on his
shirt as her phone rang. 'Are you going to get that?'

She wouldn't have—except it was her sister.

And she wished—even as she heard what was said,
even as she acknowledged that her sister was absolutely
right to have rung—just wished the call had come ten
minutes later. Because what she heard made it incredibly hard to be brave, to refuse, to turn down
Aleksi's once-in-a-lifetime offer.

'It's Georgie.' As she replaced the receiver, even if
she loathed him at this moment, she knew he was
human. Even if she wanted to be brave for a little while
longer, where Georgie was concerned she simply
couldn't. 'She wet the bed, she's in tears. She didn't
want to upset me.'

'About what?'

'She's being bullied.'

'Bullied?'

Kate's heart was in her throat. 'I knew she didn't fit
in. I know the other children can be a bit mean to her.
But they actually pinch her. They hide her glasses. They
throw her lunch in the sandpit. They call her names. She
just told my sister. She didn't want to tell me because
she knows there's nothing I can do…'

Always—no matter how busy his day, no matter

what was going on his life—always he took time to hear about Georgie. Only this morning he didn't. Instead, Kate watched as he patted the pockets of his jacket and looked for his phone—then remembered he'd thrown it away.

'I need a phone.'

'That's all you can say?' she asked, hurt beyond belief.

'I could say plenty, Kate.' Instead he took out his chequebook and put that impossible figure into words and then seven figures, and then tore it out of the book and placed it on the table. 'But you already have the answer.'

She did.

And what mother wouldn't sell her soul for her daughter? Kate tried to reason. At least this way she wouldn't be beholden to him for years—wouldn't be dangling on a string, nervous to answer back in case he fired her, worrying for the next twelve years that he might up and relocate to Europe or...

Oh, there were many reasons to take it, but only then did it dawn on her—only then did she acknowledge what was really stopping her. Only then did the truth she had tried to deny for years hit her.

It had been easy to blame Georgie for her lack of relationships—easy to say she was too busy for romance, that she didn't want a partner invading their lives. Oh, there had been so many reasons, so many excuses, and all, in part, had been true.

Yet there was a bigger truth.

From the day Aleksi Kolovsky had stepped off the plane and run a bored eye over her swollen stomach she had been attracted to him.

From the day he had walked into the maternity ward and plucked her and Georgie from the pitying stares and the incessant beat of loneliness she had held a soft spot for him.

But more than that—oh, so much more than that.

She stared for a dangerous second into eyes that were as grey and murky as the ocean after a storm, saw the beauty and the danger and the hidden depths and the strange pull that always, always dragged her in. Then she saw the mouth that both kissed and cursed, the supreme package that was Aleksi, a man who offered her escape while warning her not to love him—except his warnings came too late. Nearly five years too late, in fact. There were no hatches left to batten down, no time for rapid preparation.

The storm that was Aleksi Kolovsky had already hit, already invaded.

It was quite possible that she already loved him.

CHAPTER SIX

'I DON'T have to go back?'

Georgie's eyes shone with a hope that had been missing for a long time. Kate had left Aleksi and driven two hours to the country where her sister Julie lived, and had broken the news to her daughter.

'I don't ever have to go back to that school?'

'No, you don't.'

It was such a relief to tell her. Oh, Kate knew running away from problems wasn't the answer, but watching her daughter struggle and struggle just to belong, watching her spark fade, wasn't the answer either.

Telling her about Aleksi was harder.

She was so accepting, so delighted, so *happy* with the news that Kate found it hard to meet her sister's eyes.

'You're a dark horse!' Julie grinned when Kate joined her in the kitchen. 'God, Kate, this is fantastic. I'm so happy for you.'

'It's early days.'

'You're getting engaged!' Julie refused to be anything less than delighted for her sister, and wrapped her in a huge embrace. 'After all you've been through, I'm just so glad to see you happy. Now, go!' Julie said.

'We'll have Georgie while you sort everything out. You go and do what you have to.'

Julie had no idea, Kate realised as she drove from her sister's, how hard those words might hit her.

'Come in.'

Aleksi was dressed casually now.

Or as casually as a Kolovsky could manage.

In black jeans and a black T-shirt, with his hair wet from a shower and his jaw unshaven, Kate realised as she stepped into his stunning home that he was also perhaps just a touch uncomfortable.

'How did Georgie take the news?' he wanted to know.

'She's delighted.' Kate struggled to keep the unhappiness from her voice; she was a willing participant in this ruse, she reminded herself. Only this *so* wasn't what she had wanted.

'I'll show you around.'

She had never been to his home, although she had sat outside it in a car a couple of times, to be brought up to speed on a few things on Aleksi's way to catch a flight.

She had never, though, been invited inside, and from what she knew few women were.

Aleksi lived outside of the city. It had always surprised her. Such an eligible bachelor should surely have penthouse city views. When he needed to be close by work, or when he brought a woman back, he used hotels. It shouldn't have surprised her, really—after all, she had once worked for Levander, who had chosen to live full-time in a luxury hotel.

'I'm not a trauma doctor like my brother,' Aleksi had once said. 'I don't need to be three minutes' drive away from work. An emergency for me can be dealt with online.'

And so he showed her around. It was an amazing home, sun-drenched and tastefully furnished. The jarrah floors echoed her steps as she walked around. Her eyes took in the huge white sofas and the modern artwork that hadn't been purchased with a five-year-old in mind! Every room offered views of the bay, and it didn't end there—there was a pool, tennis courts, a gym, and if that didn't satisfy there was always the beach a mere step away.

'This is us.' He gave a tight smile as he indicated the master bedroom, and stood watching her cheeks burn as her eyes took in the bed that was centre stage. 'There's plenty of wardrobe space...'

Except she wasn't really worried about that!

Kate peered into the *en-suite* bathroom, to the spa and double shower, and she caught a strong scent of his cologne and an intimate glimpse into the private world of Aleksi—glass bottles and heavy brushes lined up in the control room where he prepared himself for each day. She was almost dizzy with the thought that for now she would be sharing it with him. Rather than dwell on that, she walked back through the bedroom, stepped out of the French doors and onto the decking area.

'The view's amazing.' Port Phillip Bay was a vast horseshoe that spread from Queenscliffe on one end to the sharp peaks of Melbourne's city buildings on the other, and Alexi's house sat in between, with each destination a possibility. She could see a pier nearby, and tried to hazard which one, but then she looked to the left and there was another. The water was so close she could hear it lap, lap, lap, and then swish as it pulled out.

'Do you swim in the bay?' He was standing beside her and she struggled to make light conversation.

'I prefer the pool,' he replied. He gave the view just a cursory glance. 'I suppose it is nice when it storms.'

'It's wonderful now!' Kate said, but Aleksi just shrugged.

'You get used to it.'

She'd never get used to it.

Even after the weekend, even after Georgie had been enrolled in her new school, ready to start midweek, even after Kate had been back at her desk for a little while on the Tuesday afternoon, there was still no getting used to anything—and not just for her either.

'Kate! *Kate?*' She could hear the incredulity in Nina's voice and then worse, far worse, the bitchy ring of her laughter. Aleksi's office door was slightly open, but even had it been closed, the stench of her words would have seeped through. 'Now I really have heard it all. Tell me, Aleksi, how is getting engaged to that bumbling whale with her illegitimate daughter supposed to convince the board you're serious about preserving our elite name?' Aleksi must have moved to close the door, but Nina halted him. 'If she really is joining our family, Aleksi, she may as well hear it. You could have any woman and you chose *her*—are the doctors quite sure that there is no brain damage after your accident?'

He had hated his mother for decades.

Not a door-slamming, palpable hatred, more an apathetic one that simmered away silently.

He cared so little for Nina, and with such good reason, that perhaps it would have been wiser to walk away after his father's death. Yet he had stayed and risen to the challenge of running the House of Kolovsky on the death of his father. After Levander had had enough of it, and Iosef didn't want it at all, Aleksi had stepped up and taken control.

He liked the power, the life, the buzz.

Or he had done.

If his brain had been damaged in the accident, Aleksi was almost grateful for it—for now he could almost see.

Almost.

The ring was on her finger, Kate's possessions were in his home, she was picking up Georgie soon, and the little girl would start her new school tomorrow. The press were about to be informed but first, though—as it was in normal families, right?—he shared the news with his mother.

'The board will never buy it,' Nina scoffed.

'This isn't for the board.' Aleksi leant back in his chair. 'This is for me. Since the accident, I've realised how much Kate—'

'Oh, please.' Nina scorned. '*You*, taking on some other man's child? *You*, a parent?' Nina laughed. She just threw her head back and laughed at the very idea. 'How much are you paying her? Then again,' she mused, 'it wouldn't take much! She'd be grateful just to share your bed and get free board...'

Where *had* the apathy gone? Aleksi's formidable temper was usually saved for the boardroom, but today he stood from his chair, walked over to where his mother sat and stared at her—stared into those pale blue eyes—and the anger that usually seethed deep within him bubbled to the surface, even though Nina was too foolish to see it.

'When I had my accident,' Aleksi said slowly, 'she was there every day for me.'

'Because you *pay* her to be!'

'When I was in the Caribbean she called. She—'

'Because, like every other woman in Melbourne, she's crazy about you.' Nina was as hard as nails. 'You don't have to get engaged to the halfwit. Are you really telling me that her child is moving in too? That the slut is bringing her—'

'When I watch Kate with her daughter—' he spoke over Nina's filth, his voice slowly rising '—I see, for the first time, how a mother *should* behave.' He was standing over her now. 'I see how a parent *should* care for their child.' Then he stopped. Not a word more was uttered, not a hand raised, but he stared at his mother till she blinked with nervousness. He opened his mouth and then closed it again, because if he spoke now he would annihilate her. And maybe she sensed it, because only when he had walked back to his desk did Nina find the bravado to speak again—her voice not quite so assured now.

'If you do care for her, Aleksi, then what the hell are you doing? The press will crucify her.' Her voice was almost sympathetic. 'There will be huge interest in the engagement.'

'Kate can handle it,' Aleksi said, but though his voice was sure he himself was not. For the first time guilt was trickling in. He was more than used to the regular probes into his private life, and the girls he usually dated were delighted at any publicity—but Kate?

'What about her child?' Nina prodded again, smothering a satisfied smile as she found her son's buttons and pushed them, though he tried to hide it. 'Of course if you are in love, if this is what you want, then this is what you must do—but to bring an innocent child into the glare of publicity… Well, I hope you are very sure of your feelings for them both.'

Aleksi wasn't the only one whose heart was plummeting as Nina spoke.

Kate's shame and anger at Nina's initial reaction was now being replaced by guilt—fear, even. Because, no matter what she could deal with, she didn't want it to impact on her daughter. Yet on her way to work she had stopped at the school. Loath to cash the cheque, still not a hundred percent sure of her decision, Kate had paid the first term's tuition with the very last of her savings and bought the uniform and books with her emergency credit card. And then, when panic had again overwhelmed her, she had asked to be shown the classroom once more. The sight of it had temporarily soothed her nerves.

This was the right decision.

It was the education her daughter needed.

As Aleksi had said, relationships broke up all the time—but at least Georgie's future was secured.

'Your choice, Aleksi…'

Kate could almost see in her mind's eye Nina shrug her shoulders, and then, of course, she moved onto business.

'Have you got the Krasavitsa projections?'

'Sorry?'

'You said you'd have them.' Nina was curt. 'I want to go through them.' There was a pause, an interminable pause, and Kate sat at her desk frowning as Nina continued. 'Don't try and mess me about, Aleksi. You assured me I'd have them well in advance of the meeting…'

'One moment.'

'You do have them?'

'Of course.' He walked out his office and to her desk.

She could see his pallor, and was relieved when he closed the door behind him. 'I'm sure you heard all that.'

'I couldn't exactly *not* hear,' she said dryly.

'Are you sure about this?' Aleksi looked over to her, and it was Kate's turn to be angry.

'It's a bit late for concern now, Aleksi—I've already told Georgie, and she knows she's starting her new school tomorrow. I'm picking her up from Julie's in an hour, to bring her to her new home, and all of a sudden you're concerned for us.' She glared at him. 'You promise me one thing,' she said. 'Never, to anyone, do you reveal this is a ruse.'

'I won't.' He meant it.

'Swear it, Aleksi,' Kate said. 'I'll sell myself for my daughter's sake, but she must never, ever know about it.'

'And she won't.' Aleksi said, 'We fell in love, remember?'

Somehow she felt as if he were mocking her—or rather, Kate realized, it was the impossibility of his words.

'When the time comes, we'll say we fell out of love. That when I got well I saw that perhaps the accident had made me maudlin for a while…' He gave her a smile, tried to reassure her, but she couldn't return it. 'We'll talk about this later. Right now I need the Krasavitsa projections…' He raked a hand through his hair—he still hadn't had it cut. 'I need you to get straight onto it. I'll tell Nina they're nearly ready, but you'll need to give it your immediate—'

'They're done,' Kate interrupted him, clicking a button on her computer. From behind where he stood the figures he needed started printing. 'You still need to go through them.'

'I need the original figures. Not the ones—'

'I've got them for you.' There was just the tiniest flicker of a frown on his face, but then normal services resumed and Aleksi picked up the paperwork and scanned the figures. It was Kate frowning now. 'You don't remember do you?'

He didn't answer.

'Aleksi, you don't remember her asking for these earlier…'

'Shh…' He hushed her, as he often did when concentrating, but Kate would not be silenced. There had been too many small things he'd missed—too many details that could no longer be glossed over.

'I'll be going home, then.' As she stood, only then did he look up. 'I want to oversee the removalists.'

'When will you be back?'

'Should I really come back to work?' Kate's eyes were wide. 'I'm supposed to be your fiancée.'

'You know I need you here.'

'You don't remember her asking, do you?' Kate asked again, and she saw him swallow, saw his eyes dart to the door to check that it was closed. 'You don't remember Nina asking for those figures.'

'Of course I do,' he said, giving her a scornful look.

He could never admit it.

Never.

Not once had he admitted to any weakness, and now, when he most needed to be strong…

'Aleksi?' Her eyes were worried. 'Your hair needs a cut.'

'I'm busy.'

'Every fortnight, without fail—'

'It suits me longer,' he said, daring her to contradict him.

'Since when,' Kate said, walking over, taking one of his hands, 'did you cut your own nails?' He withdrew his hand and she wondered if she was right. Yes, his hair was just a touch longer, and, yes, he had been phenomenally busy last week—too busy perhaps for a manicure? Yet this was Aleksi Kolovsky…

He never forgot, never missed an appointment at the salon. He made everyone else look scruffy with his fastidiousness. No one looking at this elegant coiffed man would see a hair out of place, would see him as anything other than utterly and completely in control.

Except she loved him—maybe.

Which meant *she* noticed.

'They can't know. The board can't know.' Aleksi voice was hoarse. 'My mother—it would be like blood in the water. They'd feed like sharks…'

'She will know soon,' Kate said, because after all surely his mother loved him, too?

'She mustn't.'

'What's wrong, Aleksi?'

He hated this revelation—hated standing in front of her and admitting…what? That there was a flaw in his armour and he couldn't bear it? He couldn't stand weakness, abhorred it, so he silenced her, pressed his mouth to hers and did what he still did brilliantly—because this he could never, ever forget how to do.

This made it possible.

His mouth, his taste, his scent, his maleness pressing into her, chased all the fears and doubts away.

As his tongue played with hers, as his animal magnetism drew her into him, the impossible was made easy.

He obliterated doubt with one stroke of his tongue.

She must not care, must brace herself for walking

away, but while she stayed *this* made it do-able—his kiss, his touch, the only things that made sense.

His fingers were in her hair, his hands insistent, and then they moved down over her back to caress her hips. He made her both weak and strong. Strong because he made anything possible, and weak because he could take her any time he wanted.

His erection wedged into her groin and she gasped into his mouth.

'Aleksi, how long…?' Nina opened the door of his office, her voice trailing off as she caught her son in a passionate clinch. But she was the mother of Kolovsky sons, and had long got over any embarrassment. 'I need those papers,' she said, as Aleksi released Kate from his potent grip. 'Assuming, of course, that you have them.' Her eyes held just a fraction of challenge, and Kate felt sure that Nina knew there was something amiss with her son.

'Here.' Normally he would never have handed them over without checking them carefully first, but Aleksi reassured himself that Kate had prepared them so he trusted they were right.

And then he quickly checked them himself.

He trusted no one.

'You haven't signed them off,' Nina said. 'I'm not going to work on figures that you haven't approved. Here…' She headed to Kate's desk and picked up a pen, which Aleksi had no choice but to take. After just a beat of a pause, he signed off the figures with his usual flourish.

Nina caught Kate's eye. 'We will dine tonight…' She gave Kate a smile that didn't meet her eyes. 'To celebrate.'

'It's Georgie's first night in her new home. I really don't want to take her out,' Kate replied.

'You don't bring children to dinner! Ring the nanny agency.' She took the forms from Aleksi and without another word headed out.

'That should keep her quiet for a while,' Aleksi said, once she was safely out of earshot.

'It's lucky that I had them on the computer.' Kate said, but her voice was far from even. The thought of getting a stranger to look after Georgie had her in a spin. Only now was the true reality of being a part of the Kolovsky world starting to hit home. But her thoughts were sideswiped as Aleksi responded to her comment.

'I meant,' he drawled, 'the kiss.'

It would have been kinder to Kate had he simply slapped her.

CHAPTER SEVEN

'SHE'LL be fine,' Aleksi said with a sigh, as for the third time in as many minutes Kate questioned whether they really had to go out. 'The whole point of this exercise is that we are seen.'

'It's her first night here,' Kate pointed out, although Georgie really did seem fine.

Even though she had only met Aleksi perhaps a handful of times, when Kate had had to come in at weekends or in the evenings and had had no choice but to bring her, he had always been lovely to Georgie, and Georgie, in turn, thought he was fantastic.

Of course Kate had played it all down as she'd shown her daughter around her new home. Yes, Aleksi was her boyfriend, she'd told Georgie. It wasn't a complete lie— she was, after all, crazy about him. He filled her every waking thought and then came back for a nightly visit to her dreams, and as of tonight she'd be sleeping beside him.

'Will you get married?' Georgie had asked, and only then had it tipped into a lie. Because, like love, marriage for Aleksi was something that would never happen.

'Let's just see how we all get on together first.'

'But he's bought you a ring...' Georgie's eyes fell

on the emerald-cut diamond that alone could pay for her education and beyond. 'That means you're going to get married.'

There was no easy answer to logic combined with a five-year-old's dreams of how the world should be, so Kate had stayed silent, and now Georgie was playing on the tennis court with Sophie, her new nanny, shrieking with laughter as she patted back balls while Kate prepared herself for a glittering night with the Kolovsky family.

A night out she didn't want.

'I thought the exercise was to show how responsible the new Aleksi was,' Kate said, still hoping for a last-minute reprieve.

'Which is why I've paid for a top nanny who's going to play games and have fun with her.' Aleksi clearly didn't see what the problem was. 'Hell, we'll only be a couple of hours. The last thing I want is a prolonged night with my family.' He was knotting his tie. Backwards and forwards he slid the silk through the knot, then cursed in frustration as with each attempt it fell apart.

'Do you want a hand?'

'I don't need you to dress me,' Aleksi hissed.

Kate bit her tongue, because she knew he was in pain. Knew because since that night he hadn't taken a single painkiller. But it was more than that. Since the office, since Nina's cruel observations, his mood had been black. So much for a warm welcome to their new home!

And so much for sensitivity. When she was sliding on her dress and struggling with the zip Aleksi turned around. 'You can't wear that.'

'Excuse me?'

'You wore that at last year's Christmas party.'

'Should I be touched that you remember?'

'I remember,' Aleksi said, walking over, 'because you had the tag hanging out at the back all night—just as you have now.' He flicked it with distaste. 'My real fiancée would not shop at a high street store.'

'And no doubt your *real* fiancée wouldn't have this dress size,' Kate said sharply, mortified as she tucked in the label. 'I must have forgotten to pack my designer wardrobe.'

'Buy one!' Aleksi said. 'I gave you a more than generous allowance...' Then his eyes narrowed. 'I suppose you're saving that for your nest egg.'

'It just doesn't feel right,' she admitted, 'cashing the cheque...'

'So you're doing this for nothing?' Aleksi gave her a wide-eyed look. 'You're here simply out of the goodness of your heart?'

She'd seen him so often like this at work, with his family—never once had it been aimed at her.

'Tomorrow Nikita will sort out your wardrobe—she is the top designer at Kolovsky.' He watched in exasperation as she used the tongs in her hair. 'Why the hell didn't you get someone in to do that? You know what to do—you know how to prepare...'

Yes, she did.

For Alexi's dates Kate would often organise the hairdresser, the beautician, the day spa. Which would all have been rather lovely for her—except Aleksi's usual dates didn't generally have a nanny to interview. Despite the fact Aleksi had said an interview was unnecessary. Nor did they have an almost five-year-old who wanted her mum to sit with her while she had dinner, and to spend a little while exploring her new home.

So instead she'd had to make do with a fifteen-minute make-over to transform her from drab to almost fab—well, perhaps not by Kolovsky standards. As a single mum Kate was rather used to performing great feats in record time—she did it each morning, after all, just to get to work. Now she slicked on foundation, dotted her cheeks with blush, and attempted massive renovations on her eyes.

Aleksi watched, his impatience mounting with each passing minute.

He'd finally knotted his tie.

His hair, even though it might require a cut, fell into exquisite shape, and he slapped on some cologne and tried not to think about the snakepit he was exposing her to tonight. Wished he had thought and had packed her off for a makeover—the press would be there, his mother would make sure of that, and Kate, with her high street dress and homemade hairdo, would cause a frenzy.

'A little empathy would be nice.' She glared at him as she stuffed lipstick and mints and a mobile phone into her evening bag. 'And before you tell me to buy myself some from the generous allowance you're giving me, I'm not talking about a perfume!'

'You've got a run in your stockings.' Aleksi pointed out, then stood there, lips pursed, as she took off her high shoes, ripped off her stockings and replaced her shoes.

'What?' Kate flashed. 'Am I supposed to whip out a spare pair?' Aleksi said nothing, but Kate was on a roll. 'Are my calves too pale to be seen out with you?'

He didn't like this grown-up game.

Didn't like watching her kiss Georgie goodnight and seeing how she left her mobile number *and* the restaurant number on the bench in the kitchen, because

Aleksi's silver fridge didn't possess a single magnet. Didn't like her assurance to Sophie that they'd be home well before midnight.

It had never been a factor for Aleksi before.

She could feel his tension as the driver pulled into the restaurant. She wasn't particularly surprised by it—after all, she had arranged a few family get-togethers in her time as both Levander's and Aleksi's PA, and neither brother had particularly embraced them.

This was different, though, and as the car pulled up, as she saw the throng of photographers waiting to greet them, Kate's nerves, which seemed to have been placed in temporary cold storage while she had dealt with the practicalities of Georgie and moving house, suddenly rapidly thawed and caught up.

This might be a charade for her and Aleksi, but for tonight, and for the next couple of months, this was real to everyone else.

This was her life.

And now, when she thought she might turn tail and run, he took her hand and moved in to speak quietly into the shell of her ear.

'You're going to be fine,' Aleksi soothed, his fingers smoothing a stray curl behind her ear. 'You look wonderful…'

And then he kissed her—except it tasted of deceit, and Kate wasn't stupid enough to believe his words were for her, that those tender gestures weren't for the cameras that were exploding outside the car, and she pulled away.

'It would have been nice…' she leant back in his arms, smiled into his eyes for the cameras and then spoke her truth '…if you could have said all this back at the house.'

'I thought it.' Aleksi didn't bat an eyelid, just smiled and played with her hair and lived the lie so well. 'Now I say it.'

As they stepped out, whether it was for the cameras' benefit or not, she was pathetically grateful for his arm around her shoulders as they walked the short but daunting distance to the restaurant. Kate never liked having her photo taken at the best of times, and right now it was possibly the worst of times as by happy manufactured coincidence Nina's car arrived just a moment behind them. She realised she was to greet her supposed future mother-in-law in front of the full glare of the press.

'So that was the delay in the car,' Kate turned and whispered in his ear. 'Aleksi, remind me again to never believe anything you say or do.'

He laughed—for the first time in a very long time, Aleksi laughed. There was no fooling Kate, and it was actually refreshing. He was also curiously proud of his fake fiancée as she handled Nina with far more aplomb than most could muster.

'Darling Kate!' Nina was at her false best, commandeering Kate as if she had missed her all her life, airkissing and cooing. Kate played the game too, even accepting the other woman's bony arm in hers as they were guided into the restaurant. Now, surely she should breathe—except the waiter was leading them through the safety of the packed restaurant, not to some exclusive, secluded corner, but back outside to the street they had just left.

'It's such a nice night.' Nina smiled maliciously. 'I

thought we should eat outside. Don't be shy,' she chided Kate, 'it's just a few cameras—the world wants to see the young lovers…'

They were seated. Despite the short notice, Nina had done well. There were a couple of aunts, Iosef was there with his wife Annie, and also the beautiful Kolovsky daughter, Annika, with her handsome husband, Ross.

It hurt to watch. For Kate it actually hurt to watch the way they pored over the menu, the way the private conversation continued despite the crowd—and the way Ross held Annika's hand the whole way through.

Love couldn't be manufactured and faked for the cameras, she thought with a flutter of panic, sipping her champagne, feeling every eye on her, and most of all feeling Nina just waiting for her to slip up. What mother would want to turn on her own son? Kate tried to fathom as Aleksi spoke with Ross, his new brother-in-law. What mother would so badly try to expose her son's faults for the sake of winning?

'What's wrong, Kate?' Nina asked pointedly. 'You look uncomfortable.'

She couldn't do this, Kate realized. She couldn't sit and be demure and plastic—even if she was a fake fiancée she was still herself, and for this charade to continue that was who she needed to be.

'I am uncomfortable,' Kate said, and the table fell silent. 'It must be the coat hanger I forgot to take out of my skirt.'

It was nice to see Nina's face falter for a second, but nicer—far, far nicer—was once again the rare sound of Aleksi's laughter, the feel of his hot hand closing around hers as he addressed his mother.

'See now why I love her?'

He didn't, of course, Kate told herself, reminded herself, insisted to herself, over and over again. Only now she was herself, now she was being who she really was, the night and the table were more lively. Even Iosef and Annie seemed a touch reluctant when Iosef's pager urgently sounded and they duly made their excuses.

'One of the benefits of being a doctor,' Aleksi remarked quietly, as he said goodnight to his brother and sister-in-law.

'Had I known it would be such a good night,' Iosef murmured to his twin, 'I would have arranged at least another hour.' He turned to Kate. 'It really has been nice meeting you.'

It was strange, Kate pondered, to kiss the cheek of a man who looked exactly like Aleksi, to smile and chat, to look into the same slate-grey eyes and yet feel nothing.

She almost wished she could ask them to swap—so she could get through this without emotion. Because one touch from Aleksi and her heart was on skid row.

Aleksi had dreaded this night, and no doubt would regret it in the morning, when the press did their savage best to mock the reunion and ridicule Kate, but to his absolute surprise he was enjoying himself in a way he never had with his family.

Oh, his mother was at her most irritating and caustic, but he was so proud of how Kate had just shrugged and carried on. There was no need to impress, he realized. She had this confidence, this strength that amazed him— a side to her he had never seen or appreciated before.

For the first time he was actually enjoying an evening with his family, and even Annika seemed to be relaxing—

until Nina introduced a new subject. 'I hear you are going to the UK,' she said to Aleksi, 'to try and dissuade Belenki.'

'I'm not just going to see him.' Aleksi didn't even look over to his mother as he spoke. 'I would like to meet Riminic, my new nephew…' Now he looked over to Nina and watched her face pale, watched as she reached for a glass of water.

'His name is Dimitri,' Nina croaked.

'My mistake,' Aleksi said. 'Are you going over to meet your new grandson?' he asked. 'Or doesn't a Detsky Dom orphanage boy count?'

'It's too soon.' Nina was having great trouble wearing her false smile, and all the aunts were sitting in rigid silence, awaiting her response. 'Levander and Millie said they don't want him to be crowded, that they don't want too much fuss made.'

'Well, you'll never be guilty of that.'

'Aleksi's an expert in children suddenly.' Nina smiled to the table. 'Next time you must bring along Georgie. We'd all love to meet her.'

You could have heard a pin drop.

'You've got a child?' It was Ross, Annika's husband, who broke the silence.

'Georgie.' Kate nodded.

'How old?' Annika's voice was curiously high.

'She's nearly five.'

'A lovely age.' Nina smiled falsely. 'She'll be thrilled that Mummy's engaged, no doubt—what little girl doesn't harbour the dream of being bridesmaid?'

'Aleksi…' Annika and Ross were ready to leave now; the night was wrapping up. 'Can I have a word?'

Of all his family, it was Annika he was closest to. He knew how hard things had been for her, the expectations that had been placed on her slender shoulders and how hard it must have been to turn her back on them. She was, to Nina's horror, finishing her nursing training, and was hoping to specialise in aged care—she amazed him too. Every day she grew stronger. Out of her family's clutches and in Ross's arms she grew stronger by the minute.

'Of course.'

'Away from…' Annika looked uncomfortable and frowned to Ross, who quickly flicked his eyes away. Aleksi's heart sank, and he shot Ross a black look for his betrayal.

He had been dreading this day.

Ross, a doctor, had seen Aleksi's X-Rays, showing old injuries, when he had been admitted to the hospital after the car crash—had confronted him about them. In a moment of weakness, and also to assure him that Annika hadn't suffered the same treatment from their father, Aleksi had confessed that he had been beaten in the past. Ross had promised never to reveal what he had said.

'Ross had no right!' Aleksi flared when they were out of earshot. 'I don't care if he's your husband—I hope his medical malpractice insurance—'

'What are you talking about, Aleksi?' Annika frowned. 'He's just worried—*I'm* worried.' She swallowed. 'Kate's got a daughter.'

'Georgie.' Aleksi nodded, relief whooshing through him. He kicked himself for overreacting, but he had been so sure Ross had revealed his past.

'When Mum rang…' Annika was clearly uncomfortable '…she said you were pulling some stunt but that we should be seen to be supportive. Look, I get that there are a lot of people you have to convince you are settling down, and I have no idea what Mum's up to, pretending to support you...'

'Don't worry about Kate and me.'

'I'm not.' She looked squarely at him. 'Kate seems lovely. She seems more than capable. If you are genuinely engaged then I couldn't be more delighted for you. If you're not...'

'Kate and I have worked together a long time,' Aleksi said. 'Only when I was injured did we realize—'

'Save it for the press,' Annika hissed, clearly not convinced. 'What I am saying is that if you two are just doing this to appease the board, if this is just some convenient arrangement... She has a *child*, Aleksi!'

'I am looking after Georgie,' he protested.

'So it's about the money for Kate, then?' Annika asked cynically.

'You don't know what you're talking about.'

'I know this much,' Annika flared, and Aleksi realised just how strongly his sister felt. 'If it's anything other than love guiding this, then you two had better think long and hard about Georgie. Do you really want a child caught up in all this? The press will give you both absolute hell if it comes out. Do you really want all this to land on a five-year-old?'

'She's sensible for her age,' he said defensively, although his heart was sinking with every sentence she uttered.

'Oh, so that's okay, then,' Annika sneered, and then her voice broke. 'She'll love you, too, Aleksi.'

'Annika—'

'No!' She would not be silenced. 'What little girl doesn't want a daddy? What little girl doesn't want to see her mum happy and live in a beautiful house?'

She shook her head at her brother. 'I've seen Kate looking at you. She's crazy about you, Aleksi, but that's her problem. Just don't break that little girl's heart, too.'

He had dismissed it when his mother had said it, but hearing Annika's raw plea had Aleksi more than uneasy. He looked over to where Kate sat, smiling, chatting, making light work of his mother, and he knew, as he had always known deep down, that Kate had feelings for him. So many women had. And then she turned around, caught his eye, and she smiled a smile that was just for him.

A smile that said, *Get me out of here.*

An intimate smile that was only passed between lovers.

He would hurt her.

Of that Aleksi was in no doubt—and now here was Annika, telling him that he would hurt Georgie, too.

'Be very careful,' Annika warned, only Aleksi wasn't listening. For him the night was over.

He summoned Kate and they were out of there, the cameras clicking again, Kate once again attempting to duck his kiss as they slipped into the back seat.

'We're supposed to be unable to keep our hands off each other,' Aleksi reminded her, but even as she tried to close her eyes and think of Kolovsky all she could see was the cheque still in her bag, waiting to be cashed.

She felt paid for.

'It's like kissing an aunt.' Aleksi gave in and brooded instead, sat drumming his fingers on the passenger door as they were driven back to his home.

But worse, far worse for Aleksi, was when they arrived home. All he wanted was to take her upstairs to drive out the warnings, to convince himself they were right to be doing what they were doing, to forget for just a little while that this was a dangerous game. As if sent to remind him, as they stepped into the hall Georgie stood at the top of the stairs, a teddy on her nightdress, her hair a mass of ringlets, and a very sorry nanny by her side.

'She wouldn't go to sleep till she knew you were home.'

'She's probably a little unsettled,' Kate said as Georgie came running down the stairs.

Georgie quickly corrected her mother—she wasn't unsettled; on the contrary she was absolutely *delighted* with her new home.

'We had supper by the pool and then we took Bruce for a walk on the beach.' She was chattering so fast she could hardly get the words out in order. 'There are hundreds of different channels on Aleksi's television; I saw you arriving at the dinner and they were talking about the wedding!'

'What was she doing watching the news?' Aleksi frowned to Sophie.

'It was just for a second. She was working out the remote…'

'She is not just to be plonked in front of the television—'

'Aleksi,' Kate broke in, 'I let her watch some. It's no big deal…'

'She's not even five yet,' Aleksi warned the nanny. 'She is not to watch the news.'

'Of course, Mr Kolovsky.' Sophie's face was purple with embarrassment. 'Come on, Georgie, let's get you to bed.'

'I'll take her,' Kate said, because that was what she wanted.

It was a thoroughly over-excited Georgie that she put

to bed, and it took for ever to get her to settle. Her new school uniform was hanging on the wardrobe door, as per Georgie's instructions, and she would have worn it to bed had Kate allowed it.

'I love it here,' Georgie whispered as Kate finally flicked the light off. 'Are you happy too?'

'Of course,' Kate said, and closing the bedroom door she let out a long breath, before walking along the hall to the bedroom, bracing herself to earn her keep.

'How is she?'

His suit lay in a puddle on the floor, and he lay in the bed. He didn't look up from scrolling through messages on his phone, and Kate felt suddenly shy.

She had never actually undressed in front of him. Usually, it just…well, happened. But now she stood in his vast bedroom, the bedside lights seemed to be blazing and because when packing she'd realised she truly couldn't bring *that*, her familiar tatty dressing gown was in a bin somewhere. Despite their previous intimacies, Kate just wasn't ready to undress in front of him, so instead she padded into the *en-suite* bathroom.

Her hair, of course, was everywhere. Her mascara was smudged beneath her eyes, her lipstick, despite the packaging's promise, had long, long since faded, and yet…

Her usually self-critical eyes blinked—because though she could see her faults there was something new there, something that had been missing too long. He had awoken something in her—intangible, yet somehow visible.

There was a glow that had been missing—a ripeness, a lushness, that she couldn't logically explain. As she peeled off her clothes and stepped on his scales they gave her the same old bad news—said it out loud, actually, and Kate jumped off in horror, hoping to God that Aleksi hadn't heard!

What to wear?

She stared at the neatly folded white towels that had been replaced since her shower this evening. There were bathrobes hanging against the door, as anonymous as in any hotel.

She was too nervous to go out there, so she lingered in brushing her teeth and taking off her make-up. Always till now their passion had been spontaneous, a wave that swept them up, only now she felt as if she were standing at the edge of Aleksi's glittering pool, nervous about just plunging in.

What to wear?

The question plagued her again. She didn't own a nightdress. The last time she had worn one was when Georgie had been born. Yes, she could put on a bathrobe, and then take it off when she got to bed. Brave, nervous, she opened the bathroom door. The overhead lights were off, but the dim bedside lights might just as well have been spotlights tracking her as she padded towards him, her body a contrary jumble of emotions, because she wanted him…so badly she wanted him…

Just not like this.

The French windows were open and she could hear the slow lap of the bay, except it didn't calm her a jot. She could feel his eyes on her as reached the bed and stood there.

'Are you going to wear your bathrobe to bed?'

She bit down on her lip and took it off in one fumbled motion that included lifting the sheet and sliding into bed.

She could smell his maleness, could feel his brooding mood, and she longed for the spontaneity of before—

for touches that just happened, not this manufactured simulation they had invented.

His kiss was skilled and practised, his hands insistent and probing, and she tried to tell herself she enjoyed it—tried to remind her body how just a few days ago it had craved this moment, had yearned for the weight of his body and the scratch of his thigh as he parted her legs. But her body refused to listen.

Oh, she kissed him back, moaned and made noises, but Aleksi had tasted the real Kate and knew he was getting a poor imitation of the woman he had so recently reduced to delicious begging.

And Aleksi was too proud to take favours.

'You're tired.' He rolled away from her.

'Yes.'

'It's been a long day,' Aleksi offered, and flicked off the bedside light.

'Yes.' She stared at the darkness, relieved and yet disappointed at the same time.

'They're in the bathroom cupboard, by the way,' Aleksi said, shifting onto his side to face away from her, and Kate closed her eyes at what came next. 'The headache tablets—no doubt you'll soon say you've got one.'

CHAPTER EIGHT

KRASAVITSA KATE

Aleksi stared at the headline, and then at the photo.

Always the papers crucified his dates. The sleekest, glossiest were caught mid-blink or at an unflattering angle, the write-ups were always scathing—all night he had dreaded Kate's face when she saw the cruel words and pictures at the breakfast table.

And yet here she was. On the front cover.

One strap of her dress falling slightly from her shoulder, her hair rippling down the other one, her head thrown back mid-laugh, her cleavage, her arms, her flesh so refreshing—but most surprising for Aleksi next to her was himself, and for once he was smiling. Not smirking, not grinning, but there *was* a smile on his usually stern features. As he stared at the photo he tried to recall that moment, what it was that had made Kate laugh, what it was that had made him smile—only, unusually, he couldn't narrow it down to one time.

Despite the tense atmosphere, despite the barbs and the comments and the claustrophobic air any family reunion of his usually fostered, last night there had also been moments like these.

Many of them.

'There's Mummy!' A smiling face peered over not his shoulder but his elbow. 'What's that word?'

'*Krasavitsa*,' Aleksi said. 'It means beautiful woman.'

'Well, I'm not feeling so *krasavitsa* this morning!' Kate headed for the kitchen bench to pour a coffee then, realising there was no need, instead walked over to the breakfast table, where the maid was pouring it for her. The table was positioned in a sun-drenched area, over-looking the pool and the tennis courts, the French doors were open, and as she sat before the generous feast, Kate wondered how he did it. Not a single fly buzzed around the pastries and spreads—no doubt Aleksi employed someone to ward them off from a suitable distance.

She couldn't meet his eyes so she concentrated on her breakfast, choosing some lovely fresh fruit and wonder-ing if she should treat the next two months as some kind of mini-health retreat—swimming each day, eating all the right things. She'd come out of this all glossy and gorgeous, even if she was lugging around a broken heart.

'When you marry my mum—' Georgie's words hauled her from her introspection '—will I be a bridesmaid?'

Horrified, she looked over to Aleksi, wondering what his scathing response would be, but Aleksi just smiled into his newspaper.

'Georgie…' It was Kate who answered. 'I told you—we're just seeing how things work out.' Her eyes were urgent as they darted to Aleksi's, hoping he would understand that marriage wasn't on Kate's agenda, but that she couldn't include her daughter in the charade and expect her not to voice the truth.

'I know that,' Georgie said, making puddles of milk on the table as she ate her cereal. 'Okay.' She looked again at Aleksi and rephrased her question. '*If* you marry my mum—will I be a bridesmaid?'

Oh, God, she could feel every follicle on her head jump. Her teaspoon rattled against her cup as she stirred her coffee and, worse, she could feel the sting of tears, too.

Georgie was so happy, so accepting, so trusting—and it was her own mother who was setting her up for this hurt.

'I am quite sure,' Aleksi said, his voice kind because it was Georgie asking, 'that when your mother marries you will be her absolute first choice as a bridesmaid.'

Delighted with his response, Georgie finished her breakfast and scampered off to put on her new uniform as Kate sat with the unfamiliar feeling of not having to scramble together a lunch box—it was already packed and in Georgie's bag, Sophie informed her, and then she headed out to her little charge, which left Kate and Aleksi alone.

'I've been thoughtless.'

Kate frowned. Aleksi was never thoughtless—arrogant, perhaps, rude, often, but his words were never without thought.

'I am used to…' He shrugged as he tried to locate the word, except there wasn't just one. 'I'm not used to being with someone who has other things to think about.'

'Other things apart from you, you mean!' Kate tossed back, and when he smiled she couldn't help just a little one too.

'I am usually the sole focus,' he admitted. 'You have moved home, changed your daughter's school, dealt with your family, with mine, with your daughter and all the changes she is going through…' Kate blinked at this rare glimpse of sensitivity. 'It is no wonder you *were* tired last night.' And then she realised he wasn't being sensitive. He was about to more clearly spell out the rules. 'So you need to take things more easy—don't worry about going into work.'

'I'm not to work?' she gasped.

'You're my fiancée. You can hardly be my PA too.'

'I thought you *needed* me working!'

Aleksi closed his eyes for a brief second. He did not like being argued with, but more than that he didn't want to examine the truth behind what he was saying— that he might more simply just need *her*.

'My needs are more basic than that, Kate,' he settled for saying instead. 'You need some time to get used to your new surroundings, to concentrate on Georgie, make sure she is settling in okay.' He glanced at the bathrobe. 'To sort out your wardrobe and to get some rest.'

She looked away, blushing at his innuendo but Aleksi hadn't finished yet.

'Oh, and Kate…' He waited and he waited and he waited, until finally she looked at him. He wanted to ensure he had her full attention as he addressed a pertinent point. 'You haven't banked that cheque.'

She felt a blush spread over her cheeks. 'I meant to,' she said. 'I'll do it today.'

'Good,' he clipped, and then she frowned, because he smiled.

A real smile.

Only it wasn't for her.

'Wish me luck!' Georgie stood beaming in her new shoes and school uniform and little straw hat.

'You don't need luck,' Aleksi told her. 'You're going to have a great day in your new school. But good luck anyway.'

'Do you think they'll like me?' Georgie checked with Aleksi as Kate sorted out her socks, that were already slipping.

'Do *you* like you?' Aleksi asked.

'Yes!' Georgie laughed.

'Then you've got a friend already.'

It was times like that, Kate thought as she and Georgie were driven to school, when it would be so easy to love him—except that wasn't allowed in their rules.

Still, if ever she had doubted as to whether what they were doing was right, Kate had some confirmation that morning that they were.

Oh, it was all new, and of course Georgie's little classmates were curious about her, but there was a different air to the place—a feeling of rightness as Georgie proudly showed off her pencil case contents to the little girl sitting next to her, who did the same.

'She'll fit right in,' Mrs Heath, her new teacher, assured Kate. 'Go home and don't worry.'

And she would have done that—except just as she felt she could breathe and didn't feel like bursting into tears there was something new to worry about. Two vertical lines appeared between her eyes as she crossed the playground, reading the unexpected text she'd just received.

Can we meet—need to talk.
Say hi to Georgie from me.

And then, even as she erased it, another text pinged in.

As soon as you can. Really do need to speak with you.

She rang Craig straight back. 'There's not much to say!'

'Kate, just listen.'

'No, *you* listen.' She was beyond furious with Georgie's father as she stalked towards her driver. 'Not a single word from you for months and now you want to talk!'

'I read in the paper about you and Kolovsky,' Craig said. 'I'm pleased for you, Kate, it's just…'

'Just what?'

'I can't say this on the phone.'

'Then it can't be said,' Kate responded curtly, then ended the call and turned off her phone.

'Everything okay?' Phillip, her driver, checked.

'It's fine,' Kate said, then forced a smile. 'It's early days yet, but she seems really happy to be there.'

Craig wasn't going to spoil it, Kate swore to herself. If it was money he was after—and when *hadn't* he needed a loan?—then he'd better not be holding his breath.

She was doing this for Georgie.

Not Craig, not Aleksi. She was doing it for *Georgie*.

And maybe, Kate conceded, she was also doing this for herself—though not for the money.

She was, Kate realised, buying a little bit of time with Aleksi, for herself.

It should have been a relief not to work.

She *was* tired.

And not just from the whirlwind that had taken place in her life in the past few days.

As the days ticked by, and her stomach turned from paper-white to lobster-pink, to honey-brown as she lay on the lounger between trips to boutiques and beauticians, it was, Kate reflected, no wonder she'd spent the last few years feeling permanently exhausted.

It took three full-time staff and one part-time person, on top of Aleksi's regular crew, to perform all that she routinely had.

Sophie sorted out books and clothes and homework and readers and, concerned about her charge's love for processed cheese and juice boxes, bizarrely spent entire mornings while Georgie was at school sculpting carrots into mini-carrots and celery into mini-celery and making heart and star-shaped ice cubes to liven up the water for Georgie's after-school snack!

Bruce was returned unrecognisable from the groomers. Shampooed, washed and clipped, he was walked twice a day by Kate's occasional driver, but lay mainly dozing and scented on the decking as Kate tried to summon the energy to flop into the pool.

And, of course, with a child in the house an extra cleaner was employed.

Yes, the days were full of pampering and indulgences—like catching up on the pile of books she had meant to read. But there was only so many treatments at the day spa and only so much lounging one could do.

The afternoons were the most wonderful.

She always waiting at the school gates for Georgie—even though Sophie thought it was her job. Kate could never willingly miss the sight of her daughter in a sea of children, smiling, laughing as she came out at the end of the day, once even waving a party invitation. It was so nice to take ages over her reader, to go for a walk on the beach together.

It was the nights that were hell.

Last night they'd been out to dinner, holding hands across the table, with a kiss for the cameras, but then, after a blistering row, when she really had had a headache, Aleksi had stormed off to the city and spent the night in a hotel—at least that was what she'd hopelessly assumed. Now he was back, had taken the afternoon off work, and was in the blackest of moods.

He thumped balls over the net as she lay on the lounger trying to relax, trying not to turn on her phone and see if Craig had called *again*. Kate knew she was a bit of a poor excuse for a bought and paid for fiancée—to Aleksi's intense annoyance she jumped out of her skin every time he came near her. It was her mind that didn't want this, battling with her body that so desperately did. No, she was a very poor excuse because, despite her extremely pressing finances and having already received a bill from the school for next term's fees, she still hadn't cashed his cheque.

He really was pounding those tennis balls; every time the machine slammed one out he slammed it back—slicing his shots, brimming with suppressed rage.

Long-limbed, his black hair shiny with sweat, his top off, he was incredibly beautiful, Kate thought, hiding her wistful expression behind dark glasses. Thanks to his time recuperating in the West Indies his hospital pallor had long since dimmed, and the wasting on his leg was diminishing rapidly with his punishing exercise schedule. If she didn't know better—if she didn't lie beside him at night and feel him tense in pain, hear him swim at three a.m. just to ease the cramping—then she'd think he looked a picture of health.

If you ignored the black rings beneath his eyes and the tension etched in his features, the dangerous energy to him that wasn't abating… Kate was sure it wasn't just the lack of action in the bedroom that was fuelling him.

Belenki was still permanently unavailable when Aleksi tried to communicate with him, and Aleksi wasn't a man used to being left on hold. Add to that the takeover bid against him, and Kate somehow knew there wasn't enough tennis balls on the planet to quell what was fuelling his anger.

He was walking towards her now, barely limping, yet it must surely be an effort. His breath was hard from exertion, his naked chest rising, and he fixed her with a smile that didn't reassure her in the slightest. Then he lowered his head, his mouth hard on hers. His skin was hot but his mouth was cool, and she closed her eyes—not from passion but to try to blot the tears. Because she had seen the glint of a camera lens too, and knew this display of affection was only for them.

'I think they just got their picture,' she whispered.

'Then let's give them another.' He dragged a chair over with his foot and sat opposite her, toying with the tie on her sarong.

'Please don't…' She closed her eyes in shame at the thought of being exposed in just her bikini in the paper.

'Why not?' Still he fiddled with the tie on her sarong, and she struggled to find her voice.

Her mind was not on the cameras now, but on his hand, his palm grazing her nipple, which was thick and swollen. She wished it were different. She hated her body—hated its passionate responses to him, hated that even after a passionless, manufactured kiss still she flared for him.

'Maybe I don't want to be made a fool of. Where were you last night?' She reached for his hand and removed it.

'Don't question me,' he ground out.

'Then don't expect me on tap,' she snapped back.

'Hardly!' came his sarcastic reply, and still he played with the knot.

'Maybe *krasavitsa* Kate doesn't want to read about her fiancé's indiscretions in the paper.' She took a deep breath. 'You're going to publicly dump me anyway once this is over, once you've convinced the board you're respectable.'

'Leave it.' He could not think about then. Could not stand to think about the day when all this would be over—when everything he had would perhaps be gone. When nothing remained, when she knew his shame, she would hate him too. He looked into her troubled blue eyes and he was angry. Because she knew nothing—none of them, not one of them, knew the danger, knew the trouble. He carried it all…

'In a couple of months,' she persisted, but her voice was strangled when he finally undid the knot, her hand reaching to close together the flimsy material. 'Please don't, Aleksi.'

'I would be forgiven for straying,' he said nastily. 'As all we do is kiss, and always you are covered to the neck.'

'Sorry I'm not as blatant as your usual scrubbers,' she hissed.

'Take it off,' Aleksi demanded, his voice silken, his mouth soft. But he was the smiling assassin, and she sat there, shivering in her own misery. It wasn't the camera she feared, wasn't her cottage cheese thigh on the cover of a magazine, but his scrutiny, his distaste she dreaded right now. 'It's warm; you need oil.'

When she didn't or rather couldn't move, Aleksi did, his hands removing hers from the sarong. His mouth, warm now, kissed her shoulder as he parted the sarong and then dropped it.

'Lie down.'

She could feel his breath on her shoulder, could feel the sweat trickling between her breasts, feel his hand on her stomach, and she wanted to weep in shame. But that would only shame her more, so instead she lay there.

Always her body had captured his attention.

He poured oil into his hand before he looked properly at her, and he saw that his hand was shaking a fraction. Those breasts he had once caressed naked were behind fabric and he wanted them exposed. But he wouldn't do that to her here, with paparazzi watching, so he oiled her shoulders and resisted the urge.

He loved her breasts. They were completely natural, without any telling scars beneath the areolaes. He slipped his hand up underneath her armpits, also knowing there were no scars there either. It was a little game he played, and usually his hand met the hard ridge of an implant, but there were no hard edges to Kate; she was soft, unlike him, and she was nervous but she didn't need to be. He saw her frantically try to hold in her stomach, but despite her best efforts when his warm palm met her skin there it was soft rather than taut. Her body was nothing like the many others he had been with, which had all been the same.

Finally, after all these long days and lonely nights, she let him touch her, and it wasn't just her body but her mind that remembered the bliss, and he felt her surrender, felt her accept what she had been resisting, and only then did he lead her inside.

'You're going to hurt me.' There—she'd said it. She stood in his bedroom by his bed and she wanted him so badly. Yet she still wanted to run, because there was no simple solution for her. 'No matter what I do—I know this is going to end up in hurt.'

'I'm not hurting you now.' And he wasn't. 'Just don't

fall in love with me, Kate.' Between sentences he kissed her. 'Because only then can I hurt you.' It should have sounded like a threat or a warning, but instead it was more of plea. 'Don't think even for a moment that it can be like this for ever…'

'I don't.' Kate swallowed. She just hoped it instead.

'This is now,' Aleksi said, and slid his hands around her waist. He spoke into her mouth. 'The words I say, the words we say as lovers, don't belong in the future.'

'I don't understand,' she murmured.

'When I say you are beautiful…' His mouth grazed her neck, and then one hand dealt with her bikini. Her breasts tightened briefly at the rush of fanned air, then softened to his warm tongue. 'When I say I want you… That I need you…'

'You actually mean that you won't in the future, right?' She pushed him away furiously. 'Are those words you say so you can close your eyes and go through the motions?'

'Hell! What did he do to you?' Aleksi demanded. 'What did that louse do that you can doubt yourself so much?'

'He *hurt* me, Aleksi, as you're promising you're about to.'

'Only if you think that it can last,' he reiterated. 'Because we both know it can't.'

It couldn't—how could he tell her that soon it might all be gone? That the luxury that bathed her now might soon be over? That even with his bravado, *Krasavitsa* might no longer be his? Oh, he would rise again, would come back from nothing, of that he had no doubt—but he would have to do it alone. Which was why it was imperative she took care of herself. But how could she want him anyway if she knew the truth?

He was back down at her breasts now, buried in them, wanting to get lost in them, but some things had to be said. 'Cash that cheque,' he ordered.

She slapped him in absolute fury. How dared he kiss her breast and at the same time remind her that he was paying her?

'That's what stopping you?' Aleksi would not be thwarted. 'Is that what is stopping you cashing it? Thinking I'm paying you for sex?' Her tears were her answer. 'Then I'll do it for you.' He had never been so hard, had never wanted a woman more, but it had to be business that drove them—this was *his* life that was crashing and burning, not hers, and he couldn't afford to let her glimpse the darkest part of it all.

He left her naked, apart from her bikini bottoms, while he tapped into his computer, and she stood there sobbing with humiliation and shame as he erased all her problems and created a whole set of new ones.

'There…it's done.'

'So now you can have sex with me?' she flung at him.

'Now,' Aleksi said firmly, 'we can forget about it for a while—forget why you are here.'

But she fought with him, avoiding the mouth that was searching for hers. He wanted to resume, to carry on where they'd left off. He had just paid her more money in a moment that she had earned in her entire life and now he expected to sleep with her!

'I have paid for your time, for the façade, for you to hold my hand and kiss me in public. I have paid you for the invasion to your privacy and for your exclusive company over these next weeks.' He pushed her onto the bed and pulled at her bikini while her hand strove to stop his. 'And now it is about choice,' Aleksi insisted when she was naked beneath him. 'Because the money is out of the way now—it is gone, it is done and forgotten. What happens now is your choice.'

But he gave her no choice at all, because her body wept for him…

He was out of his shorts and kissing her hard when suddenly he stopped.

'Tell me to stop now and I promise you will never have to say it again.' His erection was there between her closed thighs, his body on top of hers, his words hot breaths in her ear. He kissed her ear till she furled over on the inside. 'Apart from a kiss in the street, or a handhold on the way to an event…' he was breathing so hard in her ear now she turned her head away '…I will never lay a finger on you again.'

And then he kissed her neck, but still he spoke.

'I don't pay for sex, Kate, and I never have done—you either want me or you don't.'

Her thighs parted a fraction when her lips couldn't, and it was like opening a door a little way and the cat shooting out—except Aleksi didn't quite let himself in.

'It's your choice,' he insisted again, but he was trying to steady himself, because her beckoning warmth was doing strange things to his mind. He found himself wanting to stay just a little longer on the precipice, en-visaging the thrill of the jump, but exhilaration was already building, and then he felt her mouth, felt her kiss him, felt her open, and he accepted her warm welcome and crept in.

Not a stab, not a split second, not a dive. Instead, for Kate, there was a slow gathering and filling. He made that moment of entry last for ever. He gathered speed with his thrust, and yet it was like a slow sear deep inside her—slow enough for her to assimilate rapid sensations: him filling her further, the stretch of her body, the moan of relief from him. Then his tongue licked her ear and she felt something new, something close to blind panic, but so much more wonderful than that. All this she felt as Aleksi slid deep inside her.

He beckoned her on his decadent path with a rapid withdrawal, just to the edge, and then he dived in again and again…

And she had never, ever been so intimate with another person before.

Had never been so angry and so desperate and so relieved and so free at the same time, and she told him all that with her body.

She fought—not to get him off, but to pull him deeper and deeper inside her. And harder he went, till she thought she would scream from the pleasure of it, and then she heard that she *was* screaming. It came from another place, this voice that was hers but she'd never before heard.

'I can't.' She heard herself gasp it—then wanted to explain herself, because she wasn't saying she couldn't do it; she was saying she couldn't hold back any longer.

Only words were meaningless now. They were in a different place that spoke a different language, yet Aleksi understood it, because clearly he couldn't hold back either. He was speaking in Russian, and saying her name; he was a different man than she had ever seen or imagined. He was rough and he was tender and he was mindful yet brutal, and so was she—it was another version of Kate that he had exposed. He was so into her, this guarded, sexy, remote man, who was there with her on another level. He made her act like an animal—she was biting and scratching, and her legs were so tight around him that she felt him bucking against her calves. She offered no escape.

Kate was a delicious tourniquet around him, and he shot into her what she craved. They shared the same dizzy high—this rush, this shared sensation that lasted and lasted till she could hear the slowing thud of the bed and realised they were still on the planet, could feel again her body, which she'd surely just climbed out of.

Then she thought about the screams and the bed and the swear-words and the servants—and she did the strangest thing, with him still inside and on top of her. She stared to laugh.

And, strangest of all, Aleksi laughed too.

Then he rolled off and lay beside her and did the unthinkable.

He asked something rather than demanded it of her.

'Will you come to England with me?'

She didn't answer, just turned and looked over to him. He didn't look at her, just stared up at the ceiling, and something told her that her reaction was more important to him than she could even begin to guess.

'Tonight,' Aleksi added, and then he did look over to her. 'Just for a few days—you can bring Georgie, or she can stay with Sophie. Maybe your sister could come and stay here…'

In everything, for more than five years, Georgie had come first with Kate, and of course she still did. But there was actually room in Kate's life now for someone else.

'I'll come,' she said quietly.

'I don't want to unsettle Georgie, but…'

'She'll be fine,' Kate said, because she knew her daughter would be. 'I'll sort that out.'

Then he did something that had never come easily to him.

Kate watched as he nodded his thanks to her and then fell asleep.

Had it been anyone less complex than Aleksi, she'd have thumped him.

CHAPTER NINE

IT WAS freezing in the UK, but Levander and Millie's welcome was warm.

They had a sprawling home on the outskirts of London, and though Kate could see instantly that Aleksi and he were brothers, there was a lightness to Levander, a peace that was missing in Aleksi.

Their house was filled with love and laughter and Kate felt a pang. She wished she'd brought Georgie, but a sixth sense had told her that her daughter would be better off at *home*. Her mother had actually come down from the country for a few days to watch her, and there was Sophie, and her friends, and a party that Georgie felt was too important to miss.

It was her first break from motherhood in almost five years, and it was a guilty relief.

She and Aleksi pretended to be tired when they landed, and were in bed before seven—but it wasn't for sleeping. In the morning, having spoken to Georgie, even though she sounded just fine, Kate found she had to resist constantly phoning to ensure that everything was okay.

'It's like trying not to go back and check if you've

put the handbrake on in the car.' Kate described it to Millie. 'Even though you *know* you have…'

'I know.' Millie nodded. 'We left Sashar here when we went to Russia for Dimitri—everyone said that we needed some one-on-one time with him and that it would be better for Sashar too. Especially as Dimitri can be…' she hesitated to summon the right word '…difficult.'

He was certainly that.

Dimitri didn't say a word, didn't join in, and he didn't even seem to be taking an interest in what was going on.

'He does sometimes,' Millie said hopefully. 'He laughed at something Levander said the other day, and he has played a little with Sashar.'

'That's good,' Kate said, and Millie nodded.

'My brother's severely autistic, so I know that Dmitri is interacting a bit—we've just got to be patient.'

Which wasn't a Kolovsky virtue.

Belenki had again dodged all Aleksi's attempts to contact him.

An emergency had arisen, his PA had informed Aleksi.

'He can't help that,' Kate attempted one morning as they sat around a vast indoor pool—it was freezing outside, all the windows were steamed up, but inside the temperature was soaring—and not only due to the luxurious surrounds. Craig was texting constantly now, and she had finally agreed to meet him when she returned, just to get him to leave her alone, which had her on edge. And Aleksi was proving impossible. 'You can't plan for emer…' Her voice trailed off as Aleksi peeled off a page from the newspaper he was reading and there was his nemesis, skiing down a black run in Switzerland.

'That photo's for me,' Aleksi said.

'Don't be ridiculous.' Kate laughed. 'He'll be mortified he's been caught out.' Still she smiled. 'Aleksi, you do it all the time—it's just business.'

'No.' Aleksi shook his head. 'It isn't.'

'Then what?' She didn't get it—she truly didn't get what it was about Belenki that galled him so. 'What is it with him?' she demanded, because she really had to know—his answer, however, just confused her.

'That,' Aleksi said tartly, 'is what I'm trying my damnedest to work out.'

Their *words* thankfully went unnoticed by their hosts, but Kate was sick of his moods, sad that a lovely morning could be ruined by a photo in the newspaper of a man he barely knew—and she told him so, then flounced off to find a better mood in the water.

Levander was playing with Sashar in the pool, and Millie was sitting with Dimitri—who sat where he had been put, his legs dangling in the water, so sheltered and closed, such a contrast to the laughter and boisterousness and sheer joy that came from his little brother.

'Come on, Sashar, jump!' Levander grinned to his son, who had climbed out of the pool and was standing on the edge, nervous but excited as his father urged him on. '*Jump!*'

It took only two tries and then little Sashar stretched out his arms and flew to his father, who caught him. It went on, over and over again, and the squeals of delight made everyone laugh.

Everyone except Dimitri and, Kate realised, Aleksi.

He had been on his phone, replying to an e-mail— only now the e-mail was forgotten. Kate could feel his tension lift, feel the shift as Aleksi looked towards where his brother stood with arms outstretched to Dimitri, whose pale body was shaking as he contemplated taking that brave step.

'How about you, Dimitri?' Levander said in English, and then he repeated it in Russian. 'Jump,' Levander urged. 'I will catch you. I promise.'

But Dimitri just sat there, his eyes looking down.

Levander said it again. '*Preeguy* Dimitri, jump. *Yar tibyar piemaryou.*' And then Aleksi, who wasn't a father, who hadn't been through anything that Levander had, who had no bond with the child, spoke for his nephew.

'Leave him be, Levander.'

Distracted by the warning in his brother's tone, Levander briefly turned around.

'We're just playing. He'll do it when he is ready...' Then he turned his attention back to his new son. 'How about it, Dimitri?'

He spoke again in Russian, but now Kate understood what was being said. What she didn't understand was the tension in Aleksi, who sat beside her like a coiled spring. It was as if he might pounce at any time. Kate glanced over to Millie, who had also picked up on the strange atmosphere.

'Levander is just letting him know that when he is ready to join in...'

'That is not a game.' Aleksi's voice was hoarse. 'It will not help him. Levander!' Aleksi's voice was restrained, but urgent. 'Leave him.'

'Don't tell me how to raise my son.' Levander was less than impressed with his brother's interference.

'They've been playing for ages,' Millie said patiently. 'Levander is not pushing him. Dimitri will go in when he's ready.'

There was something Kate was missing here. Her eyes darted from Aleksi to Sashar who, jealous from lack of attention and wanting some of the fun, climbed out of the pool and ran around the side, laughing and sailing into the air. Then her eyes moved back to Aleksi, whose face was chalk-white. She could see the vein pulsing in his neck as Levander caught his son, and there was fear, real fear in his eyes, as Dimitri stood at the very wrong moment and decided to jump.

'Levander!' Aleksi called to his brother—only Levander didn't need his brother's warning.

He was watching not just Sashar but Dimitri too. He didn't launch himself, it was more a step really, and despite having just caught Sashar, Levander caught Dimitri in time, pulled him into his arms and didn't make too much of a fuss—just held him and encouraged him till Dimitri found his feet on the bottom of the pool.

The steam from the water was rising, a contrast to the icy rain slicing against the windows, and Millie climbed in and took over as Levander glared over to his brother and got out.

'Did you think I would drop him? Did you really think I would deliberately drop him for *fun*?' Levander challenged.

'To show him,' Aleksi corrected. 'To teach him.'

'I know what I'm doing,' Levander snapped. 'I know what he's been through. What sort of a sick person do you think I am? Don't tell me how to raise my son.'

'Would *you*?' Aleksi challenged his older brother. 'When you came to our family, had our father told you to jump would you have done?'

'No,' Levander admitted. 'But I am not Ivan. Dimitri can trust me.'

'Trust no one,' Aleksi sneered. 'That is what Dimitri has been taught.'

'What were *you* taught, Aleksi?' Levander asked, and he didn't sound angry any more.

'To jump,' Aleksi said. 'I stood on the dresser at the bottom of the stairs and he held out his arms and told me to jump. I didn't want to, but he told me to trust him…'

Kate felt sick. She had heard of the ritual, a strange reversal of today's events, where bonding camps made you jump from great heights into the waiting arms of strangers. A ritual that had once been passed from father to son—to toughen them up, to show them the harsh ways of the world.

'So you jumped?' Kate asked in a croak when Levander said nothing. 'And then what?'

'He let me fall,' Aleksi muttered. 'He let me fall and then he picked me up off the floor and held me as I cried. He told me I had been foolish, that I hadn't listened to what he'd told me before—*"nyekamoo doveerye"*—that I should trust no one.'

'He was wrong—' Levander started, only Aleksi didn't want to debate it.

'I'm going to rest.'

For the first time he really limped as he walked off. For the first time he wasn't being proud, or perhaps he didn't have the mental energy to push through the pain. Kate just sat, wondering if she should follow. She guessed he would rather be alone, yet she ached to go after him.

'Sometimes,' Levander said, as the pool door closed on his brother, 'I wonder if the sympathy of my family is misguided. As hellish as my childhood was in the or-phanage, I think I might have got off lightly.'

'He was wrong.' It was all Kate could say at first, her mind still whirring with conflict. Because the thought of destroying a child's trust was abhorrent to her, yet things had been different then. 'It was the way men toughened up their children then.'

'Leave it.'

'I don't want to leave it,' Kate answered. 'I'm trying to understand you.'

'Why?'

'Because I…' She hurriedly choked back the word he hated so. 'I care about you.'

'I pay you to care,' Aleksi said coldly.

'Please don't!' she begged. 'Because you know there are some things that can't be bought…'

'I disagree.'

'Well, you're wrong!' Kate sobbed. 'Because—'

"Kate.' Only then did his eyes meet hers, and he might as well have been looking at the wall for all the feeling in them. They were as grey and cold and as im-permeable as steel. 'I am not interested in a relation-ship—I am not interested in your caring. How much more clearly can I say it? All I want now is my business—not just Krasavitsa; I want the lot. And then—' he nodded as he made his mind up '—I want my mother out!'

'How can you speak of her like that?'

'I don't care for her,' Aleksi said. 'I care only for the Kolovsky Empire.'

'You're so cold,' Kate whispered.

'More than cold,' Aleksi said. 'You want to know

why I hate her? You want to know why this is nothing but business for me?'

She had wanted to know, but suddenly she was scared. Only there was no stopping Aleksi now.

'I want to understand you,' she told him.

'You couldn't,' Aleksi retorted.

'Maybe if you just let me know you, I will,' she retorted.

'When I was seven, and Christmas was close, my mother said there would be no gifts that year—that I had been too naughty. I knew she must be lying, so I searched for them. She hadn't been lying about that—there were no gifts—and instead I found out their real lie.'

'About Levander?' Kate asked, her stomach tightening as she thought of a seven-year-old boy finding out the family secret. 'I thought they only found out about him being in the orphanage after they came to Australia…'

'They knew,' Aleksi said. 'They knew all along that they had children in the orphanages—but they were too busy living their new lives to care.'

'*Children?*' she gasped.

'Levander is my father's son,' Aleksi said. 'Ivan had a brief fling with his cleaner before he was engaged to my mother. Levander's mother, when she found out she was dying, begged them to take Levander with them to Australia—she had guessed they would soon flee Russia.'

'And you found this out?'

'I found letters,' Aleksi said, 'and certificates. I confronted him…'

Kate knew some of this. She had worked at Kolovsky long enough, had heard the whispers and read the papers, so it came as no real surprise that Ivan and Nina had actually known about Levander all along—but Aleksi hadn't finished yet.

'I found out, too, that there was another child—that before Levander my parents had had a son together.' Beneath his tan his face was grey. 'Not even my brothers know that. I confronted my father with it.'

'And what did he say?'

'He answered me with his fist,' Aleksi said, 'and with his boots, and with his belt. What scared me...' briefly his eyes met hers '...was not the pain, but his fear.'

She didn't get it. She wanted to ask, to probe, yet she knew to stay silent, and tried so hard not to cry as she heard how badly he had been beaten.

'He was scared and angry and I knew he had no control. That his fear was bigger than him in that moment...' His eyes held hers, awaited her response, and yet she didn't understand, no matter how she wanted to.

'I consoled myself that in that moment his fear overrode his love for me.'

She swallowed. She would go over and over his words later, to try and make sense of them, but for now all she wanted was for him to speak. Only Aleksi was done. Turning his back on her, he stared out of the window. It was so warm inside, so light and airy, it was strange to think that on the other side of the glass it was cold and damp and frozen. She knew she had to reach him, to speak, or he would be gone.

'Nothing overrides love,' she said at last.

'Wrong answer.'

She felt her blood run cold—knew somehow that she had just failed him.

'When you are seven—when you lie on the floor and the man you love, the man you admire, the man you one day want to become beats you, kicks you… When you can see his eyes bulge and feel his spit on your face…'

Her tears were silent, but they were there, flowing down her face as she listened to him.

'You tell yourself this is not your father's doing—that he loves you—that it is the fear that makes him do this…'

'Aleksi—'

'Leave it,' he said. 'I have.'

'How can you?' Kate begged. 'You have another brother. Did you look for him?'

He just stood there.

'Have you found him?'

'No.'

And then she asked the question he dreaded giving an answer to. 'You haven't even *tried* to find him?'

He had never known shame like it—could see the struggle in her eyes as she tried to fathom what even Aleksi couldn't. 'No.'

She really didn't know what to say, so he said it for her.

'I live as my parents have done—a life of greed and debauchery. No, I haven't even tried to find him. So you see, Kate, perhaps it is better that you don't know me, or try to understand me.'

'How could you not—?'

'We should pack,' Aleksi interrupted, the conversation clearly over.

'We should stay,' Kate tried to halt him. 'Maybe if you spoke with Levander, spent some time—'

'I'm done with family,' Aleksi said, and then again he surprised her. 'Thank you.'

'For what?' she asked.

'For making me see…' He gave a small shrug. 'It doesn't matter now.'

As she put her hand up to him he dusted it off and walked out the room, and Kate knew he was also done with her.

Knew then that she shouldn't have spoken, should only have listened, because her response *had* been wrong.

As right and logical as it had seemed to her, as she replayed his words she let her tears fall as she realised what she had just done.

If, as she'd stated, nothing overrode love, then to Aleksi it must be simple—she'd just taken from him the last semblance of his father's love.

CHAPTER TEN

'THERE'S a job going in Bali…'

Kate walked along the beach and tried to take in what Craig was telling her. 'Well, not a job as such, but I've got friends there, and the surfing is good. I've been wanting to go for ages.'

'But you didn't?'

'I wanted to know you were okay—I know I'm not a good dad, but I just…' he pulled his hand through his long blond hair. 'Now you're okay, now that you and Georgie are going to be looked after…'

'You feel that you can?'

'I'll write to her. I'll send her cards, and I'll save up so she can come for a holiday. My parents are hoping to bring her out for a couple of weeks. Here…' He wasn't after money; he was here to give it. 'I know I can remember birthdays, but for Easter, for when she gets a good school report…'

She stood there as he gave her everything he could afford for his daughter—just not his time.

'We want different things for her, Kate. I want waves and freedom, and you want schools and routines…'

'*She* wants schools and routines,' Kate said, but she

wasn't arguing with him. She actually got it—he certainly wouldn't make father of the year, but in his own way he did love Georgie, and Kate would always tell her that.

'Will you let my parents bring her out to see me?' he asked.

'Of course I will,' Kate said, and even if it wasn't much, somehow she was touched, because he had at least stayed around to make sure they would be okay before he left.

He just didn't know it was all a lie.

'I've got good taste in louses,' Kate tried to joke, and she cried a little inside for herself and for Georgie.

She wished Craig well, hugged him and gave him a brief kiss, and as she walked back to the house she surprised herself—because she actually felt free.

Aleksi was having a revelation all of his own.

'Have it.'

Monday morning at nine, he had stepped off the plane and headed straight to the office. He'd been ready to fight his mother for everything, and now Nina had handed it to him on a plate.

'I can't fight you any more, Aleksi...'

He stood unmoved by Nina's tears.

'Have Kolovsky, have Krasavitsa—just please hear Belenki out. Maybe I am wrong, maybe I have been greedy, but some of his ideas are good...'

He didn't get her.

If he lived to be a thousand he would never get her. Always he would hate her, but sometimes, bizarrely, he wondered if he could summon love for her too.

'You've changed your mind.' He was tired of this—so damn tired of this. 'Why?'

'Sheikh Amallah cancelled the Princess's order, and others have cancelled too. Lavinia has told me she is leaving—that I can stick my job and she'll only work for you...'

Aleksi glanced over to where Lavinia stood and gave her a thin smile of welcome as the rebel returned from the coup. Then he dismissed her as Nina carried on shredding tissues.

'Others have too—and then I saw the samples of Kolovsky bedlinen for the supermarket chain and I knew I had sold out. I know I am a poor businesswoman. No matter how I enjoy it, I see that everything your father built I am ruining...'

'Then stop,' Aleksi said simply, because he could not make himself embrace or comfort her.

'I *am* stopping. I will concentrate on the charities. But please,' Nina begged, 'hear Belenki out.'

'I can't get hold of Belenki,' Aleksi said wearily.

'He's here,' Nina said, and Aleksi's blood ran cold. 'Rather, he arrives this morning; I am supposed to be meeting with him at two. Please talk with him, Aleksi. Always he confuses me—he is so strong, so forceful— and always I end up agreeing with what he suggests, always he tells me I am helping the orphans...'

It was guilt that drove her. Aleksi could almost see it.

He drove along the beach road back home and the adrenaline was still coursing in his veins—because he had expected a fight with his mother and then got tears and capitulation. Guilt for what she had done in aban- doning her son and a stepson to awful childhoods in Russian orphanages. She tried to purge it by raising millions for charity.

He just didn't know if he had enough left of his soul

to forgive himself, let alone Nina, for not trying to right her sins long ago.

Didn't know if he could ever find peace—and then he turned the key in his door and almost glimpsed it.

Walking into his house, Aleksi saw the dust of sand on the tiles, Georgie's boogie board discarded, and the apologetic expression of his housekeeper.

'I'm sorry, I haven't got around…'

'It's not a problem,' Aleksi said, and he meant it. 'Leave it—take the day off,' he offered, because he needed to be alone.

Since Kate and Georgie had moved in every homecoming was different he realised. Everything was different—even his fridge contents, Aleksi thought as he pulled it open.

Oh, there were still exotic fruit juices and imported beers, still fancy cheeses, but there were also juice boxes and little animal shaped processed cheeses that tasted disgusting but were strangely addictive.

He was growing used to waking up to laughter and conversation and chaos—chaos because even with a nanny and a housekeeper and the most efficient team of staff, every morning without fail Georgie lost something. Every morning there was a mad dash for the front door.

But not for much longer.

He didn't need Kate now.

Except maybe he did.

He walked upstairs to the neatly made bed and saw her book on the bedside, picked it up and checked the page.

She was at 342 and it had been 210 on the plane.

So, she had been reading it when he'd thought she was sulking—why did that make him smile?

She had tried to talk to him since his revelation, had

told him that she would try to understand, that maybe it wasn't too late to look for his brother.

Could he do it?

Could he let her in? Could he trust not her but himself?

Not just with her future, but with Georgie's?

Could she even want a man who had chosen to turn his back on his brother?

It wasn't just monogamy that Kate wanted, but his truth, his thoughts, his soul. It was a lot to consider giving, and yet... He put down the book, smelt her perfume in the room and realised he had a lot to lose, too.

More than he could stand.

He would tell her—tell her what he didn't know. About this fear that woke him at night, about the answer he was so close to remembering, about the shame that filled him each time he thought of Riminic, the brother he had left behind all these years.

How could he ask Kate to have faith in him when he didn't know his own truth?

He walked across the bedroom, stared out at the bay—a view he had seen maybe a million times but he'd never really looked at before. All it was was a backdrop, a view he paid for, to impress but not to enjoy—but he did so now. The water was so smooth there was barely a ripple, shades of grey with steaks of azure, and then if you looked deeper there was aqua and silver and brown. It mocked Kolovsky silk over and over, because nothing could be as powerful and beautiful as nature.

The bay changed—not each day, not even each minute, but with every shift of focus, every look, there was more to see.

So, so much more to see.

Nyekamoo doveerye.

His father had been dead for two years, but as sure as if he was standing beside him Aleksi heard Ivan's voice—and, to his regret, Aleksi conceded that his father was right.

She was walking. A sheer white sarong covered her, but not enough. Even from this distance he could see the curves barely leashed by a bikini.

Money did suit her, Aleksi thought darkly.

Those wild curls were sleeker and glossier now, and her skin glowed. He could see the flash of her jewellery and the golden dust of her tan, and she had a new-found confidence that he'd been stupid enough to think he might have given her.

"Nyekamoo doveerye"—trust no one.

The man was as blond as Georgie, and Aleksi just knew that it was Craig who was walking in step beside Kate now.

They were together.

There was an ease to them that sliced at his heart.

There was a togetherness that unleashed his anger like a snarling dog let loose.

Disgust churned black and bilious in his stomach.

Foolishness mocked him too, for daring to believe for a little while that she might be different—that he could be too.

But as Craig kissed her, as he pulled her into his arms and she leant on him for a moment, it wasn't jealousy that ate Aleksi alive—that would come ten seconds later—it was regret.

Regret that it wasn't him.

That Georgie wasn't his.

That there could be no *them* after all.

* * *

'Hey!' There was an elation to her as she stepped into his home that he might once have been foolish to think had been caused by him. 'What are you doing back?'

His muscles were shot with adrenaline, the hairs on his neck stood up, and he was slightly breathless. His body was screaming for him to fight, to confront, but he just stood there waiting, needing to hear her lie, and somehow, still at the eleventh hour, hoping she wouldn't.

'Where were you?'

'Just walking.' Kate smiled, because jet lag didn't factor when you'd snuggled in gold pyjamas reading, eating and dozing all the way from England. 'It's a gorgeous day. What are you doing home?'

'I came for my computer,' Aleksi said. 'The real one.'

'The one you've been hiding from Nina!" Kate laughed, and the sound of it made him sick. 'Why?'

'Belenki is here.' He glanced at her skin, at the dust of sand on her legs, and then to her face, to the lips that smiled at him but had just been kissed by another man. 'Get dressed,' he said. 'We meet him at my office in an hour.'

She didn't want to get dressed.

Aleksi was right—she was on a high. There was a dizzy elation to her that she had never expected to come today.

There was freedom, there was lust, and there was still the prickly warmth from the sun on her shoulders and the salty smell of the bay in her nostrils. And before her was Aleksi.

She could feel his tension, knew it must be because he was meeting Belenki, and as she had done once before she wanted to soothe him.

Wanted *him*.

Whatever his past, she wanted his future—so badly.

He made her bold, he made her ache with want, and although she felt his bristling anger she wanted to soothe him, so she stepped towards him.

'It's only a thirty-minute drive,' she murmured.

She pressed into him, smelt not the ocean but him, felt his hands on her arms and placed her lips on his.

And he thought about it. Feeling her hot and oiled beneath his fingers, he thought about it. So angry, he was hard; so beguiled, he wanted release. He could feel her tongue roll around his, urging a response, and although he knew where those lips had just been he let her kiss on.

He hadn't cried in decades—not even when beaten. The last time he had wept was when he had lain on the floor and his father had warned him to trust no one, and yet now there was a sting in his eyes and such tension in his lips that he couldn't kiss her back. He just felt the roll of her tongue.

God, but she had a nerve!

Her sarong was off—was it her fingers or his that had done it?—and the top of her bikini was gone. Her breasts splayed against his chest, her heat pressed into him and his fingers dug into her generous buttocks.

She was grappling with his belt, but he would not give her an inch.

He pulled her so tight into him that she gasped.

Her mouth was on his cheek and his burning anger impaled her. He dug his fingers in deeper to her flesh, and he was so turned on he wanted to forget what he had seen. He wanted her so badly that it actually hurt to resist.

He wanted her seduction, yet he craved survival more.

But still he let her.

He let her kiss him, let his body respond to her, just enough to inflame them both.

He could feel the hum of her lips on his neck, feel her frantic search for his skin, her hand tearing at his shirt, and then the nibble of her teeth on his neck. He slipped his fingers into her bikini bottoms, felt the heat of her intimate skin and like an addict he craved just once more. But Aleksi was stronger than that—he was a man who could come off pain medication in one night; he could surely withdraw more easily from her, couldn't he?

Yet she was more addictive.

Her hand was at his zipper, and it was a more skilled hand now, because she freed him in seconds.

He wanted her bikini off, but there wasn't even time for that, so he parted the material with his erection and entered her, feeling the scrape of her bikini along his length as he pushed into her. He could sense the throb of her orgasm around him, felt her sob and moan as she convulsed around his length, and he was a second away from joining her.

Yet he was stronger than that. As she ground into him, demanded his response, screamed his name, the triumph was his as he pulled back, still erect, unsated— and, she now registered, loaded with contempt.

'Aleksi?'

She had never been so naked, so exposed, so confused, tumbling down from the throes of orgasm to see his look of pure loathing.

'I told you.' He pulled up his zipper and crucified her with his eyes. 'Get dressed.'

For Kate, it was the ultimate in rejection.

This logical voice inside her mind told her he was

tired, stressed, late for the meeting, yet her gut told her otherwise.

She sat beside him as he drove in silence, her mind going over and over what had taken place, trying and failing to remember his response—she had been so deeply into him, so confident, so sure, so *open* with him, his fleeting resistance hadn't confused her at the time.

It confused her now.

She could still feel the imprint of his fingers in her buttocks, and as she stared out of the window at the bay that stayed still as they hurtled towards the city, she could recall his initial imperviousness to her kisses—only she had won him round. No, she'd *thought* she had won him round.

She just wasn't used to these grown-up games.

Her seduction had been her own, her devotion absolute. There had been nothing else on her mind other than him. Her motives had perhaps not been virtuous, but they had been pure—she had only wanted to make love with him.

The bay view had gone now. There was no view from her window other than shops and cafés and people and trams and cars. It was too busy for her cluttered mind to cope with so she turned to him, yet there was nothing there.

Just this dark brooding stranger with a mind she could never begin to fathom.

They pulled in outside the office. The doorman jumped, the valet parker was already moving. Aleksi was keen to get to Belenki—but Kate just sat there.

'What happened back there, Aleksi?' she asked quietly.

'What?' He frowned, as if he had no idea what she was talking about.

'What *happened*?' She could hear her voice rising to a feminine, needy pitch and fought to check it, fought to check herself, to reel herself back, to heed his earlier warning—that love, a future, was something he would never be prepared to give her.

'I changed my mind.' A cruel smile twisted his lips. 'Which is a man's prerogative.'

Slap.

Her hand sliced the air, struck at his cheek. He made no move to halt it. Worse, he gave no reaction to it, and she watched as the doorman discreetly closed the door and backed away, watched the smoothness of his cheek turn red, saw the shape of her fingers on his flesh. It didn't even move him.

'I trusted you.' He said nothing as she voiced her truth. 'I could accept that it wasn't for ever, I agreed to your rules, to your twisted logic. But in bed, with us, when we made love, I trusted you.' She saw him blink. It was his only reaction, but it was more than she'd come to expect and so she told him—told him exactly what he had just done to her. 'Even when you whispered that you would always want me—' she saw him blink again '—I stuck to the rules and told myself it was passion talking. But I didn't deserve that.' He closed his eyes for a second, but she would not let him shut her out. 'I trusted you with my body, Aleksi. I felt safe and gorgeous and free of shame. When we made love I thought in that, at least, we were on the same level— that whatever else we had, that was something honest between us.'

'Did you feel safe and gorgeous and free of shame when you were on the beach with *Craig*?' Livid eyes turned to her, because he wanted to see this—wanted her eyes to widen when she realised that he knew, wanted to watch her fall from the dizzy heights of her moral high ground and scrabble on the floor to pick herself up with fractured reasons and excuses.

'Actually, yes,' Kate said simply, and she opened her own door and stepped out. 'We've got a meeting to go to.'

'You were unfaithful to me,' Aleksi sneered.

'No.' She walked to the lift with her head held high—walked just a step in front of him and only spoke again when the lift doors were safely closed behind them. 'I finally felt free because Craig was telling me he was moving overseas. I finally felt free because he wasn't asking for money and he wasn't suddenly deciding he wanted to take Georgie with him. I felt free because finally we'd worked out our boundaries. You could have spoken to me, Aleksi. You could have asked what I was doing with him, asked me to explain what was going on, instead of screwing the truth out of me.'

He gave a black laugh. 'What, and give you a chance to come up with excuses?'

'I don't need your chances, Aleksi, and I don't need your mistrust.' She had never felt so weak, so floored, so raw, and yet somehow she had never felt so strong as she walked into her old office and stood at her old desk. 'And I don't need to make excuses.' She fixed him with a stare and she meant every word that she said. 'We're done.'

'So why are you still here?' Aleksi demanded.

'Because, unlike you, I have a moral compass. I have a daughter too, and the cleaner the break the less the impact on her. If you don't mind, I'd like to tell Georgie back at the house, and then we'll find a hotel.'

'Kate…'

'I don't want to hear it, Aleksi.'

'Tell me exactly what you were doing with him and maybe then…'

'You'll forgive me? Or will it suddenly be acceptable to you? I'll prove that this time you were mistaken? But what about next time, Aleksi? What happens next time you decide I'm not trustworthy?' She shook her head, and she was so angry she wanted to hit him again—only this time she stopped herself. The tears that were building inside her she would save for later. 'What you did to me back there,' Kate said, 'I'll never understand and I'll never forgive. But I'm not going to be a martyr and give you back your money—after what you just did to me I've earned every last cent of your million dollars. In fact, *you* owe *me*!'

What she was saying should have killed him, should have hurt, should have shamed him—except he was beyond all that. He was numb, frozen, locked up—because in their darkest moment he wasn't even thinking about her.

Coming towards him was a walking nightmare—one he'd never been able to wake from. One he'd never been able to adequately describe or recall, except in the black moths that fluttered and taunted his shattered memory as logic tried to pin them down. They all gathered now, as clear as day, and walked right up to him.

'Aleksi,' Zakahr Belenki announced as he stood before him. 'I believe we have much to discuss.'

CHAPTER ELEVEN

'STAY.'

Rarely did Kate sit in on meetings—and especially not since she had been masquerading as his fiancée.

His *ex*-fake fiancée she reminded herself. But stay she did, because Aleksi's face was suddenly grey.

The air was thick with tension and Kate didn't really understand why. Sure, Zakahr Belenki was a difficult customer—he had his claws in Kolovsky, thanks to Nina, and it would be hard extricating them—but Aleksi was more than up to the task.

'We seem to keep missing each other.' Zakahr's Russian accent was pronounced.

He shook Aleksi's hand and nodded to Kate, but she could feel the animosity sizzling between them and suddenly all she wanted was out.

There was danger here. She could smell it.

Despite the designer suits and opulent surroundings there was something primitive about them—two gang lords meeting. Despite the white smiles, their eyes were black as they locked.

'I don't think so.' Aleksi dismissed the polite observation. 'I have made every effort to meet. You, Zakahr, have been the one who has been unavailable.'

'Well, I'm here now.' Zakahr gave a brief shrug. 'Where is Nina?'

'*I* am head of Kolovsky,' Aleksi said. 'You speak with *me*.'

'Of course,' Zakahr replied. 'As you know, I have an exciting vision for the House of Kolovsky,' Zakahr went on, 'and it will benefit my charity with a percentage—'

Aleksi put up his hand to stop him. 'You are a brilliant businessman,' Aleksi said. 'As am I. You must know that this is only a short-term gain—that in two years the exclusive name we have built will be no more.'

'My priority is to my charity. Nina assures me—'

'Nina speaks rubbish,' Aleksi interjected. 'If Nina had her way you could buy Kolovsky toilet paper in the two-dollar shop—where,' he added, '*we* would all be working. Don't hide behind your charity in *this* office.'

'Okay.'

There was a mirthless smile on the edge of Zakahr's lips, and it made Kate uncomfortable. It was the winning edge she had seen in Aleksi when he held a full hand, and suddenly she was scared—of what, Kate didn't know, but she was scared all the same.

'Kolovsky is raising millions for your charity,' Aleksi pointed out. 'That stream will continue for as long as Kolovsky is strong—yet this plan you propose to my mother, while it might bring you an initial surge of income, will rapidly end. Kolovsky will dry like a stream in the desert if we follow this through—you and I both know it. Your aim is to crush Kolovsky.'

Kate felt her breath hold in her lungs as Aleksi threw

down the most outlandish suggestion. But then he re-iterated it.

'You *want* the business to go under.'

'Why would I want that?' Zakahr frowned. 'I am serious about my charity.'

'Don't play your games with me,' Aleksi said coldly. 'The truth, or leave!'

'You really want the truth?'

'Oh, I want it,' Aleksi gritted out. 'I want to hear how you plan to crush Kolovsky—how in two years you hope to—'

'Aleksi…' As his PA, Kate would never have dared interrupt, even as his make-believe fiancée she had no right to, but his accusations were so outlandish, his anger so palpable, she couldn't contain herself. He was walking into a trap and she wanted to warn him.

It never entered her head that Aleksi already knew it was there…

'You're right,' Zakahr admitted bluntly. 'My hope is that in two years I sit at your desk on my annual visit to Australia. That it will be the House of Belenki which produces the silks that make women weep with greed.'

Kate just sat, her mouth agape.

'Your mother brings me coffee, or perhaps she cleans the stairs when I walk in with my filthy shoes…' He stopped. 'That is the dream—but I will settle for reality. I will accept the House of Kolovsky's complete demise…'

Why?

Kate wanted to ask, but she sat there silent, waiting for Aleksi to demand the same—except he didn't.

'Don't you want to know why?' Zakahr asked finally, when Aleksi said nothing.

'I already know why,' he said quietly.

'You know *nothing*,' Zakahr sneered. 'You sat there drunk at a fundraising ball as I spoke of my childhood, of how I prostituted myself just to survive. You simply snapped your fingers for more champagne, and then the world wept when the next day you wrapped your car around a tree. You write a cheque and your work is done. Iosef at least makes an effort, Levander tries too—even your sister is making amends. But you, Aleksi, have forgotten your roots.'

'Never,' he denied.

'You live a gluttonous, debauched life that is built on shame—'

'There's no shame!' Kate countered, her voice thin and pale in the crackling silence.

Zakahr's face was bleached in hate, as if at any moment he might leap across the desk and take Aleksi's throat in his hands. But worse, and most confusing for Kate, was the fact that Aleksi just sat there, leaning back in his chair, his eyes narrowing as each accusation was hurled. So it was she who jumped in.

'The Kolovskys have already acknowledged what happened to Levander…'

'This isn't about Levander,' Aleksi said, but he didn't look at Kate. His eyes were on Zakahr.

'Your fake boyfriend is right,' Zakahr said. 'I've been through the figures—he's certainly paying you well!' he sneered in her direction. 'This isn't about Levander. This is about revenge.'

'Revenge?' Kate swallowed.

'You want the truth?' Zakahr challenged Aleksi. 'Well, here it is.'

'I told you—I already know the truth.'

Only now did Aleksi look at Kate, and she saw the

slate-grey of his eyes. Even as her eyes darted to Zakahr, even before Aleksi spoke again, Kate knew it too—realised a little more of the pain he carried.

'Kate, this is my brother, Zakahr.'

She saw the dart of surprise in Zakahr's eyes, saw him swallow before speaking.

'You know?'

Aleksi nodded.

'For how long?'

'That it was you?' Aleksi asked the question. 'Only now do I know that for sure.' He continued, almost speaking to himself. 'Ivan and Nina had another child. They had a relationship when they were young and broke up for a while—which was when Ivan fathered Levander—you, Zakahr, are my full brother.'

Then he told him about the certificates he had found aged seven, that he had found out his kin were being raised in orphanages.

Riminic Ivan Kolovsky.

Levander Ivan Kolovsky.

There had been no Zakahr.

'I changed my name,' Zakahr explained. 'Not at first. I ran away and worked the street for several years, and you don't need a name there. A charity like the one I run now offered me a way out. It was then—when I was a man, when I had picked myself out of the gutter—that I swore revenge. It was only then—when I wasn't eating out of garbage cans, when I wanted an education—that I needed a name. Perhaps you can see why I chose not to take my father's.' He looked at Aleksi with loathing. 'Did you never think to look for me?'

'I didn't know. I couldn't remember,' Aleksi said.

'You found out when you were seven—you are a man now.'

Kate just sat there—she didn't know what to say, because Zakahr was right. With all Aleksi's means, with all his money, with everything at his disposal, *shouldn't* he have at least looked?

After the longest silence Aleksi spoke. 'I thought I was going mad. I thought I had brain damage from the accident. For months now—all the months since the accident—I have been trying to work it out; I thought the accident had robbed me of my memory,' Aleksi explained, 'though now I see it actually brought things back.'

Zakahr opened his mouth to speak, but as Aleksi continued he stayed silent.

'I knew something was wrong before the accident. I was out of control, but I didn't know why. I hated seeing you at the charity ball, but after you left I tried to speak with you—I was driving to the airport when the accident happened and I didn't even know what for. I didn't know you were my brother.'

'Please!' Zakahr retorted. 'You've just told me that you *knew* you had a brother in an orphanage in Russia, you *knew* you reacted emotionally when you saw me, when you heard about my past, and you expect me to believe that it never entered your head that it might be me?'

'After the accident I could remember the beating my father gave me when I was seven as clear as anything. I could remember finding the certificates, demanding to know about you. You can believe it or not, though I swear this is the truth—until then I had no recall of it, even when Levander arrived...' He looked back on those years with different eyes now.

'It was a shock to find out about him.' Aleksi shook
his head as if to clear it, as he struggled to join
together the pieces of his mind from before and after
that fateful day. 'Only after the accident did I
remember what I had found out all that time ago. The
revelation all those years before had completely disappeared from my memory.' He shook his head again,
but in bemusement. 'How?'

'He literally knocked it out of you,' Zakahr said, and
Aleksi just sat there, stunned. 'For a child to survive,
sometimes the brain is kind and allows denial. I know
because there are things I have done that I don't
remember—just sometimes I wake up in the night…'

'And you know you've glimpsed hell?' Aleksi
murmured. He knew because he had.

After that restless night at the ball had led him to
Kate's door once more he had headed for the airport,
filled with a need to put matters right with Zakahr, to
face what he was facing now.

'I have thought of revenge for a long time.' Zakahr said.
'It has been my one sure goal—to bring you all down.'

'Have your revenge, then,' Aleksi said. 'There will
be no argument from me.'

'You might want to speak with your lawyer first,'
Zakahr responded. 'Shore up your assets, close a few
doors…' He frowned when Aleksi shook his head. 'But
surely you would want to protect the people that you love?'

'Levander, Iosef, myself—we can all take care of ourselves. I have already taken care of the others that matter.'

'I understand,' Zakahr said.

And suddenly so too did Kate, and she saw a drop of
salt water land on her lap, replaying so many conversations through tear-filled eyes. She knew now why Aleksi

had so badly wanted her to cash the cheque. Somehow, even though he had hurt her today more than she thought she could bear, he had been taking care of her.

'What about Krasavitsa?' Belenki checked. 'Your mother said before you would never step down from that without a fight.'

'Take it,' Aleksi stated emotionlessly. 'If it makes you feel better.'

He had lost everything.

He had lost her.

There was no thrill, no elation, no victory, no peace.

He had nothing to give, nothing to offer to make it up to her.

Aleksi knew that as he drove her to his home for the final time.

His past—his shame, his family's shame—had all finally caught up with them. After his mistrust, his treatment of Kate, he knew, because he had finally let himself know *her*, that there would be no going back for the two of them.

He had hurt her at her very core.

But the old Aleksi suddenly jumped on his shoulder, whispering in his ear as he hugged the bends on the beach road, grinding the gears, accelerating out of bends, trying to justify the way he'd treated her. She had been with her ex, she'd kissed him, he'd seen it…

What had *she* seen? he asked himself.

Over the years, as he'd ricocheted from scandal to scandal, what had the woman who'd loved him throughout it all silently endured?

He looked over to her and knew he was right about how she felt about him—and it wasn't vanity or presumption, as it once had been. Her love had been different, and so rare he hadn't recognised it. A steadfast love that had been there beside him through bad times as well as good, and now, because of his actions, it was lost.

'I'm sorry.'

The old Aleksi would have attempted to lighten the silence that followed his apology, would have confused her with casual words like, *We can finish what we started*, would have made her blink till she wondered if she'd misread what had happened, till he convinced her that she had.

'For what?' she asked.

'All of it.' They were nearing his house and he slowed down to slide through the electric gates. 'Had I known, had I understood that Zakahr was my brother, had I known just how toxic my family's history really was, I would never have exposed you to it. I would never have brought you and Georgie to my home at such a time. I knew something was wrong. I had no idea just how wrong it all was.'

'I don't care about your family's mistakes! All I cared about was you,' she cried.

They were home, or at his house anyway, and she climbed out of the car.

'I am sorry, too, for accusing you about what happened before...'

'For what?' Kate wanted him to say it out loud.

'For what happened,' he repeated.

'For *what*?' she pressed.

'For...' He didn't know how to describe it, but he tried. 'For holding back from you when we last made love.'

She laughed a black laugh as she went into the house—because that was exactly what he had done.

'You hold back in everything, Aleksi. You hold yourself back because you're so damn scared of falling.'

Oh, she would have said more, but the trouble with being a parent was that at times it included children. Little girls who arrived home when they shouldn't. And even though she wanted to scream and shout and kick and fight, Kate knew that instead she had to smile, to swallow down her loss and anger and pretend it didn't hurt, to convince her daughter that leaving was a good idea, that they were better off without him, that Mummy was absolutely and completely fine…

Only tears were so appallingly close, Kate realised with horror, that she couldn't do it right now.

Couldn't be brave at this second.

'Hi, there!' It was Aleksi who filled the crushing silence as Georgie climbed out of the car. 'How was school?'

'I hate it,' Georgie said, and then promptly burst into tears. 'I hate it and I'm never going back!'

Oh, yes, the trouble with being a parent was that even when you had a top-notch nanny children still wanted their mother—even when there wasn't a single bit of you left to give, still they demanded that you produce it.

'What happened?'

They were somehow in the kitchen. Aleksi got a juice box from the fridge and Kate thought Georgie might push it away, but she actually took it and then, when Aleksi left them to it, she gulped it down before speaking.

'I don't like it there,' Georgie sobbed. 'Tell me I don't have to go back.'

'Not till you tell me what happened!' Kate repeated. She knew she wasn't handling this well, knew she should wait for her to open up, but her nerves were so taut they were close to snapping. She wanted it out now and sorted, so she could get on with her own pain. She didn't want Georgie's drama today. Tomorrow, yes, and the next day, and the next too—but not today, when her own heart was bleeding and breaking. Except she was a mother, so she didn't get to choose. 'Talk to me, Georgie.'

'I just don't like it,' she said. 'The other girls are mean.'

'What did they say?' Kate asked, and she could hear the shrill note in her own voice that undid all the good of the cool juice and made Georgie cry just a bit harder.

'Why don't you have a swim?'

It was Aleksi who came in, and even though Kate loathed him, even though she knew she would be far, far better off without him, she was actually relieved when he took over the reins. She was so used to holding them alone it felt different as he steered things a little— perhaps not in the direction she would have, but maybe another route was called for.

'Have a swim, I'll get some snacks brought out, and then when you've cooled down maybe you can tell your mum what's going on.'

'Will you swim too?' Georgie's eyes swung to her mother's.

'Sure,' Kate said, though it was absolutely the last thing she wanted.

'And you?' Georgie's eyes narrowed at Aleksi, and Kate couldn't help but sense a small challenge coming from her daughter. 'Will you swim, too?'

'Of course,' he responded immediately.

Kate took for ever to reluctantly haul on her bikini, although Georgie had changed in less than a second. Aleksi was out there, and she really couldn't face this…

Her face started to crumple as she heard the laughter

from her daughter, and she looked out as Aleksi threw a ball and realised what she had to tell the little girl.

That they were moving again. That Aleksi and her mum's relationship was over. That her dad had gone to Bali, permanently...

'Catch me!'

Georgie's voice soared through the late-afternoon sky and Kate's throat tightened on a shout of warning as she saw Georgie run. Aleksi was turning to get the ball, too far from the little girl who ran to the edge. She slipped, soaring through the air, and Kate's heart was in her mouth as the world moved in slow motion—she was too close to the edge, and would surely crack her head! Only Aleksi moved like lightning, stretching though the water and pulling Georgie back with milli-metres to spare. He caught her. Oh, there was a splash, and they both went under, and Georgie had a mouth and nose full of water, but somehow he caught her.

'Never do that again.' Aleksi's voice was close to a shout, and real fear was on his features by the time Kate had dashed through the house and out to the pool. 'You could have had an accident.'

'You caught me, though.'

'I might not have...' Aleksi sat her down at the pool's edge and Kate could see that beneath his tan he was pale. 'I almost didn't!'

'But you did!' Georgie said simply.

'Georgie...' Kate realised her voice was shaking. 'You warn people properly. You don't just jump. You slipped and might have really hurt yourself.'

'He caught me, though,' Georgie insisted, but her face was working up to tears.

'Leave it,' Aleksi said gruffly. 'You're fine—you're

safe. I'm only upset because…' He was helpless at her tears. 'Because I care about you.'

'No, Aleksi, you *don't*!' she snarled, and then she turned and challenged her mother. 'Everyone at school knows it's just pretend. Lucy's nanny is a friend of Sophie…' She stared accusingly at Kate. 'She heard them talking, and she said that soon he's getting rid of us!'

'Nobody's getting rid of you!' Aleksi's voice was a husk of breath.

'But it is going to end,' Georgie said. 'I could hear you rowing.'

'Grown-ups argue sometimes,' Aleksi explained, still stunned.

'When are we going home?'

Georgie's voice was shrill and Kate felt sick. 'We're getting a new home darling.' She tried to smile, tried to sound positive, tried to make it sound idyllic as she crushed her own daughter's heart. 'Near your new school.'

'So it's true, then?'

Georgie was too proud to crumple there and then, but with a sob she ran up to her bedroom, leaving Kate with the guilt she had always known would come since she'd embarked on this dangerous game—only she had never anticipated how devastating it would be.

'Kate!' Aleksi called her back as she rushed to follow her daughter, but she ignored him, so he barred the door with his body. 'You've done nothing wrong. She'll be okay once you are in your home, once she's really settled in her new school…'

'You don't get it, do you?' Kate choked. 'You think it's about the house and the nice cars and the pool and the posh school…' God, she truly hated him in that moment. 'She doesn't give a stuff about all that. She loved *you*, she loved our little family, she actually believed that you loved us too…'

And not even Aleksi could halt her, so desperate was she to get to her daughter, so he didn't even try. He stood aside and listened to Kate somehow not pound up the steps but calmly walk, blowing her nose as she did so. Then he heard the gentle knock on Georgie's bedroom door.

Walking had been painful for Aleksi since the accident, but it was sheer agony today as he forced himself, physically forced himself, to take each step. Every instinct told him to turn, to run away, yet he made himself undertake the most daunting walk of his life.

'Why doesn't he love us?'

He heard Georgie's sobs and he could feel the sweat beading on his forehead. He so badly wanted to fling open her door, to counter Kate's words, yet he did what Kate had so rightly accused him of.

He held back.

'Aleksi has a lot going on in his life.' He heard her trying to sound calm and assured. 'Lots of difficult things are happening with his family right now. There are going to be lots of rows and arguments and he doesn't want us to get mixed up in at all…'

'But we could help him,' Georgie begged. 'We could be nice to him when they are all being mean.'

'It's not that simple, darling.'

Aleksi closed his eyes as he listened to Kate attempt to soothe her daughter.

'Aleksi isn't sure what's going to happen with his work with his home…'

'Why can't he live with us in our new home?' Georgie reasoned. 'You said we're getting a nice new home near the school.'

'We are, but…'

'So why can't he live with us there?'

'It's not going to be what Aleksi's used to,' Kate said, and she couldn't gloss it up any more.

Defeated, she sat on the bed where her daughter lay sobbing and stroked her shoulder, tried to comfort her, and wished someone could comfort her too—because all Georgie's arguments had done was ram home the cruel truth. Aleksi didn't want them. Yes, he cared, and had ensured they would be looked after, but their little world wasn't one that was for him. Soon he would be healed, back to his playground world. Aleksi would build himself up again—and it wouldn't be with her.

He had told her that from the start. She had gambled her heart and had thought she knew the odds, that the prize of an education and security for her daughter was worth the risk. But sitting on the bed, realising her future was without the man she loved, thinking of the pain she had caused Georgie, suddenly Kate was angry. The glimpses of his love, the tastes of what he could never sustain—surely it would have been better without that? Better to live not knowing what she was missing?

'I thought he loved us…' Georgie sobbed into her pillow. 'I told all the girls that I had a new daddy….'

Maybe she shouldn't have, Kate thought to herself, but who could blame her? Just as she had played dress-up as a little girl, who could blame Georgie for wanting what so many other children had? Kate wanted to give in then—just wanted to stop being brave and strong and sensible. She wanted to lie down on the bed with her daughter and wail, and bemoan how unfair it all was sometimes, but she wouldn't allow herself. For a second she wavered, felt the swell of tears in her throat, and then she felt his hand on her shoulder, comforting her as she comforted her daughter, and Kate held her breath.

'Georgie…' Aleksi's usually curt voice was soft, but unwavering. 'Nothing would make me more proud than to be your father.'

'So why are you sending us away?' Her pinched, angry and tired little face swung around to confront him.

Yes, she was tired, Kate realised, and her heart twisted in on itself. The journey that was so hard for her at times was hard on Georgie too. No matter how she tried to shield her, no matter how she tried to protect her, her little girl was tired and confused too.

'I am not sending you away,' Aleksi explained. 'Part of me wants you and your mother to leave because I think it might be easier on you both.'

'How?'

Georgie sat up as Aleksi sat down.

'Your mother told you that things might be difficult if you stay.'

'I don't care about that.'

'I see that now,' Aleksi said. 'Georgie, I have lived a complicated life…' He caught Kate's eyes in a silent plea for help.

'Aleksi isn't the settling down type,' Kate tried.

'I wasn't,' Aleksi corrected. 'Never did I consider marrying, and especially not being a parent.'

'Why?' The perpetual question came from Georgie, and Kate was glad for it.

'I did not think I would be very good at it,' Aleksi admitted. 'I was brought up to trust no one and I didn't—not anyone,' he elaborated, 'not even myself.' Georgie's tears had stopped. 'I see my brothers with their children and I wonder how they can be so sure they are doing the right thing by them, making the right decisions for them…'

He didn't know what else to say, so Kate stepped in then.

'Being a parent is a huge responsibility, Georgie, and Aleksi isn't sure…' She stopped as she felt his hand tighten on her shoulder.

'I'm not sure that I'll be the best father, but I will try…'

Kate could feel the blood pounding in her ears.

'I will do everything I can to look after you and your mother. I have a new brother, and I want to do the right thing by him too—but you, Georgie, and your mother come first. I will fight for what is mine—hopefully with honour.'

Georgie didn't understand, so Aleksi explained.

'Zakahr is my eldest brother—he has a right to the House of Kolovsky. But I will have a wife and daughter to look after…'

'We don't care about the money,' Georgie said. 'So long as we can have lots of channels on our television!'

'You deserve the very best in life.' Aleksi actually managed a smile as he spoke. 'And now I have someone to work for…' He did. All the years—the gambling, the searching, the reckless times—just melted away, because here before him was what really mattered.

'Us?' Georgie checked and Aleksi nodded.

'You two.'

'So I can tell the girls at school…'

'Tell them you are going to be a bridesmaid.'

Aleksi smiled, and Kate paled. 'You're supposed to ask *me* first.'

'Are you going to refuse?'

She looked at Georgie, and then at Aleksi, and then she looked into her own heart and she absolutely wouldn't dare refuse the gift she was staring at now—the gift of his love. There was, Kate realised, no greater love than that of a bad boy made good—it was there for the taking, a future with him, and all she had to do was say yes.

'I love you, Kate.'

He said it for the first time in front of Georgie—and Kate knew that he meant it. Because he might be reckless with his own heart at times, and even with hers, but always, always he had taken Georgie's welfare seriously—at the hospital, with her education. Always he had made sure that she was okay, and he wouldn't let her down now. So, whether he trusted himself or not, Kate did.

'Yuck,' Georgie said as it was sealed with a kiss.

'And now,' Aleksi said, quickly getting a handle on being a father, 'you can go to your room and play for a while.'

'I'm in my room.' Georgie pointed out.

So she was!

So they went to his.

'Ours,' he corrected, and then he thought of this house that was all tied up in Kolovsky. 'I will speak with Zakahr,' Aleksi promised. 'When I gave it all away I was only thinking of me...' She opened her mouth to speak, but he overrode her. 'You deserve something too.'

'I've got everything,' Kate said. 'I've never been more proud of you than when you handed it back to him. He's your brother.' She watched him screw up his eyes, and then he opened them again—to the woman who was going to be his wife. And he knew, finally knew, he could trust someone.

'Will you be there when I tell my mother?' Aleksi asked, and Kate didn't hesitate.

'I'll always be there.'

'She won't fit—there is not enough fabric…'

It had been Nina's response to the news of the wedding the following day. Her tears had soon dried and it was back to the pointed catty remarks as usual—this time about Kate's wedding dress.

And the planning for the wedding of the year had started in her next sentence!

The pleading too.

'Iosef is your twin—of course he must be your best man…'

'I love Iosef, but I have already discussed this with him.' Aleksi was pale—not that his mother noticed. Aleksi was bleeding inside now that the moment of truth had arrived. 'Iosef agrees this is the right thing to do—Zakahr is to be my best man.'

'Zakahr?' Nina frowned. '*Zakahr?* Why on earth would you choose a stranger? He's not even a colleague…'

'I thought he was your new best friend,' Aleksi taunted, 'as you've been singing his praises for months.'

'He helps with our charity. It is just business, Aleksi.'

'You really thought he liked you?' Aleksi said, gaining momentum now. 'You really thought he had the House of Kolovsky's best interests at heart?' He stared at his mother with utter contempt. 'You *fool.*'

'Don't you dare speak to me like that,' Nina retaliated. 'I am your mother!'

'And Zakahr is your *son.*'

Kate had never imagined she might feel sorry for Nina, never thought she could feel sympathy for a woman who had stood back and watched her son be beaten, who had denied him treatment for the sake of her reputation, who had abandoned her own flesh and blood in an orphanage and who had humiliated Kate at every turn. But watching the colour drain from Nina's well made-up face, watching her stumble, watching hands that, unlike her face, looked every bit her age hold onto the desk as her legs gave way, she felt sympathy override satisfaction and Kate found her a chair, helping Nina into it before she slipped to the floor.

'Riminic!' Nina sobbed the word out, and Kate realised then that she must have said it to herself every day.

'Remember Zakahr's words at your charity ball?' Aleksi was merciless. 'Remember how he prostituted himself to survive? How that boy, your son, was forced to beg, to steal, to…?'

'Stop!' It was Kate who halted him as Nina was gagging now. 'Aleksi, stop. She's heard enough.'

'She can't stand to hear it,' Aleksi said contemptuously. 'Zakahr *lived* it.'

'Forgive me!' Nina screamed, so loudly that even Lavinia came running, her bony legs struggling on six-inch heels as Nina sobbed louder. 'Forgive me, Aleksi.'

'It's not me who needs to forgive you,' Aleksi said. 'It's my brother—your son.'

'Leave it, Aleksi,' Kate said, and she was crying for both of them, for all of them, because there was no victory to be had here—just a whole lot of healing to take place.

So they left Lavinia comforting Nina, walked out of the golden doors and stood on the steps of Kolovsky as

Aleksi took a deep breath, and then another one. The sun was shining and the world was waiting, and Kate knew they'd be okay because instead of walking on ahead Aleksi stopped and took her hand.

'Are you sure you want to be a Kolovsky?' he checked, and somehow, on the worst day, he made her laugh.

'Quite sure,' Kate assured him, and they looked over to the church across the road.

If they'd had a licence, she'd have married him there and then, but instead they walked over hand in hand and booked the date.

EPILOGUE

IT *WAS* the most beautiful dress in the world—at least it was to Kate.

As soft as petals it clung to her curves, and there was a hint of daring too.

It was a Kolovsky gown, but not *the* Kolovsky gown—because Kate didn't want it either.

'Do I look like a princess?' Georgie asked for the hundredth time as the Kolovsky dressers fussed with her mother.

'You do...' Kate said through chattering teeth, hardly able to stand the thought of so many eyes on her. It was more soothing to gaze at her daughter.

Her dress was simple yet stunning: silk, a shade pinker than her mother's. She had flowers on her head and her eyes were shining—clever and gifted, yes, but just a little girl who was dressed up today when, even better, all her little friends would see.

Even the one who had once pinched her!

Georgie's dress, though simple, was filled with tradition.

A new tradition—a new order.

Aleksi's gift to his new daughter had been jewels—

jewels Georgie did not even know existed. They had been sewn into the hem of her dress. Jewels that would never see the light of day unless they were needed at some point in the future.

His way of saying that, come what might, with the House of Kolovsky, Aleksi's girls would always be safe.

It was a fairly low-key wedding, but that didn't stop the press clamouring—just who *was* Zakahr Belenki? Add to that the news that Nina Kolovsky was *resting* in a private hospital and might not make the wedding and it had them hanging from the trees.

But she made it.

Kate stood at the entrance to the church and was curiously proud of the woman she loathed.

A woman who stood tiny, shaky but straight, plastered in make-up, leaning a touch on Lavinia and trying very hard to smile.

Kate was proud of Nina's sons and daughter too.

Of Levander, who had flown his family from the UK... As she walked down the aisle she could see Dimitri smile and turn, and it made Kate smile too.

Of Iosef, who *was* Aleksi's best man—just not for today.

And Annika, who had looked out for Georgie in all of this.

She couldn't look at her husband-to-be as she walked, or she'd have started to cry—which she did when Zakahr turned around and nudged his new brother and smiled.

How did Zakahr do it?

How could he stand to be in the same room as all of them?

How did you start to forgive such betrayal?

And then she saw Aleksi, and nothing else mattered.

He kissed his bride, and then he did the nicest thing: he went over and kissed a very proud Georgie before going back to Kate's side.

Back to his *krasavitsa*.

THE DEVIL
WEARS KOLOVSKY

CAROL MARINELLI

CHAPTER ON

ZAKAHR could have walked, but he chose not to.

The offices of the House of Kolovsky were, after all, just a short stroll from the luxury hotel that was for the next few weeks Zakahr Belenki's home.

Or, to avoid the press, he could have taken a helicopter for the short hop across the Melbourne skyline.

Except he had long dreamt of this moment.

This moment of the future was one that had sustained Zakahr through a hellish youth—and now, finally, the future was today.

His driver, on Zakahr's instruction, took the long route from the hotel, the blacked-out windows of the sleek limousine causing heads to turn as it made its way through the smart streets lined with galleries and boutiques. As instructed, the driver slowed down at the original House of Kolovsky boutique. The cerulean blue building with the Kolovsky gold logo was familiar, and its wares were desired worldwide. The window display was, as always, elegantly simple—swathes of heavy silk, and one large opal that shimmered in the morning light. Aesthetically it was beautiful, but as always,

this sight greeted him on his travels, Zakahr
bile.

'Drive on.'

His driver obliged. A few moments later they pulled
up outside the offices of the House of Kolovsky, and the
moment was Zakahr's.

Cameras were aimed for their shot, and for once
he didn't mind. Impossibly wealthy, and with brooding good-looks, he had dated many of Europe's most
beautiful and famous women. His heartbreak reputation
had been exposed and examined often in the glossies.
Though Zakahr usually abhorred the invasion of his privacy, here, on the other side of the world, and especially
this morning, it did not faze him, and a wry smile was
contained as he thought of the Kolovskys watching the
news as they ate breakfast.

He hoped they choked.

Questions were hurled, cameras flashed, and micro-
phones were pushed towards him.

*Was the House of Kolovsky being taken over by this
European magnate? Or was he here covering while
Aleksi Kolovsky honeymooned?*

Had he enjoyed the wedding?

Was he a relation?

Where was Nina, the matriarch?

What was his interest in Kolovsky?

That was a question with merit. After all, this fashion
industry icon was but loose change to a portfolio like
Belenki's.

Zakahr made no comment, and neither would he
later.

The facts would soon speak for themselves.

The sun beat on the back of his head. His grey blood-shot eyes were hidden behind dark glasses, his lips were pressed together, his expression unreadable, but he was an imposing sight.

A head above everyone, he was broad-shouldered too. His skin was pale, beautifully clean-shaven, and his black hair was short and neat, but despite the im-maculate suit, the glint of an expensive watch and the well-heeled shoes, there was an air of the untamed to him—a restlessness beneath the sleek exterior that had the journalists holding back just a touch, with an unusual hesitancy to push for answers. Because no one wanted to be singled out by this man. No one wanted that un-leashed power aimed solely at them.

He strode through the street and then up the steps, scattering the press, pushing the golden revolving doors. Zakahr was in.

Perhaps he ought to stand and relish this moment, be-cause finally all this was his. Except there was a hollow feeling inside Zakahr. He relished challenges—had come ready to fight—yet when his identity had been revealed the House of Kolovsky had been handed to him on a plate, and it was now for Zakahr to decide what to do with it.

He sensed the unease of everyone around him.

It did not move him.

'Mr Belenki.'

The greeting followed him. The lift doors were wait-ing open and he stepped inside. The lift glided up.

He sensed trepidation here too, as he walked out on to

the floor that contained his office. As surely as if it had been pumped through the air-conditioning he could feel it—in the thick carpets, the walls, behind every door as he walked down the corridor. And they had every right to be nervous. Zakahr Belenki had been called in, and in the business world that heralded change.

No one outside family knew who he *really* was.

Zakahr headed to his office. He had been here several times now. Just never as Chief.

He opened the heavy wooden doors, ready to claim his birthright, but his moment was broken as he stepped into darkness. Zakahr frowned as he turned on the lights, and then his jaw clenched in anger—there were no staff to greet him, the blinds were not drawn, the computers were off.

Perhaps the Kolovskys thought they were having the last laugh?

Aleksi had at the weekend married his PA, Kate, but he had assured Zakahr that the last few weeks had been spent training her replacement—except there was no one here.

He headed for a desk, picked up a phone, ready to ring and blast at Reception to get someone up here. But the door opened again, and Zakahr stood, silently fuming, as a stunning blonde came in, wafting fragrance, carrying a large takeaway coffee.

She walked past him to a small office off the main suite, put her drink on the desk, and gave him a quick 'Sorry I'm late' as she slipped off her jacket and turned the computer on. 'I'm Lavinia,' she added.

'I know,' Zakahr said, because he had seen her at his

brother's wedding on Saturday, and hers was a face men noticed and remembered. She had huge blue eyes and a tumble of blonde hair, achieving a look both glamorous and pretty—though Lavinia wasn't looking anything like as amazing as she had at the wedding. There were dark smudges under her eyes, and an air of weariness about her that rather suggested she was more ready for bed than work.

'Is this how you make a good first impression?' Zakahr asked, used to groomed, beautiful staff members who faded into the background—not someone who burst into a room then pulled out a large magnifying mirror from her drawer and proceeded to put make-up on at her desk.

'Give me two minutes,' Lavinia said, unashamedly applying foundation and rather skillfully, Zakahr noticed, erasing all shadows from under her eyes, 'and then I'll make a good impression!'

He couldn't believe her audacity. 'Where is the PA?'

'She got married on Saturday,' Lavinia said.

She was working on her eyes now, her brush loaded with grey. Given Zakahr had been at the wedding, she must have thought her response humorous, because she gave a little laugh at the end of her sentence. As she layered mascara, she told him the necessary truth.

'The stand-in that Kate trained left in tears on Friday and said she was never coming back.'

She wasn't about to sweeten things for him—the House of Kolovsky had been in chaos since the news had got out that Zakahr Belenki was taking over, and if this man really thought he was going to walk in and find order then he was about to find out otherwise.

Lavinia knew he was irritated at her putting on her make-up but what choice did she have? In less than an hour they would be leaving for the airport, and it was essential that she looked the part. But even if none of her previous bosses—Levander, Aleksi or Nina—would have had it any other way, Zakahr was beyond irritated by her actions.

'Did Kate sit at her desk to do her face?'

'Kate,' Lavinia said, with just a hint of ring to her tone, 'wasn't exactly hired for her looks.'

He heard the edge to her voice, and suppressed a smirk at her clear annoyance. Kate was the absolute opposite of Lavinia, and it must surely eat away at this stunning specimen that an overweight, rather plain single mum had married the prize that was Aleksi Kolovsky!

'There's clearly more to Kate than looks,' Zakahr quipped. And, because he just couldn't resist, he added, 'After all, she married the boss!'

He watched the blusher brush pause over her cheek for a second, then she carried on rouging her cheeks.

'Where are *your* staff?' Lavinia frowned, peering over his shoulder as if she expected someone to appear.

'Unfortunately for me you *are* my staff.'

'You didn't bring anyone with you?' The surprise was evident in her voice—she had read up on him, of course. Zakahr Belenki had interests all over Europe. His team swept in on ailing businesses that glinted with potential gold, injecting massive doses of cash to keep them afloat, moving in like a cuckoo, and taking prime place in the newly lucrative nest. And even though Kolovsky was far from ailing, even though Lavinia secretly knew he was here for rather more personal reasons, it was quite unthinkable that he was here alone. 'You haven't brought your team?'

Her question was a pertinent one. His own staff *had* been bemused that he would travel to Australia without them—to them he was assessing the viability of a company. Why wouldn't he bring his team? But Zakahr was a leader. He never displayed weakness, and Kolovsky was his only one. He was not about to explain to his staff why this trip was personal. Still, Zakahr wasn't about to discuss it with Lavinia either, so instead he told her to bring him coffee, then stalked into his office and slammed the door.

Loudly.

Lavinia had worked for both Levander and Aleksi Kolovsky prior to Zakahr, so a slamming door barely made her blink.

Sitting at her desk, all she wanted to do was close her eyes and sleep. It hadn't made the best impression that she was late, but had Zakahr stopped to ask he might have found out the reason—it had truly been the weekend from hell. Propping up Nina at Aleksi's wedding had been the easy part.

On Friday her little half-sister had been moved into foster care, and though Lavinia was beyond relieved that finally action had been taken—Lavinia had actually engineered it—it hadn't been as swift as she had hoped. Instead of Rachael being moved into Lavinia's care she had been placed in a foster home, and the authorities were now assessing the situation.

The true precariousness of Rachael's future had hit hard, and Lavinia had spent three sleepless nights, worrying not just about the future but about how Rachael was coping at the foster home—how the little girl felt sleeping in a strange bed, in a strange home, with strange people.

Even if there was little Lavinia could actually do for Rachael at the moment, even if she could only console herself that at least the little girl was safe, the last place Lavinia wanted to be was here—and if it had been on any other day she would have rung in sick.

Except whom could she ring?

The oh-so-efficient temporary PA Kate had trained had thrown in the towel on the eve of the wedding, Aleksi was on his honeymoon, the other Kolovsky brothers had long since washed their hands of the place, and Nina—*poor* Nina—on finding out the news as to just who Zakahr Belenki was, was now in a private psychiatric hospital.

With the authorities examining Lavinia's suitability to parent, more than ever she needed a stable job, and with that thought in mind, instead of not showing up, Lavinia had showered and pulled on the clothes she had set out the previous night—a dark cami and a gorgeous, if rather short in the skirt, black suit. She had put on her favourite black suede high-heeled shoes, which *always* kicked off an outfit, and had somehow arrived a mere five minutes late—or, as she would point out later, fifty-five minutes early. Most office jobs started at nine!

Not that Zakahr Belenki had thanked her for her effort!

Lavinia poked her tongue out at his closed door.

He was more arrogant than his brothers combined—and that was saying something. She knew who he was! Knew, despite his name, that he was actually a Kolovsky—that he was Nina and Ivan's secret son.

Not that he could find out that she knew.

Happy with her face, Lavinia opened up her computer, ran her eyes over the schedule for the day. Even if she and Kate, the old PA and now Aleksi's bride, had clashed at times, how she wished she were here to sort this out.

Lavinia wore the title of Assistant PA, but was aware she had been hired more as an attractive accessory—a bright and breezy attractive accessory—which was an essential role within Kolovsky. Now, though, the team Ivan had built had, since his death, been slowly dismantled, and that combined with the astonishing news that Zakahr hadn't brought his impressive team left Lavinia with a heavy weight of responsibility.

She shouldn't care, of course.

Lavinia was well aware that some of the minor directors would be only too happy to have their own PAs loaned out to Zakahr—who in this building *didn't* want a direct route to the mysterious new boss?

Lavinia.

She didn't want it, but she had it.

And, like it or not, till Zakahr understood its complicated workings, the smooth running of Kolovsky fell to Lavinia.

She was quite sure people would say she was being grandiose—as if the House of Kolovsky needed Lavinia to survive! Lavinia knew in her heart that it didn't—but some things mattered, they really mattered, and without her inner knowledge certain things that mattered simply wouldn't get done.

Lavinia rested her head on the desk and closed her eyes.

In a minute she would lift it.

In a minute she would force a dazzling smile, would inject some lightness into her face and make them both coffee. Hopefully she and Zakahr could start over again.

She just needed a minute…

'Lavinia!'

This time she jumped!

As Zakahr had intended! Given that he had buzzed her, given that he had called her twice, given that she was asleep at her desk!

She jerked awake at the sound of his voice behind her, felt his brimming anger as strongly as the heavy scent of his cologne, and was tempted just to get her bag and head for home rather than follow his instruction.

'Could you and your hangover please join me in my office?'

CHAPTER TWO

LAVINIA was beyond embarrassed.

She sat at her desk, scalding in her own skin for a full minute, before she could even think of going back out there.

Her first day with her new boss and he'd found her not daydreaming, not dozing, but fast asleep at her desk. Lavinia was used to bouncing back, and she normally did so with a bright smile, but she didn't even try to summon one as she headed for the gallows.

'I'm sorry, Zak…' She walked into his office where he sat, but her voice trailed off when he gestured her to sit and she realised he was on the phone, talking in Russian. Whatever he was saying, Lavinia was quite sure that it wasn't complimentary

His voice was rich and low. He did not shout—there was no need to. There was a ring of confidence and strong assertion behind each word, and she was quite sure this was a man who rarely had to repeat himself.

He was incredibly good-looking, but that was pretty much the norm around here—he was no better than his brothers.

Actually, he *was*, Lavinia conceded.

As if God had made him perfect and then, happy with the formula, had kept on going. There was a salient beauty to him—one that demanded closer inspection—and, just as she would examine the shots of a new Kolovsky model, Lavinia briefly scanned his features. There was rare perfect symmetry to his bone structure, and his high cheekbones and straight Roman nose were a photographer's dream, or nightmare. For not for a second could Lavinia imagine him posing for the camera. There was nothing compliant about those grey eyes, no *give* in his demeanour. Normally she could sum a person up easily, but she was struggling to do so with Zakahr—especially now he had caught her looking.

His eyes held hers as he hung up the phone, and Lavinia felt a warmth spread over her cheeks as he refused to drop his gaze. Rarely—very rarely—it was Lavinia who looked away first, Lavinia who broke a silence that appeared to be only uncomfortable to her.

'I'd like to apologise for before—I didn't get any sleep last night, you see…'

'Are you fit to work?' Zakahr did not care for excuses, and he cut right in. 'Yes or no?'

'Yes.' Lavinia bristled as he refused her attempt to explain.

He stood, leaving her sitting, and went to make the coffee—it was the only way he would ensure it got done. Zakahr was in fact the one battling a hangover. Aleksi's wedding had been hell. He had done the right thing by the man who had tried to do the same for him, but as soon as he'd been able to Zakahr had got out of there and away from the woman he loathed.

He had done everything he could during the service not to look at Nina, the woman who was by biology only his mother, to just ignore her—not to care. Since finding out he was her son Nina had been admitted to a plush psychiatric hospital.

Karma, Zakahr thought darkly.

There was a saying he had learnt as a child—as the call, so the echo. How good he should feel that it was Nina institutionalised now, and that it was he running his parents' empire. It should have been a feeling to savour—only yesterday had found him sitting in an anonymous taxi, staring at the hospital, trying to brace himself to go in.

There was so much to say, so much she *deserved* to hear in a long-awaited confrontation—except, hearing how ill she was, at the final hurdle Zakahr had balked with rare charity, unable to add to her pain.

He had ordered a taxi to the casino, consoled himself that if he chose, soon there would be no House of Kolovsky, soon he could walk away with the name erased and pretend it had never existed—as his parents had done to him. Zakahr had tried to lose himself in noise and stunning women, yet despite his intentions nothing had appealed, and he had spent the night back at the hotel, dousing the bitter churn of emotion in his stomach with hundred-year-old brandy.

And now he was making his assistant coffee!

Seething, he handed her a cup. She tasted it and then screwed up her face and moaned about too much sugar.

He should, Zakahr realised, fire her on the spot.

Just tell her to get out.

Except despite her total lack of professionalism, despite her possibly being the worst Assistant PA in memory, for a little while at least he needed her. Begrudgingly. Extremely begrudgingly. Aleksi had given him a password—one that supposedly accessed all areas—but he had to get in to the system first!

'What is the password?' Zakahr asked. 'For the computer?'

'H-o-K.' Lavinia said, and when that didn't work for him she elaborated. 'The *o* is lower case.'

He shot her a look. 'I want to address everyone together this morning,' Zakahr said. 'Then I want you to arrange fifteen-minute blocks for everyone from cleaner to top designer. After lunch I want the first one at my desk—you co-ordinate it. I want their history file in front of me...'

'You can't.' She watched his lips purse a touch—presumably *can't* was a word rarely said to Zakahr—but he really couldn't. 'We have dignitaries arriving. King Abdullah's daughter—she's coming for a fitting.'

'And?' Zakahr shrugged.

'Once a month or so we have an esteemed bridal guest—a Kolovsky always greets her at the airport and brings her back here...'

'Here?' Zakahr frowned—because surely they would head straight for a hotel?

'Here,' Lavinia confirmed. 'Because this is the moment she's been dreaming of.' He was far too male to understand. 'Anyway, she's hardly been cooped up in Economy. She will have been in their own jet. But someone high up has to greet them—it's what happens, what's expected.'

'The designer can go,' Zakahr dismissed, but when Lavinia still stood there he offered rare compromise. 'You go—if you have to.'

Lavinia ignored this. 'And then, as their host, you will invite her to dinner later in the week, and if their stay has been satisfactory you and your guest will be invited by her family to dinner...' She frowned for a minute. 'I think it's that way around—yes, in a few days she'll ask you to dinner to thank Kolovsky for its hospitality. She's here for a couple of weeks, as the wedding is only a couple of months off.' She saw him frown. 'There are normally a number of trips—Jasmine's doing it all in one.'

'The designers can take care of that side of things.'

'The designers are busy designing.' Lavinia rolled her eyes with impatience. 'The design team will be working day and night on the first designs...'

'I have more important things to do than meet some spoiled princess at the airport.'

'Fine.' Lavinia shrugged. 'Then so do I.' She turned to go, then changed her mind. 'These things matter, Zakahr.' He was working on the computer and didn't look up, and though in truth it wasn't Lavinia's problem, on her previous bosses' behalf it incensed her. 'This is the biggest day of the Princess's life we've been entrusted with. It's her *wedding*!' Lavinia said.

But that word clearly didn't move him, and if he didn't care then neither should she—except Lavinia did.

'I've got a lot going on in my life right now, Zakahr.

And, just for the record, I *didn't* race to get here because the new head of Kolovsky was taking office, I *didn't* sit putting on my make-up to impress *you*—I'm here and ready because I knew that the Princess had to be met. I'm not at my best with our international guests—Kate hated sending me. I forget things, I talk too much, or I show the soles of my feet and such. But I turned up today to try to do what is expected, because that's what Kolovsky is about—beautiful gowns, beautiful women, and at the top of the food chain those blasted wedding gowns.'

He just sat there. Zakahr did not need to be told how things were done by some Assistant PA who fell asleep at her desk. Except he knew he just had been. She was a strange mix, Zakahr decided. Disorganised, yet conscientious. There was also a brazenness to her—a boldness in her slender stature as she awaited his response, hand on hip, toes resisting tapping. Still he said nothing.

'Fine,' she shrilled to the cold silence. 'I'll go myself.'

But first she had to make a phone call...

Back at her desk, Lavinia checked the Princess's flight details, and that the cars were all ready, and waited anxiously for the clock to edge to nine before picking up the phone and dialling.

Ms Hewitt, Rachael's case worker, sounded more angry than exasperated. 'I spoke with you on Friday. You cannot ring in for daily checks—you are *not* her next of kin.'

'I'm trying to be, though.' Lavinia resisted the urge

to say something smart, knowing that she needed these people to be on her side. 'I just want to know that she's okay, and to find out when I can see her.'

'Rachael's father is visiting her on Wednesday evening, and again on Sunday. Really, it's very unsettling for Rachael to have so many visitors.'

'She's my half-sister,' Lavinia bristled. 'How can it be *unsettling* for her to see me?'

'I'll speak with her carers and see if we can arrange something.'

'And that's it?' Lavinia asked. 'Can I at least have a phone number so that I can ring her?'

'We'll contact you if we need to.' Ms Hewitt would not be swayed. 'I'll see if I can arrange a visit.'

Lavinia somehow managed to thank her, then replaced the phone and buried her head in her hands. She hated the lack of speed—couldn't stand what was happening to Rachael—and knew that Kevin, Rachael's father, was still probably dredging up every piece of dirt he could on Lavinia. He'd done everything he could to shut her out of the little girl's life. Maybe it was better that she was at work, because otherwise she'd be standing outside the kindergarten, waiting for Rachael to arrive, and that wouldn't go down well. Lavinia knew she had to stay calm. Had to accept that nothing was going to happen fast—and that she had to prove she was the responsible one.

'Sorry to inconvenience you with work.'

Lavinia looked up to the owner of the voice that dripped sarcasm. He was holding out her jacket, and she didn't even attempt to explain herself. She knew how bad this looked. Instead she just took her jacket and clipped ahead, trying to switch her mind to the job, to being the happy, outgoing person she was at work, whatever the problems in her private life.

They used the rear entrance. A huge limo swallowed them up, with another following to accommodate the royal entourage, and they headed for the airport as Lavinia filled him in as best she could on Princess Jasmine's details. Even Zakahr's eyes widened when she told him what this gown and the dresses for the bridesmaids would be costing King Abdullah.

No wonder Kolovsky, despite everything, was still riding high.

For Zakahr, it was in fact a relief to get out of the office—to get away from the scent of Kolovsky, the surroundings—and for the first time since he had taken over he felt the creep of doubt. He had given himself a month to come to a decision. He was starting to wonder if he could stand to be there for even a week.

For years he had watched the House of Kolovsky from a distance, researching them thoroughly. Levander, Ivan's illegitimate son, had been brought over from Russia as a teenager and given the golden key to Kolovsky. There was no mention of Riminic, Nina and Ivan's firstborn.

Riminic Ivan Kolovsky they had named their baby, as was the Russian way—Riminic, son of Ivan—then at two days old they had taken him to Detsky Dom. Some orphanages were good, but Nina and Ivan had not chosen well. The Kolovsky name meant only hate to Zakahr.

At thirteen he had left the orphanage and had done what he had to to survive on the streets. At seventeen he had been given a chance—shelter, access to a computer, to a different path. Discarding his birth name, he had followed that path with a vision—and that vision included revenge.

As rumours had escalated that Levander had been raised in Detsky Dom, of course the House of Kolovsky had rapidly developed a social conscience, raising great sums for orphanages and street children.

Zakahr had been doing it since his first pay cheque.

And so he had made contact—attending a charity ball Nina had organised as guest speaker, telling the glamorous audience the true hell of his upbringing and his life on the streets. Nina had been sipping on champagne as she had unwittingly met her son.

'It's not just a gown.'

Lavinia dragged him from his thoughts. She was still in full flood, Zakahr realised. She'd probably been talking for five minutes and he hadn't heard a word!

'It's the experience, it's working out the exact colour scheme, it's watching how she walks, her figure, her personality—that's why she has to come to us. For the next few days the Princess will be the sole focus of our designers. Every detail has to be sorted out while she's here. The team will be in regular contact afterwards, of course—and then a week before the wedding our team will fly to her and take care of everything. Hair, make-up—the works. All the Princess will have to do is smile on the day.'

'And how many weddings?' Zakahr asked. 'How often do we have to do this?'

'Once, sometimes twice a month,' Lavinia said, and

then, when she saw his face tighten, it was Lavinia who couldn't resist. 'And what with it coming in to spring in Europe we're exceptionally busy now. You'll be doing this a lot.'

'Great,' he muttered. Talking weddings was so *not* Zakahr.

They sat in silence, and the car was so lovely and warm, and she was just so, so tired, that Lavinia leant back in the sumptuous leather. She wasn't at her desk now, so she did what she would have done had it been any of her old bosses there, and closed her eyes.

Even if she wasn't quite what Zakahr was used to, he begrudgingly admired her complete lack of pretence. Rather more privately, after another sleepless night, he felt like doing the same, but instead he took the opportunity for closer inspection.

She really was astonishingly pretty—or was *attractive* the word? Zakahr couldn't decide. Her jacket was hanging up, her arms lay long and loose by her sides, she had wriggled out of her stilettos, and sat with her knees together and her slender calves splayed like a young colt. Though there was so much on his mind, Zakahr wanted a moment's distraction—and she was rather intriguing. He actually wanted to know more about her.

'How long have you worked for Kolovsky?'

'A couple of years,' Lavinia said with her eyes still closed. 'I did a bit of modelling for them, but I had an extra olive in my salad one day and Nina said I would be better suited in the office.' She opened one eye. 'I'm aesthetically pleasing, apparently, but I'm just not thin enough to model the gowns.'

She was *tiny*! Well, average height. But her waist could be spanned by his hand, her legs were long and slender, her clavicles two jagged lines. Zakahr, who trusted his personal shopper to sort out his own immaculate wardrobe, realised he knew very little about the industry he had taken on.

'What did you do before that?' Zakahr asked her once more closed eyes.

'Modelling—though nothing as tasteful as Kolovsky. It wasn't my proudest period.'

Zakahr didn't say anything.

Lavinia just shrugged. 'It paid the rent.'

It had more than paid the rent.

Hauled out of school by her raging mother one afternoon, the sixteen-year-old Lavinia had become the breadwinner. She had wanted to finish school, had been bright enough to go university—and though she hadn't known what she wanted to be at the time, she had known what she didn't want!

Lavinia had also been bright enough to quickly realise that her mother had no need to know just how many tips she was making.

For two years she had squirrelled away cash in her bedroom.

At eighteen she had opened a bank account and started studying part-time.

At twenty-two, six months after starting work at the House of Kolovsky, and with the requisite employment history, she had marched into her bank, taken her money and bought her very small home.

A home she now wanted to share with Rachael.

Just the thought of her sister alone, with a stranger getting her ready for kindergarten this morning, had Lavinia jolting awake. Her eyes opened in brief panic and she looked straight into the dark pools of Zakahr's gaze—a dark, assessing gaze that did not cause awkwardness. He didn't pretend he hadn't been watching her sleep, he did not use words, and somehow his solid presence brought comfort.

'Rest,' Zakahr said finally.

Only now she couldn't. Now she was terribly aware of him, felt a need to fill the silence. But he was staring out of the window, his expression unreadable, and Lavinia was filled with a sudden urge to tell him she knew who he was, to drop the pretence and find out the truth.

The drive took a good thirty minutes, and was one Zakahr had made a few times in the past months as he had slowly infiltrated Kolovsky. Each time he'd left Australia his heart had blackened a touch further at realising just how lavishly his family had lived all these years while leaving him to fend for himself.

'It's just coming up...'

Zakahr frowned as Lavinia interrupted his dark thoughts.

'Where Aleksi's accident happened...'

There wasn't much to show for it—the tree that had crumpled his car simply wore a large pale scar—but it *did* move Zakahr.

A troubled Aleksi had been trying to halt Zakahr in leaving after his speech at the charity ball, unsure as to his own motives, not even realising that the businessman he was dealing with was actually his brother. Something had propelled him to race to the airport in the middle of the night with near fatal consequences. Though little moved Zakahr, Aleksi's plight had. At seven years old Aleksi had uncovered the fact that he had not just one but two brothers in Russia, and he had confronted his father with the truth. Ivan had beaten him badly enough to ensure that it was forgotten. Only the truth had slowly been revealed.

Out of all of them, Aleksi was the only Kolovsky he had any time for.

'Have you known him long?' Lavinia fished, but Zakahr didn't answer. 'I was surprised Iosef wasn't his best man...' Lavinia tried harder '...given they're twins.'

He was, Lavinia decided, the most impossible man— completely at ease with silence, with not explaining himself. He didn't even attempt an evasive answer—he just refused any sort of response.

'Five minutes, Lavinia,' Eddie the driver warned her and, sick of her new boss's silence, Lavinia opened the partition and asked after Eddie's daughter as she pulled out her make-up bag.

'Six weeks to go!' Eddie said.

'Are you excited?' Lavinia asked, and then glanced over to Zakahr. 'Eddie's about to become a grand-father.'

It could not interest Zakahr less, and his extremely brief nod should have made that clear, but Lavinia and Eddie carried on chatting.

'I can't stop my wife shopping—we've got a room full of pink!'

'So it's a girl!'

Lavinia seemed delighted, and Zakahr watched as she snapped into action—touching up her make-up and combing her long blonde hair.

She could feel him watching her, sensed his irritation, and her blue eyes jerked up from the mirror. 'What?'

He shrugged and looked away before he answered. 'I don't like vanity.'

'I'd suggest that you *do*!'

'Pardon?'

'You've dated enough vain women,' Lavinia pointed out. 'According to my impeccable sources.'

'Five-dollar magazines?' Zakahr was derisive, but still he was intrigued. Lavinia wasn't remotely unnerved by him, and it was surprisingly refreshing. 'Are you always this rude to your boss?'

'*Was* I rude?' Lavinia thought about it for a moment. 'Then, yes, I suppose I am. You wouldn't last five minutes in this place otherwise.' She was annoyed now—he just didn't get it. 'And it has nothing to do with my being vain—this isn't *me*!' Lavinia said. 'This is me at work. Do you really think the Princess wants someone greeting her in jeans with oily hair?' She was on a roll now! 'And another thing—while by your calculations I was five minutes late, I was actually fifty-five minutes *early*. Most people start work at nine. And because *work* insists I look the part, when I got to *work* I ensured that I did,' she concluded, snapping closed her lipgloss as the driver opened the car door. Then, having said her piece, she suddenly smiled and did what Lavinia did best—got on with the job. 'Let's go and meet the Princess!'

Zakahr had realised back at the office that it would be extremely offensive for him not to greet the royal guests, and he was more than a little grateful to his dizzy PA for her strong stance. Because it wasn't just the Princess—the King himself was here. Zakahr quickly assessed that one bad word from this esteemed guest and even the great Kolovsky name would be dinted.

Zakahr swung into impressive action—greeting the guests formally in the VIP lounge, and immediately quashing any disappointment that neither Nina nor Aleksi was here to greet them.

Lavinia *was* very good at small talk, Zakahr noted, back in the limousine. She chatted away to the shy Princess and her mother, and very quickly put them at ease. And every layer of lipgloss, Zakahr conceded, was merited—because it was clear the royal family expected nothing less than pure glamour, and Kolovsky could deliver that in spades.

'The team are so looking forward to finally meeting with you,' said Lavinia now.

She was nothing like the pale, wan woman who had stepped into his office this morning. She was effusive, yet professional, and as they stepped out of the limo it was Lavinia who paved the way, speaking in low tones to Zakahr about what was taking place.

'We take them through to the design team now.'

The King remained in the car, his aides in the vehicle behind, and they all waited till they had driven off before the colourful parade made its way to the centre of Kolovsky. Every door required more authorisation, but then they were in.

'Thank you.' Zakahr was not begrudging when praise was due, and as they left the Princess in the design team's skilled hands he thanked Lavinia. 'It would have been unthinkable of me not to greet the King!'

'I know!' She gave him a wide eyed look. 'They don't normally come—the men, I mean. Lucky!'

He didn't know why, but she made his lips twitch almost into a smile. He contained himself as Lavinia showed him the wedding displays, all locked behind glass and beautifully lit. She headed straight for the centrepiece.

'This,' she said, 'is the one they all want. The Kolovsky bridal gown.' He stared at it for a moment. 'Beautiful, isn't it?' Lavinia pushed.

'It's a dress,' Zakahr said, and Lavinia laughed.

'It's *the* dress! It was supposed to be for the Kolovsky daughter, or one of their son's brides—well, that's what Nina and Ivan intended.' She didn't see his face stiffen. 'It's the dress of every woman's dreams,' Lavinia breathed, peering closely and steaming up the glass as she did so. 'It actually *is*,' she added. 'I dreamt about this dress long before I ever saw it.'

Zakahr was not going to stand there and engage in idle chit-chat about a wedding dress, and without a word he walked off. But she caught up with him, trotting along to keep up with his long strides, and—annoyingly for Zakahr—carrying on with her incessant chatter.

'I used to fall asleep dreaming about my wedding, and I swear that was the dress I was wearing—it really is the dress of dreams.'

'You fell asleep dreaming of your *wedding*?' They

were in the lift now, and he couldn't keep the derisive note from his voice.

'I was eight or so!' Lavinia shrugged, then coloured a touch as his eyes assessed her.

'You don't dream of it now?' Zakahr checked, and he watched her ears pinken a fraction.

'Sometimes I do.' She shocked him with her honesty. 'Then the alarm goes off and it's back to the real world.' She gave him a little wink as the lift door opened. 'Or I hit the snooze button.'

Was she being deliberately provocative? Zakahr couldn't be sure, and it irked him. There was an edge to Lavinia—an openness that was inviting, a smile that was beguiling—and yet there was a no-nonsense element to her too, almost a wall. The combined effect, he reluctantly admitted, was intriguing.

'We have much work to do,' Zakahr said as they reached the office suite. 'We'll start the one-on-one interviews tomorrow, but this afternoon I will address everyone—liaise with HR, but I want *you* to arrange it.'

'It's not possible,' Lavinia told him. 'People have meetings scheduled, and there are—'

'Anyone not present has effectively handed in their notice.' He cut her off mid-sentence. He would accept no excuses, and Lavinia's lips pursed as he left her no room for manoeuvre. 'Just do as I ask.'

'The thing is—'

Zakahr halted her. 'The thing is I am in charge now. Whatever your relationship with your previous boss—

disregard it. When I say I want something done, it is not up for negotiation.

'Which night do we dine with the King?'

'Wednesday. But I don't do dinner.' Lavinia shook her head. 'They only trust me with the occasional airport run.'

'Well, for now you do the social side of things too,' Zakahr said. 'You have a promotion.'

'I don't want it,' came her immediate response.

Lavinia loved her job—she'd vied for pole position with Kate at times—but she didn't actually want to do Kate's work. And it wasn't just the fact that she wasn't remotely qualified. There was Rachael, her studies, Nina—just so many demands on her time right now it really was an impossible task.

'You will be remunerated.'

'It's not about money,' Lavinia said. 'I'm busy...'

'Too busy to work?' Zakahr frowned. 'I'm not *offering* you a promotion—I am telling you that I need a PA, and you either step into the role or I will have to consider my options.'

'You'll fire me?'

'If I don't have a PA what is the point of employing her assistant?'

She felt the knight sweep towards her. Click-click: he knocked away her pawn, and of course it was checkmate. But instead of saying nothing, instead of pleading her case, Lavinia refused to give him the satisfaction. Rather, she blinded him with a smile and accepted defeat with grace. 'Congratulations!'

'Pardon?'

She loved that she'd confused him. 'I'd love to accept the role, Zakahr.'

'Good. Move your things out to the main office,' Zakahr said. 'Then go through your diary and cancel your social life.' He was completely immutable. 'For now your time is mine.'

CHAPTER THREE

LAVINIA had never worked harder in such a short space of time.

Firing off e-mails, replying to e-mails, then resorting to repeating—not quite verbatim—Zakahr's warning, she sent a final e-mail with the word 'COMPULSORY' in capitals, and a little red exclamation mark beside it—though she did wrangle from an unwilling Zakahr exclusion for Jasmine's design team. Then she cleared the main function room of a group of sulky models and designers who were trying to prepare for a photoshoot for the sulkiest of them all—Rula, a stunning redhead who was to be the new Face of Kolovsky. Finally checking the PA system, Lavinia had done in an hour what it would take most a full day to achieve.

Not that Zakahr thanked her as she raced back to her office to collect her bag. He merely glanced up as he came in.

'Everything's in place.' Lavinia spritzed her wrists with perfume. 'I'll be back before two.'

'Back from where?'

'Lunch!' From his expression she might just as well have sworn. 'I'm surely entitled to a lunch-break?' In support of her argument, Catering wheeled in a sumptuous trolley of delights for Zakahr, but it did not appease him.

'We will work through lunch,' Zakahr said. 'Come and eat with me.'

'I really can't,' Lavinia said. 'I've got an appointment. A doctor's appointment.' She ran a hand over her stomach and Zakahr pressed his lips together.

She knew every trick, he realized. Knew with just that fleeting gesture no man would pry into women's business—and Lavinia was certainly that: a woman.

'Sorry!' Lavinia added.

She didn't hang around for his reaction. Instead she darted out to the lift, just a little bit breathless at her lie—because if Zakahr knew where she was going on her lunch-break he'd do more than sack her. It was, she knew, the ultimate treachery. He'd go ballistic if he knew where she was heading.

But she couldn't *not* go.

'Hi, Nina.'

Nina didn't look up—she was talking to herself in Russian—but Lavinia hugged her. Trying to keep the shock from her voice, she chatted away—except Lavinia *was* shocked. In a couple of days the other woman had surely aged a decade.

Nina had somehow got through her son's wedding. On day leave from the plush psychiatric hospital, and sedated from strawberry-blonde head to immaculately shod feet, she had worn a smile and a fantastic Kolovsky dress, and with Lavinia's help had managed to get through the service. But clearly the public effort had depleted her.

Her hair hung in rats' tails, her nail polish was chipped, and there was no trace of make-up. The silk she usually wore was replaced by a hospital gown, and all Lavinia knew was that Nina—the real Nina—would absolutely hate to be seen like this.

'I'm going to do your hair, Nina,' Lavinia said, rummaging in her locker and finding some hair straighteners. 'And then I'm going to do your nails.'

Nina made no response. She just sat talking in Russian as Lavinia smoothed out her hair. Only when Lavinia sat and worked on her nails did Nina speak in English—the questions, the statements, always in the same vein. 'He hates me. Everyone hates me.'

'I don't hate you, Nina,' Lavinia responded, as she always had since the day the news had hit.

A terrible day that was etched for ever in her mind.

Aleksi had returned from his accident to find Nina had taken over, and a terrible struggle for power had ensued. Nina had taken advice from Zakahr, who from afar had fed her ideas that would make huge profits but, as Aleksi had pointed out, would also cause Kolovsky's demise.

Then Zakahr had swept in, and for Aleksi realisation had hit: the man toying with Nina was actually his brother.

Lavinia could still recall the moment Nina had found out that Zakahr was her son. She had held Nina as she'd collapsed to the floor while Aleksi had told her in no uncertain terms of what Riminic, the child she had abandoned, had endured in the orphanage, and then in graphic detail what the runaway teenager had gone through to survive on the streets.

'They will never forgive me.' Around and around Nina went.

'Your family just need some time to process things,' Lavinia said patiently. 'Annika has been in to see you, and Aleksi has rung from his honeymoon. I know Levander has been in touch from the UK, and Iosef *has* been in to see you.'

'They are all disgusted with me.'

Lavinia let out a breath and focussed on painting a middle nail. Sometimes she truly didn't know what to say. 'They need time,' she said.

'I had no choice,' Nina pleaded, but Lavinia would not be manipulated. She was used to her mother's ways, and in a lot of things Nina behaved the same.

'There are always choices,' Lavinia said. 'Maybe you made the best decision you could at the time.'

'I should have tried to find him,' Nina said, and Lavinia, who never, ever cried, felt her eyes suddenly well up.

The nails she was trying to focus on blurred, and for a moment she couldn't answer—because, yes, Nina *should* have tried to find him. And, yes, when they were so rich and powerful, surely, *surely* she should have tried to find her son. And it dawned on her, fully dawned, that the brooding, closed-off man she had met this morning was actually the baby Nina had abandoned.

'Why didn't you?' Lavinia couldn't stop herself from asking. 'Why didn't you even try?'

'I saw how everyone hated me when Levander came to Australia—when they found out I knew his mother had died, and that Levander had been raised in Detsky Dom orphanage...'

Lavinia blew her hair upwards. Nina was getting more and more indiscreet, and the rumour that had quietly blown through Kolovsky—that Nina had known all along—was, to Lavinia's horror, confirmed.

'Levander wasn't my blood, and still they hated me. I couldn't face it if they knew there was more—that I had left my own son too.'

'Well, you have to face it.' Lavinia bit down on the sudden white-hot fury that shot through her. 'You have to face it because the truth is here.'

'Does he ask about me?' Nina begged. 'Does Riminic ask about me?'

'Nina...' Lavinia shook her head in exasperation. 'He doesn't have a clue that I know who he really is—to me he's Zakahr Belenki, someone Kolovsky was doing business with, and he's taken over now that Aleksi is working solely on the Krasavitsa fashion line and you are not well. That's all he thinks I know.'

'He is beautiful, yes?' Nina said. 'How could I not see he was my son? How did I look in his eyes and not recognise him?'

'Maybe you were scared to,' Lavinia offered. She glanced up at the clock on the wall. She was loath to leave her because at least Nina was talking now, but she had no choice. 'I have to go, Nina.'

And then, in the midst of her devastation, as always Nina remembered.

'How is your sister?'

Lavinia toyed with whether to tell her or not. She had always confided in Nina, but now it just didn't seem the right time.

'She's doing okay.'

'She likes kindergarten?'

'She does,' Lavinia said quietly, thinking of Rachael's serious little face—a guarded face that rarely smiled. She was reminded of Zakahr.

'You keep fighting for her.'

Nina stroked Lavinia's cheek, and Lavinia truly didn't get it. She had seen the worst of Nina—had heard her bitch and moan, had worked alongside her even as she tried to have Aleksi ousted. With all the shame of her past—the fact she hadn't fought for her own son—there was so much to despise, and yet Nina could be so kind.

'Give her my love.'

'I will.' Lavinia stood up. 'I'd better get back.'

She really *had* better get back—hospital visits didn't really squeeze into lunch-breaks, and she'd have to run through the car park to make it back to the office.

But as she raced out of the lift she saw Zakahr had beaten her to it.

'How was the doctor?' he asked.

'Not great.' Lavinia put on her best martyred face, but instead of being cross with her Zakahr actually wanted to laugh—she was such an actress.

'Poor you,' Zakahr said, and she caught his eye, not sure if he was being sarcastic—not sure of this man at all.

He unsettled her.

All morning he had unsettled her—in a way very few did.

She would *not* be intimidated. Lavinia utterly refused to be. Only it wasn't just that—it was the lack of roaming in those eyes, the stillness in him as he looked not at her, not through her, but *into* her that made her breath quicken, made the ten-second lift-ride down to the main function room seem inordinately long. And when the lift doors opened she forgot to step out.

'After you,' Zakahr said, when she had stood for a second too long.

And because Zakahr didn't know the way to the stage entrance Lavinia had to lead, awkward now, with him walking behind.

'Hopefully everything's in place…' She hung back a touch and walked in step with him, tried to make small talk. But Zakahr, of course, didn't engage in that.

Lavinia was just a little impressed with what she had achieved—and just a little praise would have been welcome. Effectively the place had been put into lockdown, and now, as they stood in the wings, instead of models and the new season's display, it was Zakahr Belenki who was the star of the show, with wary, disgruntled staff waiting to hear their fate.

He wasn't in the least nervous, Lavinia realised, as he leant against the wall reading e-mails on his phone while the head of HR read out his credentials to the tense audience. Even Lavinia had butterflies on his behalf, yet Zakahr was as relaxed as if he were waiting for a bus.

'Hold on a second…' She put her hand up to correct his tie, just as she would have for Aleksi, just as she would have if Nina had had a strap showing as she was about to walk on. But on contact she immediately wished that she hadn't. The simple, almost instinctive manoeuvre was suddenly terribly complicated. She felt his skin beneath her fingers, inhaled the scent of him as she moved in closer, the sheer maleness of him as she moved his tie a fraction to the centre and went to smooth his collar down.

His hand shot up and caught her wrist.

'What are you doing?' Zakahr was the least touchy-feely person on the planet. Flirting, unnecessary touching—he partook in neither. Lavinia seemed a master at both.

'Sorry!' His reaction confused her. There had been nothing flirtatious about her action, but Zakahr seemed less than impressed. 'Sheer habit,' Lavinia explained. Only her voice came out a little higher than normal, and her breath was tight in her chest as those eyes now did roam her body. His hand let go of her wrist, but instead of dropping to his side, the warm, dry hand slid around her neck. Lavinia stood transfixed. For a second she thought he was going to pull her towards him—for a full second she thought she was about to be kissed—but instead his fingers stole down the nape of her neck to the tender skin there, tucked in a label he couldn't even have seen beneath her thick blonde hair. And then he mocked her with a black smile. She could see the flash of warning, and she could see something else too—the danger beneath the slick surface of him.

'That's better,' Zakahr said, his hand still on the back of her neck. 'It was annoying me.'

'I was just…' Lavinia attempted to explain again that she had just been straightening his tie, but her voice faded as Zakahr shook his head.

'No games!' Zakahr said. 'Because you have no idea who you are playing with.'

The applause went up, and without a further word he headed out, leaving Lavinia standing in the wings, her neck prickling from his touch, stunned and unsure as to what had just taken place.

And then he smiled.

A slow smile that moved around the room like the rays of the sun.

Those grey eyes somehow met everyone's, and before he had even opened his mouth the audience was his.

'There is much fear and speculation today,' Zakahr said, his accent more pronounced over the microphone. 'I cannot end the speculation, but I hope to allay your fears.'

He did.

Everyone had a voice, he told his captive audience, and he would listen to each one. He expected the House of Kolovsky to continue to flourish, and was looking forward to getting to know the staff.

A smile of relief swept the room—only it didn't reach Lavinia, and neither did his speech. It was his earlier words that rang in her ears as she watched from the shadow of the wings.

'You have no idea who you are playing with.'

But she did.

Riminic Ivan Kolovsky—a man surely with no allegiance to the empire, a man who had learnt hate from the cradle, a man who had practically warned her himself to steer clear.

She didn't trust him. She wasn't even sure if she liked him. And he was absolutely out of her league. So why, Lavinia asked herself as her hand moved to the back of her neck, as she felt the skin he had branded with his touch, did she really want to know him some more?

CHAPTER FOUR

THERE was no one less fun to work for.

It was straight down to business after yet another sleepless night.

Not only did she have Rachael to worry about, there was now that incident with Zakahr. She *hadn't* been flirting, she'd thought indignantly as she'd lain there. Or maybe she had? Blushing in the darkness, Lavinia had rolled over, replaying that seemingly innocent gesture over and over, replaying: Zakahr's warm fingers on the back of her neck, her being momentarily trapped at his bidding.

Even though she'd hauled herself to work early, Zakahr, of course, was already there. She made him coffee and took it in, but he neither looked up nor thanked her—just asked for some staff files and re-minded her that he wanted to commence interviews at nine. Lavinia rued her night of imaginings—clearly it hadn't troubled him a jot.

Lavinia ached for the old days—gossiping by the coffee machine, chatting with Aleksi. Even Kate would have made things so much more bearable. But with Zakahr it was just work, work, work.

Her lunch break consisted of a mad dash for the vending machine and yet another energy drink.

'Annika's on the line.' When a moment later Zakahr still hadn't picked up his sister's call, Lavinia buzzed him again, and then knocked on his door. 'Annika's on the phone for you.'

'I'm busy with interviews. Who's next?' Zakahr asked, raising an eyebrow at the large energy drink she was carrying. It was Lavinia's third of the day.

'I'm just trying to get hold of her—it should be Alannah Dalton, Head of Retail,' Lavinia said, handing him the file.

'And?' Zakahr asked, because Lavinia's little off-the-record additions were actually spot-on.

'A right old misery. She moans about everything—thinks the whole world's out to get her...' Her voice trailed off, and Zakahr looked up to see that Lavinia's eyes were closed and that despite her make-up there was a sallow tinge to her cheeks.

'Are you going to faint?' He sounded weary at the thought of it.

'No,' Lavinia whispered. 'I'm just...' For an appalling moment she thought she might be sick, but it abated and she took a deep breath, licked very dry lips. The world was swimming back into focus. 'I had no sleep last night.' She saw his jaw tighten. 'I know it's not your problem—it's entirely mine...'

She sat on his large sofa and put her head on her knees for a moment. He just sat at his desk and watched, neither worried nor impressed—if anything, he was bored by the drama of her.

'I'll be fine,' Lavinia said a couple of moments later.

Only she wasn't.

She made it out of his office even as little dots danced before her eyes. She gulped down water, ate four jelly beans and a bag of crisps that had been hiding in her desk, and took a call from Alannah.

Lavinia buzzed Zakahr. 'She's on her way from the boutique. They had an important client.' She didn't actually hear his response, because there was a loud ringing sound in her ears.

When Alannah Dalton didn't appear, and neither did Lavinia respond to his intercom buzzer, Zakahr marched out of his office, less than impressed, to find her once again head-down at her desk.

'I'm not asleep,' Lavinia said without moving. 'And I really am sorry.' She had to tell him—well, not tell him everything, but she had to admit a bit of the truth—it was either that or get fired. 'I've got some personal problems. I hardly had any sleep over the weekend, just worrying, and it was the same last night...'

Now she did lift her head, and Zakahr rather hoped she'd put it down again. Her lips were white, her mascara was sliding down her cheeks, and he was now worried rather than weary. He was used to more staff, used to snapping his fingers and producing solutions, but in a situation of his own making there was no one.

He went to the en suite bathroom, ran water onto a hand towel and brought it back to her. He wasn't entirely convinced by her story, but she was clearly ill, so he took the towel, and she accepted it without thanks, burying her face in it as Zakahr stood silent till finally she came up for air.

'I'll be better tomorrow.' Lavinia was insistent. 'I'll be back to normal.'

'I'll get my driver to take you home—' Zakahr started, but he halted as she winced. The thought of walking, of getting into a car, clearly had her dizzy all over again. 'You need to rest...'

He led her to what had actually been her old office, before Zakahr had insisted on the promotion, and she fell into the familiar cushions with relief. It had never been more blissful to lie down. But now that the world was back in focus embarrassment was seeping in.

'I'm really sorry.' There was colour coming back to her face now, though her make-up was on the towel which she had pressed to her forehead. 'I can explain.'

'Just rest for now,' Zakahr said. Seeing that she was shivering, he did the right thing and took off his jacket and covered her. Then he pulled the blinds. By the time he had finished she was sound asleep.

Zakahr rang down to Reception and had someone sent up to replace Lavinia for the rest of afternoon, while he carried on conducting staff interviews. Alannah Dalton *was* a right old misery, as Lavinia had said.

He was a skilled interviewer, and he listened as the staff ranted and raved, and saved their own skin by blaming others.

He learnt a lot.

Confirmed a lot.

The cracks in Kolovsky had started long before Ivan's death—of course he pursued this, but on too many occasions his mind wandered to the woman asleep next door, no matter how many times he tried to halt it.

'Were there staff favourites?' Zakahr asked them all.

It was as simple as that.

Of course he had to listen to a lot that did not interest him in order to get to the bit that did. It was common knowledge that Lavinia had been sleeping with Aleksi, and maybe Levander too, before him. Lavinia, he was repeatedly told, always kept in with the boss.

Zakahr kept his face impassive as over and over this was reiterated, but he almost felt regret as he realised that the smile he was starting to like, the chatter, the jokes—everything that was Lavinia—wasn't pleasing exclusively to him.

In a break between interviews Zakahr walked into the darkened office and stared down at her for a full moment. With her face relaxed by sleep, her mouth minus the gloss, she looked younger, prettier—innocent, almost.

Though clearly that wasn't the case.

He found her file and bundled it up with a few others, and then he settled back for a read.

She had been hauled in to HR several times—always at another colleague's request—and Kate herself had made a couple of complaints, but there had never been any action taken.

Zakahr was quite sure he knew why.

At five p.m., she stepped into his office, with a red mark from the cushion on the side of her face.

'I don't know what to say!' She handed him his jacket, which he took without a word. 'Thank you, though. I'll see you tomorrow—assuming, of course…' Lavinia tried to keep her voice upbeat, but even she could hear its waver '…that I still have a job?'

'Do you even *want* this job?' Zakahr asked.

'Of course I do,' Lavinia responded immediately—because now more than ever a solid working history was vital.

'Then can I suggest you go home to bed and sleep tonight?' Zakahr said tartly. 'And that you eat something instead of relying on caffeine…' She exasperated him—why, he didn't know. She was too pale, too thin and too careless with herself, and even though it was far from his problem for a moment it felt like it. 'Let's both get something to eat.'

Lavinia shook her head. Because even if she was starving, even if all she'd have the energy to rustle up this evening was egg on toast, the thought of being out with Zakahr—of an evening away from the office, actually talking to him—had her body on instant alert. She'd heeded his warning. She wasn't about to toy with him. His company out of office hours would be perilous at least!

'I'm really not up to a fancy restaurant today—and we're eating out with the King tomorrow. Right now I just want to go home, have a bath, and go to sleep.'

'Home, *eat*, bath and then sleep,' Zakahr said through gritted teeth, not trusting her to do so. Taking it into his own hands, he stood. 'You need to eat, and so do I.'

CHAPTER FIVE

HE TOOK her somewhere very dark, very low-key, and actually rather relaxing.

'How do you know about this place?' Lavinia had grumbled as they'd turned into a back street and he'd led her to what must be one of Melbourne's best-kept secrets. As she slipped into deep velvet seats Lavinia peered around and saw it was filled with the rich and the beautiful. 'I've lived here all my life and didn't know it existed.'

'Concierge,' was Zakahr's concise reply, but then he stopped being her boss for a moment and gave her a brief smile. 'The food is good.'

And she *did* need to eat. She ordered a snow pea and asparagus risotto, which was smothered in pepper and fresh parmesan, and layered butter on a warm roll.

Conversation came easily, and Lavinia surprised Zakahr by tucking in to her food the moment it arrived— and even if she only managed a quarter of the large plate he watched with surprising pleasure as colour came back to her complexion and that sparkle came back to her eyes.

'Better?' Zakahr asked.

'Much,' Lavinia admitted—because the food *had* been lovely, and the company pleasant rather than challenging. Far from feeling awkward, for the first time in ages Lavinia found herself unwinding.

'You need to take better care of yourself.'

'I take very good care of myself,' Lavinia responded, but then relented. 'Usually.'

Zakahr waited for her to elaborate—his skilled interview technique continued long after office hours. He chose to give away little about himself, and the easiest way to accomplish that was to ask about *her* life—but though Lavinia spoke easily about work, weddings and the like, she was surprisingly reticent when it came to her current problems. In fact, when Zakahr subtly asked the nature of her problems, Lavinia turned the question on *him*.

'Just family stuff—but then you'd know all about family dramas, wouldn't you?' She watched his steak knife pause, and after a moment he actually put down the cutlery and took a drink of water before speaking. He was unsure if he'd misheard, because it was such a guarded secret—one the Kolovskys dreaded getting out—surely the Assistant PA couldn't know?

'Do you come from a large family?' Zakahr asked instead of answering.

'I've got a half-sister.' She saw him frown, and realised she was making no sense. And though she was really too weary to explain herself, so much had been bottled inside for so long that Lavinia found herself opening up. 'My mum died last year.'

'I'm sorry,' Zakahr said, as was polite, but Lavinia gave a tight shrug.

'She lived longer than expected,' Lavinia said. 'I'm rather amazed that she made it into her forties—my mum was someone who really didn't take care of herself.' She pushed the risotto around her plate—hungry, but not, angry, but not. Just sharing her burden, just voicing it, might bring fresh perspective.

'What about your father?' Zakahr pushed.

'I don't have a father,' she said. 'Well, I don't...'

'You don't keep in touch?'

'I don't know who he is.' She gave a tight smile that was born from embarrassment. 'Neither did my mother.'

'I see.'

'I doubt it.

'Look.' Lavinia gave up with her food. 'My half-sister is younger than me—*much* younger. She lives with her father and his new partner. It was bad enough leaving her there when my mother was alive—I know what I went through as a child—but now that she's gone...well, I know that Kevin doesn't want her, and nor does his new partner. I'm trying to get custody, but they're opposing it...'

Zakahr looked up, unable to imagine the high-fashion, rather dizzy Lavinia taking on the role of single mum. But since the moment he had met her she had surprised him.

'I thought you said that they didn't want her?' Zakahr frowned. 'What is her name?'

'Rachael, and she's four.' Her tense mouth softened

even as she said the name. 'They *don't* want her. But Mum had a life insurance policy, and there's a small trust for her—they'd get paid. Not a huge amount, but enough to make it worth their while to keep her. They deny it's about money, of course, but I know I'm right.'

'So how do you know that they don't want her? Really know?' Zakahr asked—because he dealt only in fact.

'Her dad's got two older boys who can do no wrong, and his partner's got two little girls from another relationship. And now they've just had a baby of their own.'

'A large blended family,' Zakahr said, but Lavinia screwed up her nose.

'Rachael doesn't fit into the blend,' Lavinia said. 'She's clever, she's a serious little thing, and they just have no time for her. I buy her clothes, but I go there and the girls are wearing them while Rachael's in rags. She spends most of her time in her room.' He saw the flash of tears in her eyes as she took a large gulp of water. 'It's the hardest thing to explain,' Lavinia admitted. 'It's actually *impossible* to explain. I used to see her once a fortnight, and if I argued or pointed anything out—well, I just didn't get to see her the next time.'

'So you've stayed quiet?'

'Do you know how hard it is to stay quiet when you know a child is suffering?'

Zakahr said nothing.

'I arranged some childcare for her—it had a kindergarten programme. I told Debbie…'

'The partner?' Zakahr checked, and Lavinia nodded.

'I told her that it might give her a break, that I knew

Rachael was hard work—I made it sound like I was doing them a favour. But in fact I wanted her away from them, and hopefully for one of the teachers to see what was going on.'

'Which they did?'

'She had some bruises on her arms,' Lavinia said. 'And they were worried about some of the stuff she'd been saying. She was taken into foster care on Friday. I thought I'd get her—I really thought it would be automatic—now I'm being *assessed.*' She shrilled out the word. 'I've got my own record with them,' Lavinia admitted. 'I was bounced in and out of care for most of my childhood—'

'And that goes *against* you?' Zakahr checked. 'You are responsible now—you have a good job...'

'I didn't always,' Lavinia said, and she was so weary with it all, so tired of trying to justify herself, she simply stopped. To Zakahr she would be honest. 'The "modelling" that I used to do—after my mum pulled me out of school at sixteen—I was actually a stripper for a few years. Then I did some dancing...'

'I'm assuming not classical?'

There was nothing derisive in his voice, no shock in his eyes—all he did was listen—so much so that Lavinia even managed a wry smile.

'Steer me away from all poles!' she said to his bland expression. 'I just can't help myself sometimes.'

'You modelled as well?'

'That's how I ended up at Kolovsky—it was a fashion week, the agents were frantic, Kolovsky were a bridesmaid short... It was luck, really.'

'You'd still be dancing without Kolovsky?'

'God, no,' Lavinia said immediately. 'I'd all but given up on Mum by then—I still gave her some money for Rachael, but it all went on gin. I was looking for another job. This one, though, paid far more than I'd dreamed. It was a Godsend.' She caught his eyes. 'I know I haven't made the best impression, but I really do need this job— now more than ever. Two years as Assistant PA, a recent promotion to PA...' She gave a tight smile. 'Well, it beats an unemployed ex-stripper.'

'Have you taken legal advice?'

'What can a lawyer do?' Lavinia asked. 'It's up to the authorities.'

'A lawyer can ask questions.' Zakahr thought for a moment. 'You say Kevin is good with his sons?'

Lavinia nodded.

'So why not Rachael?'

'Maybe he prefers sons...' Lavinia started, then changed her mind. 'He seems to dote on the new baby, though, and she's a little girl.'

'Get advice.'

Lavinia rolled her eyes. It was all very well for Zakahr, with his billions, to suggest a lawyer. 'I'll just keep working on Ms Hewitt!' She smiled over to him, but Zakahr didn't smile back. In fact he was annoyed— not with Lavinia, but with his brothers, with his so-called family.

Hell, he'd known Lavinia a couple of days and already knew her story. She'd been Aleksi's lover—surely he should have sorted this out for her? And what about

Nina? They had lawyers galore at Kolovsky—surely someone could have stepped in?

'You need to speak to someone,' Zakahr said, reluctant to be dragged into a problem that wasn't his, but unable to stay quiet.

'What I need,' Lavinia corrected, 'is to keep my job. So, thank you for listening, and I promise after a good night's sleep I'll be back to my usual self!'

He rather liked her *un*usual self! Still, that wasn't the issue.

'Listen to me, Lavinia. You can't deal with this without a lawyer.'

'I *am* dealing with it,' she insisted. 'I know the system well enough—Ms Hewitt was my own case worker years ago. You know, it really *is* a shame you can't choose your family!' Maybe she should just stay quiet, not admit that she knew, but Lavinia didn't work well being subtle, and frankly she'd had enough of playing games. 'Zakahr—I know who you are.'

'You shouldn't listen to gossip.'

'Everyone's too scared to gossip about *you*,' Lavinia said. 'I was there when Aleksi confronted Nina with the truth that you are in fact her son.'

'Was,' Zakahr corrected.

'*Are*,' Lavinia said.

'They are not my family.'

'So why are you here?' Lavinia challenged. 'If you want nothing to do with them, why are you here?'

'To claim what is rightfully mine,' Zakahr lied; he was hardly going to tell her of his intention to destroy it.

'You could talk to her...' Lavinia knew she was

venturing into dangerous territory—knew this was absolutely not her place—but Nina's devastation was real. 'At least hear what she has to say...'

'I can forgive tardiness, I can forgive rudeness, and I can accept that in some things for now you know better.' His voice was like ice. 'But don't *ever* try to advise me on my family.'

'Fine,' Lavinia said. 'But what gives you the right to advise on mine?'

'I'm right,' Zakahr snapped.

'So am I!' She reached for her bag.

Zakahr sat for a moment, unable to believe she knew—that that was all she had to say on the subject. Conversation was not something Zakahr often pursued, but despite the difficult subject matter, despite broaching topics that were completely out of bounds, he was enjoying her company. Except Lavinia was looking at her watch.

'I really have to go home.'

'I'll take you now. I'll ring for my driver,' Zakahr said, deciding it would be nice to see where she lived. Only Lavinia wouldn't hear of it.

'I'm fine to drive.'

They walked through the streets, both in silence, back towards the darkening offices.

'What did she say?' It was Zakahr who broke the silence—curious despite himself. 'What did Nina say when she found out I was her son?'

'She screamed—wailed.' Lavinia didn't soften the brutal details of that day. 'It was one of the saddest things I've ever seen.'

'She doesn't deserve sympathy.'

'She wasn't asking for it,' Lavinia said.

To Zakahr it felt strange to be talking about this. For so long it had been private knowledge. In the last few weeks it had come to the fore, with harsh words spoken with his so-called family, but now, like a cool breeze, Lavinia had swept into the most closed area of his life, and to be walking at eight p.m., to be talking about that which was never discussed, with a woman he had only just met, was as unfamiliar as it was refreshing.

She challenged him—made him question his own thoughts…duplicated them on occasion.

'Maybe you should hear what she has to say.' She was gentle rather than probing, but it touched the rawest of nerves.

'There's nothing to talk about with her—you yourself cut ties with your own mother.'

'No,' Lavinia corrected. 'I simply gave up trying to change her.'

Zakahr didn't want to think about it. Zakahr, as they reached the staff car park, wanted instead the easy solution.

Lavinia was incredibly pretty.

Her mouth, devoid of lipstick, was full and plump, and despite a few hours' sleep in the office still her body seeped with exhaustion. He thought how nice it would be to take her back to his hotel.

How much nicer for her, Zakahr thought, rather than driving home, to come back to his luxurious suite, to be pampered.

Sex, for Zakahr, was the equivalent of benzodiazepine.

It helped one sleep, and when the bottle ran out it was easily replaced. He had no qualms about one-night stands, one-week stands.... He caught a waft of her fragrance. Maybe, he realised, here was a woman who could hold his interest for a month.

'Thank you.' She smiled up at him as they reached her car. 'It's been really nice to talk.'

'We can talk some more.'

There was an invitation there, and Lavinia's body reacted to it—whether it was embarrassment at sleeping the afternoon away, or just that it had been so pleasant to actually talk about her problems, for a while there her guard had been down and she'd simply enjoyed his company. But there was a knot in her stomach as she faced him. Not the knot of anxiety that was familiar these days, but a knot far lower in her body, which tightened as she stood there. Her mouth, which had chatted easily all evening, felt now as if it were made of rubber as she tried to ignore his thinly veiled offer.

'I need my bed!' Lavinia said, then corrected herself. 'Bath and *then* bed!'

Zakahr was about to agree—in fact that was exactly what he had in mind—but he knew women, knew how to be subtle, knew exactly what he was doing... He lowered his head. A slow, soft kiss, a teasing taste, and then bath and bed would be arranged—except at his hotel.

Only Lavinia had other ideas.

It took a second to register her lips on his cheek, the feel of that plump mouth on his skin, saying goodbye as she might to any friend—a fleeting exchange after a pleasant evening.

'Thanks again.' Lavinia climbed into her car, hid her blush with her hair as she leant forward and put the key in the ignition. 'I'll see you in the morning. Have a good night.'

Lavinia drove out of the car park on autopilot, put in her card and willed the boom gate to rise, willed herself not to look in the rearview mirror, fighting a sudden urge to screech the car into reverse. So badly she wanted to go to him. She had felt rather than heard his invitation, and even if her mind had said no her body had felt more than inclined to accept.

How?

Lavinia turned into the city street and met a red traffic light. Now she looked in the rearview mirror, seeing not herself but her image—the woman Zakahr thought he saw.

What would he think if he knew the truth? That this outwardly assured, flirty woman had no experience with men—that even his casual kiss would be her first?

Lavinia was an extremely skilled flirt.

Her mother had taught her well, and now it happened without thought.

She could beckon a man to bed with one eye and warn him off with the other. It wasn't a case of being manipulative—for a while it had meant survival. And survival had been necessary for a teenager in some of the sleazier jobs Fleur had encouraged for her daughter.

Now twenty-four, and working for Kolovsky, she still retained those skills, but they were used more subtly. Of course she'd flirted with her bosses. But, rather as with the stunning garments they produced, she'd simply admired them, enjoyed them, loved to have a little play with them and dress up. Despite the rumours to the contrary, it had all been strictly fun.

Flirting with Zakahr, however innocent, was proving downright dangerous—like teasing a tiger behind bars. Here was one man Lavinia wasn't sure she could handle if he suddenly got out—and it was a relief to be away from him.

As she drove off, there was also relief for Zakahr. Normally he had no compunction about getting involved with staff, none at all—even his regular PA Abigail was an occasional lover—but he was here in Australia with the intention *not* to get involved. And certainly not with someone like Lavinia, who not only knew his past but was dealing with Rachael.

It had killed him to sit and listen to that—he didn't want to go through it again.

Zakahr poured vast amounts of money into helping damaged children—each company he resurrected was always structured to work closely with a charity. It came with unexpected benefits—staff were more eager, it promoted a sense of purpose. Yes, Zakahr walked the talk, but despite his great work there was no contact. He had left that part of his past behind, and never wanted to visit it again. Despite his impassiveness, hearing Lavinia speak of Rachael had swirled the black river of hate that ran through him.

No, Lavinia and her problems he did *not* need.

There was a lipgloss rolling around on the floor of the car. He kicked it under the seat opposite, but a moment or so later it rolled out again to him. He cursed, and picked it up and put it in his pocket.

The car slid past the casino, but that wasn't the sort of high Zakahr needed tonight.

He walked into the hotel and, instead of heading to his suite, headed to the plush bar—because he *did* need a good night.

He ordered a brandy, then saw a pretty face and jewels and lipstick and a smile across the room, hoping he might return it.

It was that easy for him.

But, no, Zakahr did *not* have the good night Lavinia had wished him. Because he pulled out a lipgloss instead of his pen when he went to sign for champagne, and, wondering if she'd hexed him, Zakahr downed his brandy in one and to the smile's disappointment headed up to his suite.

He took off his jacket. It smelt of her.

He took off his shirt, because that now smelt of her too.

He poured another brandy. The room's flowers had been replaced—an arrangement of lilies—and Zakahr felt a soft, thick petal. It felt like Lavinia's skin surely must... He stopped himself. He did not need names to faces.

Less than a week into his month, his decision was made. The House of Kolovsky would be no more—now all he had to do was execute it.

She'd get another job, he told himself. Yet his gut churned with sudden unease.

Zakahr headed to the bathroom, ran the tap and

splashed his face with water. As he reached for a towel he caught sight of his back in the angled mirrors—scars like tattoos all told their tale, and Zakahr had lived through each hellish one.

Rarely did Zakahr examine them, but he did now.

He saw the thick knot of flesh over his scapula, the dark purple circles that like the memories did not fade, and he was sixteen again, surviving the brutal streets—streetwise and hardened, but as scared as hell.

Here was the bigger picture, Zakahr told himself. *This* the reason he was here and he mustn't forget it.

Couldn't forget it.

God knew he'd tried.

CHAPTER SIX

'You need to sign this.' He did not look up as she handed him a document. He took a long drink of his coffee to escape the scent of her. 'Contracts are screaming for it—Aleksi should have done it before he left.'

'I'll read through it later.'

'They need it now.'

If they didn't she wouldn't be standing in his office. She was doing her best to avoid him, tapping away on the computer, seemingly engrossed in her work. But Contracts had demanded his signature, and like it or not Lavinia had to face the man who'd filled her thoughts all night, trying to pretend she wasn't the least concerned that tonight they were going out for dinner—and it wasn't dining with royalty that was daunting Lavinia.

'Rula is to be the new Face of Kolovsky—they're shooting this week, and her contract still hasn't been signed off.' Still he made no move. 'It's an important document.'

'Then it deserves close attention,' Zakahr retorted. 'Which I don't have time for now.'

'So what do I tell them?'

'That's entirely up to you.' He took another drink of his coffee. 'Out.'

He was loathsome, Lavinia decided as she hung up the phone after not the easiest of conversations with Contracts. He was loathsome, horrible and arrogant, and she was mad to even consider fancying him. In fact she refused to—so she checked her horoscope instead.

The stars are urging you to take the advice being given…

Fat lot of help that was—some advice on pompous, tall, dark and handsome bosses would be nice.

'Lavinia.'

With a jolt she looked up, and for a second was confused. But Iosef always did that to her, given he was Aleksi's identical twin. Though he had plenty of the Kolovsky dash, he was a smudge more down-to-earth than Aleksi, who wore only the best suits and had his hair trimmed weekly.

Iosef was in black jeans and a T-shirt, and didn't look in the best of moods.

'Is he in?'

'He is!' Lavinia smiled up at Iosef—he had always been her favourite of the Kolovsky brothers, and they'd shared a little flirtation in the past—well, till he'd fallen head-over-heels and married Annie.

'How is it going?'

Lavinia rolled her eyes.

'What are you doing at this desk?'

'I'm the new PA!'

Iosef actually laughed, and for a moment so too did Lavinia.

'What's he like to work for?'

'He makes the rest of you look positively docile. I'll just let him know that you're here.'

'No need.' Zakahr was at the door, his expression boot-faced. 'Carry on surfing the net, Lavinia.'

Zakahr closed the door. Iosef was already sitting down, and Zakahr was rattled that he hadn't waited to be asked, at his clear familiarity with the place.

With Lavinia.

For now he pushed that from his mind.

'How are things?' Iosef asked, not remotely embarrassed at being overheard. Arrogance was a strong genetic trait. 'How are you finding it?'

Zakahr did not answer.

'How's Lavinia doing as PA?'

'Are you here to make small talk?' Zakahr could not be bothered with small talk.

'I have just come from visiting our mother.'

'*Your* mother,' Zakahr corrected. 'Her choice,' he added, because from the day she and his father had abandoned a newborn baby in Detsky Dom she had no longer been his.

'I spoke at length with her psychiatrist yesterday. She is in a fragile mental state.' Like Zakahr, Iosef did not mince words. He did not want to be here—he understood completely his brother's take—but always with family there was a strange sense of duty. 'I was not going to come to you with this, but I've spoken with my wife and we now agree you should at least be told. What you do with the information is up to you. Nina wants to meet with you, to speak with you...'

'And then it will all be okay?' Zakahr sneered. 'I would check this psychiatrist's qualifications—because if she is in such a fragile state does he *really* want me to say all I have to? All I want to? Does he think I am going to walk in and forgive her?'

'He has warned her how damaging this confrontation could be for her at this stage of her treatment—but still she is desperate to see you.'

'Tell her it's too late,' Zakahr said. 'Thirty-six years too late.'

Iosef nodded and stood to leave. He had not come here to argue or to plead, and he had known this would be difficult—that Zakahr wanted nothing to do with them.

When he got to the door he changed his mind. 'Annie and I are having Annika and Ross over on Saturday for dinner. It would be good to see you...' Iosef hesitated. He knew so little about this man who was his brother, and was trying hard to do the right thing. They actually *weren't* having Annika and Ross over, but if Zakahr would only agree he knew his sister and her husband would come. 'If you want to bring anyone...'

'You still don't get it.' Zakahr leant back in his chair. 'I am not here for a tender reunion with my *family*.' His lips sneered the word. 'Aleksi I have respect for. The rest of you...'

'We didn't know.'

'You didn't *want* to know,' Zakahr said, but Iosef shook his head.

'We are all devastated by this, Riminic...' And Iosef could have kicked himself. He had spent the morning hearing his mother wailing and crying the name of the baby she had abandoned, and now he stood before the man who loathed his past so much he had wiped it clean and changed his name. 'Zakahr...'

'Get out.' Zakahr did not shout it, but it was non-negotiable. Just hearing the name Riminic made the bile churn in his stomach.

Riminic Ivan Kolovsky.

Riminic, son of Ivan.

He could feel the sweat on his forehead as the name played over and over. All Riminic had done, all Riminic had endured.

He never wanted to hear that name again.

Nina could die screaming it, but *he* never wanted to hear it.

Riminic was gone, Ivan was gone, and if he had his way so too would be the House of Kolovksy.

'Zakahr!' Lavinia's voice came over the intercom and he pressed his fingers together and to his lips. The light breeze of her voice hauled him from the eye of the storm. 'I need to pop out for an hour.'

'Another appointment?'

'Actually, yes.' She hesitated before continuing, 'Then I've got to get my hair done, and I'm meeting Katina back here at five to sort out my outfit for tonight...'

'Your point is...?'

'I won't be back this afternoon. You'll have to manage without me.'

There was the crackle of the intercom, an unseen

blush, a call to flirt, an inappropriate response there for the taking. She willed him not to, and thankfully Zakahr obliged.

'Fine.'

'How?' Ms Hewitt asked for the twentieth time, and the answer was, as always, impossible.

In an effort to look more presentable on paper, Lavinia had officially promoted herself to PA, but Ms Hewitt was now questioning how she could hold down such a responsible job *and* be a full-time carer for Rachael.

'I'm sure I won't be the first single working mum.'

'Rachael will need a lot of attention,' Ms Hewitt said.

'Then I'll go part-time,' Lavinia said. But even that didn't appease the case worker. Not that anything Lavinia could say was going to convince Ms Hewitt that Lavinia was a responsible adult—she still saw Lavinia as the angry, troubled girl she had been all those years ago.

'Have you really thought this through at all, Lavinia?'

'I've thought of nothing else,' Lavinia said.

This whole hour had been pointless. Now the clock was edging towards four. She had her hair appointment soon, then the dinner to get ready for—not that she could tell Ms Hewitt *that*.

'How long till you reach your decision?'

'Lavinia, it's not a cut and dried decision. We're about keeping families together, not pulling them apart.'

'I *am* her family,' Lavinia attempted again, but it

fell on deaf ears. 'Can I at least see her—it's nearly a week now!'

'You can see her tomorrow afternoon for an hour—but, Lavinia, Rachael needs calm. She doesn't need to know that the adults in her life are fighting over her. When you see her, just keep things light.'

'I can't tell her I want her?'

'Her father *wants* her.' Ms Hewitt's words were abrupt. 'She has a family that wants her. Yes, it's a family that might need extended support…' Lavinia opened her mouth to argue, but Ms Hewitt overrode her. 'But making false promises to Rachael isn't going to help matters. Try to keep things even.'

God, why was *she* being made to feel like the bad guy?

It took every ounce of will-power to stay calm and thank Ms Hewitt, but as Lavinia sat at the hairdresser's she was shaking with silent rage as her thick blonde hair was curled into spirals and pinned.

'Problem?' Zakahr checked as she stomped back into the office after her appointment.

'Only of my own making!'

Oh, she'd sworn her distance from him, but Zakahr was *there*, just at the right moment, and asking a question. It was like a champagne cork popping. Her rage was fizzing out, years and years of rage spluttering over the edges with such ferocity Lavinia's eyes actually stung with tears.

'She'll send her back to Kevin,' Lavinia said.

'You don't know that.' Zakahr wished he hadn't asked the question—wished he hadn't heard Lavinia's response. He gave his brief, soothing answer and turned to go.

'She sent *me* back to my mother time after time.' Lavinia's words hit his turning back like arrows. 'I'm supposed to keep things *even* with Rachael and not make promises I can't keep. I'm not even supposed to tell her I want to raise her.'

'*Can* you raise her?' Zakahr challenged—because he believed in action rather than words, and before he offered his support where a child was concerned he had to be sure. 'Or is this just a cause for now?'

'It's why I bought a house—I've got a room for her at home that I'm waiting to decorate. I've wanted Rachael in my care since she was born. But I'm not supposed to confuse her with all that.' She shook her head, cross with herself for bringing her problems to work, for exploding in front of him. 'Just leave it.' She brushed past him, heading for the safety of her office.

'Ms Hewitt is wrong.' Zakahr halted her. 'All this stuff about keeping your distance, not building up her hopes.' He could see Lavinia do a double-take, could see her try to speak, to tell him this was not his concern—except right now it was. 'Take her to your home, show her the room, tell her that no matter what happens, what is decided, it is always there for her. Say that you will do your very best to get her there—that even if you are not able to look after her now you are thinking of her, and that the room is *hers*, waiting.'

'Go against everything I've been told?' Lavinia's knuckles were white on the office door. 'I could lose her.'

'You're losing her every day you are not honest,'

Zakahr insisted. 'How many milkshakes, how many dolls, how many clothes will fill her soul? She needs to know that you love her, and that you are doing everything you can for her—even if she can't see it, even if it doesn't feel like it.'

'Build up her hopes?' Lavinia challenged. 'And then what if she finds out she's going back…?'

'She might not,' Zakahr said. 'And if she does…' he was exasperated because it was surely simple '…buy her a phone.'

'She's not even five!'

'A cheap phone.'

'She'll lose it. They'll take it off her.'

'Then buy her another—and another,' Zakahr said. 'You can text her a kiss each night.'

'Ms Hewitt said—'

'Are you going to change your mind?' Zakahr demanded.

'Of course not.'

'Because *that* is Ms Hewitt's concern. I can guarantee it. That Rachael will be too much like hard work—that Mr Right will come along but he won't want children, or not someone else's. *Are* you going to change your mind?'

'No.'

'Then let them accuse you of loving her too much. So long as it doesn't wane, their argument won't last.'

'I don't know…' Lavinia admitted. But when he said it like that, it made sense. 'I want to tell her, but…' She shook her head. 'I need to think.'

'You need a lawyer…' Zakahr said.

'I need a drink,' Lavinia corrected, pulling the ring on an energy drink as Katina waltzed in with an armful of gowns. 'And to get ready.' She gave him a thin smile. 'Thank you for listening.'

Zakahr shook his head. 'I wish *you* would listen.'

CHAPTER SEVEN

'No.' KATINA was definite. 'It's not your colour.'

'It's stunning,' Lavinia begged—because the dress *was* heavenly, and more importantly they had not a moment to spare.

But Katina would not budge.

'You represent Kolovsky. You're dining with a king. I choose.' Katina pulled down the zipper and Lavinia wriggled out. Katina bundled up the peach dress with a warning to Lavinia to do her make-up as she left her standing in her panties and bra. 'You're running very late.'

She *would* have put on her war paint—except her make-up bag was at her desk.

Had it been Aleksi, or even Levander, she'd have just padded out there—not caring if they were there or not. She'd even have answered the phone had it been ringing. The brothers were so used to it they wouldn't notice. But Zakahr came from the staid world of finance.

With Zakahr—Lavinia swallowed—it was different. Very different indeed.

'Would you mind fetching me my bag?' She settled for popping her head around the door and calling out to him. But Zakahr was in his own office, and he could not believe her gall.

He walked out to tell her so—and there was her skinny shoulder and her clavicle, and the deep red silk strap of a bra. He *got* that this was normal around here— he had been down to the design rooms and the dressing rooms and had seen far more than a shoulder—and he was also exceptionally used to women in their natural form in his own personal life.

'It's in the second drawer,' Lavinia directed.

He practically threw it at her.

'Thank you.'

'You could have waited till you were dressed and got it yourself,' he said tartly.

'And spilled foundation on a Kolovsky creation? I don't think so,' Lavinia called back. But despite her quick comeback she was blushing right down to her toes, and she leant her head on the door for a moment as she closed it.

Why did he have to go and be nice about Rachael? Why couldn't he have ignored her, as he had all morning? How, *how*, was she supposed to get through tonight?

It was too dangerous to ponder, so she drained her energy drink and then slapped on some foundation, rouged a cleavage where there was none, and painted her face with more than her usual care. By then Katina had returned. Lavinia frowned at the rather bold colours, but she held up her arms as the dress slithered down her skin, delighting in the rich caress of the silk. And, yes, when she stepped back and looked in the mirror Lavinia accepted that Katina had been right!

'It's perfect,' Lavinia breathed, craning her neck for a view from behind as Katina strapped her into the highest of heels. 'I'd never have chosen these colours.'

'I told you…' Katina said, and she stepped back, scrutinising Lavinia carefully. And she was never one to lavish compliments—at least not with the staff. 'I wasn't sure you could carry it off.' She handed her a sheer golden net overcoat, and before she left warned Lavinia she had to sign it in when she brought it back in the morning.

'But for now you're all mine!' Lavinia grinned at the mirror.

Her hair had been curled into long thick blonde ringlets, and loosely piled on top of her head, and her eyes were bluer than ever, thanks to lashings of mascara. But her lipstick was neutral, and she added one final layer of gloss before stepping out to where Zakahr stood, fiddling with his tie at a full-length mirror, reeking of expensive cologne and, on reflection, looking thoroughly fed-up.

Until he caught her eyes in the mirror.

She saw him blink as he slowly turned around.

'You look amazing!' He couldn't *not* say it—there was no disputing the fact; Zakahr felt his tongue on the roof of his mouth as she teetered towards the mirror in a blaze of gold and red and orange.

'I know!' She gave him a wide grin, and it was so unlike any of the usual responses to a compliment he almost smiled. Then she handed him a tie and jiggled with the dress, rearranging very small breasts into some sort of cleavage. 'I know I didn't want the job, but I love the perks!'

'Kolovsky silk?'

'Of course,' Lavinia said. 'As is this tie.' She handed him Katina's choice, but Zakahr stared at it in disgust. 'It would choke me,' Zakahr said, and then corrected himself. 'I choose my own ties.'

'Not when you're accompanying me!' Lavinia said. 'Put it on.'

And, given he now ran the place, he supposed he must.

It was grey, but there were flecks of a colour there from beyond the spectrum, and a silvery tinge that turned his suit into evening wear.

'You know,' Lavinia twittered on, 'Kolovsky silk changes depending on the wearer's mood.'

'Rubbish.'

'That tie was a midnight-blue. I swear it.' Lavinia blinked at the transformation. 'Now it's cold and grey.' She gave him a sweet smile. 'It matches your eyes.'

He couldn't help but stare at her. The dress shimmered gold, and there were flashes of red that moved as she did, dancing like an aura around her body.

'I'd better not spill anything. Katina will never forgive me!'

'You don't get to keep it?'

'God, no!' Lavinia said. 'It's just on loan for the night—like me!' She picked up his wrist and glanced at his watch. 'You've got me till eleven.'

Eleven a.m., preferably, Zakahr thought. Because when she was close all he wanted was to kiss her. He could feel her thin fingers around his wrist, smell her fragrant hair and see the fiery reds darting across the heavy silk, shimmering and then darkening. It was as if it blushed around her breasts, the curve of her waist. Her skin was pale, and there was a lot on display, long limbed and slender. He wanted to lower his head and brand her skin. He wanted now the pleasure that must surely be his soon. She was, Zakahr decided, if she'd only stay quiet, completely gorgeous.

'Should you cover yourself…?' Zakahr started, but Lavinia knew those rules at least.

Words like *pashmina* and *wrap* and *shrug* were not in Zakahr's vocabulary. He watched as she pulled on the golden net, covering her arms, skimming down to mid-calf. She looked like a captured mermaid, and he wanted to tear off the net, to free her, to say to hell with Kolovsky and the dignitaries downstairs, to lay her on the office floor and take her now.

'Come on, then.' She seemed completely oblivious to the charged air. She just clipped ahead of him in heels that were impossibly high, squirting perfume as they walked and informing him that an exclusive restaurant had been booked, and was one that they used regularly—the rear closed off for their guests. It was an extremely upmarket vegetarian restaurant, where Aleksi usually took his guests—which saved any cultural awkwardness.

'I'd kill for a steak,' Zakahr said, and sighed.

'And no alcohol,' Lavinia warned.

'Lavinia.' They were in the lift. 'I *have* done this before.'

'You nearly didn't go to the airport,' Lavinia pointed out.

It was morning in Europe, so the car-ride was taken

up with Zakahr firing off e-mails on his phone. Already her feet were killing her, but Lavinia distracted herself by chatting to Eddie and annoying Zakahr as she did so.

'I'm working,' Zakahr snapped as her laughter sailed through the car.

'We're *all* working!' Lavinia pointed out, winking at Eddie as she did so. 'Just some of us manage to smile as we do so.'

She wasn't so assured a moment later.

'The press are here.' Lavinia swallowed as they approached. 'The restaurant's usually discreet. How would the press have found…?'

But quickly Lavinia realized, as she stepped out of the car, that it wasn't the royals who awaited them that had captured the nation's interest. It was the man who walked beside her.

'Oh, God…' Absolutely Lavinia wasn't prepared for this—she was used to cameras in a more controlled setting—and the unexpected frenzy that circled them had her spinning momentarily, wondering if she should have foreseen this, if there was a detail she had overlooked in tonight's preparation.

'Just walk.' He sounded completely at ease, and he made it sound easy—except her legs wouldn't obey his simple command. Then, perhaps realising she was struggling, he offered assistance, put his arm loosely around her, to guide her.

But as his hand touched her waist the contact almost shot Lavinia into the throng of photographers. She could feel his hand on her waist more than she could feel her sore feet!

'Come on.' It was twenty-four steps to the restaurant. Lavinia knew because each one took effort. She could smell him, she could feel him, but more than that he was aware of her too.

She knew that.

Knew because when they entered the restaurant it was just herself and Zakahr—their guests hadn't arrived— and it daunted her. The conversation that had flowed so easily was horribly awkward now.

'They should be here soon.' Lavinia flashed a smile at a passing waiter, just for something to do. 'Could I have champagne, please?' But even as she said it she remembered her own warning. 'Actually, make that a Diet Co...' Her voice trailed off, because that didn't actually go with the dress. 'Just a sparkling water, please.' She sighed and rolled her eyes. 'Lucky me!'

And then she looked across the table and saw him smiling—not grinning, just looking at her and smiling, his dark lips suddenly dangerous, those cold grey eyes warming. And it was attraction—pure, naked attraction—in surely its most potent form. And for the first time in her life she was sampling it.

She sat there as his eyes roamed her.

She breathed in, and then she breathed out, and then she couldn't remember how to any more.

She could feel a pulse in the side of her neck. She knew his eyes were upon it, and she wanted it to be his mouth.

'I'll get you champagne later,' Zakahr said, and for

the first time with a man Lavinia felt the floor slip beneath her, felt the frantic dash of her feet to find solid ground. Because for the first time with a man Lavinia felt suddenly out of her depth.

'I'll stick with water,' she said. 'It's far safer.'

Thankfully their guests arrived, and Lavinia was more than a little relieved when, after she rose to greet them, the King's aides subtly moved her further down the table. The men and women were sitting separately, which meant that, without the distraction of Zakahr, Lavinia could concentrate on the Princess.

Unlike the Queen, Princess Jasmine was veiled, as was the tradition for unmarried women of their small, prosperous land.

'The women of today know what they want.' The Queen smiled in the direction of her daughter. 'Jasmine knows exactly the dress she wants—though it is hard to capture that along with all our traditions. Throughout the marriage service slowly she will be revealed. Then we have the problem that some of her maids are married, others are betrothed, some from different lands...' The Queen shook her head in exasperation. 'Kolovsky is the only Western designer we could trust to fulfil all our wishes.'

'Oh, they will,' Lavinia said assuredly, then turned her attention to Jasmine, her interest completely genuine. 'So what sort of dress *do* you want?' she asked. 'I can't wait to see what the designers come up with.'

His so-called brothers had overlooked a rare asset, Zakahr realised as he worked through dinner. It could have been the most awkward of dinners. Jasmine, out in public, was veiled, and Lavinia ate like a bird, so food was hardly top of either woman's agenda, but it was the conversation and laughter that flowed.

Yes, Lavinia spoke just a little *too* much, and once he noticed she actually interrupted the Queen, but—used to entertaining, and all too aware of its pitfalls—Zakahr, on a professional level, found it was actually a relief to have Lavinia with him. King Abdullah required close attention—the King was extremely clever, and he wanted to speak business, which Zakahr did best—and it was made easier knowing the rest of the guests were being attended to. After all, was there anyone on this earth who could talk weddings like Lavinia?

Zakahr doubted it.

Not once, he noted, did her eyes glaze over as the Princess described the Kolovsky designers' visions for her and the bridal party. In fact Lavinia kept halting the Princess and asking for more detail, which the Princess and her mother were only too happy to provide.

'My daughter is enjoying herself.' As the Princess and her mother's laughter filled the table the King followed Zakahr's gaze. 'Lavinia is charming.'

She certainly was. Zakahr's eyes lingered, and perhaps she felt them, because suddenly she looked up and she met his gaze—only she didn't smile and look away.

Lavinia could hear the glasses chinking, the laughter, the noise of the restaurant, but all she could see was this beautiful man as his eyes caressed her from across the crowded table. There was heat in her cheeks, and she was trapped by his stare, dizzy at her own thought-processes. Startled, she finally pulled her eyes away, tried to concentrate on the conversation, but her mind was still with Zakahr.

The restaurant was warm, and maybe the difficult week was catching up with her, Lavinia told herself as her temples pounded to the beat of her own pulse.

She took a sliver of dragon fruit, felt the cool fruit on her tongue, but it didn't cool her head.

'Excuse me.' She headed for the opulent ladies' room, turned the heavy gold taps and ran water over her wrists. Then she sat on the lounger.

Lavinia pressed her fingers into her eyes as something close to panic washed over her.

Piece by piece, Zakahr had dismantled her armoury.

She could deal with men—any man, Lavinia told herself.

She was *trained* to keep men at a distance.

Except so easily he disarmed her.

She took a couple of slow deep breaths, told herself she could deal with it, and then removed her hands from her eyes and stood. There was a huge gold mirror, and Lavinia looked at her sleek reflection, looked at the dress and the jewels on loan, and the ringlets that were starting to loosen, and she wanted to be *her*, Lavinia thought. She actually wanted to step into the mirror and escape.

Wanted to give in to the beat of her body, to be the woman of the world Zakahr thought she was...

'Everything okay?' Zakahr checked as she walked past.

Coffees had been served; the table was relaxed.

Jasmine had moved seats and was now speaking with her father.

'Of course. It's been a good night.'

It *had* been a good night—so much so, the King did not wait for the end of the meal to extend his own invitation.

'We would love to have you as our guests before we return to our land—I will have my aide contact you.' He shook hands with Zakahr. 'It has been worth the trip—though I was sceptical,' the King admitted. 'I wanted to use our own designers—I did not see why we had to come to you. Usually it is the other way round.'

Out of the restaurant and out of the noise, exhaustion hit Lavinia. She was so tired she was dizzy—as if she'd drunk a whole bottle of champagne—and her feet were positively killing her.

"Where's Eddie?' Unlike Zakahr, Lavinia noticed that their car had a different driver.

'He got called away.' This driver was far more polished than Eddie, and politely rebuffed Lavinia's further questioning. Zakahr Belenki was the man to impress and, partition closed, the car slid through the night.

Zakahr sat opposite her. He watched as she unstrapped her shoes, and there was a moan of bliss and a look of rapture on her face as she peeled them off—both Zakahr wanted to revisit later, and he was quietly confident that he would.

'Where are we going?' Lavinia frowned at the unfamiliar direction.

'I told you there would be champagne.'

'No champagne for me!' Lavinia snapped a smile.

'I have to drive home.' She didn't bother with the partition, just pressed the intercom and gave the driver her instructions

The car pulled in at the large multi-storey car park, where the staff parked their cars—except it was closed for the night, and cars could only exit now. The driver was clearly a little torn between leaving Lavinia to walk alone through the concrete jungle or having his esteemed passenger sit and wait. 'Would you mind waiting, sir,' he asked Zakahr, 'while I escort Lavinia...?'

'I'll walk her,' Zakahr said, quite sure they'd soon be returning.

Lavinia didn't usually *do* shy—she was used to beautiful people, used to working alongside strong, male energy, and had survived at Kolovsky by *not* being overawed or intimidated—but she was shy as they walked through the concrete enclosure of the car park. She carried her shoes, but wished she'd put up with the pain and kept them on—because beside him she felt swamped.

'Thank you.' She turned and smiled at him when they reached her car, then looked in her bag for her keys.

Zakahr could see one heavy ringlet falling over her eye and had to bunch his fist in order not to move it. He could not read her, could not work her out—usually he did not have to, did not want to. The flirting game was a mere means to an end for Zakahr.

Lavinia, Zakahr knew, could prove tricky at work, but sometimes in her company he escaped the loop of revenge and hate. He had smiled, he had laughed, and it was she who made it happen. Zakahr wanted more.

'Are you sure you don't want that champagne?' Zakahr asked.

She was about to deliver her firm response, only her mind was at odds.

She wanted champagne.

She wanted his bed.

She wanted the woman in the mirror to step into passion.

She was, Lavinia thought, quite possibly going crazy.

'Lavinia?'

She heard her name but she didn't look up. She found her keys and stared at them. She heard the tip in his voice, heard his unvoiced question. Still she didn't look up, because so badly she wanted to say yes to him. His fingers took a lock of her hair as she stood there, and there was an urge to sink into him, to kiss the wrist she could see, to lean on to his chest, to have someone hold her up for a little while.

She was scared to look up, because her warning look was off. But she did it anyway. She looked up into lust and into the blissful escape of him.

She knew the danger, but so sweet would be the reward.

Lavinia turned the key.

One kiss goodnight, she insisted to herself.

He lowered his head slowly, wondered if her mouth would again meet his cheek, hoping that this time it would swell to his.

Only it didn't swell. Instead it rested against his lips.

Her forehead pressed to his, and her mouth did not move at first. It just slowly met his. Her first taste of him, and she savoured it. She felt the pulse of his lip, and she let herself feel it, and then his lips moved across hers, his kiss slow and measured and so skilled that for the recipient no experience was required. All she had to do was accept it, move with it, give in to it. And then she got the reward of his tongue—it was so cool and luxurious it was like drinking gold. There had been no teenage kisses for Lavinia—her youth had been spent warding off men—and now as a woman she tasted heaven.

Kissing bored Zakahr.

He had kissed many—so many; he started at this point only as a means to swiftly moving on. A means to an end because it was what women wanted.

Only *this* kiss he enjoyed. This kiss he chose to linger over. She tasted sweet, and her mouth was soft. He tasted deeper. His hands roamed her body—not to progress things, but to stay a rare while longer. He felt her waist, and then down to her bottom as his tongue stroked hers. She was gorgeous, but too slender, on the cusp of ripening, and Zakahr wanted to be there to witness it. He was imagining more curves to her body, in his arms a taste of potential that he wanted to explore, but he halted that strange thought-process because Zakahr didn't *do* futures. Zakahr lived for one night.

Now he could lift his head and without a word take her by the hand back to the luxury of his car—could kiss her again as they headed for his hotel. Except still he wanted to linger, wanted to kiss her some more, and Lavinia was happy to oblige.

The caress of his hands was exquisite. She could feel the heat on her skin, imagined him leaving a trail of red on gold, but with the taste of his lips there was room for no other thoughts. He was strong and male, but there was a glimpse of tenderness, a skill to his lips that taught and she followed, a danger to his kiss that took her to places she'd never intended to go.

The feel of his hands was sublime—his mouth a retreat from the hammer of her thoughts. Only now did she realise the panic of her existence. Because for the very first time her mind met with beautiful silence. There was just one thought to follow, one need, one want to succumb to, and instead of someone else's tonight the need was *hers*.

His hand moved to the padding of her bra, stroking her through the silk, but the dense material dimmed the pleasure. She kissed him—deeper she kissed him. She didn't want it to end, and neither did Zakahr. He almost breathed an apology when she removed his hand from her breast, but moaned into her mouth as he realised it wasn't modesty she was requesting in the deserted car park. Lavinia guided him to the zipper, and he slid it down just enough to slide his hand inside and free her.

She hated her non-existent breasts—should have been embarrassed that he first met with padding—but his quickening breathing spelt desire. His thumb met her nipple, his palm cupped her small breast, and she swelled in his hand. His fingers were stroking the tender flesh beneath her arms, and it was as if her thighs were too heavy for her legs. Her body whimpered for more, and Zakahr grew harder at her pleasure.

'Come with me…' He could not continue this here—would not. 'Come with me,' he said again, his mouth, his tongue working hard between the words. The pad of his thumb on her nipple and the heat in his groin were intense, and there was no relief as he pressed it into her.

No relief for Lavinia either.

She wanted to.

So cautious with men, tonight—with him—she didn't want to be cautious any more. She wanted to give in to the begging of her body and let him lead her away.

She wanted him to pick her up now and carry her to his car.

She wanted to fall on his million-thread-count sheets and be looked after.

She knew she could not.

Knew when his lips left hers the night must be over.

She could feel him pressed into her and she pushed back, felt his hand dig into her bottom as he pressed her in harder still. She didn't want this to end. Her kisses were frantic, and it was Zakahr who halted them.

'Come on.' He *had* to stop now. 'Come on.'

The world came crashing in.

Her world. She was supposed to be being responsible—not standing kissing in a car park at midnight, not pressed up to a man she had known less than a week.

'I can't.'

The statement was almost cruel. She could feel his hardness, knew her bold exploration of his body's reaction had brought them both close to the brink. And now she was changing her mind. Lavinia would have given *anything* for it to be otherwise.

She'd dropped her keys. Somewhere in this she'd dropped her keys and her handbag and her shoes. She sank to the floor to retrieve them, mortified because she knew she appeared nothing more than a tease.

'Don't play me, Lavinia…'

'I'm not,' she attempted—except she had. Lavinia knew that. She'd never had the intention to go back with him; had been a completely willing participant in a kiss that had got out of hand. She tried to keep her voice even. 'We have to work together…'

She'd worked with Aleksi, he almost pointed out. But he bit down on that caustic remark. Zakahr did not get her, was unsure as to the game she was playing, though quite sure that she *was* playing.

'I just don't think it's right that I go back to your hotel.'

'Why?' Zakahr asked, and then said, the barb on his tongue one he could not swallow down, 'Do you prefer car parks?'

CHAPTER EIGHT

IT WAS just a kiss. She almost convinced herself as she parked her car in her reserved space, burning with shame at what had taken place on this very spot.

He thought her cheap.

Lavinia knew that.

Thought her a tease and a flirt—*if only he knew the truth.*

Lavinia handed over the dress and signed the book, and then took the lift up to the office, bracing herself to face him—she would deal with this the only way she knew how.

Wearing a high ponytail, high heels, silver eyeshadow, and a silver top under a grey linen suit, she swished into the office a full twenty minutes early, bearing chocolate croissants and a smile that made people want to join her.

If Zakahr had been expecting awkwardness—her notice, even—he got neither.

'About last night...' As she placed his coffee and a pastry on his desk, Lavinia somehow managed to look him straight in the eye. 'I'd like to apologise for my behaviour.'

'*Our* behaviour,' Zakahr corrected. 'We were both there.'

'Well, I just want you to know that it was completely out of character for me.' She did her best not to notice the slight rise of one eyebrow. 'I've been running on too little sleep, and that combined with too many energy drinks yesterday…'

'I wasn't aware they were so potent.' He actually admired that she faced him head-on. 'Lavinia…'

Zakahr closed his eyes for just a moment. Really, he should just accept her apology at face value and move on. Soon he could move on—except she worried him so. He'd been here less than a week, the internal auditors were coming in… In three short weeks Lavinia would be out of a job, and somehow he had to warn her.

'Maybe I was hasty…' He had to word this so carefully—could not let her even glimpse the real meaning behind his words. 'When I insisted you became my PA I did not realise you had so much to contend with.' He watched her rapid blink. 'I don't want a PA who has to survive on energy drinks…'

'I slept well last night.'

Lucky for her, Zakahr thought. Because every time *he* had closed his eyes their kiss had replayed.

'Next week will be different. I'm seeing Rachael this afternoon—'

'Lavinia,' Zakahr broke in. 'I need someone who can work sixty-hour weeks—who can drop everything and do as the job demands.'

'Are you firing me?'

'Of course not.' Zakahr wished that sometimes she

wasn't so direct. 'All I'm suggesting is that, given your situation, maybe you should start thinking of a job that has more child-friendly hours.'

'Such as?' Those bright eyes flashed a shade darker, and Zakahr had no answer. 'With all *my* dazzling qualifications...?'

'I could give you a glowing reference.'

'Saying what?' Lavinia challenged. 'Lavinia's computer skills are excellent? She checks her e-mails hourly...?'

'You're good at your job.' Zakahr was aware of her lack of formal qualifications, and uncomfortably aware that another job that paid like Kolovsky would not be easy for Lavinia to come by. 'You're personable, you're good with clients...'

'And I love my old job,' Lavinia finished for him. 'Once you've hired a PA I can go back to it.'

He couldn't help her without revealing the truth. He had tried, Zakahr told himself—her future was not his responsibility.

'Fine,' Zakahr clipped, and glanced at his watch. 'I have to go down to Design.'

It was an unusual situation for Zakahr. Usually he was openly assessing a company—closing it or salvaging it. Once it was acquired by Belenki he hand-picked staff to ensure its smooth running, but here at Kolovsky, in order to maintain the façade before pulling the pin, the day-to-day running he was usually too busy for was up to him.

He sat through the most mind-numbingly boring visual of the first images for Princess Jasmine's wedding dress.

He had absolutely no *passion* for the product, as Lavinia would say, but he did his best to hide it and congratulated the designers. Cross-eyed with boredom, he headed out—just in time to catch Lavinia lounging against the wall and talking into her phone. But she was clearly waiting for him, because she turned it off when she saw Zakahr approached.

'You need to approve some shots and sign that contract.'

Zakahr rolled his eyes.

'Urgently,' Lavinia added, handing him a large folder. 'It's the new range,' she explained. 'We have to get these out today.'

'Are you going back to the office?'

Lavinia shook her head. 'It's almost lunchtime.'

'So soon?'

'It's almost one.' She completely missed his sarcasm and drifted back to her topic as Zakahr flicked through the folder. 'Just sign them and I'll drop them off. I shan't be around this afternoon—I've got to go down and have Katina sort out an evening wardrobe for me.' Lavinia gave a delighted grin. 'I'm starting to love my new job!'

He was about to ask how, given she was so rarely there, but Zakahr was fast realising sarcasm was wasted on her. If anything, it made her laugh. Lavinia was the oddest person he had ever met—utterly beautiful, but stunningly direct.

'Gorgeous, isn't she?' Lavinia commented, peering over his shoulder.

Zakahr wasn't so sure. Rula certainly *could* be

gorgeous, with her tumble of auburn hair and cool green eyes, yet she was beyond thin. Even the thick Kolovsky silk she was draped in did nothing to add a curve, and the underwear shots were to Zakahr unappealing.

'She's so thin.'

'I know.' There was almost a sigh of envy from Lavinia, but she rolled her eyes at herself. 'God, I am *so* glad to be out of that game.'

'What game?'

She put two fingers to her mouth. 'I couldn't do it,' she admitted.

'Too squeamish?'

'Too hungry!' Lavinia corrected.

'This is what Nina would have had you aim for?'

Lavinia just shrugged. 'It wasn't for me.'

'I'll have a look through these and get them back this afternoon.'

'Are you sure?' Lavinia checked. 'In that case I've got ten minutes.' She stopped at a door. 'I'm just going to have a quick peek. Are you coming?'

'Sorry?'

'The fabric Princess Jasmine has chosen?'

'I've just sat through a half-hour presentation.' Zakahr's head actually ached because he'd been so bored. It bemused him that she expected him to be keen, that they all were so devoted to *material*! 'I've seen the images, the swatches...'

'It's not the same.' Lavinia pushed open the door and they stepped inside a vast room, with shelf after shelf filled with rolls of fabric. The fabric codes were all in a computer, and an assistant located them and brought the rolls to a desk, where they were laid side by side. As she ran her hand over them finally Lavinia could properly picture it.

Zakahr, not for the first time, stood bored, hard-pushed to feign even mild interest—where was a financial crisis when he needed one?

'Thank you.' Lavinia, satisfied now that she could actually speak with the Princess about her choices, went to walk out. But suddenly she changed her mind, pressing in an access code, pushing on a heavy door and beckoning him in. 'Here.'

She gestured down a long aisle of fabric, and then down another one, through a maze of silk. Zakahr followed the blaze of silver ahead, with ponytail swinging, past endless corridors of colour till Lavinia stopped.

'This is my absolute favourite.'

Zakahr stared nonplussed at the neutral fabric, watched as she pressed a button till a metre or two of the silk had rippled down. Lavinia ran it through her fingers.

'Isn't it beautiful?' Lavinia said, and then she paused. She had been about to say *your father*, but she knew how that irked him, so without missing a beat Lavinia used his name. 'Ivan spent months getting this right—this is one of the original fabrics that made Kolovsky so famous.'

'It's beige.'

'No.' She held her hand up to it. 'It's more a cream—and look…' she slipped her hand behind it '…now it's pink. The fabric is called *koža*.'

'That means skin.' He was a little bit curious now. He

held it between his fingers, watched as the pinks faded to more golden hues, and it actually *felt* like skin—cool skin. He could see her hand stroking the fabric, see it running through her long fingers, and for the first time Zakahr realised that material could be beautiful—so beautiful. He prolonged the contact as he asked himself how it could be that a piece of material could be erotic.

How could simple, neutral cloth provoke reaction?

But, watching her hand stroke the fabric, watching her fingers while feeling the *koža* beneath his, he actually felt as if she were touching him.

'It's divine, isn't it?' Lavinia breathed. 'Normally they use this as a slip dress. It couldn't actually *be* a dress—you'd look as if you had nothing…' Her voice petered out as she watched his strong hand run beneath the cloth, saw the ripples it made as if she was wearing the fabric he held, as if it were her skin beneath his fingers, as if he were stroking her…

'Why?' Zakahr asked in a voice that wasn't quite as steady as he'd like. 'Why do you say these things?'

'I don't!' Lavinia said, and she was cringing. 'Whatever I say around you…' She couldn't explain it. It was like innuendo city—every road led there!

'What do you want, Lavinia?' Zakahr already knew what *he* wanted, but she had to want something—of that he was sure.

'I don't know,' Lavinia admitted. She wanted his kiss, she wanted everything they had almost had, but she was quite sure—positive, in fact—that if he knew her truth he wouldn't want her. 'I'm trying not to think about you.'

'Maybe stop fighting it?' Zakahr suggested. 'Why would you resist something so nice?'

'I'm a mother-to-be!' She tried to make a joke, but Zakahr didn't smile.

'So—soon you can be responsible, soon you can stay in every night…' He voiced everything that she wanted to happen, everything she feared. 'You can say goodbye to your passionate—'

'I'm really not,' Lavinia said. If he knew how boring she was he'd run a mile.

'I dispute that.'

'Are you saying I should just walk away from Rachael? That I should give up…?'

'Of course not,' Zakahr said. 'But you are single *now*. You can be selfish. You can do what you want. And,' he said, 'you want *me*.'

It wasn't a question. It was nothing she could deny. Because so very badly she *did*.

'You told me with your mouth.'

'It was just a kiss.'

'With your tongue.'

She just stood there.

'With your hips,' Zakahr said, and watched her redden at the memory of her groin pressing into his. It was as if it were now, her body flaring as she stood, and he refused to leave it there. 'You told me with your hand,' Zakahr said, and in a cruel repeat he did what he had before—but without her guidance this time.

She watched, curious, fascinated, wanting, as he

raised his hand slowly, slipped it inside her jacket. Her nipple jutted through the sheer fabric to greet him. He rested his forehead on her head, and for Lavinia the relief was exquisite.

All night she'd denied this, all day she'd remembered—and now she got to relive it.

'Why *do* you fight it?' Zakahr asked, but even as she tried to fathom an answer, even as she tried to do just that, he overrode her with a single word. 'Don't.'

'Don't?'

'Don't fight it.' Zakahr stroked slowly, and when still she stood he slipped his hand up her cami to the heaven of no padding, no bra, just the taut swell of her.

Lavinia ached for more contact. She could feel the throb between her legs. But she just held his gaze. She would not stop him, because so badly she wanted him, but he would do nothing more till she begged it of him.

When he held her she forgot not to trust him.

Zakahr liked sex.

Not the build-up to it, nor the come-down after it—though no lover of Zakahr's could tell. He was detached, he performed, he got what he needed, she got what she wanted.

But here, in this stand-off, he was loving the build-up, was here, right here in the moment, aroused by her pleasure.

He stroked on till her neck arched backwards. He stroked on till her lips clamped hard on her plea. He stroked on till it was Zakahr who ached for more contact.

He pushed up her cami, saw her pretty naked breast, and lowered his head.

Lavinia could not believe the bliss of it, the thrill of it. There was nowhere to go but backwards. She leant on the fabric behind, his mouth her only contact, and she watched.

She watched his tongue flick her nipple, watched him softly blow, closed her eyes as he suckled, and then watched again as he drew his lips back on the length of her nipple.

He was so hard. There was no choice for Zakahr but to cease contact—and for Lavinia there was both regret and relief when he did.

'I have to go.'

'You don't.'

'Actually, I do.' Lavinia pulled down her top. She could see a damp circle form as the fabric met her breast, and pulled her jacket over to cover it. 'I'm meeting Rachael…' This was madness, she knew—just madness. 'I'm supposed to be proving to Ms Hewitt what a responsible woman I am.' Her voice choked at the irony of it all.

'I could come with you,' Zakahr said. 'Perhaps if she thought you were in a steady relationship…'

'Steady!' She shot out an incredulous laugh. 'You've got *temporary* written all over you.'

He didn't even try to deny it.

It was madness, Lavinia told herself again. Dangerous too. 'I have to go.'

She practically ran—which was just as well, because Zakahr too craved distance.

What the hell was wrong with him? That he'd even suggested going with her was… He was cross with himself as he strode back towards the lift. Cross that now another afternoon would be wasted, pondering the mystery of her, another night of ruing her games. He wanted her in his bed, not his head.

'This just came.'

The receptionist rushed over, and Zakahr took the thick gold envelope, recognising its royal seal. But his mind was still on Lavinia as he scanned the invitation.

She was way too distracting, Zakahr decided.

Then he read the invitation again, and decided maybe some distraction was merited—just not at work.

An idea was forming, and his lips stretched in an unseen smile as a plan took shape. Back in the office, Zakahr picked up the phone—and then glanced at his watch, realising it was too early to make a call to the UK. But with his decision made he fired off an e-mail to Abigail—he had already put her on standby: it would come as little surprise that he wanted her to join him immediately.

Then he made another call, delivered a rapid RSVP to the lavish invitation while flicking through the photos of Rula and admiring the private secretary's discretion as he went through the finer details.

Actually, it would be great having Abigail here, Zakahr decided, as Lavinia's phone rang out again and again, till finally it diverted to his. Abigail didn't take endless breaks, and if she was away she ensured that at least his calls were covered.

'Belenki!'

'Sorry, Zakahr...'

He clicked on his pen as someone in Legal asked if he had signed the contracts. He was about to say yes, to tell them they could send someone to come and get them, then he looked again at the photos on his desk. He thought of an already too-thin Lavinia, who had been considered too big for Kolovsky, and then Zakahr thought again.

'I'm not signing them.'

There was a beat of silence, followed by a shout of incredulous laughter, then a suggestion that he was joking.

Zakahr assured the voice on the phone that he wasn't.

CHAPTER NINE

ALL of it—*all* of it—would be made so much easier if only Lavinia was sure Rachael wanted her.

Lavinia picked her up from her foster family—saw her pinched little mistrusting face peeking out from behind her foster mother's leg.

'She's tired,' Rowena said, after introducing herself, and then told her a little of Rachael's day. 'She's had a big morning at kindergarten.'

'I won't keep her out long.' Lavinia forced a smile she couldn't feel as she offered her hand, but her sister didn't take it.

Rachael trailed Lavinia to her car and quietly let herself be strapped in. 'I thought we could go for a milkshake,' Lavinia said brightly.

'I hate milk.'

'Since when?' Lavinia grinned, but Rachael didn't answer.

'Maybe we could go to a park?'

Which was far easier said than done. Lavinia had no idea of the local area, and they ended up on a rather sad strip of faded grass, with a slide, a rickety old see-saw and two swings—not even a duck in sight.

'Is Rowena nice?' Lavinia attempted, when Rachael climbed down from her dutiful swing, but Rachael just shrugged.

'I *am* trying to get things sorted for you,' Lavinia started, but there were so many things Ms Hewitt had said not to discuss with her.

'How?' Rachael asked.

'I just am.' Lavinia had to settle for that. 'Let's go on the see-saw.'

'Before you take me back?'

They didn't even last the hour. Lavinia tried to console herself it was because Rachael was tired, but the reality was that their time together was hard work.

'I'll try and see you again next week,' Lavinia said, not wanting to make promises Ms Hewitt might not let her keep. Securing her into her seat, she went to give Rachael a kiss, but she pulled her head away.

She dropped her back to the foster home, gave her a hug that wasn't returned, and, driving back to work Lavinia, who never cried, was precariously close to it. She'd had so much pinned on that hour, and there were so many things she had wanted to say. Nothing had transpired. If anything, Rachael was more distant than before.

She dashed to the loo in the foyer, blew her noise, touched up her make-up—though she needn't have bothered.

No one even noticed Lavinia enter the office, so furious was the argument taking place. The room seemed filled with people from Legal, Accounts and, loudest of all, Katina.

'*N'et.*' Katina's lips were white with rage. 'You cannot do this! It's too late. You *cannot* do this.'

'I'm not doing anything,' came Zakahr's clipped response. And, just as Lavinia had surmised on the first day, he didn't shout, didn't raise his voice—such was his authority he simply didn't need to. Zakahr overrode everyone.

'You *have* to sign!' Katina insisted. 'You have to—'

'I don't *have* to do anything,' Zakahr interrupted, and Lavinia froze in realisation. The shots of Rula were scattered over his desk, but Zakahr was ignoring them. As chaos reigned around him he was typing away at his laptop as if there was nothing more annoying than a fly in the room.

'You're trying to ruin the House of Kolovsky,' Katina spat. 'You tried before, with your cheap suggestions to Nina, and now...' Katina was so furious she tripped over her words. 'Now with this decision you will ruin it.'

'Why?' Now Zakahr *did* look up. 'Because I refuse to endorse a few images? *This*—' his manicured hand swept the photos on the table '—is not the vision I have for Kolovsky. Now, if you'll excuse me, I have work to do. I suggest you have the same.'

Katina cried.

One of the hardest women Lavinia knew actually cried as she left the room.

'That's months of work you've just destroyed,' Lavinia said when they were alone; her heart was thumping in her chest yet Zakahr seemed unmoved. He stood and stared out of the window, down to the city streets below.

Maybe, Lavinia reasoned, he just didn't comprehend what he had just done—or maybe, and she paled at the very thought, maybe Katina was right...

'*Are* you here to destroy Kolovsky?'

'You're being ridiculous.'

'Am I?' Lavinia asked. 'You tried to destroy it before.' She watched as his shoulders stiffened. 'When Nina didn't know you were her son you bombarded her with ridiculous suggestions—you were going to put a Kolovsky *bedlinen* range in supermarkets...'

'A one-off!' Zakahr did not turn. 'With a portion of profit going to my charity. Why would I want to destroy what I own?'

'Because you hate her?'

Hate was a word that sounded wrong coming from Lavinia; there was no venom behind it, just a bewildered question.

'What is it with the overreaction?' He turned, irritated now. 'This has nothing to do with my family or destroying Kolovsky. Why the melodrama? I've said that Rula can come back for a re-shoot when she is a healthier weight, or they can find another model. I refuse to put my signature on a page that encourages a seventeen-year-old girl to starve.'

'You can't change the industry.'

'Really?' Zakahr frowned. 'I thought I just did.'

Her questions had been too close for comfort; Zakahr dismissed her with a turn of his head and stared unseeing out of the thick windows, only resting his forehead on the cool glass when he heard the door close behind Lavinia. To keep up the façade it would have made more sense just to sign. A week or so from now it would be over anyway—there would be no Face of Kolovsky—yet he could not put his name to this madness, could not condone what his parents had.

He turned as the door opened and Lavinia entered.

'I've thought about it, and you're right.' Her words surprised him. Her opinion should not matter, and neither did he need her approval, yet even if not sought there was a curious pleasure in having it. 'I was wrong,' Lavinia added. 'You can make a difference.'

'How was lunch?' Zakahr asked, changing the subject, because guilt was a visitor he did not welcome. She trusted him, Zakahr realized. Trusted in his decisions, trusted that his intentions were for the greater good. For the first time he had trouble meeting her eyes.

'Spent bouncing up and down on a see-saw.' Lavinia smiled, but it changed midway. Somehow she just couldn't feign happy right now. 'It was hard work,' Lavinia admitted. 'Maybe I'm kidding myself—maybe she doesn't even want to live with me...'

'Don't doubt yourself.'

'It's hard not to,' Lavinia choked. 'She doesn't want to spend time with me.'

He did not want to get involved with this part of her—he wanted only Lavinia the woman. Yet she came with a whole lot more, and Zakahr knew his insight could help. Surely he could share that without getting involved?

'She resents you,' Zakahr said.

'Me?'

'You come in dressed in your gorgeous clothes,

smelling of perfume, like some fairytale princess come to rescue her, and then you send her back.'

'I have no choice.'

'I'm just telling you how she feels,' Zakahr said. 'She would probably prefer that you do not come.'

God, he could be brutal.

'How can you *say* that?'

Because he knew it. Because he'd lived it. Zakahr gave a rare piece of himself.

'When I was in Detsky Dom a family looked to adopt me. I was a good-looking child, clever...' Zakahr's voice was analytical. 'For two weekends they came and took me out. I stayed in their hotel—they wanted me to enjoy, to be grateful, to laugh...' His eyes were actually darker, if that was possible, almost black with the memory of many years ago.

'So I shouldn't visit?' She hated what he was saying, but she hated the ramifications more—couldn't stand the thought of not visiting Rachael. Again she had read him wrong.

'You *never* miss a visit,' Zakahr said. 'No matter how rude, how appalling her behaviour, how ungrateful she is, *always* you are there. She's testing you,' he said. 'She's waiting for you to prove that she's right.'

'Right about what?'

'That you don't really love her—that one day you will turn your back. Rachael is testing you. To her, she's just expediting the inevitable process.'

'I'm not going to change my mind.'

'Good—because while you were out Ms Hewitt rang,' Zakahr said, and watched her eyes widen. 'She only got as far as speaking with Reception, but she is ringing back next week for a reference check. That must mean they are seriously considering you.'

And suddenly ruined photoshoots and skinny models and tricky access visits, even the stunning man before her, all faded as a long-held dream perhaps began to be realised.

'I could be getting her...' Lavinia was actually shaking. 'They're actually taking my application seriously.' Her hand moved to her mouth as the news sank in. 'I could have her next week.'

'Don't go racing ahead...'

'I could, though.'

'Then you should enjoy this weekend,' Zakahr said. 'You more than impressed the King. He doesn't want to reciprocate with dinner—he has a yacht chartered in Sydney, his family are enjoying their visit, and he has asked us to join him on the yacht on Saturday, stay overnight as his guests.'

That brought Lavinia back to earth—a shaky earth, a changing earth, an earth that moved beneath her feet, that blew her towards Zakahr whenever he reached for her.

'We can't.' Lavinia shook her head.

'It would surely be rude to refuse such an offer?'

'You can easily refuse.' Lavinia's mind flailed at the prospect. She wanted to say yes, but was scared to. 'You don't have to say yes. The King would understand...'

'Maybe I want to say yes.'

She heard her own swallow as Zakahr paused.

'Perhaps you want to too?'

She had to tell him—had to somehow find the words to explain that the woman he saw, the sensual woman he had held, only came to life by his hand.

'It is separate rooms?'

'Of course.' Zakahr sounded affronted. 'The King would not be so crass.'

Finally she could breathe—but only for a second.

'I will ring his aide.'

'I haven't said yes.'

'Then say no.'

She was trapped. Not by his directness, but by her own desire. Trapped because even if he was dangerous, even if she should say no, even if she knew he would soon break her heart, for the first time in her life Lavinia wanted to say yes—wanted to give in to the call of desire.

'Don't assume…' Lavinia attempted.

'I never assume,' Zakahr said.

Which he didn't.

He just *knew*.

CHAPTER TEN

'How's your daughter?' Lavinia asked Eddie as he held the limousine door open for her. Today she was the guest of a king, today she was the 'plus one' of Zakahr, so there was no question of her driving. But his limousine was out of place at eight a.m. on Saturday in her ordinary suburban street.

'I'm a grandfather!' Eddie gave a proud smile, but it was a touch wan. 'They've called her Emily—she's tiny, but a real fighter.'

She would have to be. Lavinia knew that Emily had been born not only premature, but with a heart condition that would need surgery. 'This is for Emily.' Lavinia said, and handed him a package and then another smaller one. 'And this is for Princess Jasmine, so it's to go on the plane. Can you tell them to be careful with it, as it's fragile?'

As is your heart, her inner voice warned as she climbed into the limousine. To her surprise, she saw that Zakahr was there.

'I thought we'd be coming to pick you up.'

'You are my guest today and tonight,' Zakahr said. 'And shall be treated as such.'

Even so, she took the seat opposite him. The implication, however subtle, was there—she was not his PA today but his guest, and she would be his lover...a woefully inexperienced lover. Somehow she had to find the courage to tell him.

Wanted to tell him.

Wanted him.

Lavinia turned her head away, tried to think of something light and witty to say, but nothing was forthcoming. She knew she was playing with fire, knew all about the heartbreak reputation she was ill-equipped to handle, but for the first time in her life there was a man who didn't evoke her usual caution—there were feelings, experiences that she wanted to explore, and she could only envisage doing it with him.

She could handle it, Lavinia had told herself when she'd accepted his offer, and, really, since then she'd been too busy to think.

Everything would be taken care of, Zakahr had assured her. She did not have to do anything other than choose her wardrobe. And, given she had the Kolovsky design team at her disposal, and because he was male, he assumed it was as easy as that. Yet, as a female, the moment she had said yes to his dizzying offer a frantic dash to the imaginary finishing line had ensued.

Yes, her wardrobe had been skilfully sorted by Katina, but there had been stockings, panties and new lipstick to buy, a trip to the hairdresser's, then a last minute bikini wax to ensure that *all* her hair was neatly taken care of. And then the extremely difficult task of buying a small gift for someone who literally had everything!

All Zakahr had had to do was roll out of bed.

He hadn't even shaved.

She flicked her eyes to him, and then back out of the window. Her heart was leaping, as was her stomach, at the daunting sight of him. She had only ever seen him in a suit, but Zakahr in smart-casual was just as giddying—perhaps more so. He was, from her quick peek, wearing charcoal-grey linen trousers and a white fitted shirt—impossibly elegant, dangerously relaxed, achieving effortlessly what Lavinia had spent the past hours striving for.

'Will it be very grand?' Lavinia asked, nervous not only at the prospect of Zakahr.

'The King is supposed to be a marvellous host, so I'm sure it will be pleasurable. You got on well with Jasmine at dinner.'

The journey was awkward—so much so that in the end Lavinia opened the partition and spoke with Eddie, asking more about his granddaughter and sympathising with him as to the stressful times that lay ahead.

Zakahr checked his e-mails, trying not to listen, trying not to hear that Eddie's son-in-law was taking time off work to be there for his wife and new daughter, and that Eddie was stepping in to help them out financially, so they could concentrate on Emily rather than worry about bills.

He did not want to hear it.

Would not *let* himself hear it.

He did this month in, month out—year in, year out. It was no different from any of the other companies he had closed—still, it was a relief when they turned off for the airport, bypassing all car parks and queues.

For once it was Lavinia being driven straight on to the tarmac, but only as she climbed the steps to a small jet did a different set of nerves catch up—an unexpected set of nerves. For a second she stalled.

'Okay?' Zakahr checked as he walked up the stairs behind her, and Lavinia forced legs that felt like jelly to move forward, smiling to the waiting cabin crew and stepping inside.

It was divine, but it did not soothe—not the plush leather seats or the thick carpet. As she sat, even idle conversation wasn't happening, and she wished he'd flick open a newspaper so she could just close her eyes and go into herself as the plane started taxiing. But instead Zakahr was looking at her as Lavinia tightened the strap over her lap.

'Are you a nervous flyer?'

'It would appear so.'

'It's only an hour.'

It was going to be the longest hour of her life, and Lavinia blew out a long breath at the prospect.

'Why didn't you say something before?' Zakahr frowned. 'You could have taken something—'

'I didn't know,' Lavinia interrupted, and then turned to him. 'I've never flown.'

'Never?'

'I've never been to Sydney either.' Lavinia was more than a little embarrassed by her admission, and to mask that her voice came out a little more snappish that she had intended. 'So don't expect me to play tour guide.'

Again she had surprised him. He'd been sure that she was used to being whisked away. But she was like a glorious butterfly, cooped up in Kolovsky and unable to fly.

'It's very safe.'

'Sure.'

Zakahr recalled *his* first flight; there had been no nerves, just the feeling of excitement that he was finally on his way to make real his dreams. An elderly man sitting next to him had talked to him, so Zakahr did the same now. He told Lavinia about that first flight, when he had been a teenager, on his way to England, hardly speaking the language, hoping that an old friend from the orphanage he had contacted would be meeting him, his nerves that Immigration would turn him around.

He did something else too.

Zakahr held her hand as he spoke, and she could feel it hot and dry around her cold one, and instead of worrying about the noise and the speed she was listening, trying to imagine being so young and so brave.

A light breakfast was served, and still he spoke. Lavinia chose warmed blueberries smothered in cold yoghurt, the ripe fruit bursting on her tongue, and she finally got her champagne, with a small hibiscus flower placed inside the glass that slowly unfurled as the bubbles streamed over it. And it wasn't just the flower opening up under her genuine interest. So too did Zakahr.

'How did you start?' Lavinia asked. 'If you had no formal qualifications?'

'I lied.' A slow smile spread over his face. 'Only at first. I didn't have to for long. I was clever, I had confidence—people respond to that.' He told her how he had waited on tables and cleaned houses for a year, studying not just the language but his options, working out what it would take to get on that first step of a golden ladder, then buying a second-hand suit. 'Not any suit,' Zakahr said. 'I found good second-hand shops. That suit was more expensive than a regular new suit, but with the right shoes, the right briefcase, the right haircut, the right address...'

'The right address?'

'I made sure I cleaned at the right address. Every morning at ten the letters landed on the mat.'

Lavinia gaped at how he had reinvented himself.

'For one year I saved for my interview outfit. I had three shirts, five ties, one suit... With my first pay packet I bought another second-hand suit; after one year I had my first suit tailor made. I had no need to lie about my qualifications then. I knew that once I was in they would not want to lose me.'

'Wow!' Lavinia blinked. 'I can see I've gone the boring way about it.'

'Boring?' Zakahr questioned, because here was a woman who never had bored him.

'I'm not brave enough to lie,' Lavinia said. 'Anyway, I actually needed that bit of paper to get in to university.' She saw she wasn't making much sense. 'When I finished school I went to TAFE part-time.'

'TAFE?'

'Like college,' Lavinia said. 'I finished my schooling, but it took for ever—four years, part-time.'

'You still study?'

'Chemistry.' Lavinia nodded. 'Though that's happening ever slower—more so if I get Rachael. At this rate, by the time I'm thirty I'll have my degree and be teaching.'

'You're studying for a Chemistry degree?'

'Painfully slowly,' Lavinia admitted. 'But, yes.'

It was like watching a pleasing movie and then being handed 3D glasses. All the colours, all the nuances that were Lavinia, were amplified with every look, and he knew that there was more. Normally it would have troubled him—for when it wasn't business Zakahr never wanted more detail, never wanted extra involvement. Only with Lavinia he did.

They were preparing for descent, the short journey over, their table cleared. Aware she would be nervous, he carried on talking and offered his hand. But she just laughed and didn't accept.

'I'm not nervous any more.' Lavinia grinned. 'The closer we get, the better I feel. I think I rather like flying after all.'

She just adapted, Zakahr realised, staring out of the window. Sydney was spread out in the most stunning riot of ocean and rocks, and it was impossible to see this view and not be moved. He could smell her hair as she leant over him, could feel her elbow in his chest as she drank in the view. And he didn't want her to pull back, would have loved to undo the belts and pull her onto his lap.

As Lavinia moved back to her seat, her cheek moved past Zakahr's face, and whether it was his will or want she hesitated, turned to him with eyes that were crystal-clear. Contact would be both the solution and the problem—releasing a volatile energy she wasn't sure she could deal with. But how she wanted to…

It was Lavinia who kissed him, but there was nothing bold about it—no first move—because the moves had long since been made.

She kissed lips that she wanted, that wanted her, she tasted champagne on his tongue and the only place in her mind was *here*.

There was an awakening within her that he had triggered—one she had suppressed, one she had ignored, one that needed to come to its own natural conclusion. Like caesium reacting with water, her body fizzed and danced on the surface of his caress. He spoke her name into her mouth and his fingers bunched in her hair, and he kissed her deeper, with the delicious warning of intent, his mouth more possessive now, telling her without words that tonight would be explosive.

But first there was a truth that needed to be told. She had to untangle her lips from his, every cell protesting at the disengagement, but she knew that her provocation, the bold, sensual woman he'd kissed, was a product only of *him*, and tonight it would be too late to reveal.

'This could be a weekend of firsts…' Lavinia pulled her mouth away a smudge, and Zakahr smiled in triumph at her confirmation that tonight they would finally be lovers.

'Zakahr…' She didn't know how to just come out and say it—so, being Lavinia, she just came out and said it. 'It will be my first time.'

'You haven't been on a yacht?'

'No,' Lavinia said, and it was an impatient no. 'Well, yes—I *haven't* been on a yacht…' It would be far easier to go on kissing him than to say it. 'That's not what I meant.' She took a breath. 'I haven't slept with anyone.'

'Lavinia…' He actually smiled at the impossibility. 'I think we both know—'

'*What* do you know, Zakahr?' Lavinia asked. 'Or what do you assume?'

It was only then that he realised she was being serious—except it made absolutely no sense.

'I know all the rumours. I know people assume I was sleeping with Aleksi, some think Levander too, but they're just that—rumours. People judge me because I can have a laugh, a flirt. Because of my past people just assume that I'm easy, cheap…' She shot him a look. 'You did.'

'I did not,' Zakahr immediately corrected her, because even if his relationships were generally without substance there was no disrespect for the women who had been his lovers. Sex was a necessary reward, and Zakahr would have loved to give more of himself to each and every one of them, but there was no self to give. 'I assumed from *your* actions,' Zakahr went on, 'that you wanted me as I wanted you. It was not your refusal that offended, but the mixed messages, Lavinia.' He could not get his head around it. 'You cannot go around leading—'

'I don't,' Lavinia said. 'I've only ever been like that with you.'

Her words hung between them as they came in to

land. Lavinia leant back in her seat at the force of land-ing, though it was pale in comparison to the power of the man beside her.

There was no second offer of his hand, his distance immediate. He had thought her teasing at first, but now he knew he was hearing the truth, and it was too much for Zakahr.

'I am not looking for a relationship.' As the plane slowed down, he turned to her. His sentence was curt, but there was nothing lost in translation—he wanted the coming weeks over, and he wanted no part of the family that still invited him in. He did not want his mother, or his siblings—he wanted distraction, not involvement. Lavinia was to have been a stunning reprieve in grim proceedings.

Zakahr wanted Lavinia, but he wanted the silver-eyeshadowed, smart-talking Lavinia—the one who laughed and poked her tongue out at the world, who knew men, knew the rules that he could deal with. What he struggled with was the *other* Lavinia—the Lavinia who seemed to be dragging him into a world that he had always refused to inhabit. Lavinia oozed feeling and emotion. Zakahr did his best to avoid both. Yet there was no one without the other with the woman beside him.

'Was I asking for a relationship?'

'Please…' He halted, because again he was assuming—but it was an assumption based on long his-tory. Always women wanted more than he could even begin to give.

'Can't we just see what happens? Any day now I could have Rachael.'

Zakahr closed his eyes, and Lavinia had the temerity to laugh as his face paled.

'Zakahr—it's because of that that I don't want a relationship with *you*. I might take a risk with my own heart, but never with hers,' she said. 'I know the sort of family I want to give Rachael—' it was Lavinia's turn to be brutal '—and that's something you could never provide.'

There was a conversation there, but he chose not to pursue it—he did not want to hear what he could not give. The crew were out now, the cabin door was opening, and he could see the car and the King's aide waiting on the tarmac. Zakahr unclipped his belt, just wanting the hell out, but Lavinia caught his arm.

'I want to be twenty-four...' She caught his eyes and stared into them, and to the dangerous place beyond. 'I am in no position to have a relationship, but I want to be with you. I want one night...' She didn't know the words, she didn't know how to articulate—to tell him that even if she must accept he wasn't interested in for ever still she wanted *now*. 'For one day, one night, I want to forget so that I can remember.'

He could not respond. He did not know how to respond—because he wanted more than one night. He had been going to propose a full week—a week that would both resolve his past and secure her future.

'Zakahr...'

He pulled his hand away and then stood. Only then did he respond. 'As I said on our first day—you have no idea who you're playing with.' He shook his head in disbelief, angry with her for her misplaced trust. 'Again, I tell you—you need to be more careful.'

There was no chance for further discussion.

The King's aide met them on the tarmac, and they were driven to the wharf, making polite conversation along the way but never to each other.

Lavinia could feel his tension, knew he felt beguiled, and only as they stepped out of the car and walked along the jetty towards the yacht was there a chance for terse conversation.

'You should have told me.'

'It's not something you just slip into the conversation. When was I supposed to tell you?'

'In the car park it might have—'

'I'd known you less than a week!' Lavinia retorted, but her cheeks were burning as she recalled their blistering kiss—hardly her usual response to a virtual stranger. 'Oh, well.' Lavinia tossed her hair. 'Just because I'm off-limits on your strange moral compass, it doesn't mean we can't enjoy our time here.'

It would, Zakahr quickly realised, be *impossible* to enjoy his time here.

As they boarded they were warmly greeted by the King and his family. Jasmine, amongst her own family and in the privacy of the yacht, was unveiled, revealing a smiling, happy face, and she was clearly delighted to see Lavinia again—a completely different woman from the shy Princess they had first met. Their laughter filled the salty air, reaching Zakahr's ears as he took refreshment with the King on deck.

The stunning vehicle that was to be their home till tomorrow was soon moving out of Darling Harbour, and though it was a visual feast—the huge Harbour Bridge, the splendour of the Opera House—it wasn't the scenery that over and over again forced his gaze. It was Lavinia—completely at ease with the royals, delighted in her surroundings, and the company he wanted to be keeping. He had, as Lavinia had pointed out, *assumed*.

Not just from her job, or the rumours, but from her bold kisses, from the desire of her body—yet her purity muddied the waters for Zakahr.

He liked *uncomplicated*—would soon be walking away. A brief, albeit passionate, affair with Lavinia would have eased the stress of the day. This, though, however she denied it, was teetering Lavinia-style towards a relationship.

Refreshments taken, they were shown by staff to their accommodation. Yes, Zakahr realised, this day and night would be more than impossible—it would be hell. And, thanks to his careful instructions when he'd accepted the invitation, it was a hell of his own making.

Lavinia had no idea what to expect—for not only hadn't she flown, apart from a trip on the ferry to Tasmania she had never been on a boat, and the yacht they had boarded outreached even her wildest imaginings. It was as luxurious as any five-star hotel. They had walked through a lounge filled with scattered sofas, and a huge bar with large plasma screens, and there was a vast dining area where, Jasmine told her, they would dine tonight. But lunch would be served on deck. There was even a dance floor.

As they took the steps down to the next level an aide took Zakahr to his suite and a female aide took Lavinia further along a narrow corridor. And though it was becoming clearer by the moment how luxurious this trip would be, Lavinia gaped in awe when she first glimpsed her suite.

A large four-poster bed was the centrepiece, with heavy walnut furniture, thick carpets and a dressing table. There was even a sunken spa.

'It's stunning!' She roamed the vast suite, opening doors, admiring her already unpacked clothes and her toiletries set out in the bathroom. 'What's this...?' she asked, stopping in front of another door.

'Adjoining,' Mara the aide said, lowering her eyes. 'The King understands there are differences...' Clearly a little embarrassed, Mara explained that lunch would served shortly on deck and left.

It was very like having a red button with a sign saying not to push it—only it wasn't Lavinia resisting temptation, it was Zakahr. Refusing to be embarrassed, Lavinia gave the wooden door a sharp rap, and then opened it to find Zakahr lying scowling on his bed, gorgeous in the dark grey linen pants and white shirt, sulky and thoroughly fed up with his lot.

'Hi there, neighbour!'

He didn't reply.

'Don't worry—I shan't be creeping in at night. You can sleep safely.'

'Ha-ha,' came Zakahr's response.

'Sorry to rot up your plans.' Lavinia perched on the end of his bed. 'But I told you not to assume…'

Zakahr shuttered his eyes. She was right—he *had* assumed. So much so that now he had Abigail arriving on Monday. His intention had been to have Lavinia safely tucked up in his bed for the remainder of his stay in Australia, distraction merited, but only at night. He looked over to where she sat. How much easier would it be to just reach out and pull her towards him? There was almost a thread between them in that moment—one that could draw them closer or snap—and Zakahr knew he had to break it. For there could be no involvement. They were from two different worlds, opposite sides of the world, and soon Lavinia would be carer to a child. Zakahr had tried relationships. They did not suit at the best of times, and this, for Zakahr, was the worst of times.

'If you've waited this long you should wait to be with someone you're serious…' He couldn't finish, because he couldn't stand the thought of a future Mr Lavinia—or, worse, a one-night stand because she didn't want to be alone, with some lowlife who wouldn't take care of her.

'We'd better go up for lunch.' Lavinia stood. 'Imagine them giving us adjoining rooms—I can't imagine why they thought us a couple.' She gave him a wink before closing the door. 'See you on deck.'

It was a casual lunch, with Lavinia chatting with Jasmine and her bridesmaids as waiters mingled with plates—and it was lovely to be out on the water, to be away from her problems for a little while.

'He's very handsome!' Lavinia looked at a photo of Jasmine's husband-to-be.

'I know.' Jasmine smiled. 'Lucky for me I am the youngest of five girls. My father had a lot more say in my older sisters' husbands—and he was not my father's first choice for me. He is a friend of my brother's,' Jasmine explained. 'They were at university together, and sometimes he would come to the palace. I had a terrible crush on him for years. My brother spoke with my father a few months ago, told him how unhappy I would be if I followed *his* choice. I am very blessed to have such a wonderful family.'

The Princess smiled as Zakahr walked over and joined them, and though she returned it, for a second Lavinia struggled: it was things like that that hurt at times. Lavinia certainly didn't show it—but so many times she'd wondered how much easier things might have been if there had been brothers and sisters by her side. Even now her world seemed so small—there were friends, of course, but those friends had their own families. She ached sometimes, literally ached, for a sister to ring her up, or have coffee with her, a family to moan about too, to visit for Christmas and birthdays.

'I was just saying to Lavinia how nice it is to come from a large family.' Jasmine politely invited him into the conversation.

Zakahr respectfully declined.

'It is my pleasure to meet them.'

They spoke for a few minutes about the King's cousin, who spent four months a year in Australia. It was his boat they were on. They spoke, but they only talked, and

Lavinia realised then that had she not known his past he would never have revealed it—saw first-hand just how little Zakahr let anyone in.

'I need to speak with my father.'

Jasmine excused herself, and Zakahr revealed the real reason he had come over—he had seen Lavinia's slender shoulders pinken, seen her nose and cheeks redden a touch, and even if she wasn't to be his lover she promoted reluctant responsibility. 'You need to apply sunblock.'

'I know!' Lavinia whispered. 'I forgot to bring any.'

'Ask Jasmine if she has some…' His voice trailed off. Jasmine's skin was lovely and brown; it was Lavinia who was lily-white. 'You need it.'

'I'm scared to ask,' Lavinia admitted. 'They're so polite they'll probably go and helicopter some in, or something…'

'I'll sort it.' He was back a few moments later, having had a word with one of the crew, and handed her a tube. 'They will also put some aftersun in your cabin.'

'Hardly a cabin!' Lavinia smiled.

People were starting to drift off. The afternoon sun was too fierce to stay on deck, and the King announced that he might sleep for a while. Jasmine wanted to watch a film. Lavinia was on the King's side.

'We meet at seven for dinner,' Jasmine's mother informed them. 'Relax for now, Lavinia. Enjoy the boat, your room…'

They were just the nicest people. Lavinia had been rather worried that she'd have to talk and entertain right up till bedtime, but they were the most lovely hosts. The Queen sat in the shade with a book, Jasmine and her bridesmaids curled up to watch a film, and a very guilt-free Lavinia slipped down the stairs to the cool bliss of her suite. Peeling off her clothes, down to her bra and panties, she winced at her pink shoulders. They didn't hurt yet, but possibly would by evening.

She rubbed in cool aloe vera aftersun lotion, swore never to leave her room again without sunblock, and then stretched out on the bed, enjoying the gentle lulling motion of the yacht. She was relaxed, yet not. Aware that Zakahr was close, deciding that perhaps his reaction to her news was possibly for the best.

She wanted to be made love to by him, she wanted him to be her first, but her assurances to him that she expected nothing were perhaps more what he'd needed to hear than what she had wanted to say.

He captured her mind in a way no man ever had, Lavinia thought as she headed into a lovely long sleep. With him Lavinia was—possibly for the first time in her life—completely herself.

She'd told him of her past, told him of her present, even her hopes for the future.

It wasn't Zakahr who enthralled her.

Neither Belenki the businessman.

Nor the focussed Riminic, who had chosen to reinvent himself, who had Lavinia slightly spellbound.

It was the whole montage of him—the smile that could make her stomach fold, the dark humour and those glimpses of a softer side, a protective side. To have that, to be wrapped in it, to be held by it even for a little while, would be hell to let go of.

'Lavinia?'

He *so* did not want to go in there, but it was after six, and there were no noises from her room, so Zakahr realised that it was up to him to wake her. Unlike Lavinia, Zakahr did not relish down-time—he had no desire to make small-talk with his hosts, nor did he know how to relax. Bed in the afternoon was what he had hoped for— but not alone. He had taken off his shirt and stretched out on the bed, and spent a restless afternoon playing heads or tails with his conscience, thinking what they should be doing now. On too many occasions had come dangerously close to her door.

What was preventing him, Zakahr was not quite sure.

He had broken many hearts in his past, and Lavinia was willing—there was a strange sense of honour that kept him back, though. A sense of the damage he could wreak, a wanting to spare her from the hurt that was inevitably to come.

'Lavinia!' He knocked again and then pushed it open. 'It's after six.'

She jolted awake with the horrible realisation that she had less than an hour to get ready to dine with the King, and with no Katina on hand or a hairdresser to help this time. Sun, sea and a champagne breakfast had ensured Lavinia slept well—now she heard the sound of laughter from above, and a rap at the adjoining door, saw Zakahr standing in the doorway.

'Oh, God…' Lavinia did her best not to dwell on the splendid sight of him—naked from the waist up, he was more beautiful than her many imaginings. His pale skin was shadowed with a smatter of chest hair like a charcoal smudge that led down to the now crumpled linen trousers; he looked sulky, restless and never more beautiful. But it was easier to snap than to admit it… 'Why didn't you wake me?' Her high, terse voice was a contrast to his drawl.

'I'm trying to give up the habit!'

There was no time to think of a reply. Lavinia jumped off the bed, wincing as her bra strap stuck into her sunburnt shoulders, then wincing for a different reason as Zakahr turned to go and she caught sight of the scars that laced his back, the ripple of muscles rising beneath almost in defiance.

He must have heard her intake of breath, or just realised he'd left himself exposed, because she watched those muscles stiffen, saw his neck turn a fraction, as if to witness her response, but then he changed his mind, closing the door behind him, and Lavinia stood for a moment, trying to take in not just what she had just seen but her own response to it.

Lavinia never cried.

At five years of age she had worked out that tears were entirely wasted—that it was far more productive to just smile and carry on.

She *chose* happiness—forcibly wrenched herself from bitterness and anger, yet it drenched her now. There was fury that shot towards Nina, that ricocheted to Ivan, to all of them, to anyone who had touched him—a possessive fury she had met before when she'd heard about the bruises on Rachael.

Except this was a man, Lavinia told herself. A man who did not need her protection and certainly did not want her compassion or her heart.

So she did what she did best—swallowed unshed tears, applied make-up to her sunburn, and then concentrated on her hair and face. She had just slipped on her dress, a trifle worried she would be overdressed, when Zakahr knocked at her door.

'We should go up.'

She hadn't overdressed, Lavinia realised, because Zakahr would never get such things wrong. For dinner he had shaved, and was now suited, utterly ready to dine with the King—and, she thought as her heart quickened, utterly and completely able to bed her at will. She wanted to fall on him, she wanted to kiss him, she wanted to be pushed on to the bed and be made love to by him. There was nothing virginal about her thoughts.

'Two minutes,' she bargained.

'One,' Zakahr allowed—though she did not need it. His eyes tried not to roam her body as he sat on the couch. She was dressed in black, sheer lace and velvet like thick black grapes, hugging her body, and Zakahr wanted to peel and taste each one. Her blonde hair spilled over her shoulders and she must have just sprayed scent, for there was a potent dose of Lavinia in the air.

'You look nice.' Even Zakahr knew that was too

paltry. 'You look fantastic. The dress…' *The woman in it*, was unspoken, but Zakahr ignored his impulse and kept his voice even. 'The pattern…'

Lavinia laughed. 'Devoré.' She smiled at his nonplussed reaction. 'You've got a lot to learn.'

So did she, Zakahr thought, stamped with a fierce need to teach her, but changing the subject instead. 'What's that?' he asked when, having slipped on high heels, she picked up a wrapped present from her dressing table.

'A gift for Jasmine.'

'I'll arrange a gift on Monday.'

'I'm sure you will!' Lavinia said as she fiddled with her dress in the full-length mirror. 'Or rather you'll ask me to have something very tasteful, beautiful and expensive arranged, to thank the King for his hospitality. This, though—' she turned and smiled '—is just a little present for Jasmine from me!'

Was there an affront there? Zakahr could see no reason for one, yet there was just a slight mockery to her voice that he chose to ignore.

'Let's go.' He stood just as the yacht lurched slightly while it anchored.

Lavinia, grimly holding on to her present with one hand, made a quick grab for the four-poster bed with the other and balanced herself in her heels. And then as easily as that she caught his eye—she did nothing, no dance, nothing provocative, just smiled as she held onto the bedpost.

'I told you—I just can't help myself sometimes.'

And as easily as that he smiled, paused for a second.

There was a short laugh, and then he walked behind her up to the deck—ruing how easily she lightened him, the verbal shorthand that had developed between them, and the irony that for the first time as he walked into a room with a woman, still smiling at their little joke, even if she was out of bounds, it was the closest he had felt to being part of a couple.

The table was elaborate. The Opera House was lit up, a stunning backdrop, and the food and company were exquisite. Surely there should be pride tonight in his achievements—a moment to savour the triumph so close? But the laughter and the company and the woman beside Zakahr found him reluctantly glimpsing an alternative.

There was that unwelcome visitor guilt too, as the meal came to its conclusion. Jasmine and Lavinia were talking between themselves, and Jasmine was opening her present.

'Remember I was telling you about our traditions?'

Lavinia's make-up was fading, and he saw her blush spread down her neck and sun-kissed arms, clearly embarrassed by Jasmine's enthusiasm as she opened the package.

'It's just a tiny little thing. I know you have new, but there are old traditions…'

'It's beautiful.' Jasmine held up the small blue glass horseshoe. It was flimsy and fragile, but had been chosen with so much care. Jasmine was delighted with her gift.

'It is nice to see my daughter make a friend.' As the evening concluded the King strolled on deck with

Zakahr. 'In our position friends are easy to come by—genuine friends are much rarer. I am sure it must be the same for you.'

'It can be,' Zakahr admitted.

They walked for a while, admired the stunning view, but even as they spoke, even as the King bade him goodnight, Zakahr's mind was on Lavinia.

He stared unseeing across the water, realising that the King was right—though for a long time it had suited Zakahr. His position, his wealth, guaranteed he was never short of company—it had suited him, but it just didn't feel so right now. He had suppressed a smile as Lavinia had educated the Princess as to the wonders of social networking, making her promise to post some wedding pictures online, and whether or not Jasmine was being polite, tonight she had agreed. The King was right. They were already friends, and would no doubt stay in touch after the wedding—and then he remembered what tonight he had chosen to forget.

There would be *no* friendship. This time next week the Kolovsky name would be mud to King Abdullah. There would be chaos, and she would be in the thick of it—he had to get her away from there.

CHAPTER ELEVEN

LAVINIA smiled a mirthless smile as, after the most wonderful night, she entered her suite and saw the lit candles.

Petals were scattered on the bed, and even if there had been no alcohol on deck, down below there was champagne, cooling in a bucket. The spa was filled too—all no doubt on Zakahr's instruction, before he'd found out she was a virgin.

She had taken the chance to slip away as Zakahr walked with the King, had said goodnight to her hosts, and now she stood alone and her smile was no longer mirthless. In fact, Lavinia laughed.

She didn't just laugh, she peeled off her dress and shoes and absolutely refused misery, popping the champagne cork and then stripping off her bra and panties.

Zakahr heard her as he walked past and so badly he wanted to join her—to make love to her and, yes, whether she understood it now or at some time in the future, to take care of her in the only way he knew how.

He went into his suite, took off his tie. There was a large brandy waiting for him, which he downed in one, but it did not make a dent. No drink could douse his emotions tonight—but it was a different emotion that rose now, as he knocked on the adjoining door and waited.

Lavinia lay in the spa, champagne in hand, heart in her throat, more than ready to say yes, which she did in a voice that was just a little breathless.

'You've been busy,' Lavinia said as he walked in and slowly took off his jacket. 'I thought you were walking with the King, not stripping roses of their petals and rushing around lighting candles.'

He looked at the candles, the petals, the bubbling spa, and then to her.

'I did a good job!' Zakahr continued the joke. 'I didn't know I could be so romantic.' And then he was serious. 'Are you sure?'

She was absolutely sure.

The bubbles were dispersing, slowly revealing her body to him, and rather than shy she had never felt more sure in her life—Zakahr was the only man she could imagine being like this with. Yes, she had stripped in the past, but she had bared only her body then. With Zakahr she could reveal herself.

'I am a bit scared, though.' She looked up at him and clarified her words. 'Not of you, of *it*.'

'You won't be soon.' It was an assured promise, and even if it still scared her she believed him.

He soaped her arms, her shoulders, her neck, till all traces of make-up were gone, and he saw just how young and vulnerable she was, even if she was tough at times too. He knew she was scared, and was grateful that it was him—because he knew that he would take care of her, knew she would be scared only till he was inside.

He pulled the plug and helped her stand. Lavinia had never been shy of her body, had revealed it too easily, but now, feeling his eyes roam her with affection rather than lust, there was a chasteness that had been missing before, tempting her to cover her breasts as she climbed out of the spa. Instead he pulled her into him, shielded her with his kiss, and feeling his mouth, feeling her hot damp body press into his shirt, for a little while she forgot to be shy.

It was a different kiss than any they'd shared before. Zakahr held her oiled and naked and warm against him, felt her dampen his shirt, and it was another kiss he relished. His hands roamed her waist, her hips, her bottom, her wet hair against his face, till the sheen on her skin evaporated and not even his hands could warm her. He felt her shiver in a mix of exposure and want.

'Come to bed.'

She had never expected tenderness. He pulled back the bedclothes and took off her towel, and she climbed in and lay there, nervous, though not, watching him undress. He slipped off his damp shirt, and there was only beauty tonight in the male form.

Scars and all, he was exquisite. Her eyes feasted on him, and he stood in the warmth of her gaze for a moment before climbing in beside her. For a long while he just held her. Then he turned on his pillow and his mouth found hers.

It was a different kiss again—a slow, tentative kiss to accustom her. And slowly she did—to the feel of being in bed with a man, to a naked body beside her. It was a building kiss, a kiss that spread through her body till it knew what to do. He tasted of brandy—or was it her? A luxurious mingling? Still he kissed her, and her leg slipped against his, felt the roughness of his hair and the solid strength of his thigh, and then his hand slid back to where she had once guided him. He lowered his head, his tongue sliding down her neck. She could feel the wrap of his legs around hers, the scratch of hair between the tender skin of her thighs, and the solid, warm weight of his erection, pressing into her stomach and slipping further down as his body moved. His mouth met her aching nipple and his hand moved lower. He could feel her warmth, feel her trepidation. His mouth worked her breast, and his fingers tenderly probed, and it was Zakahr who was nervous on her behalf. Always he was sheathed, but he thought of her virgin flesh and wanted to *feel* his way in—he wanted all of the experience, and not just for him, so wary was he of hurting her.

'When are you due?' His mouth moved to her ear.

'I'm not… I'm on the pill…'

'Never trust a man when he says this.' Those grey eyes met hers. 'Except me. I have never done anything before without protection.' He never had—had sworn he never would—except he was parting her from her innocence, and he knew that tonight he needed to be more gentle, to feel his way. And he would.

She could trust him.

Not in anything else, but in this she could. And he knew she did.

He had a streetwise side to him, a knowing, a danger

that for tonight was being put on hold. Yes, she could not justify it—she knew some of his depraved past—but it was trust that had led her to his bed, and trust that guided her now.

And it was the same for Zakahr.

So many women had wanted him—all of him. Had thought that a baby would change him—would mellow him. Nothing would.

His tip was moist, and with it Zakahr moistened her. He stroked himself around her and Lavinia lay, her breath high and shallow in her chest, nervous, curious. Then he lowered himself onto her, because he *did* want to kiss her throughout. He kissed her till she was drunk from it, and without ordered thought she was kissing him back. He kissed her till he was in just a little way, and then he kissed her some more.

He held back, but his mind surged forward to pastures new. He wanted her pleasure, he wanted her escape, and without the usual barrier the pleasure was more intense for Zakahr. That he was her first took on vital importance. He whispered words in her ear that were far more than the sweet talk he usually delivered—he whispered words that were dangerous from a man like Zakahr, words he never used.

He told her neck she was beautiful as he licked it, told her cheek he would not hurt her as he kissed it, and inched in just a little deeper, whispering into the shell of her ear that he would *never* hurt her, that she was safe, that she was okay, that he would make it so.

He dizzied her brain with endearments.

He slowly moved and gently she stretched. With each

word, each gentle probe, she opened willingly, and when he completely filled her he showered her senses further with every word she craved. He sounded as if he meant it, so he said it some more, and he felt as if he meant it as her hips rose to greet him, and her lips gasped for air, and her head thrashed with unfamiliar sensation.

Zakahr consumed her, he filled her and he thrust now within her, and it was so breathtakingly wonderful that Lavinia actually wanted it to stop, because she hadn't agreed to this, would never have agreed to this—to the absolute devotion her body held for him, to the complete disregard for the rules she should be abiding by. There could be no holding on to her heart when she was holding on to him.

Her nails dug in his back and her ears accepted his words and her body throbbed beneath his. And then she was coming, and sucking on his skin as he spilled deep within her, and then biting on his shoulder just to stop herself from saying it—because she couldn't, she mustn't. Except she already did… And he was still holding her, and kissing her, and then she rolled and turned away, waiting for it to fade, for sense to prevail. And still she wanted to say it.

Zakahr pulled her warmth towards him, kissed her shoulder and lay there. She was aware for ages that he didn't sleep, that he lay awake beside her, and so many times she had to stop herself from blurting out to the darkness, telling herself it was impossible…

Except it was possible.

She just did.

Already she loved him.

CHAPTER TWELVE

HE WOKE to the absence of regret.

Zakahr noticed because it was usually a familiar bedmate—uneasy with intimacy, he saw it as weakness and always awoke wishing she were gone. Not this morning. Faced away from her, his back exposed, he would normally roll on to his back or climb out of bed. But he had left it too late, because she had already stirred beside him. In silence he lay there, felt her cool hands on his back, felt her fingers tenderly probe his scars, and he braced himself for the inevitable—the demand for information on the strength of one night, as if he were just going to roll over and share the darkest part of his life.

He waited for her questions, but they never came.

Still her hand softly roamed him, and as her fingers explored he relived the hell of each scar, reminded himself why he was right to be here, that the plan in action was deserved. It did not have to affect Lavinia, but that meant he had to trust her, and he tensed at the very thought of it—trust was an enigma to Zakahr.

She felt him tense, but kissed his back, his shoulder, his neck. Lavinia willed him with her mouth to turn to her. Bold, she unfurled beside him, stretching into the new skin of a body that felt different this morning—aware and tender. His skin was warm next to hers, and her hands explored him, past the jut of his hips to the flat of his stomach, inching downwards till she held his morning erection in her hand and adored it. She had been scared—not just last night, maybe all her life—but with him she wasn't any longer. All was beautiful.

Here, now, was where he would turn—here, where he would normally end the intimacy. Yet he lay there and let her explore him, closed his mind to everything but her and then turned to face her. He never wanted to get out of the bed. He felt her mouth kiss his chest and then work down, felt her lips soft, warm and tentative, and then the cool of her tongue. He wanted to give in to her, but he would not. He wanted her, and it had to be now. He slid her up the bed, hooked her leg around his and drove into her.

Last night had been slow and tender, but now there was an urgency—one Lavinia wasn't sure she could match—but there was also an intensity there that excited her, a loss of control in this guarded man as he bucked inside her, an instant need that from nowhere somehow her body easily met in a storm not building but hitting, spreading from her centre and outwards, and she clung onto his shoulders and gripped with her legs, bit on her lip to stay quiet.

He could feel her dense orgasm capture his, felt the shatter of release as he entered a place he had never sought, as he drove hard within her. He could hear her calling his name, and he was saying hers too.

They coupled.

It was a word he had never considered, never used, but in the midst of orgasm its meaning was crystal-clear—so clear he could actually *see* its meaning, feel her vibrations match his as she pulled him deep into her centre. He felt her fading twitches massage the last throes from him and he did not want it to be over, still lingering even after his body was spent. He lay on top of her for a moment, and her hands were still on his back. Zakahr wanted to recoil, to climb off, to get out—because the intimacy was killing him, because somehow he had to detach. And yet *still* he lingered, still his body refused to obey his demand, still he kissed, still he was inside her—still she was in his head. And somehow, if he was to keep her for a little while longer, he had to trust her.

'We should get up for breakfast…' She lay in his arms, unfazed by his silence. 'When do we leave?'

'In a couple of hours.'

She picked up his wrist and glanced at his watch. 'This time tomorrow I'll be back at my desk,' Lavinia grumbled.

Maybe this wouldn't be so hard after all, he decided. Maybe this was what she'd intended.

'Why not take some time off?' Zakahr said. 'Concentrate on getting Rachael.' He saw just a smudge of a frown. 'You could stay with me…'

'Sorry?'

'Move in with me.'

Lavinia laughed—she just laughed.

'I'm serious. You just said you don't—'

'It was a comment, Zakahr. I was grumbling about

work—not fishing. Why would you ask me to move in? Any day now I could be guardian to—'

'Just for a while.' He saw the smile wobble, made himself say it. 'Till I return to the UK.'

And she'd known she could never keep him, had accepted as best she could that it could never last, but did he have to remind her so soon? She tried to sound casual, tried not to reveal that her heart was breaking. 'And who's going to do my job if I suddenly leave?'

'You don't have to worry about that,' he said evenly. 'I called Abigail, my PA, on Friday. She should be there by tomorrow.'

'Oh, but I do worry.' She sat up, pulling up her knees and whipping the sheet tightly around her, hating how easily she was being replaced. 'I like my job…' She shook her head. 'I *need* my job—I'm not leaving.'

'Lavinia, I tell you—you won't have to worry…' He reached out to caress her back, his fingers reaching for her shoulders, running the length of her prominent spine, glad now he hadn't signed that contract—righteous, even, in his decision. She *was* far better out of it. 'I like spending time with you—I want to spend time with you.' It was an extremely unusual admission from Zakahr. 'I'm trying to help…' He forced the words out. 'Soon there will be no job…'

She went to turn her head, but froze. Katina's bitter words, which he had dismissed so readily with his assurances, now repeating.

'You're going to destroy—'

'I'm closing it,' Zakahr interrupted.

'Destroying it.' Her lips were white. Hugging her

knees tighter, she curled up at the wretchedness of it, her mind full of Rachael, how her employment status might change things. If she did get custody, how was she supposed to support her? 'I can't believe you'd do this.' The implications were trickling in now—her colleagues, Nina. The ramifications grew bigger with each cascading thought.

'What about Jasmine…?' Lavinia was appalled. They were here as their guests, and Zakahr was planning on closing Kolovsky! 'She's getting married in a few weeks…'

'Lavinia—I've been doing this for a long time. People will be looked after—there will be redundancy packages, agreements reached. You cannot make this personal…'

'It *is* personal, though!' And she said the words she had the first day they had met. *'It's her wedding…'*

'Her father will be able to sort it… It's a dress…' This wasn't going as well as he had hoped, and he moved to calm her. 'You are going to be fine. You will be away from all the fall-out. You can stay with me, and I will make sure you don't have to look for another job. When I'm gone, you will be able to concentrate on just yourself and Rachael—you can do your studies…'

Her spine straightened beneath his touch, ramrod straight, and the muscles over her shoulders tensed rigid as he named a price—a price, Zakahr surmised, that was beyond her wildest dreams, that would secure her future, so of course she was silent—of course it was a shock. And then her head turned in fury, till the blue eyes that had always smiled darkened in fury.

'You'll *pay* me to be your mistress?'

'I want to look after you.'

'While you're here,' Lavinia snarled, 'you'll pay me to sleep with you.'

'You're twisting things.'

'I don't have to twist anything. It's pretty blatant.'

'This way—' Zakahr started. But Lavinia would not let him continue.

'This way I'll be your prostitute.'

'You're being ridiculous.'

'Actually, no. I'm an expert on the subject—my mother was a prostitute, Zakahr. I've done everything I can to claw my way out of that pit, and you'd hurl me straight back in...'

'I am offering you a chance to change your life.'

'For the greater good?' Lavinia scoffed. 'What happens in ten years, when the gas bill's late or Rachael needs schoolbooks? Will I justify it then? You're offering me money, and at the same time you've taken away everything special about last night.'

She wanted to spit at him, but she wouldn't lower herself. Zakahr had done that enough already. She was out of bed in a trice, jumping out as if it were on fire, and wrapped in a sheet she turned to him. 'I don't need your charity, Zakahr. In fact, you're the one I feel sorry for—the only way you can get affection is to pay for it!'

She would have loved to dress and leave, but there really was no easy escape given they were on a yacht—so Lavinia locked herself in the bathroom, showering away every trace of his scent, repulsed at what he had said and trying hard not to cry, trying to wash away all evidence of what had taken place. He could not possibly have shamed her more, and all Lavinia wanted was *out*.

Stepping out of the shower, she wrapped herself in a towel and wondered how she could go out there and face him—wondered how on earth she was supposed to face not just him, but Jasmine, the King. How she could ever go back to work knowing what was to come? She realised she would have to deal with this the only way she knew how.

He heard the shower turned off, waited for her to come out—except she was taking ages, and for once Zakahr did not know how he should react. Cursing his choice of words, but not the sentiment behind them, because he *did* want to take care of her, he was bristling, too—he did *not* have to pay for affection. Women threw themselves at him. And yet...

Zakahr closed his eyes. He neither wanted nor needed affection—did not want the questions that came with companionship. Rather, he preferred the detachment that money allowed. He lay, wondering how best to deal with Lavinia, which words might soothe, for already she knew far too much. He would comfort her, Zakahr decided, dry her tears—even apologise if he had to...

Except as the bathroom door opened and Lavinia came out he was stunned at what he saw.

There was no trace of tears, her hair was glossy and tied back in a low ponytail, her make-up was on and—most confusing of all—she smiled over to him and, without a trace of embarrassment or shame, dropped her towel and pulled on her underwear.

'You'd better get ready.'

In purple panties and bra she hurried him, and Zakahr watched as she put on a simple white cami, then topped it with a smart lilac trouser suit. She looked fresh and poised and incredibly beautiful, and—worse for Zakahr—she was still smiling.

Worse still, she was looking him straight in the eye.

He had expected tears, arguments, perhaps, even that she might have reconsidered—it was a life-changing sum, after all. But instead she was looking at him, smiling at him, talking to him as if none of it mattered, as if she was enjoying his company, even—and it hit him then like a fist in the stomach. She was performing—just as she had for those revolting men she had once danced for.

Lavinia—the real Lavinia he had started to glimpse—was closed.

CHAPTER THIRTEEN

'MORNING.' He walked in on Monday to the scent of freshly brewed coffee and pleasing perfume. The computers were on, as he sat at his desk his diary was open at today's page, his schedule updated, and of course there should be nothing but relief when he looked up and it wasn't Lavinia bringing him coffee but Abigail instead.

The journey back to Melbourne had been hellish. There had been no grand gestures, no flouncing off. Instead Lavinia had chatted away about nothing, thanked him when his car had dropped her off, and then walked up her garden path and closed her door.

She wouldn't be back—of that he was sure. And it was for the best, Zakahr told himself. For without Lavinia buzzing in his ear, messing with his head, finally he could execute his plans.

'I want this sorted by the end of the week,' Zakahr told Abigail.

'I thought we had longer.'

'I want it done,' Zakahr said—because he just wanted to be on that plane and heading home. But even his head protested at that word. Home? To where? London?

Switzerland? Or would he stop over in Singapore? Home to what? His family was here.

He *had* no family, Zakahr reminded himself.

'Aleksi Kolovsky called,' Abigail unwittingly taunted him. 'He says it's nothing urgent. He just called from his honeymoon to see how things were going.'

Zakahr shrugged and flicked his hand, which told Abigail to disregard it—that it wasn't important. They had worked together for years. Abigail was married— very happily married—which meant she would never jeopardise things with sudden demands. But they were still occasional lovers, and Zakahr could not fathom that now, even as Abigail flirted a little and offered him a cue.

'It seems a little strange…' Abigail smiled '…just us in Australia.'

'It won't be for long.' Zakahr did not pursue it. 'I'm making the announcement on Friday—you'll need to arrange the press—but till then try to keep it business as normal as far as you can. Though I *do* need the auditors in.' He recited his orders. 'I want the team flown in by the weekend. I'm leaving straight after the press conference on Friday.'

He saw Abigail frown. Normally Zakahr stayed to wrap things up, was steadfast in his decisions. He stood by the burning building as it fell, answered questions, and fended off the reporters.

'Won't you be needed here?' Abigail checked. 'At least for a few days?'

'I've been away long enough. It will be pure admin.' He turned to his computer, and because she wasn't

Lavinia, Abigail took her cue. Did not question a detail, nor argue a point. But there was one thing he needed to clear up, so he headed out of his office, to where Abigail was now working, and briefly brought Abigail up to speed.

'There was an assistant,' Zakahr said. 'Lavinia. I doubt she will be back, but just in case, she is to know nothing…' His voice trailed off, for there she was, walking in, just as she had on that first day, offering a quick apology for being late and carrying a large takeaway coffee. Only this morning her make-up was fully on.

'*I'm* Lavinia.' She offered her hand to Abigail, who after a moment's hesitation shook it. 'Just ask me anything you need to know, or need me to do.' And, swishing past Zakahr with a bright smile, she wished him a good morning, then headed for her old office.

With that she set the tone.

It was business, but it was so not as normal—Lavinia was just caught up in the dance of pretence, while knowing it was all a charade. She loathed Abigail, with her pussy-cat smile and her long red nails that lingered too long on his arm—loathed the scent of the woman who was so devoted to Zakahr that she would accept him without question. Not that she let Abigail see how she felt.

'Rula's agent insists the new contract is signed before her client puts on weight.' Lavinia listened as Abigail passed on the message. 'They've drawn it up; I've got it here. I'll bring it through and let Katina know.'

'Here.' She made the other woman a drink, rolled

her eyes in sympathy as Abigail juggled with an angry Katina on the phone.

'He'll sign it soon,' Abigail said crisply to the chief designer, 'and we'll get it couriered. Go ahead with the alterations. One moment.' She handed a file to Lavinia. 'Could you ask Zakahr to sign these? He knows what it's about.' She returned her attention to the phone call with Katina. 'That's your department. Zakahr does not need to be concerned with those details.'

Zakahr didn't look up when the door was knocked upon and opened. Abigail had said she was bringing the documents in, but whether it was her scent, or her walk, or just her presence, before the paperwork even reached his desk he knew that it was Lavinia.

'These are for you to sign.'

He looked at her immaculate French polished nails, then dragged his eyes up past her immaculate clothes to her groomed face. There was no trace of tears, no malice in her eyes—there was nothing.

A nothing he wanted to refute—because he *knew* she was hurting.

She was unreadable, and that was what killed him— she was closed off to him, and he did not like it a bit. But he consoled himself that it was for the best—his plans were coming into place. Soon it would be done with—soon he could resume his life. If only Lavinia stopped challenging him. Zakahr had no conscience where his family were concerned, and he had considered it the same in business—figures, facts were what he dealt with. Numbers, the bottom line. It had to be that way—and yet a lowly assistant was like a loose cannon now, bursting into his office and asking for answers, her lips smiling but her blue eyes glinting with confrontation, forcing self-examination when Zakahr would rather not.

'Just one thing,' Lavinia said as he picked up his pen. 'If you do go ahead with your plans, just understand that with a stroke of your pen you're about to terminate her career.'

'Rula will get other work…'

'Rula will be known as the Face Kolovsky didn't want.' Lavinia tossed her hair. 'And thanks to this contract she'll be several kilos heavier!'

'She'll be all the healthier for it.' Zakahr signed with a flourish, but his teeth seemed welded together as he passed her the forms.

'Has she rung yet?' Lavinia asked, and Zakahr shook his head in impatience.

'Why would Rula ring *me*?'

'I meant Ms Hewitt,' Lavinia retorted—because even if it was hell right now, even if her heart was breaking, there were other more important things on her mind.

'No.'

'She did say that she would?' Lavinia checked, and for just a fraction the mask slipped. 'That wasn't another piece of your plan to get me away from this place?'

'No.' Zakahr almost tasted blood. It felt as if he were swallowing shards of glass as he heard her take on things. He could see how it looked—the night away, Abigail flying in… 'I will let you know when she calls.'

* * *

He didn't.

She limped through to Thursday, but it took every ounce of strength she possessed to go to work. She should just leave, just walk away. Except she wouldn't give him the satisfaction—and there was, despite all evidence to the contrary, still a flare of hope in her heart that Zakahr would not go through with it, that he would be the wonderful, intuitive man she knew he could be, the caring man who had listened about Rachael.

And the devil himself she was sure *did* have a conscience. Because while she smiled and carried on as before, while she made extra effort with her appearance, Zakahr didn't seem to care less. He'd stopped shaving—since Sydney his face had not met a razor—but unfortunately it made him look sexier.

What wasn't so endearing was that for the first time since he'd taken over Zakahr had the same suit on for a second day in a row—and, Lavinia was positive, the same shirt. And he wasn't wearing a tie.

She wondered whose bed he'd just rolled out of.

'I don't give "warm wishes".' He placed two letters she'd actually been asked to draft on her desk beside her, and Lavinia should have jumped—after all, she was scrolling through Positions Vacant—but she refused to jump to *him*.

'And I'm not a typist,' Lavinia said. 'What do you prefer—yours truly?'

The irony wasn't wasted on Zakahr, and he gave a thin smile. Even though they barely spoke, when they did, thanks to Lavinia—who had always refused to bend to him—they managed pretty much as before.

'Yours sincerely,' Zakahr said. 'If you can manage it.' He glanced at her computer screen. 'Anything good?'

'A few!' Lavinia said. 'Don't worry—I shan't ask for a reference.'

It shouldn't concern him at all. But as he sat later, going over and over the events of tomorrow with Abigail, over and over his mind drifted to Lavinia.

What would she do?

He'd seen the jobs she was looking at—and he knew the types of qualifications they required. She'd need a pretty good job to match her wage. She was, he admitted, one of the sharpest people he knew—but by her own admission on paper she was qualified for little.

It wasn't his problem.

He'd never have got where he was if he'd worried about individual staff—Zakahr had to be ruthless. He'd come from nothing. She could do it, too.

'Your mail.' Lavinia knocked and went in, handed him his personal mail—which was one of the few jobs still left to her.

'Thanks.' He didn't even look up at her, and Abigail sat in silence, clearly waiting for Lavinia to be gone.

'Oh, Abigail.' Lavinia smiled sweetly. 'The beauticians rang—they can squeeze you in for your Brazilian after all. Just so long as you don't need your bottom done! I said I wasn't sure, and that you'd call them back.'

'That was cruel.' Zakahr couldn't help but grin as a purple-faced Abigail excused herself for a moment.

'No,' Lavinia corrected, 'that was bliss!' She turned to go, but then, blonde, dizzy, still absolutely stunning, she turned back. 'I've just had Alannah on the phone. She's a bit upset there are internal auditors going into the boutique.'

'External,' Zakahr corrected. 'They're an international firm I regularly use. Just tell her something—I don't know.' He shrugged. 'Tell her I don't trust anyone else's figures—even Nina and Aleksi could not agree on Kolovsky's worth. Tell her there's nothing to worry about.'

'Lie to her?'

'It's your job to keep things normal,' Zakahr said. 'If you can't handle it…'

'Fine—I'll tell her. I'm going to the boutique anyway. Abigail's given me quite a shopping list!'

As Zakahr took a phone call, Lavinia flounced out. A boot-faced Abigail scowled at her from her desk.

'If you ever do that again…'

'You'll what?' Lavinia challenged. 'Fire me?'

'I'll speak to Zakahr!'

'And tell him what? That I'm a bitch?' Lavinia just laughed. 'Oh, I can be…'

Unfortunately Zakahr chose that moment to put in an appearance. 'Come,' he said. 'I'll speak to Alannah myself. You can have a lift.'

It was their first real time alone since the weekend, and for Zakahr, even if it was awkward, it was actually a relief to get out of the office. As they moved out of the city Zakahr watched as Lavinia looked out of the window. Perhaps feeling his eyes, Lavinia turned and gave him a smile. It didn't look false, and that was the part that gutted him—he knew it had to be.

'How are you doing?' he asked—because despite everything he did want to know.

'Good!' she said.

'Lavinia...' Zakahr could not stand the bright smile. 'Can you drop the act...?'

Never. She would smile, she would carry on, she would laugh and she would talk. But she would never let him in again.

'Ms Hewitt just called.' There was a slight inclination of her head. It was the only indication of how much this mattered to her. 'That is why I wanted you away from the office. I confirmed that you have worked for Kolovsky for more than two years...'

'Did you tell her that after tomorrow I wouldn't have a job?'

'Of course not.'

'She'll find out anyway.' Lavinia shrugged. 'I've got an appointment with her at lunchtime.'

'I told her that you are responsible—that you have...'

Except Lavinia shook her head—didn't need to hear it. Instead she opened the partition and chatted with Eddie about his tiny granddaughter.

When they got to the boutique she didn't wait for Eddie to come round and open the door—just shot out of the car and walked ahead of him. And it was Lavinia who held the heavy door open as Zakahr refused to hesitate. He had seen many House of Kolovsky boutiques on his travels, but he had never been able to bring himself to go in, loathing them from the outside.

'Age before beauty!' Lavinia said brightly—only today she didn't make him smile.

He was very good with Alannah and her team. Lavinia had to give credit where it was due. In fifteen minutes he had the worried staff convinced this audit was nothing out of the ordinary, that it would all take place after hours, and that none of the clients would know, nothing would be compromised.

Lavinia picked up Abigail's order, which was actually two dresses, a jacket and a sheer silk shirt, a thick coat, and a gorgeous heavy silk scarf that Lavinia could quite happily have throttled her with—because if it was worth a fortune today, as Abigail knew only too well, tomorrow it would be priceless.

As they went to walk out of the boutique, as always Lavinia's eyes lingered a moment on her favourite signature piece. He must have followed her gaze as Zakahr's hand moved to the garment and there was a flare of recognition in his eyes.

'*Koža*,' Lavinia said. 'This is what it looks like when it's made up—this is the one I was trying to explain.'

It was nothing more than a slip dress—really it should merit nothing more than a glance. Except Zakahr was for a moment mesmerised.

'How…?' The simple, albeit beautiful, cloth he had held in his fingers now hung ruched and softly fluted at the bottom. There was no zip that he could see, no darts, just one simple seam at the back and two thin straps.

'Magic,' Lavinia said. 'Which is another word for bias.' She watched him frown. 'Cross-grain?' she attempted, and now it was Lavinia who rolled her eyes. 'You really are a fashion virgin.'

'At least I don't pretend otherwise,' Zakahr said, and Lavinia's little smile of triumph faded, taken over by a blush.

'I don't have to pretend any more,' Lavinia said. 'Thanks to you!'

And he heard the implication of a future with another and Zakahr didn't like it. But Lavinia would not linger. Instead she turned her attention back to the slip dress.

'Ivan really was a genius.'

'What was he like?' Zakahr surprised himself by asking—but from Lavinia he knew he would hear part of the truth.

'A bully,' Lavinia responded instantly. 'He snapped his fingers and Nina jumped—everyone jumped. He loved his women; he flaunted them in her face. His latest mistress was even standing there with Nina at his deathbed…' She thought for a moment. 'Poor Nina.' She would *not* be silenced; she would always speak as she found. 'She used to be all bloated and miserable. I'm sure she drank—I'm sure he hit her…'

He wished she'd stop.

'But he *was* a genius.' She looked around the boutique at the amazing things his twisted mind had created. 'And, God help her, Nina loved him.'

They walked out of the boutique to the waiting limousine, and as Eddie waited for a suitable gap in the traffic Zakahr looked at the familiar cerulean blue building. There should be triumph building, surely? Except when he turned away he saw Lavinia staring at the building too, a faraway look in her eyes, and he remembered their first journey and how different things had been.

Her phone bleeped and she read a text message. For a second she closed her eyes, and then gave a wry smile. 'Jasmine.'

Just for a moment he swore he saw a flash of tears in her eyes, and Zakahr knew that despite the smile and the talk and the clothes she was struggling inside. He did the kindest thing he could.

'I won't be needing you tomorrow.'

She was silent for a moment before she spoke. 'Am I just to watch it on the news?'

'Resign,' Zakahr said. 'I'll ensure you get a good package.' He saw the clench of her jaw and corrected himself. 'A fair package. You can say you were so opposed when you found out that you resigned on principle...'

It was actually a relief.

There was sadness—an aching sadness—but there was actually relief.

'Can I come back for my things this afternoon?'

'Of course.'

'Can you be out?'

It killed her that he nodded.

CHAPTER FOURTEEN

THIS had nothing to do with Zakahr.

She sat in Ms Hewitt's cluttered office and, though her world was falling apart, she knew she couldn't blame this part of it on him.

'Your references are wonderful,' Ms Hewitt said. 'Lavinia, I am so impressed at how you have turned your life around, and I don't doubt you would be a wonderful carer for Rachael. But we go to every length to keep a family together, and with extra support we feel Rachael...'

Lavinia had begged and pleaded her case, all to no avail, and now it came down to this. 'Will I still get to see her?'

'Of course.' Ms Hewitt was the kindest she had been. 'I've spoken to Rowena and suggested you have time with her this afternoon, and I've also recommended in my report that you have overnight access once a week—which is more than before. Your role as a big sister to Rachael is one we take seriously.'

'And the decision is made?'

'There'll be a case conference on Monday,' Ms Hewitt said. 'I just wanted to tell you what to expect.'

'Is there anything I can do?'

'Lavinia…' Ms Hewitt took off her glasses. 'You can get a lawyer—you can challenge things, delay things a little—but nobody is on trial here. It's not about winning or losing. It's about what's best for Rachael.'

She *was* what was best for Rachael.

Despite the decision, right at her very core Lavinia knew that.

And she would be a good parent; the next hour proved that—because, even though she was bleeding inside, she fronted up to the hardest gig of her life and smiled when she collected Rachael.

'Where are we going?' Rachael asked as Lavinia started the car.

'We have to go to my office, just so I can collect a few things,' Lavinia said. There were essentials there, like her make-up bag and her MP3 player, but hopefully Zakahr wouldn't be there—still, given the hour, she thought it better to warn Rachael.

'My boss might be a bit funny,' Lavinia explained as they parked the car and walked along the city street and through the golden doors. 'He's a bit of a grump—and you wait till you meet Abigail.' She pulled a face, which involved making her eyes go crossed. Unfortunately at the same time the lift doors opened. Unfortunately Zakahr was in the lift.

His eyes looked to Rachael, and then away.

He did not want to see her—did not want to think of what he was doing to either of them.

Could not.

He could feel Rachael's eyes on him, wished the lift would go faster.

'Is that your boss?' Rachael asked, and Lavinia's eyes widened a fraction. Rachael rarely initiated conversation, and Lavinia rather wished she hadn't chosen now to start.

'It is,' Lavinia said.

'The grumpy one?' Rachael checked, and without looking Lavinia just knew Zakahr's tongue was rolling in his cheek.

They did a little dance as he went to step out. Zakahr was desperate to get out of the confines of the lift, but then he remembered his manners—though he wished he hadn't, because now he had to walk behind them.

See more of them.

Lavinia, polished and glamorous. Rachael, her dark curls in knots, her socks grubby and mismatched, wearing a T-shirt too short and shorts too long. He could see why Lavinia was upset that the clothing she bought for her sister wasn't being passed on to the little girl.

He just didn't *want* to see.

'I won't be long. I just need to get my things,' Lavinia said as they reached the office.

Zakahr brushed past without response.

'Right, can you sit there for five minutes? I just need to empty out my desk,' Lavinia said as brightly as she could as Rachael sat on the sofa.

For Zakahr it was hell.

Zakahr's job meant *not* getting involved.

Figures he could deal with—sob-stories he just tuned out.

For his business to survive he had to be ruthless.

He did not *want* to know about Eddie and his sick grandchild, he did not *want* to know that Lavinia's mortgage was a monthly concern, and more than that, he did not *want* a face to the name of Rachael.

Zakahr stared unseeing out of his office window, tried to tell himself that this time tomorrow he would be on a plane, that all he was leaving behind was not his problem.

Yet it wasn't that which consumed him.

Somehow—even though he had deliberately not thought about it, had done his level best not to think about it—somehow he had pictured Rachael as a mini-Lavinia. A blonde, precocious child—a resilient, happy little thing. What had shocked him to the core—what he was having so much trouble dealing with at this very moment—was that Rachael reminded Zakahr of himself.

He could feel her mistrust, her fear, her resignation, her expectation that hurt would follow hurt.

He could not stand to be involved.

He did not want to be involved.

He gave millions to charity, he spoke at functions—but there were no pictures of Zakahr donning a baseball cap and smiling beside a child. He kept his distance.

He was being manipulated, he was sure.

Deliberately not thinking, certainly for once not analysing, he pressed on the intercom.

'Lavinia?' When she didn't come immediately, he marched out of the office. 'Can I see you now?'

'One moment.' She was getting Rachael a drink from

the water cooler, refusing to let him rush her, and Zakahr returned to his office, sat at his desk. Ages later, but more like a moment, she came in.

'Is this the sympathy card you're playing?' Zakahr challenged as soon as the door was closed. 'Because if you're using her…'

'*I'm* not the one who uses people, Zakahr.' Lavinia was as direct as ever. 'And just in case that black heart of yours is having an attack of guilt, though I doubt it, there's no need. I didn't get access to Rachael, so my lack of a job doesn't affect her future one bit. Now, if you'll excuse me, I need to get my things.'

'She's going back?'

'Yep!'

Lavinia shrugged, but Zakahr could see the effort behind the apparent nonchalance. It was as if her shoulders were pushing up bricks.

'She'll adapt. Oh, and Zakahr…' She gave him a black smile. 'On the drive here I heard them announce tomorrow's press conference on the radio. Enjoy your revenge—hope it's everything you've dreamed of.'

'What did you expect, Lavinia?' He could see that she didn't get it. 'Did you really think that I'd come here to make things up with my family? Have you any idea—?'

'I've got a perfectly good idea of what you must have gone through,' Lavinia shouted. 'Because I lived it, Zakahr—because so many times I wished that my mother had turned her back on *me*. The same way I wish Rachael's father would turn her back on *her*.'

'What Nina did—'

'I'll tell you what she did,' Lavinia said, 'this woman you hate so much. She did something she bitterly regrets—has done many things she no doubt bitterly regrets. But she will always be my friend.'

'Your *friend*?'

'My friend,' Lavinia admitted. 'She gave me a decent job, gave me a chance in life. I didn't just dream of weddings, Zakahr. I used to lie in bed at night, listening to my mum entertaining her *friends*, and wish that I'd find out I was adopted. To this day sometimes I wish my mother had done what Nina did. Believe me, sometimes I think it would have been kinder.'

'Well, I think that rules out a career in counselling!' Lavinia said to a nonplussed Rachael, and then she kissed her nose—whether Rachael wanted it or not.

'Love you,' Lavinia said, and kissed her little fat cheek, which was probably the wrong thing too. But there was almost a smile on Rachael's cross little face. 'I love you so much.' Which was, no doubt, according to Ms Hewitt, putting too much pressure on her. But Rachael was smiling, and Lavinia gave her a little tickle, and then she was actually laughing. 'I want to eat you up, you're so cute.'

And it was so nice to just be sisters—one big, one little, one funny, one serious, but sisters.

And they *should* be together.

Ignoring potential wrath, Lavinia didn't take Rachael for a milkshake or a boring swing in the park, and neither did she take her back to Rowena straight away.

'Where are we going?' Rachael stood on the elevator in a large department store as they went up past children's wear, past toys, past books, till finally they were in the bedding department.

'We need to sort out your room,' Lavinia said, trying to work out how much room she had left on her credit card. 'Let's choose some nice bedclothes.'

'Am I coming to live with you?' Rachael asked, and Lavinia could hear the hope and fear and doubt in her sister's voice. It almost broke her heart that she couldn't give the answer they both surely wanted.

'Not for now,' Lavinia admitted. 'But I'm going to keep trying to make that happen. I don't get to decide...' She saw Rachael's little pinched face tighten. 'But you *are* going to have your own room at my house.' Then she qualified it a touch. 'Wherever I live there will be a room there for you—even if I can only get you one night now and then, or even if we have to wait till you're sixteen.' Lavinia had an appalling thought. 'I'll be in my thirties!' She was surprised that Rachael actually smiled. 'Come on.'

It was, in spite of a broken heart, in spite of losing everything dear to her, one of the best hours of her life.

She didn't listen to the experts, she listened to her heart—and, yes, it was Zakahr's advice she took.

They chose pinks and greens for her bedspread and pillowcases, and a butterfly dreamcatcher, and then Lavinia got Rachael the cheapest mobile phone. They took their wares *home*, and made up the bed and put up curtains, and Lavinia set up the phone and taught Rachael how to text.

X

'I'll send you a kiss every night,' Lavinia said. 'And, if you can, you can send me one back.'

So Rachael had a go at texting, and Lavinia's phone bleeped, and she got her first kiss from Rachael.

'Come on,' Lavinia said. 'Let's get you back to Rowena.'

And this time when she offered her hand Rachael took it.

'You know, we're going to be okay,' Lavinia said. 'I'm going to make sure of it.'

And she did try to hand her back with grace—did her absolute best to trust that Ms Hewitt maybe did know best—but as they walked up the garden path Lavinia could feel her heart cracking as Rachael looked up at her.

'I want to be with you.'

'You'll be fine,' Lavinia said as bravely as she could. She saw Rowena's shadow as she came to open the door, and then her heart surely stopped beating.

'Lavinia, I don't want to go back to him.'

And she knew you should never make a child promises you couldn't keep but, handing her over to Rowena, Lavinia hugged her tight and made one. 'I'll do everything I can.'

'Promise?'

Lavinia nodded. 'I promise.'

She let her go, smiled to Rowena and even managed

a wave as she drove off. But hearing Rachael's plea was more than she could bear, because on Monday she *was* going back to her father.

There wasn't time to break down, there wasn't time to cry, there really wasn't much time to think.

All Lavinia knew was that she'd do anything for that little girl.

Anything.

CHAPTER FIFTEEN

SHE could do this, Lavinia told herself.

Lavinia paced the city streets, high heels clicking, and she didn't care.

Kevin wanted money, a significant amount of money, and she knew where she could get it. She just had to work out how.

There was the Kolovsky boutique—the place every woman wanted to be—and she stared in at the window and saw the silk and the opals. And then she saw her reflection, and it would have been so easy to rest her head on the window and just weep, but if she started she would never stop. Instead she swept into the store and selected a Kolovsky wrap—one of the last designs of the founder, Ivan Kolovsky, spun in golds and reds and ambers, in the same thread as the dress she had worn that night she had first kissed Zakahr. The staff knew her, of course, but they blinked a little when she told them to charge it to Zakahr Belenki.

'And this, too,' Lavinia informed them, grabbing a *koža* slip dress. And then she saw another wrap, a turquoise one, filled with silvers and greens like a peacock on display, and she knew who would love this one.

Ignoring Alannah's incessant questions and requests for a signature, Lavinia left—and ground the gears in her car all the way to the hospital.

'Here.' She wrapped it round Nina's shoulders. 'Ivan designed this one.' She smoothed the silk around her friend's shoulders and tried to comfort her. But she wouldn't stop crying, wouldn't stop wailing.

'He's called a press conference for tomorrow. It's over,' Nina sobbed. 'Tomorrow it is all over.'

'Stop it,' Lavinia said, because it was too much like her own mother.

'He hasn't been in to see me. He'll never forgive me. Riminic won't come to see me.' Round and round on the same pointless loop. 'He's never going to forgive me.'

'Perhaps not!' Lavinia was cross, but she was kind. 'Maybe he'll never forgive you, Nina. But you know what? You can forgive yourself. You did a terrible, awful thing—but that's not all you are. You've done many good things, too—look how you helped me. You gave me a good job, you helped me with Rachael, with so many things.'

'I want my son.'

'You *have* your son!' Lavinia said. 'Whether he forgives you, or loves you, still you have your son…' But there was no reaching her, and the doctor moved in with medication. Lavinia shooed him off. 'You want more Valium, Nina? Or why not have a drink, like my mum did? Or you can get up, get washed…'

'It hurts,' Nina insisted, thumping at her chest, and Lavinia couldn't do it any more.

'*Life* hurts,' Lavinia said. 'But you can't just give in.

Sometimes you do what you have to at the time, and then work out how to forgive yourself afterwards.'

And so, now, must she.

For the first time in almost a week Zakahr shaved. He stood with a towel around his hips and tried somehow to shave and not fully look at himself in the mirror.

His suit was chosen for the morning, his speech written, his case packed. Soon it would be over.

And then came a frantic knocking at his door.

'Yes?'

Zakahr stood back as a mini-torpedo swept into his suite.

'I've changed my mind.' She was breathless, could not look at him, but she was determined. 'That offer.'

'What offer?'

'For money.'

'Lavinia…' he sounded bored '…you told me very clearly that money was the last thing you wanted.'

'I've changed my mind.' There was a frantic air to her, an urgency as she rained his face with kisses.

'Lavinia…'

Zakahr peeled her off him. He did not want to deal with this. He did not want to deal with *her*, Lavinia, the person who made him sway, this woman who clouded his judgment. So he pushed her away with words.

'I might have known you'd revert to type.'

'I'm my mother's daughter.'

'Just go.'

She could not. She would not.

So she did it—she pulled off her dress to reveal the

koža slip beneath. She was shaking, and ashamed, but worse—far worse—he remained unmoved.

'Here.' He strode across the room to his desk, pulled out a cheque. 'For the other night. Now, get out.'

And she had what she wanted, there in her hand, but it wasn't enough. It could never be enough—and it had nothing to do with money. She was kissing him again, pressing her lips on his unwilling mouth. He turned his face away.

'Is it money you want, Lavinia, or sex?' He wanted *her*, not what she was doing. He remembered her abhorrence at the idea and tried to save her from herself. Pulling at her wrists, he pushed her away from his body. For even as he rejected her she would surely be able to feel he was lying.

Both, she almost sobbed. But that wasn't the entire answer. There was a third—an addition that she could not bring herself to admit.

She didn't want him to go, yet somehow had to accept there was nothing here for him to stay for.

He had taken her heart—he might just as well have had the butler pack it amongst his shirts—and the fire died in her.

'What do you want, Lavinia?'

'Not this,' Lavinia admitted, and she stared at the cheque and then handed it to him. 'Thank you.'

'For what.'

'For not letting me…' She screwed her eyes closed. 'Please—just take it.'

He didn't.

'I don't want to make money this way—and the stupid

thing is you're the only man I could have tried to… I'm so ashamed.'

'You didn't do anything.'

'Not for that…' When still he wouldn't take the cheque she screwed it up in her hands. 'I promised myself I'd do anything it took to get Rachael, but in the end…'

'You don't need that money,' Zakahr said—which was great, coming from a billionaire.

She picked up her dress, and it was an almost impossible task to get out with dignity. But as she stepped into her shoes, rejected and broke, Lavinia was the one who could look him in the eye.

'I thought I wanted you…' She shook her head. 'But I don't. I want a family for Rachael—I want cousins and grandparents and brothers and sisters and aunts and uncles for her. I want everything for her that I never had, and everything you so readily could.'

She went to open the door. She knew she often said the wrong thing, but sometimes she couldn't stop herself, and now it was building and fizzing and welling inside her, and she probably wouldn't have said it if the damn door hadn't stuck.

'So you were abandoned?' Lavinia finally wrenched the door open, turned around and stuck her chin out to him. 'Boo-hoo—get over it.'

And, in high stilettos and a *koža* slip, she marched right out of his life.

CHAPTER SIXTEEN

IT WAS his longest night.

He drove first to the hospital, sitting outside, knowing it was too late to go in. Then he drove to Iosef's home and watched the lights flick on and off—even heard the baby crying at midnight in the dark, silent street and saw the light flick on again. Then to Annika—a sister he had hardly spoken to. He sat outside the sprawling farm she shared with her husband Ross, listening to the horses and the peace and wishing it might come to his soul.

It could.

Well, according to Lavinia.

She'd taken thirty-six years of history, challenged a lifelong dream and told him he could do it.

'You don't need money.'

He'd leant on her doorbell till she answered, still in the *koža* slip, nursing a tub of ice cream and a glass of wine. Somehow, he could tell she had not been crying.

'I had already arranged a lawyer for you. He will contact you.'

'He rang before,' Lavinia said, and taking that phone

call had felt a whole lot different from taking money. 'He seems to think I have a good chance.'

'You have *every* chance,' Zakahr said.

He walked into her house and it was the first time he had felt at home.

There were her stolen goods all over the sofa, and a make-up bag on the coffee table, and a woman who somehow reached him.

'How am I supposed to forgive her? How can I stay…?'

'You choose to.' She smiled at him, but it was a tired one. 'She was fifteen,' Lavinia said, pouring him a glass of wine. She had listened to Nina's grief for so long now she knew her story by heart. 'She was scared and pregnant and they hid it from everyone. She was poor, his family would have been angry, and Ivan told her they could not keep you.'

She didn't elaborate on that part—they both knew the consequences.

'For years they were apart. Ivan had a fling with a cleaner—that was Levander's mother—then he met your mother again. She was nineteen then, and soon pregnant with twins. His family still objected to the marriage— she was beneath him, they said. She tried very hard to show them she was better, and she did not see how they would accept her if they knew there had already been a child. You would have been four.'

She tried to picture him at four, but it didn't make her smile.

'There was a chance to flee Russia. She was heavily pregnant, and Levander's mother came to the door, begging that they take him. Nina did not want Levander if she could not have her own son.'

He looked at Lavinia and her eyes were clear, her words very definite.

'I'm sorry.'

And she was. It wasn't her fault, it had nothing to do with her, but sorry she was as she told him his history.

'How did you forgive *your* mother?'

'I don't know that I actually did—I just gave up trying to change her. Can you forgive Nina?' Lavinia asked—because now she'd stopped being angry she knew it was a big ask.

'She really helped you?' Zakahr answered in question.

'They all have.' Lavinia nodded. 'They've been like a family.' She thought for a moment, because again she'd probably said the wrong thing. 'Not a lovey-dovey family—we fight all the time...'

'A real family, I guess.'

Zakahr closed his eyes. He would wear every scar on his back easier knowing that Nina had in some way been there for her.

'I love you,' he said. And he'd never thought he'd say it—and neither had Lavinia—and now to hear it, to know it, to feel it, for once she was lost for words. He could not gauge her silence, but if he had to make it clearer then he would. 'I'm crazy about you. So crazy all I can think of is you. So crazy I would give up a lifetime's revenge to have you.'

And then she climbed on his knee and kissed him—a bold kiss, a loving kiss, a Lavinia kiss, that started on his mouth and then moved across his cheeks and over his eyebrows. Her thin fingers roamed his hair. He knew this was a for ever he had never—not once—let himself glimpse. He could be himself. The past wasn't something he ran from or something that ate him up with a need to avenge. The past could just *be*, and that meant he now had a future.

It was a kiss that was both passionate and loving—a kiss that was both urgent and patient. She felt the exhaustion as his past left him, and the hope as the future greeted him, and it was a different kiss too, for Lavinia.

She tasted his tongue, and the lips that were designed for her. She wasn't unsure and she wasn't shy and she knew with him she was revered.

She straddled him and kissed him as his hands caressed her body through the silk. He kissed her breasts through the fabric his father had created, and then his mouth moved lower still, and she felt him, warm through the fabric. He kissed her stomach and slid the fabric up over her hips. She knelt on him till it was her flesh his lips were touching, and he kissed her stomach deeply as her fingers pressed in his hair. It was a kiss that told her his babies would grow there.

She slid down his zipper and lowered herself onto him, and it was third time lucky for Lavinia, because this time *she* got to love *him*.

She got to kiss him as he came deep within her. She got to kiss him as her body learnt how readily available true passion was. Because it was fast and intense and incredibly beautiful—a lot like life.

'Marry me,' he said because he wanted her for

ever. He kissed her again, and then asked her again.
'Marry me.'

'On one condition.'

She whispered it into his ear.

He'd have agreed to anything—just not that.

He closed his eyes, because it was impossible, but how could he ever say no to her? He was still within her, and he could never deny her. And then he opened them, and saw that Lavinia was absolutely and completely serious in her 'one condition'.

Hesitantly he agreed. Tonight could only be for ever if he would do this for her. Then this love would be for keeps.

Everyone would just have to wait till the wedding to find out.

EPILOGUE

LAVINIA had no shame.

She *was* the bride-to-be from hell, and she didn't care who knew it.

As a child she had fallen asleep dreaming of this day, had blocked out the noises from the bedroom next door with dreams of her prince, and quite simply it had to be perfect.

Perfect! she informed each Kolovsky in turn.

If they couldn't move on or get along then she didn't want them at her wedding—and that included Zakahr.

The brothers would wear matching Kolovsky silk ties, and so too would Ross, Annika's husband. Annika and Nina were to wear shoes in the same silk.

'It's too much!' Katina grumbled. 'You need *subtle*— let us do what we do best.'

'It's *my* wedding!' Lavinia insisted.

And it was.

The dress that had waited to be worn by a Kolovsky bride and had been shunned each time was taken out of the display cabinet and fitted for Lavinia, and it was absolutely the best dress in the world.

She could feel the jewels in the hem that had been sewn in by Ivan.

Opal earrings from Nina dangled at her ears.

And she wore her mother's watch. It was the one thing Fleur had refused to pawn, a gift from her favourite client who, Lavinia had secretly dreamed, was maybe, just maybe, her father. Today she felt so sure and complete that Lavinia was quite certain he was.

'Big breaths,' said Hannah, the Salvation Army worker who had always been there for her while she grew up, and who would give her away on her biggest day.

'Are they all there?' Lavinia begged—because she wanted each and every one of the Kolovskys to share this.

She loved them all, every depraved, debauched, re-formed one of them, and this day was not perfect without them all here.

'Levander's there,' Hannah said, peering into the church. Levander was easily spotted, because Zakahr had chosen him as his best man—two Detsky Dom boys made good, thanks to love.

'I'm here,' Annika, who was bridesmaid, pointed out. 'And I've seen Aleksi and Iosef go in.'

'And they're standing with Nina?' Lavinia checked.

'They are,' Annika said. 'You can stop worrying now.'

And she did. Standing at the doors of the church, it dawned on Lavinia that she could stop worrying now.

Zakahr had been right. Kevin had refused the DNA test Lavinia's lawyer had suggested. Rachael was not even his. And now the little girl was getting used to her new family. Too shy to be a bridesmaid, today she was being held by a doting Nina, and that serious face more often these days broke into a smile.

'You look wonderful,' Annika said to Lavinia, and it felt strange for Annika. She should be jealous—after all, her mother was so close to Lavinia—but how could she be jealous of a woman who had healed such a fractured family? 'You *are* wonderful,' Annika said, which was terribly effusive for her. And what was more she gave Lavinia a kiss.

The walk up the aisle was up to that moment the best walk of her life. But Lavinia wanted to gallop—because she wanted to walk back down it with *him*.

Zakahr smiled when he saw her—a smile that came from his soul. Because, unlike his sister and brothers, he knew her truth. His secret virgin walked towards him, and never till then had Zakahr considered himself lucky. But resentment was a memory now. His soul was devoid of anything bitter, and every piece of his past was worth it for this moment—because without pain he would not have recognised such joy.

Yes, he knew her truth, and she knew his—knew every story behind every scar—and still, steadfastly, she loved him.

Which was why he would do anything for her.

'You look beautiful,' he said when she joined him.

'I know!' Lavinia beamed and kissed him. 'So do you.'

There was a lot of talking, and a bit of singing—only

Lavinia didn't really hear it, because they were getting to the part that mattered the most, and her heart was hammering, and her hands were shaking.

He took them in his as he offered her his vows. And he held them and remembered what she'd whispered in his ear the night he'd asked her to marry him.

He could see his dazzling, happy wife, perhaps the strongest woman he knew, for the first time ever crying as Zakahr opened his mouth. Lavinia was crying because she knew how hard this was for him, but she knew, absolutely, that he could do it.

And he did.

'I, Zakahr Riminic Kolovsky...'

She heard the gasp from the congregation, turned and saw Nina holding Rachael, crying and smiling, and all his brothers and his sister standing proud.

She could only love him more as she stumbled through her own vows.

It was the most wonderful party.

The press were baying at the door, a helicopter hovered overhead, but no one inside cared. There was love in the air, and plenty to go around, and Lavinia danced and chatted and ate, and insisted everyone danced some more.

No, Zakahr did not dance with Nina, but they shared a drink and admired Lavinia—the one solid link between them.

Forgiveness wasn't a place Zakahr had arrived at yet, but he was making the journey. And if it was hard, still it brought rewards—there were enough Kolovskys to ensure he had far fewer trips to the airport!

'I never want to take it off!' She stood in the honeymoon suite and couldn't bear to take off the dress, just twirled at the mirror as Zakahr lay on the bed and watched.

Then she turned sideways and ran her hands over her latest phantom pregnancy, pressed in the fabric in a search for changes.

Zakahr suppressed a smile—she wasn't even late yet, though Lavinia insisted she felt bloated.

'Can we have lots of babies?'

'Lots,' Zakahr said. 'All boys!' Because he'd have his work cut out keeping tabs on mini-Lavinias.

Lavinia smiled and thought of lots of little grey-eyed, dark-haired boys, and gave a smile for the little girls she'd make sure they had too. 'I want a big family.'

'We've suddenly got one!' he said as she came over.

Lavinia held up her hair as Zakahr took care of a long row of buttons, his mouth tracing her spine.

'They're *my* family, except I feel like I'm marrying into *yours*, Mrs Kolovsky.'

'Say it again.' She was shameless.

'Mrs Kolovsky,' Zakahr duly said as he peeled the bodice down. 'Mrs Lavinia Kolovsky.'

She made it easy to say—so easy to become the person he was born to be, the only man to change his name on his wedding day!

Then Zakahr stilled for a moment, realised she wasn't imagining things as he saw the unfamiliar swell in her pale flat breasts, saw the changes in her body that would change their future.

'What?' She smiled up at him.

'Everything,' Zakahr said. 'You're everything to me.'

Special Offers

Every month we put together collections and longer reads written by your favourite authors.

Here are some of next month's highlights— and don't miss our fabulous discount online!

On sale 21st June

On sale 5th July

On sale 5th July

Save 20%
on all Special Releases